ARTHUR REX

Arthur Estes

ARTHUR REX

DOUBLE DRAGON

A DOUBLE DRAGON PAPERBACK

ISBN 978-1-78695-346-9

Double Dragon
is an imprint of
Fiction4All

Published 2020
Fiction4All
www.fiction4all.com

Cover Art by Deron Douglas

Part One

Fifteen hundred years ago an old man struggled through the most terrible of winter storms. He should have known better. After all, he was wise to kings and counselors. His reputation extended throughout the greenwood kingdoms of ancient Britain.

He was more than wise – he was sly and immersed in the powers which today we have long scorned. But in those times such powers terrified. Why did some possess those powers? That was mysterious as the eclipse of the sun.

Soon, after certain events, this fortunate one wouldn't feel strong or chosen, only responsible. He would be sure he had failed everything and everyone he'd come to treasure on this small earth.

Chapter 1

A hundred and forty-one times you've glanced over your shoulder, the old man chided himself silently, now that you are definitely in danger. Then he spoke aloud. "Because you are a special sort of fool."

The bleak winter moor landscape, all lichen-covered rocks and gorse, didn't help. His words jumbled against the saurian hills and died away.

His scrawny mount snorted and twitched his ears. The old man whipped his head in the other direction. His animal, too scrawny even for eating, at least possessed sure instincts.

But the old man discovered nothing, just more of the somber landscape he'd witnessed during a week's steady travel on this lonely excuse for a road.

How far he'd gone didn't seem that important. It was important that the journey, the travail, was almost done. His certainty came from shrewd guessing and, honestly, from his dreams. An old man on a bony horse could hardly expect anything better; nor could a plowman, smithy, baker, stone carver, or housewife, people who did all the work in the old one's world. But the old man considered himself cleverer than most several times over. It was a severe weakness and he knew it.

The cleverness began with how hard he made journey. Strictly speaking, one with his powers didn't have to suffer a long stint on a sway-back animal. But who would pay any attention to a grandfather on a broke-down nag?

He glanced in all directions one more time.

"So far," he mumbled, "so good. Not great, but good enough."

I am still in their world.

His shoulders sagged at the truth. Years and years, many of their lifetimes, brought him to this place on winter British moor.

"Fool," he mumbled again because it seemed so right. "Fool, fool."

For variety he added, "Idiot, idiot, idiot."

He drew his threadbare cloak over his head. Suffering, he reminded himself, is what these beings do best. Now that you've thrown your lot in with them don't expect much more.

He glanced ahead. He stopped and wiped his eyes.

Among the winter-stunted trees and heath, a spring-time eruption of purple, crimson, and golden carpeted the valley below.

His heart beat faster. Impossible, the old man thought, under normal circumstances. Somebody's been fooling with things. But this is exactly what I want. And require. And I may demand.

He gave his animal a gentle kick.

The path led steadily downhill. They entered the narrow valley. The old man fell quiet and watched and listened more carefully than ever.

The path I'm following followed is barely wide enough for a dog cart, he noted. How does anyone around here feed himself? Where are the farms and pastures? Maybe they live off the air itself.

His horse snorted and stopped. A young lady, barefoot, wearing a green smock, stood in the road. She gave the old man a wide smile, as if she understood nothing, turned, and fled.

Around the next sharp turn he entered the village. It wasn't much in term of numbers, only a row of stone cottages, perfectly hewn and sparkling clean. Each was identical. Beside every doorway a young man or woman stood, wearing the same smock of forest green as their neighbor. Everyone was smiling. There were no children or the old, only the very healthy young, quiet and yielding as the old man and his mount passed.

At the end of the village road a last building appeared. It was another matter altogether. It wasn't large, a rectangle of stone sitting at an odd angle to the path. But its stone was pitted and weather-worn smooth and so deeply grown with moss that it seemed to have sunk deep into the ground. How can anything human-made be so old in the middle of this nowhere? The old man asked himself, but he felt fear and jubilation simultaneously.

A cathedral, he decided. He noted that the broad doorway and the walls where the moss hadn't taken hold showed relief carvings. Not of the usual Celtic or Roman crosses either; these were of lizards, scorpions, spiders, wolves, foxes, wild horses, lions, and huge bears.

He shivered. You know, he accused inwardly. Twaddle, he accused right back and felt his heart thump against his ribs. It's far, far too late. No, he argued back, pull this animal's head around and give him your spurs. You are safe till you enter that place. Age and its suffering are worthy. At least compared to what you don't know.

A crowd of villagers quietly surrounded the horse. A man politely but insistently took the reins from his hands.

"Mind you," the old man sighed, "this is borrowed property."

A striking woman, taller than the rest and wearing an elaborately embroidered costume, stepped forward. She gazed up, dark-eyed, and took his hand.

"Come along now. We've made a place for you."

Her hand felt so soft, warm, and alive.

"Don't you desire what we have? We know you do."

He sputtered. "I am very weak."

"Not at all. Look around. Where is the hurt and decay here? You are in pain now. Imagine – your youth returned, joined with your wisdom."

"Scary indeed," he mumbled.

"Must hurry," she insisted. "Hurry, hurry now."

She tugged and the old man slid from his horse. He stumbled. The young ones with their strong limbs held him upright.

"If only," he said shakily, "I knew you were real."

They laughed a little, not too much, but just right.

He was half-carried toward the cathedral doors. The old man started to make a wisecrack about needing a better maintenance crew, but a flash of distant light against the clouds caught his eye. He stopped cold.

"My lord?" the woman questioned.

"I am no lord," he said quietly,

"Why are you distressed?"

"I am not sure. Give me a minute."

She pulled him a little closer. "We have been preparing for you for many days."

"Been keeping an eye on?"

"We shall not take you back."

"Perhaps I have been too hasty. I am very sorry --."

"No. Come along. Otherwise you will be very sorry," she snarled.

He glanced over his shoulder. The dense clouds now concealed the horizon. You're surrounded, the old man told himself sternly. Even if you bolted it wouldn't do any good.

"Come along now," the woman whispered.

He managed a bitter smile for each of his final escorts – two men and two women; each so similar that might have been hatched from the same clutch of eggs.

"Impressive place. All your idea?" Merlin managed.

He got a brief smile and no more.

The men held the doors open. The women held onto him firmly. The stone interior, wild and horrible creatures frescoed on its walls, seemed to be cut from one immense block of stone.

She stopped before a stone alter. Her friends hung back. She clapped her hands, shut her eyes, and intoned what to the old man seemed mumbo jumbo.

The stone, all several tons of it, opened up and revealed stone stairs.

He peered down; the stairs didn't seem to be much. They led into pitch black. From below water gurgled and splashed.

The woman's face glowed. "Don't be afraid," she purled, "It's what you truly desire."

And the old man felt his legs shake. Despite his better judgment, he prayed she was right.

"Don't listen to your fears," she continued. "Look at you...old and weak. You've been betrayed. Your spirit is meant to live as long as this universe."

"A very tall order," Merlin said quietly.

He felt his heart pound. Outside, he knew a winter sky was turning to cobalt. The moon shone with its eternal beauty. The earth would turn on its axis; the sun would burn tomorrow no matter what he did today.

All life on this planet, he told himself, lives no longer than a May fly, a single day, compared to the scheme of things. That was betrayal, he thought angrily. He cleared his throat. "I consent to whatever – what do I owe you?"

"You sound frightened. Why?"

"A reasonable notion, considering what I'm asking."

"This?" She pulled her cloak aside. Her throat, shoulders, and arms gleamed smooth and healthy.

Surely not innocent, the old man noted, but youthful – yes.

The woman took him by the hand. "Your time is now."

"But..." he sputtered.

The woman gave him a hard shove.

The old man grabbed the nearest stone pillar. "My mightiness is failing me," he gasped. "How does this magic work exactly. Will my soul end up a warthog or tulip bulb?"

"You only need to believe." She gritted her teeth and tried to wrench him lose. Her friends joined in, each taking an arm or leg desperately grasping the stone.

"Search," the woman huffed as she yanked. "And yea shall find."

"I did. I gave in to my vanity. I abandoned my post...my king...the boy...my people...my everything."

Suddenly woman turned away red-faced in anger. Her escort scurried behind her.

Not me, not now, he accused silently, not this stooped, wrinkled thing. I have cities to build, the mighty to set straight...the young to teach...as I have so many times. I am owed my time. I have grown old and blind in their service.

"Stop!" He thundered.

The woman whirled around.

"Did I say please?" The old man managed.

"Quickly," the woman hissed, "before you are lost."

He took the first winding stair, then another. A dim light came from below; the walls glowed. Thoughtful, he remembered thinking before his legs gave way.

He struck many steps on the way down. At the bottom he rolled up like a pill bug and lay stunned. The stone opening above slid shut.

He blinked. A cave – that's all it was, he noted, with a rushing stream bordering the far end and bare as a dungeon, which, of course, is the idea.

He struggled to stand. His knees still shook. He tasted the water, clear and cold, good for watering horses or making soup. Nothing seemed miraculous, say for one thing.

"Gravity," he muttered to himself. "Totally earth-bound."

He squeezed his eyes shut. He willed a stone nearby to wobble – nothing more.

Nothing. Again.

No.

Once more.

No.

What have you done?

Now, he though frantically, no blaming. Evaluate. Situation: seconds ago you owned the powers of a renowned and – frankly - feared wizard. Now that's gone. You're stripped clean. You're weak as kitten.

Not exactly.

A kitten has claws.

Stripped clean.

How do fangless villagers trap tigers? They dig a steep hole and disguise it with leaves. They hang a goat carcass over the trap.

Does it work?

A tiger, immense, brutally strong and silent, can't deny its nature.

His enemies know it.

One of them anyway.

"Mordred!" he roared.

The sound went nowhere. He felt his nicks, scrapes, and the boils on his feet. His felt his breakable bones, his fragile skull, and his thumping heart.

The glow from rocks faded. He stood in total darkness and felt the terror of the wholly vulnerable.

It hissed above his head. The old man backed away and kept his back to the stream.

"You win," he said quietly.

A form uncoiled along the rock. It glowed faintly, just enough, the old man decided, so that I can see what's about to happen.

It was made of dozens of segments, a pair of jointed legs for each segment. Each leg twitched and clacked against the rock. The head appeared last: Narrow eyes glared from a flat, bony skull. Protruding from the mandible, a double set of pinchers clacked and drooled.

The old man's stomach churned.

"Can you speak?" he croaked.

For a few moments the creature slithered and coiled. "Why shouldn't I?"

"Just my prejudices…do you have a name?"

"Blut." It hissed and slithered and extended its neck toward the old man. "What do you care? What power do you have over a name?"

"Me? Currently I can only dream. How mighty I once was till…your magus is too much for me. I am …vain."

The creature hissed impatiently. "And I am hungry." He coiled even closer. "Hold still. It'll be much quicker that way."

"Let me guess. You intend to tear my body into pieces, consume the delectable parts and gnaw the long bones and toss the leftovers into the stream behind me."

"Excellent idea."

"Last question before lunch. Who is your magus? Just to be absolutely sure."

The creature hissed angrily. " Mordred."

It hurled forward, furious, its aim off in haste. The old man whirled sideways and dived head-first into the stream.

The frigid current shot him forward. He tried to swim. The current drew him deeper and deeper. His body struck one rock – all sharp – after another. His lungs burned for one impossible fatal breath. His skull smashed into what felt like an execution's axe and he knew nothing at all.

Chapter 2

Pain owned a color – orange and pale red. He gagged. Water flowed from inside to the sand. His eyes flew open; he struggled to sit upright.

He lay at the edge of a clear river. His skull throbbed. I hurt way too much to be dead, he sighed inwardly. He dragged himself a little farther up the bank and tested arms and legs. He saw that he was a harlequin of scraps, bruised and nasty cuts.

Slowly – very slowly – he stood and let the world settle.

The sun floated low in the east, near where it had been before he tumbled down the stairs. I have been lost for an entire day, he decided. Or maybe a week. Or maybe a year.

He studied the cliff where the river flowed from beneath the mountain. To the right the cliff rose gradually. He rested till he felt a little stronger and climbed hand over hand until he reached the top of the rise. That exhausted him. He rolled over and rested till he could walk again.

The cathedral, or whatever it should be called, stood nearby. He glanced around and crept close to it. Nobody appeared. He crossed to the village that he found completely empty, every perfect piece of furniture in place down to napkins on the tables. Crockery waited in the kitchen; clothes hung from hook; all, crisp and clean, was exactly identical to everything else.

The old man slowly climbed a low ridge behind the village. The village and church occupied the highest point in all directions. He stood and studied the southern horizon where Londonium and the Thames waited, so far away. The charcoal-colored winter landscape still lacked snow. "I can smell it," he mumbled to no one in particular, "and it will come soon enough."

Snow, with all its peace and beauty, would fall on certain hills where he longed to be.

His eyes grew damp.

He took a deep breath and felt, deep inside, a weak stirring of returning power. It makes a certain sense, he thought, now that I am no longer buried alive. Such places take on powers on their own. The rumors are true. I can swear to it now.

But caution is the watchword. I've never experienced this before, having such a vital part of me stripped away.

He took a deep breath. I am strong enough now, he told himself, and fully aware of what's going on. Two old legs are better than nothing.

From the far horizon came a flicker of green and yellow.

He leapt up.

The colors flashed again and again, like summer lightning.

He stared at the horizon for the longest time.

He sank down. He tried to turn away.

Impossible.

He would never forget.

"Death," he muttered.

He wasn't sure about the next bit of time. He became aware that he was staring at a patch of ground with a single oak leaf decorating it.

"Now," he sniffed, "Hate yourself. Feel free. But there is yet a chance. I won't call it hope."

He stood. His knees wobbled. He found a broken limb for a staff and awkwardly worked his way down the hill.

The stick seemed a good type, so he spoke to it. "I have a plan. I am still weaker than a newt, shorn of my powers, but – and here's the great maybe – they may return. Bit by bit. Especially with fresh air and exercise. How far must I force these complaining knees to scamper? Why, two hundred good Roman miles. Utter defeat is one thing, hopelessness is another. Agreed? No? Too bad."

He hobbled down the road double-time. At a hundred yards he halted. "Now," he puffed, "let's not get sassy. Give us a quick rest and we've got it beat."

The world began to spin. What did the Roman Emperor joke on his deathbed? Merlin asked himself. I am becoming a god. Well, the old man thought, I am becoming a man.

He cackled at his joke. His realized that he had an audience. From the cottages and woods came a collective rustling. The perfect people emerged from hiding. He was surrounded on three sides.

That was the first thing. It lasted seconds. He barely had time to turn his head. Even he, a veteran of endless tricks, was surprised. A series of frames passed over where they stood. This is what happened to me, he thought quickly.

With every passing, quick as it was, perfection shifted. The beautiful people – their bodies stooped. Their faces elongated, especially the noses, and their hands grew long nails.

And tails.

The old man stood transfixed.

Populating the roads the fields, the hillsides were black-furred, nude tailed, slash-toothed rats. They hissed and snapped at each other, twitched their beady eyes and sniffed the air.

The old man backed away.

"Nice ," he gulped.

Each was as big as a wolf. They focused their glistening eyes on him.

He did what he could do. He turned away.

And ran.

He ran for his life.

The slopes and fields teemed with oily backs. They gained ground to his left and right. They're toying with you, the old man thought as he gasped for air. They'll go for the eyeballs first. Counting down – five, four, three –

He never believed in luck. Fate was another matter. His bony mount burst from the forest, eyeballs rolling in terror.

The old man grabbed a handful of his scraggly main and swung himself aboard. The oily wer-rats squealed in rage. The roan, from sheer terror, managed to pull ahead – just barely.

The next steep hill saved them. At the top the man glanced over his shoulder. A storm cloud now swirled over the valley and the village. A twisting wedge descended from the cloud and struck the earth like a banshee. The valley disappeared into mist and debris. The funnel bounced back into the cloud and vanished.

The silver-blue winter sky shone clear again.

The old man let the roan trot. "A neat trick," he said to her, "He lost sleep plotting that one. Such exaggeration. No sense of proportion."

They rode through the night, out of the moon-haunted moor and onto a crumbling Roman road. Eventually the sweat-darkened animal let his head droop in exhaustion. The old man let him plod along. He caught himself nodding off in the saddle.

What day is it? He asked himself. He knew he hadn't been gone too long. By the new Christian way of counting it was the year 539 and close to their savior's birth. In the spring they always put on a fine show about his rebirth.

Rebirth.

What would the black-robes be thinking right now with fire and brimstone burning their ears? Evil, it was plain enough, though not from their devil, who seemed a stand-in for the darker nature of their flocks. It was too late, but Merlin imaged how he'd explain it to him. The fight is between Mordred on one side and the fine wizard you see before you and his price on the other. You know him, the scarred warrior living in the castle keep. I mean your protector and liege.

The old man imagined the astounded look on the priest's face. Pagan, he'd mutter... your kind caused this.

Perhaps he'd think slyly. Therefore you can save us...Just this last time.

Maybe, the old man would have to sigh.

Then the priestly fellow, if sensitive, might throw up his hands and wail why?

The old man would have to shrug. The answer, such as I know, is far beyond your understanding.

And though he couldn't say it directly, it's beyond me. I know this: we came here to teach, share, and learn. It was our nature.

Merlin's chin bounced against his chest. Eventually he dreamed deeply. The warrior-king appeared in his dream, a grizzled middle-aged man. Once he'd been a boy. Merlin had personally chosen and got the boy anointed through the ceremony of the stone.

"Arthur!" the old man called in his sleep.

His dream eye saw Arthur with his armor stripped away, his tunic torn and blood-soaked.

At first he refused even to look at the old man. "Where were you?" he finally demanded.

The old man's heart ached. "I was tricked. I was - ."

He stopped. He didn't expect to be forgiven. He couldn't forgive himself. He took a deep breath. "Are you passed over?"

"You mean am I dead? Don't be a ninny. How else could you talk to me like this?"

"I had hopes -"

"Now, now. As you eternally lectured me, hope is no more than sausage."

"Hope is all I have." The old man's face burned. He wiped his eyes with his bruised hands.

"Come now. Don't make a fool of yourself."

"At this age, maybe it's what I do best."

"And what is it you are doing now?"

"Riding like a bat from Hades to save what I can."

"A bit behind the ball, aren't we?"

The old man hung his head. Tears coursed down his cheeks.

Arthur sighed. "Look now. Once I was a homeless waif. I remember living behind the town dung heap. You came along, cleaned me up, taught me a few manners, guided me through the ceremony and the rest was history. A little abbreviated, true, but what can you do? From dung pile to throne. One pile to another. At least the scent was better... Anyway – why me? I mused about it now and then. I was not your first Arthur, as you explained. Can't be the last...unless that Mordred thing is about to win the entire game. Of course – you and your kind: what do you need one of us mere human beings anyway? Don't you want to be the top of the heap, too?"

The old man sniffed. "You underestimate yourself. All your kind do. A powerful and wise leader, brave to a fault, embroiled in human life – who else would lead your kind? "

"But you - ."

"A great wizard? See how that's turned out."

"I see that you are still in a bloody hurry anyway."

The old man gave his own great sigh. "I hurry because – because – you might be just a dream."

The wizard's eyes flew wide open. He glanced around once, and gave the tottering roan a last hard kick in the ribs.

If you happened to be a poor peasant in the year 530 or so – and that included virtually everybody – the sight along the road might have made you laugh, and in those flinty days laughter was hard to come by: A grizzly old man, wrapped in a threadbare cloak, mounted on a swaybacked animal as tired-looking as himself. Funnier still would have been the old man's grim and determined face, in contrast to his thin legs and hollow chest. But Merlin was true to his word, as wizards had to be above all things: true to words and their power. After all, that was their reason for being.

Merlin, when he was new to the earth and humankind, use to worry about the details to such things. That was a long time ago. Now speed was all that mattered. They met no one as animal's hooves pounded against the ancient pavers.

England, old Britain, was almost empty by then, not as it had been six hundred years ago, when the Romans kept order with a matter-of-fact attitude and an iron fist. The old British, the Celts really, were dispersed after the Roman withdrew. Blond, long-headed Angles, Saxons and Jutes, with their rough German words and bad tempers, raided from across the North Sea. Plunder was excellent as they tore apart the villas, the manors, the farmlands, the commerce, the forums, the Roman law, mostly from sheer misunderstanding. Raiding meant burning, stealing, and slaying the slow, stupid, or brave. Rooms filled with art of objects of silver and gold, soft clothing, glassware, sculptures, perfumes and so much more were simply too much temptation. Sitting down and thinking things through – reaching compromises, learning the local languages, and casting eyes about for peaceful profit and integration: not a chance.

From the far west, from the green hills of Wales, soldiers held to the high ground and wilderness. Their king, half Britain, half Roman, would be known as Arthur by the people he saved. Not that they were many. Their weapons, dress and training came from the Romans they once served. Those that could rode horses as an improvised cavalry to deal with the invaders flooding the landscape.

Generations and generations to come would make Arthur wealthier, more handsome, wiser, and, honestly, nobler than perhaps he ever really was. There were no knights of the round table. There were no knights actually, no courtly love, no grand castle, nothing more than fighting and surviving in a twilight world.

In the twilight world people came more and more strongly to believe in the world of the night, the moon, and magic. There was no other way to reconcile suffering and chaos. Merlin served Arthur, his king, to advise and protect him – anything to make sure he and his people survived. And that was enough: just to survive. Arthur, for his part, with his sharp eyes, scarred face and iron will, saw the old man, whose advice he listened to patiently, as much more than a strange necromancer, a self-proclaimed wizard. Arthur had no use for foul concoctions of lizards and bat's wings and incantations in forgotten Latin. Arthur connected lines from A to B. He looked for practical solutions. He was human and so, as Merlin completely understood, everything was a mystery to him.

Merlin knew otherwise, or at least he knew more. Cause and effect, time and space, the boundary between life and death – all those were facts, or ideas, or fears Merlin could change with the powers at his fingertips. The danger, of course, lay with the power. Merlin knew that some wizards used their nature to live as rulers within the dimensions that made up life on earth. They took on the character of the human lives with which they merged. They learned to laugh, love, hate and want what they didn't have. They knew jealousy, scorn, fear and joy. They forgave, forgot the forgiving, fought and made peace, and started the cycle all over again.

They weren't many actually and if people actually knew where they came from, how right their intuitions were about those special ones, people would never be the same. Their world would turn topsy-turvy, as people would say one day.

Except for traveling through this universe and shuttling through the centuries, Merlin's kind looked like everyone else. Some, like Merlin, devoted their existence to righting wrongs, defending the weak, and tending to humanity like devoted gardeners.

A few were bad – very bad. That's worth repeating. The dark ones learned to conceal their true natures, as would be expected, as they roiled the human world with Merlin and his ilk, and the people the kindly ones came to think as their own.

Chapter 3

By the third day his animal was spent. He galloped deep into the night anyway. The wind changed direction and brought low clouds and a heavy, blotting snow. Merlin caught himself sleeping in the saddle. He knew he wouldn't last much longer, the animal even less.

Arthur's fort – Merlin knew he was getting close, but without his special talents he wasn't sure how far away it still was. The world had changed to a winter wonderland of blue and white and deep snow. They picked their way carefully, sometimes floundering off the road into the deep drifts.

But they pushed forward anyway. Not that they had much choice. Merlin felt such gnawing hunger that he'd gladly eat hay. "I'd fight you for it," he murmured to the horse.

Over the centuries, it would become a gleaming Camelot, a paradise of gleaming turrets and theme-park perfection. The reality was a little grimmer. Arthur's capital actually was no more than a hold-out for a beleaguered people. It was a Celtic hill fort, built mostly of rough-hewn wood, with one-room huts making most of the dwellings. A stone tower and a wooden wall around the tower – the last stronghold– was proof of Arthur's determination against hopeless odds.

The fields around the fort, at least in the summer, glowed green. The deep woods surrounding the fields were carefully managed; within the town and village outside the walls the wells ran deep and pure. Arthur even kept a roman bath, a pretty basic one at least, just for old time's sake.

But Camelot was rare, if not unique, in those days. In a way, Merlin was glad for the snow. It hid the old ruined forums and the desolate wheat fields they'd passed all that day and night.

Suddenly the animal sank into snow deep as her belly. He stumbled and pawed, trying to rise out of the drift.

The animal would have refused to go any farther, but the urging in Merlin's voice compelled him to struggle on. He found the strength to keep going until the pale dawn began to rise.

Merlin finally pulled on the reins.

Scattered along the low hills they found the remains of burned houses. At the crown of the hill were the shattered ruins of a big hill fort. Merlin dismounted and led the animal behind the wall of a destroyed house. He pulled an armful of frozen hay from the roof.

The entire landscape stank of charcoal and burned flesh. The stallion chewed as fast as he could anyway. Merlin stared at the hilltop fort and trudged through the snow toward the ruins.

The hilltop fort lay more even more destroyed than the village. The palisade walls were pulled down; the ruins of the stone tower resembled a jagged tooth sticking out of the snow.

Merlin watched for a long time. Eventually he turned around and trudged back. He gathered straw and wood and piled it against the wall. He fished out a steel and flint from his pocket and began striking sparks. Over and over he tried. "Bah!" he spat, but after many tries, a thin plume of blue smoke rose from the straw

Even in the daylight the air felt bitterly cold. Merlin stoked the fire until. The animal snuggled closer to the roaring flames.

Merlin kept his eyes on the fire. Even tears wouldn't come. He stared at the flames for a very long time. He had no idea how long. He became aware of two men working their way down the snow-bound road. They were heavily wrapped in cloaks.. They saw Merlin and stopped in their tracks. The older man raised his only weapon, a bent stick, and shook it in Merlin's direction.

"Who would you be, varlet?" he demanded.

"The what? No matter. I tremble at your approach, mighty warriors. Anyway, don't stand there and freeze," Merlin said evenly.

The younger man pushed the older man forward. Merlin guessed that they were father and son. The family resemblance was rather remarkable. They trembled in the cold; they were grimy, pale and, Merlin was sure, starving. "I was about to have a bite." Merlin said. "Maybe I can find a few extra crumbs."

Merlin lifted up a bag hanging from the saddle. He was sure he'd recovered some of his old powers, the ones that he'd lost in the cave. The stirrings were sporadic and weak. Surely, he thought to himself, I can do a little something. If not -

He searched inside the bags and found three steaming, fresh loaves of soft bread - summer wheat, too. Merlin gave a proud little cough as he distributed the largess.

The two men grabbed the loaves and tore into the crust. After a few minutes the older man forced himself to take dignified bites. Merlin tore off bits and ate slowly.

"Did I catch your names?" Merlin asked.

The older man swallowed. "Here is Bodo, my son. I am Falkirk, son of Umber, the one who worked with iron. Maybe you remember him–"

"I do," Merlin answered, "a good man."

"Pleasure." Bodo the son managed between his chipmunk-stuffed cheeks.

"And who might you be?" Falkirk asked politely.

"Merlin. Or what's left of him."

The father put down his loaf of bread. "The wizard? I thought I recognized-- you've changed." He swallowed. "Anyways, I thought you wizards could live wishes alone."

"You mean I am a just ragged old man. The truth never hurts, does it? To the important thing. Who did all this?"

"You don't know?"

"I want to be sure."

Falkirk closed his eyes. "A thousand horsemen, maybe ten times a thousand. I have never seen so many animals, each with a fierce warrior on top, swinging their curved swords." He swung man, swung his right arm back and forth like he did, cutting his own wheat.

"Who led them?" Merlin asked tensely.

"A skinny runt, with hooded eyes and sharp little teeth. You must know him." Bodo managed.

" Mordred." Merlin hissed.

30

"There was no surrendering." Falkirk continued. "The boy and his kind killed for sport. The survivors took to the forest. We were coming back from Wexford, where my brother lives, taking some knives to him. I practice my father's craft now and then –

"And your king? What about Arthur?" Merlin could barely bring himself to ask.

"Arthur?" Bodo asked softly. "We can help with that."

The boy stood, took his last huge bit, chomped, and brushed off the snow. "This way," he mumbled with a mouthful. He started down the snowy expanse of the Roman road. His father and Merlin followed behind.

South of the village and east of the road ancient oaks grew in a dense stand. The grove, Merlin knew, had been sacred to generations of people. The trees, each with its own name and spirit, seemed stooped and dead in the winter landscape.

The grove ended at a pool of water, which, unlike all the other lakes and rivers nearby, still flowed and bubbled. It was a spring, a large and ancient one, with deep, emerald-colored water and a decoration of frozen willows along the edges. Merlin stopped. A low mound, so fresh that there was no snow on top, rose by the spring.

Bodo's father rested his hand on Merlin's shoulder. "My son and I, as we came up the Wexford road, heard on the other side of the hills what hell must sound like – the yelling, howling, and the screaming of the horses, the screams of the dying. The devil's horsemen had already broken into the fort. The village was already burning and the poor people already dead, most of them. The fighting went down the other side of the hill, toward the river. I have seen fighting, wizard, but nothing like this. It wasn't so long and it was done, the battle already lost, our people breaking and getting cut down. The monsters looted a little while and the devil led them away. The boy and I came down after they were gone, but nothing was left but the dead."

"How did you find your king?" Merlin asked. He had to know, though he didn't want to know.

"Just as you see. My son I came here to hide. This has always been a protected place, if you know what I mean. "

"I do," Merlin answered.

"We found him here laid out in the snow. My son I raised the little mound out of respect. Do you want a final viewing?"

The wizard felt his face turn pale. He thought he could prepare himself for what lay underneath the thin layer of dirt. He repeated to himself over and over that this was his duty, the ultimate result of his choice to live among these mortal lives.

Merlin nodded.

The man and his son worked quietly a few minutes, shoving away the dirt. Merlin turned his back. When the old man gave a polite cough, Merlin turned around and looked down on the face of a man about forty, pale and resolute, and troubled even in his death.

"They'll never be another like him," Falkirk said plainly and quietly.

"They'll be another." Merlin felt the blood of anger rising to his face. "I swear to it. Did you hear it? I swear."

Father and son glanced at each other. The anger from one so powerful frightened. Falkirk said quickly, "The burial of a king – I don't know if we've done the right thing. You tell us what to do."

Merlin shook his head. "You've done what you could." He took a long and deep breath. "Now we only need a warm place to sleep tonight." The wizard turned and began walking slowly, so sadly, through the oak forest.

The old man and Bodo hung back. The boy tugged at his father's sleeve. "What do we know about this old coot anyway? I mean, we might as well sit here and beat a drum and yodel at the top of voices for those monsters out there to come cut our throats!"

"Tsh. He might hear you."

"So? Mister his holiness the wizard seems to be in a fine pickle."

"Meaning?"

"Meaning all I see is a cold and old and tired and hungry old goat. It seems a true wizard would have a pig on the spit, a warm and snug mansion on the other side of the hill and a couple of foul-tempered dragons to keep him safe."

"Maybe he's having a bad day."

"Bah!" his son spat. "What's our plan provided we make it through the night?"

"Back to my brother's. These are hard times, if you haven't noticed."

"What other times are there?"

His father sighed. He remembered wonderful times, when every season seemed to be summer and the kingdoms, not matter how far you journeyed, rested fat and happy in peace. It didn't last, of course. Why things changed so much, good to evil, he didn't know. He doubted the wizard knew or surely he and his kind would do something about it. Instead, the father shrugged, and led his son out of the forest.

Merlin's offered the very basic comforts: a fire in the corner of the ruined house and the three of them wrapped up like grubs in their cloaks. Merlin listened to the knife grinder's son complain under his breath. Even the boy's father threw a few hopeful glances in Merlin's direction. Merlin shivered as badly as his guest did. He knew, though, what the danger was; and they were in the worst sort of danger. He might have given explanations, about how powers and spells and such left traces wherever they were summoned, like bonfires in the night. The single thing they had going for them, the three and the animal, was surprise. In life-and-death situations Merlin knew that was everything, more than killing armies blackening the landscape and powers of any sort.

Merlin wrapped a little tighter in his cloak and rolled closer to the fire. That was all he could do, and he hoped, he prayed, it was enough.

The father though stayed awake longer than anybody else. He listened to his son's rattling snores, bad as the boy's mother, when she was living years ago. Eventually even the wizard whistled and snorted and mumbled something about the start of things all over again. Their nasal music helped to keep him awake a little longer in the frozen night; he listened for the thud of war horses against the hard ground. He hoped he'd never hear such a thing in his lifetime, but he couldn't take the chance. He'd lived this long by never taking chances. As he lay shivering and restless, the northern lights, stronger than he'd ever seen them before, flickered hugely across the sky beautifully green and gold.

After a while the lights faded and the deep, iron-cold settled into the shallow valley, over the burned-out fields, ruined houses, and the forlorn and eyeless tower.

Chapter 4

The mount meant to eat his way through the night. Instead he woke with a start and a mouthful of frozen hay. The bitterly cold air seemed to shimmer. The animal's ears twitched. A low, drumming thunder had brought him out of sleep. It echoed off the far side of the hills around their camp.

The men, though, simply snored. The animal gave the nearest cloth-wrapped lump a solid foreleg thump.

Merlin sat straight up. "I am slain!" he called out aloud.

His new friends sat up straight and stared at the old man.

The animal chewed hay and studied Merlin with baleful eyes. The two other men burrowed out of their straw beds. From the north came the faint thunder. It grew louder as they listened. The two older men glanced at each other.

"What's it mean?" the son squeaked.

Merlin stood slowly. "Why, it means it's time for fighting."

"Brush the straw out of your hair," the father ordered his son. "Dignity first. And don't try to be a hero the first time out, despite what your heart tells you."

"Who?" Bodo blinked and glanced behind him. "What about some breakfast?"

"The victors can eat themselves sick," Fallkirk noted quietly. "The vanquished don't have to worry about it."

"Gentlemen, I want you two to guard my back. Stay in the background, if you please."

"Meaning?" Fallkirk asked.

"I want you and your son to hold the fort here."

"Excellent idea," Bodo crowed, "but then, he is the wizard, isn't he?"

Merlin tossed a saddle onto his mount and slipped on the bridle. The horse stood ready, steaming moist air from his nostrils. Merlin paused before mounting up. "Whatever you two hear - don't come running."

"He's the wizard," Bodo nudged his father in the ribs. "Let's not forget."

"It was an honor gentleman, in case we don't meet again."

"Avenge us," Fallkirk said automatically.

Merlin jabbed the animal in the ribs. With a protesting whiney the weak animal galloped. Its hoofs struck the frozen earth; Merlin turned the animal off the road and up the low hills and toward the rumbling thunder.

Father and son watched them ride away.

"Father," Bodo began.

"Yes?"

"The man carries no weapons."

"Evidently not."

"How many of them are there? "

"You've seen them. Thousands."

"The odds don't seem very good."

"He is a mighty wizard."

"Not mighty enough to save his king."

His father thought about that for a few seconds. "A good point."

Bodo shrugged. "Then I think we should hurry along."

He headed down the icy road, fast as he could. Fallkirk paused a few seconds more, thinking that they were missing something. What he could not say, but in the end, he hurried after his son. Well, he decided life could be worse. I could have been born a wizard. One against thousands: it made no sense at all, but that was the poor wizard's problem.

Chapter 5

The hills, in the summer, glowed with green pasture and blue flowers. Low trees, scattered here and there, made pools of shade. Now there was only frozen earth and deep snow, even as they topped the rise. The horse cantered, throwing snow from his forelegs. Merlin paused long enough to break a branch from one of the icy limbs. There, he noted silently, that should do. It wouldn't take much, if everything went well enough. He hoped so. He felt stronger. He knew he'd have one chance. Well, he thought to himself, that's one chance. Still, it wasn't much – it wasn't anything at all – but that's all there is.

They topped the ridge and faced a shallow valley. The snow was thin down there and the sun filled the valley with a morning light.

But the valley was occupied with something not so warm and loving -- an army on horseback, more mounted men Merlin had ever seen.

They advanced up the valley in a wide half-moon formation. Merlin spurred the animal, who galloped faster and stronger than Merlin thought possible. In a few minutes they blocked the thousands advancing up the valley, in as much as a single man on a horse could block an entire army.

Surprisingly, most of all to Merlin, that's exactly what they did: they stopped. Merlin let his eyes sweep their faces. They seemed happy enough. Maybe they just enjoyed the humor of the situation.

One horseman trotted out from the pack. He rode a bone-white animal, huge and strong, with flaring nostrils and a pounding gait, the most magnificent specimen, Arthur thought to himself, I've ever seen. The animal's saddle was black leather. His mane and tail were woven with golden braids and the bridle glittered with silver.

The man perched on the animal wore the engraved, embossed, and ancient armor of a full Roman general. A huge, blood-red cape streamed from his shoulders. At his side, he carried a huge sword, far too big for his thin arms. In fact, that was the problem: the impressive trappings decorated a warrior who seemed be no more than a peevish-looking boy.

The warrior-boy noted that the single man and miserable nag standing in his way carried no weapons at all other than a switch, with which he scratched his chin. He carried no shield, spear, javelin, or even a dagger good enough to cut up the roast chicken that the boy knew wizards were fond of cooking for themselves. Still, he approached Merlin warily and watched the old man's hands very carefully. The silly old fool simply played with his little switch.

"How well you look, Mordred," Merlin called.

"You seem well preserved, wizard."

"Hah. If only you knew."

"Maybe I do." He drew his sword and let it clink back into the bejeweled scabbard.

"You know what they say about he who lives by the sword." Merlin sounded so cheery.

"Not really."

"You'll learn."

"You're going to teach me? I'm a quick study." His voice was hoarse. He lowered his chin. His eyes flashed. "The first thing I learned: how to count."

He motioned with his hand. The army, with much rustling and jangling, advanced slowly toward Merlin.

Mordred grinned. "I'm sorry for what's about to happen…no, that's not true. Amazed, actually. How often does one get to see a true wizard get what he deserves? Many things have to come together. The wizard needs to be old and weak, and days removed from his rightful powers."

Merlin scratched his cheek with the little branch.

"Come now, old man. Where's your weapon? Let's make this fun."

Merlin shrugged and twirled the little branch.

Modred seemed confused, but glanced around, and, then, deciding it was safe, howled with laughter. Curiously, he laughed alone.

Mordred stopped laughing. "What do you plan to do? Give us a hiding and send us to bed?"

Merlin shrugged. He raised the twig slowly, just enough so that every eye was focused exactly on that one simple thing.

"Tell you what. I'll give you a weapon. Just because that's the way I am. " Modred nodded. The soldier behind him drew his long sword and heaved toward Merlin. It landed, hilt up, in the snow beside his animal.

Merlin twirled the twig slowly in his hand.

Mordred leaned forward. "Look. I know that you're weak as a kitten. You couldn't levitate a cabbage. In your human form we can cut you into

41

fish bait. Just turn around and – go. I'll hold these ruffians back, great and amazing that I am."

"Don't strain yourself."

The closest men behind them heard. Snickers and guffaws erupted. Modred turned beat-red. "You are playing me for a fool."

Merlin smiled, sat upright and let his voice ring through the cold air. "What could old imperial wizard like me do? Turn each and every one of you into swine?"

Merlin gave the twig a little flick.

"Swine."

Mordred's eyes bulged. His huge war horse snorted and reared. The horsemen closest yanked their animal's reins and shied away.

The entire host, thousands and thousands strong, twisted and snorted and whinnied and cursed and cried aloud.

Mordred turned royal purple and jerked his horse in tight, frustrated circles. "Play fair!" Then he bellowed over his shoulder. "Don't you imbeciles see what he is doing!"

"What am I doing?" Merlin asked mildly.

"You know perfectly well what you're doing!"

Merlin's eyes flashed.

"Swine!" Merlin bellowed.

He stood in the stirrups and raised his arm. The twig changed instantly into a javelin. He drew the javelin back as far as he could and threw it, high, high into the air. All the while, he prayed under his breath, let this work, let this work.

Every warrior eye followed the javelin as it arched into the sky. It nosed over and streaked toward the earth. Good, Merlin thought to himself, best I can hope for. He glanced at the warrior's faces nearest. All were slack-jawed and blank, awed as the spear seemed to pause in the air, then strike the frozen earth with a thoroughly satisfying thunk.

On the brow of the hill, Falkirk watched from the cover of boulders. His son cowered below the ridge, trying to glance in all directions at once. His father didn't notice. He'd tried to flee, but couldn't make himself. Instead, he'd come to witness the final battle of a brave man, if that's what wizards really were, and, so far, the wizard managed to remain in one piece. As he watched the old man reached inside his sleeve to produce a javelin and threw it high into the air. It was a good toss, prefaced by some curses that Falkirk couldn't make out at their distance.

It certainly got the attention. Falkirk gave him that. The spear hit the ground and quivered.

The deepest stillness Falkirk ever remembered followed. An especially hairy and wide-faced thug uttered, much to his surprise, a succinct and very convincing -- oink.

None of the ferocious ones laughed: they stared.

The man oinked again, evidently unable to do anything about it.

Left and right, by twos, then by tens, then by dozens, then by ranks, then by hundreds, men tumbled from their muscular steeds and roll in the snow – oinking and grunting as they fell on their hands and knees. Scampering through the snow they panicked, backs arched, creating a cacophony of piggy sounds, snouts digging at the snow as they scattered across the landscape.

Falkirk realized that his mouth had fallen wide open. An army of utterly ruthless, blood-drinking men disintegrated into -- something. If it weren't for the hoary faces, beefy arms, and crude tattoos the scene wouldn't have hurt so much. After all, Falkirk knew after years of life, that men acted the fool whenever they could get away with it. The old peasant shook his head; this was different. These swi – merciless killers - believed. For all real purposes, they had become exactly what the rather seedy old wizard wanted them to be: porkers.

As Falkirk watched the swine, who hate the wet, cold and each other, scattered farther and farther across the landscape, until the chill valley was empty, say for the thousands of bored horses, who pawed and nibbled at the frozen grass.

Merlin hadn't moved. He didn't have to. The other one – the hatchet-faced, evil boy – hoped up and down in his saddle, sputtering and scarlet with rage.

"Fiend!" he spat at Merlin and glanced over his shoulder. "That was no magic!"

"Just a few suggestions. Did you take notes?"

"Take note? Of what? Cheating! Trickery!"

"Take a breath. You're tired. Your anger weakens you. Add conquering and destroying a good man and his people at the same time – my, we've been busy. Not good."

"Release them." Mordred gritted his teeth so hard they cracked.

"From what? Their own imaginations? As for you – there's no excuse. Besides, you don't really care. You're simply afraid of me. And for good reason. You wonder if I still have it. Maybe I am crude and vengeful. Let's find out."

Mordred turned his horse and galloped away, hard as he could for a few hundred yards. He wheeled the animal around and charged Merlin.

Falkirk winched. The boy's hatchet face, Falkirk saw, meant murder.

The boy drew his sword as he charged. Falkirk couldn't keep his eyes off the blade--long and curved, sharp and glittering in the bright winter light. Merlin didn't move even a finger. Falkirk sucked in his breath. So this is how wizards took care of their business – as bloody and awful as peasants.

Falkirk averted his eyes. He waited for the crash of the horses and the twin cries, one of Mordred's triumph and the other of Merlin's death. Falkirk had heard the death cry so often before. Worst of all was its terrible sense of surprise. Falkirk wished his ears would go deaf, if only for a few seconds.

The first cry echoed off the snow.

But only one.

Falkirk glanced up. Mordred's huge animal flayed about in mid-air, four feet above the frozen ground, snorting, chest heaving, and eyes bulging white in fear. Merlin sat calmly where he was and gave a little nod. The animal levitated a few more feet, and turned around, or was turned around, until it faced in the opposite direction toward the north and the distant hills.

Then off it went, sailing through the hard blue winter sky, wholly unwilling, kicking and snorting, but smoothly rising until it hung all by itself high in the air as if it were the most natural sight in the world. It vanished as a tiny, if alarmed, speck against the eternal horizon.

"Is it over?" Bodo sighed, his voice muffled from under his rock.

"I wouldn't say so."

Years later, when resting by his son's hearth, Falkirk often thought about that day. He never felt sure about what he saw. He always trusted his own eyes, except at night and when he was bewitched, of course.

The problem was, of course, that bewitching was a very secret thing. Knowing the exact moment of bewitching ruined the whole experience. What he saw on the day, on a clear winter's morning, could be miraculous or terrifying, depending on the point of view.

Mordred: the boy, still encased in his Roman armor, sprawled on the snow, discarded, it seemed, and waiting for the slaughter. But his little ferret eyes were bright and darting while Merlin watched the war horse soar away on his maiden flight.

The armor, fine and miraculously wrought, disengaged itself piece by piece, as if repelled by whom it protected, and whirled through the sky and reassembled itself in the snow a hundred yards uphill.

Merlin twirled the twig between his thumb and forefinger and whistled little hunting tune. Falkirk blinked, or thought he blinked. Something happened. He was never sure what. A space seemed to open in the clear air, not a room, or a shape, but a space. Colors followed. Only once would he ever try to explain it all to his son, but all he got were

46

blank stares and whispers about the old man going gaga. The colors were everywhere, but they weren't just colors. He tasted them and heard them, like cords struck from a harp. Harmony and beauty – Falkirk had never thought the words in all his forty years, far too many days already for a good life, and suddenly, without knowing why, he felt the world well up inside him, as if he were ten years old again.

Waves came up from the space and swept over the petulant boy now sprawled in wool shift and naked feet. The waves thickened and focused on the boy. Quickly, despite the boy's blazing eyes, the waves engulfed him, tightened and rolled over his form, until, when Falkirk blinked again, he saw the boy lying in the snow wrapped up tightly in rough brownish linen.

Death shrouds, Falkirk decided, much like the ancient old, dried-up thing a dark-eyed man had brought up on the Roman road once and tried to persuade everyone in town to pay a penny to see it. A mummy he'd called it. That was it: a mummy, wrapped up to be preserved that way for eternity, or until the end of time, whichever came first.

Merlin tossed the stick into the snow and dusted his hands.

"That'll teach 'em," he muttered.

Falkirk stood slowly and brushed off the snow.

Merlin took notice. "I thought you two were on your way."

"Your magnificence, my honored father taught me never to run from a fight."

"This might have been one of those times. However, it all worked out. Impressed?"

Falkirk gave his son a kick and nodded slowly. The boy backed out of his hole and stared down at the countless horses meandering through the landscape, munching frozen grass. He whispered to his father, "What'd he do with them? The hairy ones. I'll bet he ate them, didn't he?"

Falkirk gave his son another kick and kept smiling at Merlin. The boy leaned forward, saw the mummified form of Mordred floating in the air and dived behind his father. "By Sharrick's bones, he's made them into breadsticks."

Falkirk pulled his son up by the ear. "Mind your manners," he whispered fiercely. "Anyone who can do this, you better be polite to their face."

Bodo winched his ear lose and dove for the ground again. "The breadstick's just floating there, old man, if you didn't notice."

"Let's hear his explanation," Falkirk whispered. Actually, he didn't want to know, but he doubted he was going to have a choice.

"Come down here, please. I'm tired of yelling up the hill."

Falkirk grabbed his son by the scruff of the neck and tugged his son along with him.

Merlin did seem tired; he face was flushed and sweaty. As they approached, Falkirk swore that the horse, as it craned its neck toward them, gave him a knowing wink. Merlin mopped his face and offered his hand to them both. "It seems that someone had my back after all. I have one more favor to ask. Do you gentlemen ride?"

"A horse?" Bodo asked.

"That's the one. We're going on a little journey and there's plenty of horseflesh in the vicinity without much employment."

Falkirk's moth fell open. Each war horse, even without saddle and accoutrements, was worth a yeoman's earnings for an entire lifetime. He sputtered, "I can learn."

"Not much to it, really. Just climb aboard and hang on for dear life."

Merlin's animal whinnied in what sounded exactly like a giggling sneer.

Falkirk pulled his son by the sleeve. "Boy, we have work to do –

Bodo dug in his heels and gave a polite cough. "Don't you think this might attract attention?"

He pointed to Mordred's form, undulating in the breeze.

"You've got a point." Merlin snapped his fingers and the body dropped like a rock.

"Why don't we just dig a hole and plant him here?" Bodod asked. "Respect for the dead and all."

"What makes you think he's dead?" Merlin asked.

Bodo frowned and studied the frozen blue eyes. "Just a guess."

"Well, you'd be wrong."

Bodo shrugged: the old boys were getting soft-headed. Better thee than me, he decided, and trotted through the snow after his gaga father, who was chasing frightened horses up and down the hillside.

Chapter 6

Eventually a few of the animals gave up and let themselves be lead back into captivity. The three – two men and one wizard – made a triumvirate. Merlin took the lead, of course, though, Bodo noticed, most of the time he kept his eyes downcast and muttered to himself. He led a horse that pulled a crude little sled they'd fashioned with branches and rawhide bridles. On the sled, the inert and stiff Mordred, who, Bodo decided, if he weren't dead as a flitter, did a great imitation. His father came next, riding erect and pretending he'd been born to the purple. He even crammed an ill-fitting helm onto his head, draped a baggy shirt of mail two sizes too big over his shoulders, and let a long Saxon sword jangle off his belt. Bodo followed a few yards behind, the wary and wise one, he elected himself, and at least smart enough to glance over his shoulder every hour or two.

Eventually, though, Bodo even gave that up. They rode for three more days through a landscape that grew increasingly lonely. Falkirk noted that they were heading steadily west and toward the sea that swallowed the sun. His son muttered now and then about being led to the gates of Hades, because that was all that lay to the west, where the dead sailed away on the clouds. Falkirk listened and knew what his son said was true; he shivered at the thought of meeting his late wife. It was bound to happen sometime, he knew, but he'd like to postpone it just a little longer, please and thank you.

On the third day they reached the grey ocean. The Roman road they'd been following ended at the ruins of a fort. By then, too, the weather felt much warmer and almost all the snow was gone. The boy had never seen the ocean before, and tried not to seem impressed.

"What lake is this?' he muttered to his father.

"'Tis his majesty, the sea." His fathered answered, trying to seem wise, though he'd only seen the ocean once before.

He glanced around nervously for his wife, though he wasn't sure how she'd make herself known.

While Falkirk cast furtive glances, Merlin road his horse to the edge of the sea and said, "We've reached the end of the road."

"Indeed, you munificence," Falkirk muttered.

"Literally and metaphorically."

"My thoughts exactly," Bodo answered quickly.

"Now - here's what we're going to do. We're going to build a boat. The timber is on that hill. All we've got to do is cut is down, drag it down the hill, cut the logs into boards, wear our hands raw carving and shaping, pin the boards to the keel, and caulk every seem. I want her thirty feet long at least, pinched into high bows bow and stern, with a single sail and a wide sweeping oar for a rudder. How's that sound to you gentlemen?

"And the pay?" Bodo piped up automatically.

"A penny a day plus all the horseflesh you've brought with you."

Bodo frowned.

51

His father kicked the boy's shin. "You're more than kind, your demi-majesty."

"I was thinking," Bodo began slowly, "a wizard might use his amazing powers to cut corners – y'know, lift a log, cause them to gather themselves together into the proper form, all under proper human supervision, of course."

Merlin shook his head. "Might as well burn a bonfire in the night."

"Is that a bad thing? I mean, really. Pride in your workmanship and all."

"Not in this case. I don't want him ever following the trail back."

"You mean Dilbert, I'm guessing." Bodo nodded toward the mummified form of Mordred, still tied down to the improvised sled. "Seems like our friend is begging for a resting place, don't you think?"

"In due time," Merlin muttered. "Now. Let's make ourselves busy."

They all worked, especially the scrawny wizard, who, with bare arms and head, cut trees, shaped logs, dragged boards, and smelted iron from broken tools left at the fort. At night they slept on straw beds inside the old fort, a comfortable enough bivouac, especially since Merlin always seemed to produce a decent dinner by his fishing and hunting skills. The only maggot in the works: Merlin insisted on bunking the lad Mordred against the wall within their spooky circle of firelight.

Falkirk learned to sleep with his head toward the east, through the open doorway and the hills, snow-free and already hinting at the approaching spring. Home, he sang to himself, though properly speaking, he and his son had no home; but they had a homeland, and his older brother, arrogant though he might be, still could make a place for him and his young son. It would be good enough. We are fortunate not to be born high and mighty, for look where it gets you, Falkirk mused.

He often listened to the old wizard, who muttered feverishly in his dreams in the middle of the night. The great wizard never knew a single good night's rest, though why Falkirk decided he never wanted to know.

Eventually all was done and the boat floated on the oily, cold waters of the bay. She was thirty feet long, with high bows and stern, a wide sweeping oar off the starboard side, and a low mast with a triangular sail woven from reeds. She was unpainted, a little rough around the gunwales and showed the skill of strictly amateur carpenters, but she floated and that was all that mattered.

For three days they collected supplies – water in clay jugs left in the fort, dried fish from racks they'd built by the bay and wild greens that grew up and down the hills. Merlin insisted that they pack the boat and cover the supplies with a woven tent, where he planned to sleep when he could.

Finally there was the last day and night. Merlin seemed not to make much about it, just a gruff announcement that everything was done and he'd catch the outgoing tide at first light. Maybe he just he didn't want to think too much about it, Falkirk decided, and that was fine with him.

Father and son woke to Merlin's bumping and scraping outside. He'd pulled the boat close to shore and was loading, on his own shoulders, the last of his supplies. Bodo blinked in the sunlight and scratched his stubble. He called out, "Where is it you're sailing, master?"

"I'm nobody's master. And the answer is – America."

Falkirk frowned. "Never heard of it."

"It hasn't been discovered yet."

Bodo frowned. "You're taking a trip to a place that doesn't exist yet."

"One day the whole world will hear about it."

"What's it going to be like?"

Merlin snugged the last clay jug in place. "Rather noisy."

Falkirk felt a pang for the old wizard who, more than likely, was unhinged by everything that had happened to him, and was about to sail until he dropped off the edge of the earth. Well, maybe that's the way he wanted it, rather than hang around as a has-been for countless years, begging for scraps at stranger's tables and sleeping in their stables. He cleared his throat. "How far is this journey going to be, if I may ask."

"Too far and yet not far enough."

Falkirk nodded. A riddle: that's all he expected. "But why?" He asked before he could stop himself.

"Do you really want to know?"

Falkirk blushed. "Not at all."

"A good choice."

A high-and-mighty reply, Falkirk, knew, but he'd asked for it.

Merlin glanced up at the sky. "Gentlemen, it's time."

He crossed the beach to where the horses waited and chewed their morning hay and turned around to face Falkirk and his son. "All these animals are yours, except this one." He put his arm around his poor roan and spoke to him.

Bodo leaned closer and frowned. He'd seen many warriors speak to their animals, which, after all, were more important to them than their wives. The old wizard nodded his head, and listened as if the animal were speaking back. He glanced at his father, who didn't seem alarmed at all. Both codgers were going soft in the head. He was glad this whole thing was done, weeks of building a boat so an old man could sail away and drown. Then there was what happened back in the cold valley. There was no telling what his majesty Merlin might do in a bad mood, or just because he could. His father was old, but he, Bodo, had a whole lifetime to plow through and, now, with a fortune in horseflesh at hand, he felt the world offered a something.

Merlin untied the animal's hobbles and gave him a gentle slap. The stallion looked in Merlin's direction and, with a haughty snort, galloped to freedom.

Merlin turned to father and son. "Gentlemen, it has been an honor."

Bodo glanced around to see who else might be referring to, but by then Merlin was shaking their hands. "Take care, both of you and watch your backs."

Sensible advice, Bodo decided. Then he remembered and blurted out, "What about your friend?"

Merlin nodded. Bodo glanced to the boat and shivered. In the bow, snuggled among a bed of cowhides, lay Mordred the Mummy.

"Pretty quiet company," Bodo muttered to himself and, for a fleeting moment, felt pity for someone else.

Merlin splashed through the surf, and climbed into the little boat's stern. He pushed the broad oar in a half circle until it caused the sail to stiffen with the offshore breeze. The bow cut through the waves as Merlin steered the bow toward the middle of the bay.

Father and son watched the boat's bow dip and fall against the chop. Soon it passed through the bay and sailed into the grey-metal sea.

"Looney old coot," Bodo muttered.

"Feel for him, do you?" his father asked.

"I feel he's soft in the head."

"He's sacrificing himself for the good of us all."

"How exactly?"

"I'm not quite sure."

Falkirk watched until the small craft disappeared over the misty line of the horizon. He turned to the fine animals waiting for them. As he approached, they snorted and pawed the ground. "It's been quite a time, hasn't it?" he asked aloud. The creatures bobbed their heads as if they understood. Falkirk smiled to himself: The world is a wondrous place, despite how we mess it up. Too bad we leave it so soon.

He stroked the horse's smooth muzzles. His son banged around inside the old fort, kicking and turning everything over. "Where'd he leave it?" he called out.

"What's that?" his father called back.

"Gold! Maybe the old coot left stacks of it somewhere."

"Why would he do that?"

"Why do you think?" Bodo shot back. "Gold!"

Falkirk shrugged. He let his son tear the place apart until he finally plopped down outside, sweating and angry as a hornet.

"Feel better?" his father asked cheerily.

The son grabbed the bridal of one of the horses and began stalking down the road. His mother's son, Falkirk, thought to himself, not without a resigned contentment. "So be it all," he said to the whole world, and taking the bridal, led his two animals down the road after his son.

Chapter 7

Years would pass and their corner of the world would know comparative peace and prosperity. There would be enough to eat most of the time, decent clothing against the winter, and no epidemics. Life and death, love, marriage and birth would follow as it should.

Father and son settled in the father's brother's village and built their own place of wood and wattle. Eventually the son married a young woman who liked strong young men with disagreeable personalities and children were born, healthy and pink, one after another.

Over the winter fire, when sleet pelted outside, the father, now a truly miraculously old man, told stories to pass the time. The children listened, wide-eyed, to his telling of the destruction of Camelot and their father and grandfather's encounter with the great necromancer, Merlin. They believed, as they should then.

But as the children grew older, they began to doubt and asked their father, who had evidently witnessed it all, if what their 'naner told them really happened.

At first their father grumpily told them to mind their own business. After all, he was a busy man with eight mouths to feed, corn to plant, sheep to shear and mead to swill behind the rector's crumbling hut.

One an especially snowy day, though, his youngest three children cornered their father at the door after the old man finished spinning his tale for an innumerable time.

"Was it true?" they demanded while jumping up and down. "Did old Merlin really turn a thousand times a thousand evil men into mice?"

Their father rolled his eyes. What he remembered from that distant time simply confused him. He finally decided that he had never been meant to see it and never expected to see anything like it again.

And he hadn't.

Truthfully, while they labored to build his boat, the wizard, Merlin the Everything, advisor to kinds, and destroyer of armies, seemed like anyone else. A little more lively and there was the winkle in his eye, sure enough, and, except for the unexplainable, just another skinny old man.

Still –

Bodo took a deep breath. "True? I suppose so."

The youngest squealed and hopped like jaybirds.

Their father hadn't expected that. "Wait a bit. It wasn't mice. It was swine." He shrugged. "So don't be so impressed."

The little one didn't seem to care. Bodo sighed: the distinction didn't seem to mean much to them. Well, he decided, once his father went to his reward the tales would pass away with him. The younger people seemed so level-headed. Too many went to school, spent their time reading and doing ciphers, whatever that was worth. Bodo gave another sigh and hurried outside before he got pestered to death. After all, when you thought about it, Bodo mused on his way to the rector's hut and a meeting of the village elders and the brewer of the shire mead, when all was said and done, the old wizard really did climb into his boat, stuffed his mummy friend into the front, and sailed away – very, very far away – never to be heard from again.

Not quite, as it turned out. Bodod found himself, after his children spread the word that their father witnessed all those miracles, in demand as a story-teller, complete with invitations to free food and drink. Silly stories were one thing, but all a man could eat and drink were quite another.

So the story of the fight in the snowy valley, and Arthur, and the peaceful little kingdom, good and great Arthur, nimble Merlin, devious Mordred was heard over and over again.

Bodo actually grew fond of telling his tales, even to the strangers passing through the shire. He might have stretched the truth a little, so that he became a stalwart warrior in an iron helm and a trusty sword, fierce at Merlin's side, while his father, old and weak-kneed, sought safety under the rock.

Eventually, Falkirk passed to his reward and was buried in the Christian church yard, the first of his family to be memorialized that way. Eventually, too, Bodo grew old and frail and died after a bad fall from a hay wagon. By then his children were parents and remembered the stories their parents and grandparents told; and the tales were repeated at warm hearths on bitter winter nights.

Bodod's children, in turn, grew old and passed the tales to another generation. Arthur, Merlin, and Mordred lived again – and again and again, one generation into the next. The wooden fort became a mighty one of stone, with curtains and deep, tall towers, the village grew into a glittering city, and Arthur's retainers with their leather shields became knights in steel armor, strong of chin and missing not a single tooth.

Arthur himself became noble, as wise as Solomon, a foot taller than the real issue, brave (true enough), and compassionate to a fault (true also). Merlin became a wise clerk, with grey robes, a pointed cap, and grumpy. Except for the grey university robes and pointy cap, the tales weren't too far off the mark.

Mordred remained who he was- cruel without reason, if ever there is a reason for cruelty, and clever and able to draw all round him into a maelstrom of misery and death.

Everyone who heard the tales would know someone like him; of all the characters, he seemed the most unavoidable. Glance over your shoulders, people reminded themselves with each telling. When and where will such a being return? Each person kept their own answer close to their hearts.

Gawain, Guinevere, Lancelot, the round table kitsch – all that was added much later by professional scribblers with an eye calculated for a specific medieval castle market.

Of course, very gradually, people all over the world professed to no longer believe and magic and wizards. Maybe they protested too much.

Merlin was remembered; that was the important thing, and in a way he couldn't complain about, if he had been around to take note.

And Merlin wasn't there. But like everybody, he had to be somewhere. As he informed Falkirk and his son Bodo, he was somewhere that didn't exist at that time.

It wasn't his choice. Even all-powerful wizards are swept along by fate. And fate sent him in a tiny boat, little more than a wooden chip, on a huge, frothing, wine- dark sea. He hoped to survive – that was all. On the strange shores- his real test would begin there.

Other lives, generations unborn, would be caught up in the story. Merlin felt the deepest pity for them, for, though he could do a great deal, their choices and bravery would be their own – if they were up to the challenges. There was no guarantee.

So easy to say.

That chance was as good as any other. Merlin knew it, as simply as he knew anything else, and that kept him awake though the cold and dark and even the bitter loneliness.

Chapter 8

Merlin sailed northwest for days, close by the cold wind and against a seething sea. He suffered the cold and wet and seasickness. He drank just enough sweet water to get him through each day and ate even less. On the third day he turned the boat's bow to the southwest and crossed into the royal blue of the deep Atlantic. The wind blew steadily from the northeast to southwest. Merlin knew how far the wind would blow – farther than from Londonium to Cairo, all of it cold ocean, endless horizon, and the thin blue sky arched above everything.

At the end of the first week the loneliness began to bother him acutely and, he admitted himself, he was plainly homesick. The British Isles had been his home for so long. He felt the deepest urge to come about and sail for home again.

That would sacrifice everyone, one day or another. He reminded himself of that fact every waking hour. He didn't know exactly when or precisely how, but it would happen. Toughen up. You have your duty and you shall carry it out. Yes, he sniffed; I've been in one place for just long enough.

"I need a holiday," he announced to a pair of Skuas circling his head. They cocked their heads, screeched, and soared away on the updrafts.

"A long quiet, ocean voyage, maybe," he called after.

And a long ocean voyage he got. He held the sweeping-oar so long that his palms blistered. Waves rolled dark blue and green, frothing and white, sea stallions, as he kept hard on his course.

He knew what lay ahead. The continent of America he could hardly miss, though, in five hundred years, Master Columbus would manage to miss the continent and think he was in India or Japan or China or somewhere.

But one long, dangerous, sunburned, seasick, wind-lashed voyage across the Atlantic left no trace for others to follow. After all, he was a single man (the thing in the bow was another matter) tossed about on a tiny boat on a few million square miles of ocean. He was swallowed up, literally gone west, where, as far as anybody he'd just left knew, the shades of the dead went to rest.

Merlin let the days flow past. Some days he slept sitting upright for a day or so with the tiller-oar in his hand.

Eventually sea became peaceful and green and the sky filled with bright, warm light. He smelled the land three days out: the scent of leaves, grass, and loam. His heart sang. He let his voice boom across the water. Land appeared in the next twilight, a long, dark line draw across the western horizon.

The next morning creatures of the shallow sea came out to pay their respects – gulls, terns, lumbering turtles, and a pod of smiling dolphins. Merlin knew them all and, if he weren't traveling incognito, he would have had a chat. Dolphins would talk your ears off he reminded himself. They made up the WYSIWYGs of the animal world – hyper-active extroverts, always running full blast.

The dolphins rolled onto their backs, considered him with their bright eyes, and assailed him with a barrage of clacks and squeaks. Merlin pretended not to understand. They produced string of frustrated cackles and speed away.

Merlin sailed close by the coast for another full day. The forest stretched along in an unbroken mass. In the afternoon he gave the tiller a hard shove and sailed into a wide bay. He let the sail catch a hard gust and drove the bow of his little boat high on the brown sand.

He could barely walk. The land still seemed to roll like the ocean and he desperately needed food and water.

But the journey wasn't finished. The hard part might just be ahead. He rested the first day, caught fish in a clear stream nearby, cooked them, and ate and drank his fill from the stream. The energy flowed through is bones and the sun was warm. He made a bed underneath the trees and slept from the early afternoon till the next morning.

The next morning he went out with an axe, adze and hammer and nails saved from the boat building, and pulled the cocoon from its salt-rimmed resting place.

He broke apart the boat and fashioned a small sledge from the scraps. Wheels wouldn't have helped; where he was going there were no roads. In fact, the entire continent, three thousand English miles wide, was bound together by trails, perfect for one human being to walk single file, but had not gotten round to roads.

He spent four more days catching and drying fish. He was proud of himself, living off the land leaving no trace of where he was or what he was doing.

By the fifth day he was ready. He made a backpack from what remained of the sail, filled it with provisions, and even topped it with a tidy bedroll. The cocoon he dragged to the sledge and tied down. He'd made a harness by twisting ropes from sail scraps and, after making sure the harness was as comfortable, leaned forward and began trekking.

Trekking: not walking. A well-worn trail began almost at the water's edge and he followed that. The sledge did its job. By leaning forward and pulling steadily he could make fair progress, provided he paced himself. Getting there was the thing, not how fast he went.

The journey would last two hundred English miles, about two weeks' worth of travel by foot. He didn't expect to be alone the entire time. People were all around – he spotted the lazy smoke from a campfire on his last day – and he planned how to deal with that. First of all, smile and exchange pleasantries. Display no weapons. Keep moving.

The land was level and sandy for the first few days, and warmed by spring sunshine. The air smelled so sweet from the blooming flowers, purple, white, yellow, and blue. After the cold sea he felt he had paradise, even if it was very lonely.

Maybe the people were inland, he guessed, finishing their planting. They'd move down to the seacoast later in the hot summer. He didn't see another human being for another full week until he had worked his way off the coastal plain. The trail, wide and hard-packed wound its way steadily and very gradually upward.

At midday he heard the boy singing as he came running pell-mell down the trail. He and Merlin collided around a sharp bend. The boy, with a square head and black hair, stopped short, stared full into Merlin's face and gasped. He sputtered and took off, scattering pebbles as he went.

Merlin kept going. He couldn't do otherwise. Within a few hours, Merlin heard sounds in the woods around him – quail exploding from their nest a few dozen yards before he got that close, and muted snaps of branches.

He labored to the top of a low rise. A dozen full-grown men, armed with spears, arrows, clubs and flint knives blocked his path.

Merlin smiled.

They didn't.

Merlin kept trudging. They parted and followed him quietly, keeping close enough to bash out his brains him with a single blow of their clubs.

No worse than I expected, Merlin reminded himself. He might defend himself if need be, but the trace left by mortal combat would glow for eons. That, of course, would put an end to everything.

Merlin began singing a sad ballad about someone whose father was a silkie, a sea spirit, and how one winter the silkie returned to claim the boy. The bard wasn't bad, really, but Merlin knew his scratchy voice would wake the dead. There was snickering and guffawing. Good, he thought and kept singing.

Some men poked at the cocoon, and when Merlin tore away the cowl to show Mordred's withered face they shied away. They got the idea: Merlin dragged death with him. With his ghostly skin, emaciated frame Merlin was death itself as well. The men spoke among themselves and quietly increased their distance. They followed him for an entire day, did a great deal more conferring while Merlin chatted away, giving his mute audience an earful of his life story.

Eventually the lead man – the man with the most tattoos and the attitude of supervisors everywhere – began motioning to Merlin.

Go – and keep going.

Merlin didn't have to be told twice. Death was welcome to keep moving, please and thank you. Pity he who had death wrapped up and intended to bury it all on his own. At least he'd stay dead.

"Let's pray," Merlin muttered under his breath.

On the tenth day Merlin saw the undulating line of the Blue Mountains, the Appalachians. The hills welled up sharp and grand and blue. Wisp of damp clouds clung to the flanks and the peaks. At night Merlin listened to wolves howl and cougars shriek.

Merlin built a fire at night and kept it going. His fear was primal; much of his own ancient strength had returned, but he was determined to keep to his plan.

He climbed – and climbed some more, and climbed more after that. Eventually he stumbled into a forgotten valley so narrow that even the noonday sun never reached the river flowing through the valley floor. A cold, shallow, frothing river, running with translucent, jade-green water – an amazing place Merlin would love to share, if he weren't alone.

Or almost alone.

Across the river, a sharp, strangely-shaped hill rose above the river bank. The other mountains rose and fell in rhythm with one another, like frozen waves, but this one twisted upward craggy and half-formed.

But it was good for one thing.

Merlin camped for one night at the foot of mountain and shivered all night long.

He woke the next morning to a chill fog, ate a little, drank from the river, and strapped his burden doubly tight to the sled and began climbing.

Merlin pulled and tugged; he managed a few hundred yards up the steep slope in the first hour. Not too bad, all things considered, he said to himself. He glanced up and studied the seventy-degree slope rising another four thousand feet.

"Just get it done by nightfall," he mumbled aloud. Who would want to be there at night? He asked himself, and didn't wait for an answer. He worked carefully and took on crumbling volcanic ridges again and again. A bad fall would end everything. The mummy might end up the rushing river and carried downstream for miles. Worse, it would be free, though not free the way any person would think.

Merlin didn't worry about himself – at least not too much. He'd never felt so human. He felt hunger, thirst, pain and gloom and despair – not too bad for an amateur, he told himself. It mattered, though; as the cranky shaman, the knotty old man with flinty eyes and a scraggly beard, he was seemingly like any other man ever born – and just as invisible.

Eventually the crest came into view. The sister mountains nearby ended in narrow ridges or round tops. This mountain ended in a shallow caldera a mile in diameter.

Merlin made it there in the late afternoon, as black summertime clouds scudded through the valley. Yellow lightning flashed. Dry, angry thunder echoed against the slopes.

Merlin hurried. He needed to leave that place; he felt in his heart, his brain, his skin. Scruffy weeds and twisted trees – grey and dead – covered the undulating surface of the caldera. A chill wind blew fitfully. Merlin heard voices in the wind, snatches of words, spells and curses and warnings, just enough to let him know he was in the right spot. Nobody else would come here; not anyone with any sense or awareness of the world around them. Not even the dead, Merlin thought to himself, would dare; only the very unlucky.

Merlin found what he needed, the entrance to a cave overgrown with wild roses.

He pulled out a Roman sword he'd carried all the way from England and hacked away the thorns. The thunder muttered angrily. The entrance was barely big enough for Merlin. But it was easy to conceal: better still. He raised the sword and hacked away the cords that bound Mordred to the sledge.

He pulled the mummy inside the cave. The cave became huge just a few dozen yards farther along. Merlin used his flint to spark dried moss and lit a rough torch of pine knots. With his free hand, he grabbed Mordred's feet and dragged along, hard and fast as he could.

The roof of the cave soared far above. Stalagmites and stalactites met each other in weird columns. In the shadows they seemed alive. Merlin shivered and glanced over his shoulder.

Bones from mammoths and wolves and saber cats littered the floor. Huge animal skulls gaped at him from the dark corners of the charnel house.

Merlin dragged the thigh bones of the big elephants into a catafalque and rolled Mordred atop the bony bed. "There," he said roughly, "least we aren't going to catch our death from cold."

Merlin stepped back. The torch was flickering. The shadows closed in. He saw what he was afraid he'd find: in one corner, the skeletons of a dozen human beings, stone weapons still in some skeletal hands, clubs buried in the skulls of others. They lay where they fell, with threads of hair still clinging to skulls. Merlin looked on the remains of a massacre, a fight by smoky torches for the possession of a magic place. Twelve thousand years of time didn't make it any less gruesome. So long ago, Merlin knew, people were so much more aware of such places and powers. They were right to fight for this place, if they wanted chaos and death; and that's what they found. The danger, Merlin guessed, was that another tribe or even another family might get the power; and that was worth killing each other for, even if nobody survived.

Merlin glanced around a last time. Sweat rolled off his face. His breath came hard; he couldn't take a deep breath. His skin tingled. He was sure, though he didn't want to think about it, that from the corner of his eyes he glimpsed the shimmering ghost of those that died here. That was a human belief;

Merlin normally had nothing to do with it. He feared that they might be right. He didn't want to know.

He hurried out, faster and faster, though he didn't have far to go. No matter how hard he ran, it seemed that he wasn't getting any closer to the dim light of the entrance. He ran harder, until, with all the energy he could call up, he felt the first breath of cool air rich with the scents of trees, and rain.

He squeezed through the entrance. It seemed to have gotten smaller, though that couldn't be. The place wasn't alive, Merlin reminded himself. It hadn't intended to trap him there. He would know, he reminded himself. After all, you know almost everything.

Merlin rested outside. The thunderstorm broke and drenched him. Lightning crackled through the blue-black clouds. Merlin wrenched the sledge apart and, using a long piece as a fulcrum, pried a boulder into the shallow gulley that lead to the entrance. Smaller rocks he picked up with his hands and tossed row entrance, and when, that was done, he used the long timbers as a crude shovel. As the storm raged, he filled the spaces between the boulders and rocks with black mud.

Merlin worked in the stinging rain until he had filled the gulley to the brim. He stepped back and studied what he'd done. The rain was already smoothing out the soil as if it were just a fresh grave.

Merlin sat on the ground and let the rain do its work. The sounds of the pounding rain never seemed so beautiful, nor did the smell of the wet earth. He rested a long while, until the storm blew itself out and drifted to the southwest. As the rain dripped from the trees, Merlin stood, picked up what supplies he'd kept in his sack, added his sodden bedroll, and, using the Roman sword, cut a decent hiking stick. He tucked the sword into his belt and, with that, he was done.

He took a deep, breath, turned away from the mountain and began a slow descent into the valley.

He traveled for weeks, living off what he could catch and wild grapes when he could find them. He followed the trails made by buffalo, deer, and elk. He traveled until the weather turned into high summer and days filled with brilliant sun and sodden heat.

He saw no other people, just a faint trail now and then and, a few times, the remains of an old village, deserted and grown over with honeysuckle vines. Much of the time he walked softly through forest of huge trees. Often only cool, greenish sunlight reached the ground.

He wandered steadily west. Eventually he reached a huge river, broader and deeper than any river he'd ever seen. He made a camp by rolling river and fished along the deep bank. He cooked and ate fish in every possible way for three weeks, until he never wanted to see another fillet, ever.

He gave himself time to reach a decision: up or down the river, or make a raft and cross the river and keep heading west.

On the twenty-second day, on a day of still, misty heat, as he was poking around for edible chestnuts, a gaggle of children suddenly tumbled out the woods. They stopped short and stared at the pale, haggard man. One child called out to him and, as a single entity, the children squealed and surrounded Merlin. They sang, chanted, grabbed his hands and pulled him away from the river.

Merlin didn't think running away would help. Better, he decided, not to run away. Why would he be running? The children tugged him along to a clearing. He surprised a group of forty adults, all raven haired- and dark-eyed. They were working on a stone weir, a fish trap, set across a stream that feed into the muddy river.

They glanced at each other and waded out of the stream. They quietly surrounded him. His pale skin and blue eyes caused them to stare and mutter. Merlin expected that. He kept his eyes to the ground and didn't move. Give it plenty of time, he reminded himself: no loud greetings and handshaking, that sort of thing.

He glanced at their faces. They seemed intrigued. Their children were happy and trusting. Nobody carried weapons; all those were good signs. Merlin guessed that these people lived by farming, fishing, and hunting. Without doubt, they traded with the people in all other directions, like people all over the earth. They survived the way people had for tens of thousands of years.

Merlin gave a little smile. The oldest woman stepped closer and studied his face for a long time. She rubbed a finger along Merlin's cheek and muttered as she did. Ghostly skin, no doubt – that's what fascinated her, Merlin thought. Can't blame her. After all, it seems reasonable. She pinched his arms – hard. When Merlin cried out she laughed. No ghost here, Merlin guessed she meant. He rubbed his arm and she turned around and called out to everybody as she did.

With that, they came running and laughing. He was surrounded again, this time by the adults as well, who pinched his skin on their own, tugged at his hair and poked here and there. But they kept laughing and pulled him along toward the stream. He was amazing, but let's see what he's good for-- that's what Merlin summarized they meant.

Merlin splashed into the stream and began hauling rocks. For a while, they simply watched, maybe amazed that he had legs, arms, eyes, and a willingness to be one of them. Gradually, the others joined Merlin, singing and joking as they went. Unlike the drab people he'd known back home, these people seemed well-fed and happy; after all, Merlin reflected, they gathered what they needed from millions of square miles of paradise.

That was important. After all, Merlin figured he'd be among these people for a long time. How long, he didn't know. That depended on one thing – fate and, as far as he knew, no single sentient thing, not matter where he or she or it resided in the wholeness of everything – nobody knew how things would play out.

But Merlin intended to play his hunch. He knew what had happened before.

Mordred.

Merlin heaved a big stone atop the fish trap and everyone cheered. Merlin cheered, too, though he wasn't sure why. Everyone scampered out of the water and ran upstream. Evidently the hard work was done. Women and children waded into the river and began driving fish downstream and toward the narrow neck of the trap.

They sang as they slapped at the water with branches. Merlin took a place at the far right side of the line and sang along, though he had no idea what he was saying.

The water teemed with fat, blue-black and silver fish. Merlin thought about the fish bake tonight and some of the delicate green plants, natural herbs, he could add to his part of the bake. He was sure that they brought along corn, squash and what else he couldn't say. That would be good enough; he would start language lessons that very night.

He wondered what name they would give him. He doubted he'd have much choice. The name meant everything. His only fear: that they would expect him, gradually or right away, to predict something about the future. That he couldn't do.

The night was warm and, for a long while, still. The fish bake went as Merlin expected. He served as the entertainment and danced and sang like the court fool. Arthur -- his old Arthur -- would have roared with laughter to see his knobby-kneed wizard gamboling around a big campfire. You do what you have to, Merlin thought, and kept right at it.

There was the new moon. A few hours later Merlin heard the rumblings of heavy thunderstorms crossing the wide river. By then the campfire was only glowing embers. The people were sleeping, wrapped in animal skins or capes made from woven leaves. The storm stalked closer and closer on the legs of purple and green electric bolts smashing into the earth.

Merlin drowsed. Wind roared through the tops of the trees. A spire of wind swirled through the clouds, twisting as it went, and tore through the crowns of the huge elms that sheltered them. Merlin jumped to his feet.

"Mordred!" Merlin roared.

The people leapt up too and, seeing the ghostly man afraid, cried out and ran for the safety of a hillside nearby. Merlin stood stock-still, his chest heaving, as the wind dissipated among the high crowns. The thunder quietly muttered; there was no rain at all. Merlin settled down eventually. The people returned, studied him cautiously, and, for the rest of the night, kept their distance.

Merlin managed a weak smile. I need to rest, he reminded himself, and recover a sensible way of looking at things. Other than that, all I can do is wait and hope, though I know that hope is the thinnest of reeds.

Part Two

Chapter 9

TINTANGEL, the loneliest city in Florida, its few hundred residents liked to boast, doubted every stranger. After all, they were rare enough. After all, the Florida panhandle, some people sniffed, was just southern Alabama down to the high tide.

They were right. The Cyclops, the town's single red-light, blinked to scarce traffic, red, green to yellow, at the intersection of Cornwall and Wales Street. The sky burned scalding hot; listless breezes rustled the dry palm trees. A freeway ran twenty miles to the north, too far for truckers to stop for lunch and diesel.

Nobody really knew how Tintagle survived. Orrville, ten miles south, dazzled the eye with miles of condo canyons and shops selling beach paraphernalia at heart-stopping mark-ups.

Things are kindly quiet around here, residents would say, if the extraordinary visitors happen to ask. That was, the visitor think while he smiled politely, the understatement since the pyramids. If the visitor wandered past Cleburn's Grill and Civil War Emporium, he'd see a shabby gingerbread Victorian of sunbaked shingles. A wooden sign on the crabgrass lawn warned the visitor away: the Hilltop Home for Boys.

Boys in the plural – not all really bad boys, just boys the juvenile court couldn't fob off on somebody else. They didn't live alone, of course. Cherish Heaven Wheezel had started caring for other people's boys at age thirty-five when her husband, somebody else's boy, left her for a waitress and moved to Canada.

Some declared that the next twenty years were her way of getting even with the male sex. That wasn't so. She stood for certain standards which could be summarized pretty evenly: You can't have too many rules and this House isn't Never-Never Land.

The typical client population included six to ten boys, ages four to sixteen, with more younger than older. Upstairs, the clients lived in three big bedrooms furnished with donated bunk beds, sheets, quilts, curtains, a purple carpet, third-hand clothes and boxes of chipped toys for the little ones.

The shag, grape-purple carpet was important for an accidental reason. It spread across the entire second floor fungus-like. Wheezel slept in the far bedroom, closest to the stairs just to prevent what usually happened while she snored and tossed and turned and muttered about Herbert, now a Canadian citizen: Boys padding downstairs to break rules, especially, or almost always, the two oldest.

The two oldest boys, plenty old enough to know better, occupied the room on other end. One was Lawrence Edgar Lance, sixteen point five, with that bristly carrot- red hair that boys hate and more freckles than the entire population of Brazil. His neck was frankly scrawny and his Adam's apple huge; his feet were too big, his voice cracked and, because of his habit of bumping into things skull first, everybody called him Lumpy.

The other boy meant to stay awake that hot night. Lumpy, once he got horizontal, blinked out. The other boy waited and bounced peanut shells against the wall as he chewed the kernel. He might have been a year older than Lumpy, a little bit shorter, with dirty blond shaggy hair and narrow green eyes. He chin ended in a stubborn knob.

Stubborn: that was his mantra in school. He was drifting. He was a drifter – that's what any two of teachers would say and his social worker, too, if she had time to think about him.

Wheezel, busy as everybody else, had another take: the boy was peculiar.

After all, he didn't even have a proper name. When Wheezle got the baby boy – the only infant she'd ever taken – the sketchy paperwork, filled out in somebody's chicken scratch, listed under first name A (1) boy and last name: You Guess. So Al he became.

He'd lived in Hilltop longer than anybody else, ever. Other boys came and went, like the Criswell triplets with their quivering baby blues, or graduated, like Percy Quill, to the state pen after taking off for Vegas in the Tintagle PD's only cruiser on a Christmas day. Still others moved on to foster homes, or unto the reluctant, palsied arms of ancient great aunts and resentful uncles.

But they moved. Al was just always there, Christmas after Christmas, and every September when school began again. He just was. He waited, though for what he wasn't sure. Nobody else knew either.

But children do one thing: they grow up.

Chapter 10

The Cyclops' single eye blinked a few dozen yards away at the intersection where Cleburne's and the county courthouse and Alligator Grocery Market took up three sides of the square. Waiting for Wheezel to drift into a snuffling sleep was easier for Al than dreaming.

The chimes on the courthouse ratcheted and struck ten o'clock. Al slid off the bed, twisted Lumpy's nose on the way past, ignored the squeal, and took his post by the bedroom door. Lumpy got out of bed and shuffled close by, rubbing the offended nose, and hissed, "You gonna do me grievous damage one day."

Al glanced down the hallway. He heard what he needed: a dieselchug-a-chug snoring from Wheezel's room. Al peered down the hallway.

"You think?"

"Yea, I do."

"You think too much."

"I'm working on it." Lumpy swallowed

"Atta boy," Al said and opened the bedroom door wide.

The boys slipped into the hallway, carrying their shoes in their hands. The purple shag muffled their progress down the hallway. The old stairs creaked, but by then it was too late. Wheezel kept the backdoor key under the refrigerator in the kitchen. Al had known about it since he was eight years old.

That Friday he and Lumpy felt special anyway. Al was a junior that year. In another year and a few months he'd finish high school and fall into the great Then What? For an orphan that meant work somewhere, or maybe the army. College? Not a chance.

On the other hand, other than Wheezel, Al answered to nobody in particular. After a few more seasons he'd be free and wild. He and Lumpy cashed in at the Turpentine Consolidated High by having No Papa, No Mama, and no Uncle Sam, as the old song went. No parents meant having nothing to lose, very heady stuff for anybody under age forty. Just associating with the boys seemed a risk, or at least just a little bit wrong, maybe dangerous, and certainly sweet.

Therefore the boys got rides. Most of the other kids had cars, including Lester Conway who tried never to be impressed by Al's shaggy hair (one haircut a month, tops) and clothes with honest-to-goodness moth holes chewed in them. He wasn't impressed when Al asked for a ride Friday about ten if you and Quigley were heading over to Orrville.

Lester let his hooded eyes at slid to half-mast. Yea he muttered when Al muttered the question.

'Bout ten?

Give or take, Al waved and branched off to Algebra.

At nine fifty eight Al opened the kitchen door and let it creak closed. He and Lumpy jogged across the damp grass of the big backyard where katydids sawed and sang in a chorus of thousands. Lester's plum blue coupe slid to a stop by the curb. Al and Lumpy hopped in and slammed the doors. Quigley, a blond surfer sort of girl, turned and flashed her smile. Her teeth actually caught the light. "How're you two boys?"

Lumpy shrugged.

"Leprosy's acting up," Al answered.

"That's nice." Quigley swung her blond ponytail back around.

Lester gave his wheels the gas and settled down to drive exactly at the speed limit. He father was Tintagle's entire police department, the one whose cruiser Percy snitched. The man never got over it; he threatened, if his son every got into any trouble whatsoever, to make sure his son was walking to age fifty-five.

Maybe he could do it. Nobody really wanted to take a chance. The drive over to Orrville didn't amount to much anyway, a straight shot down sandy state highway 29. Eventually Lester checked both ways three times and pulled into the Majestic Oyster Theater on the edge of Orrville.

Lester cleared his throat. "Gents, your ETA back here is Twenty-three hundred hours. At twenty-three plus ten I'm outta here, hear?"

His father was ex-military, an oxymoron if there ever was one.

"Huh?" Lumpy frowned.

"He's cutting out by ten past eleven," Al answered.

"Yea, that's what I thought."

He and Al climbed out of the car. Lester gave it the gas and scattered gravel. Al and Lumpy watched them disappear.

A few hundred yards down the road an all-night quick shop lit up the night with yellow neon. They paused in the gravel parking lot.

"You've still got the equipment?" Al asked.

Lumpy patted his back pocket and swallowed.

"Cold feet?" Al checked.

"My feet are just fine," Lumpy squeaked.

A bell over the door jangled. A tiny man the color of waterlogged driftwood hunched over the counter and mumbled and scratched at a crossword puzzle. Lumpy wandered toward the back of the store.

Al stepped up to the counter and slapped down a twenty dollar bill.

The ancient man barely glanced up. "What's yere problem?"

"Six pack of Blue Lagoon, por favor"

"Por what? Let's see some ID, Cochise." He jabbed his thumb at a sign tacked to the wall: IF YOU DON'T LOOK SEVENTY, YOU GET CARDED.

Al slapped down a yellow card. The ancient one picked it up with two fingers and peered through his trifocals. "What the heck is this?"

"Canadian military ID. Me and Jean — we're Canucks. Canadians. Killer Canadians, eh?"

The old one frowned deeper and deeper until his mouth made a perfectly upside down U. He shredded the yellow card which Al had spent ten dollars buying from a lobster-red spring breaker. The man thrust his head forward on his chicken neck. "Get outta my store before I call the cops, you buncha doped up long-haired hippie freakazoids!"

Plan B: Lumpy, hidden behind stacked jars of pickled pig's feet, pulled out a string of firecrackers. He struck a match and lit the string and tossed them on the floor. Bam! Bam! Bam! Bam!

The man dived behind the counter. Al tossed down a twenty and snatched up the pack of Blue Lagoon. He and Lumpy bolted through the front door and into the hot night. They ran and ran down highway 29, farther and farther out of town, until their sides hurt.

The traffic was scarce so far out. The dense pine woods pressed close. Lumpy grabbed Al's shoulder. "You're killing me, your majesty"

Al slowed. He felt hollow in the inside. He wondered if the old man died of fright or broke his hip or something.

Lumpy seemed to concentrate of just breathing. His lungs rattled.

"Sure you can handle this?" Al asked.

"You only got one life, right? Whatcha got?"

Al held up the pack of Blue Lagoon.

Lumpy whistled. "Sweetness itself. I feel better already, my friend."

Al glanced around. A billboard with a metal catwalk and a ladder rose a few yards off the highway. The lamps that once illuminated it were burned out; the jeans advertisement came from the year Al was twelve.

Al and Lumpy climbed the ladder. They settled on the catwalk twenty feet above the piney woods. They dangled their feet off the edge. Ahead, to the east, the neon rainbow of emerald, crimson, and blue of Orrville filled the summer night.

Lumpy pried open a can of warm Blue Lagoon, let it froth, and slurped. He coughed and frowned.

"Damned straight."

Al pulled a tab, swallowed, and tipped the can over the edge. He let beer shower the honeysuckle vines below.

"Hey! What's the idea?" Lumpy hopped up. "I don't think you appreciate the finer things in life."

"Like dog pee, you mean?"

"I beg your pardon."

"Beg all you want."

Lumpy wrenched free another can and held it high. "Maybe we should save the rest, you know, for a rainy day?"

"Great idea."

"You never know."

"You've got that right."

They didn't talk for a few minutes.

Lumpy concentrated on his own anxieties. He glanced at Al, who didn't seem to realize time was passing. Teachers, bus drivers, kids in the hallway, Wheezel, and Lumpy, more than anybody else, had to bring him back, remind him of what was going on. He was taking trips through his mind; that was the popular excuse, but it seemed worse than that.

After all, he'd had lots of practice with social workers and interning psychologists to talk about his feelings. Besides, what happened wasn't a feeling. Feelings were bad enough just by themselves. Al took journeys. Maybe he wouldn't return, he reminded himself now and then. That is if things got bad enough.

Al shivered.

"I wouldn't want to be anywhere else," Lumpy ventured.

"You really mean that?"

"I sure do." He glanced at Al. "Why else would I say it?"

"Just wondering."

"Just?"

"What really happens after you cut the apron strings. Graduate, I mean." Al asked suddenly.

Lumpy frowned. "Maybe the U.S. navy. You don't have to do a lot of walking."

"Going to be a swabbie all your life?"

"I mean, when I'm old, thirty or something, I might want to build houses."

He glanced at Al. "I want people to move into them, Mom and Dad and two point five kids. Families and all that stuff--."

Lumpy stopped quickly.

Al couldn't stop himself, "What do you remember?"

Lumpy glanced over angrily, searching his friend's face. "What's that supposed to mean?"

"Doesn't mean anything."

"What am I supposed to remember?"

"Forget it."

"Okay. I remember this freaky girl with her hair all done up in ribbons like a kid and singing a song. Just to me. And dancing with me in a room with ugly paper bag brown walls."

"What about her face?"

"What about it?"

"I'm just asking."

"I've got nothing."

Lumpy's jaw was set. Al leaned back and, for what seemed a very long time, they sat quietly and apart from each other and watched the neon lights glow over Orrville.

Finally, Lumpy popped open a Blue Lagoon. "What about yourself?"

Al felt a catch in his throat. He didn't answer quickly. He knew he shouldn't. The tone wouldn't be right.

"Nothing," he finally said.

"Just like a blank wall?"

"I guess."

"Wow. You must have been floating among the bulrushes."

"Not really."

They were quiet a little longer. Lumpy said quietly, "Do you ever want to know?"

Al didn't answer.

Lumpy said, "After I start building houses, after I make a pile of money, I'll find out where she works and drop in on her. Just like that."

"You'll do that?"

"Sure. I'll be rich, remember?"

"What do you think she does?"

"She's a counselor or makes pottery or something. Of course, I may take one look, climb back in my BMW and drive off. Depends on how I feel at that very second."

"Makes sense."

"You think so? What about you?"

Al shook his head.

"Why not? Everybody's got to have parents. It's in the rules."

"Your rules maybe." Al said automatically.

"You're looney," Lumpy took a long swig. At the end he frowned and studied the label. He dusted his hands and stood. "Come on, son. We've got things to do."

They climbed down and met Lester in the parking lot of the Oyster Majestic. The drive back was quiet. Lester seemed nervous; Quigley said a few crazy, dreamy things and smiled the entire way back.

He dropped Al and Lumpy off by the crepe myrtles on the far side of Wheezel's property. Tintagle was absolutely still and quiet. Al glanced up at the courthouse clock: one thirty.

The porch boards didn't squeak.

The back door was still unlocked.

Al slipped inside the kitchen with Lumpy right behind and managed to step on Wheezel's bare toes.

She waited in ambush by the refrigerator, hair in rollers and her nightgown tied around her neck. "Arghhhh!" she howled and sucked back a few more words, since there were little children in the house.

"Jesus Christ and General Jackson," Lumpy cried and hopped around the table, avoiding colliding with Al who'd just leapt halfway across the room.

Suddenly the room blazed with harsh light. Al, who understood now what a heart in your throat really felt like, witnessed Wheezel, rocking in a dining room chair, still muttering unsure words under her breath and rubbing her toes.

Wheezel took an especially long time. She rubbed and rubbed her toes until she straightened her spine and studied at her prey.

Al thought she seemed oddly quiet – eyes still streaming tears and cheeks beefsteak tomato red, but , instead of yelling, she gave a huge sigh and said, politely, "Good evening, gentlemen."

"Hiya," Lumpy squeaked.

"What brings you gentlemen out at this hour?"

"Birdwatching," Lumpy shot back and glanced with pleading puppy eyes at Al.

"I don't suppose you'd like to tell me the truth?"

"No, ma'am," Al said evenly.

Wheezel sighed once more. "I was starting to look on you as an adult."

"Then we'll be saying good night."

"Hold your tongue. Whose idea was this?"

Lumpy cut his eyes toward Al.

Al swallowed.

"Very well," Wheezel said quietly, as if she was already thinking about something else. "You sons of Ulysses are confined to the property for two weeks. Lump – Mr. Lance, you are not smiling."

Lumpy swallowed. "Inwardly, Ms. Wheezel, I'm all aglow."

"And don't forget it. Get out of here."

Lumpy cast a pitying glance at Al and thumped up the stairs, two at a time. Al tried to follow. Wheezel blocked his path. She waited till Lumpy disappeared. "I was serious about what I said."

"Yes, ma'am."

"Don't 'yes ma'am' me. Before you know it you'll walk out of these doors a free man. I hope you won't regret your time here. An old woman does what she can. Anyway, I'm missing my beauty sleep." She opened her mouth to say more and stopped. "Now, get out of here," she said simply.

Al felt a strange chill, and climbed the steps, careful for the first time not to wake the little ones.

Chapter 11

Al found Lumpy hiding in his bed. He peeked from beneath his pillow.

"No blood?"

Al flopped into his bed. He felt worn out. He hadn't felt that way a few minutes ago. He didn't feel angry, just sorry that he'd kept an old lady up past her bedtime.

Lumpy commenced his nightly nasal symphony. Al buried his head under his pillow. Now he felt angry at somebody, though Lumpy couldn't do anything about it. He and the Lump had been around each other too long, he decided, though that couldn't be exactly right. He didn't have anybody else to get tired of, unless it was Wheezel and everybody reminded him that he had every reason to feel gratitude and devotion and love toward her.

Al pretended to sleep. That didn't work. Eventually he sat on the bed and opened the bedroom window open as wide as it would go. The onshore breeze, carrying the sea-salt smell with it, billowed the cotton curtains at the window.

Earlier in the season, one of the interns cornered Al every Saturday morning for a month. He'd insisted that Al call him by his first name – Roy. He wore dress slacks and cowboys boots.

The man sat in the parlor and rocked in Wheezel's favorite chair. Al didn't know what to do with him.

Dreams that were more than real, Al blurted aloud.

Roy's ear's pricked right up.

Al couldn't stop himself. Dreams, he tried to explain, had you doing crazy things like marrying your lit teacher, or talking to trees, though that didn't seem so crazy –

Al dug himself deeper and deeper. He fumbled, trying to make it seem reasonable. They weren't dreams: they were memories, the way most people recalled a trip to the beach. Sitting by the window, with the damp, hot Florida night rustling around him, Al brought the memories back: a rough, thick wool cape around his shoulders on a chill, sleet-filled morning. Or words from a language that he'd never heard except in his memories. He could speak it if he wanted, but that was one thing he never, ever dared.

And more: a wooden fort sat on a grey-green hill, a little village with mud streets, the way a spear balanced in his hands, the tiredness after a long and awful fight.

Al shivered in the heat.

He rode a big, strong horse at full gallop. An old man, with a scraggly white beard, older than Wheezel, rode beside close by him. Al felt the stiff leather shirt he wore, and the reigns tight in his left hand. With his right hand, and his strong arm, he drew a sword, a heavy, long, real weapon.

Roy wouldn't let it go. Al was supposed to have feelings about his dreams. Hard to do, Al told himself, when they weren't dreams. He knew what memories were. He made up stories about his feelings, frowned thoughtfully and sniffed at all the right places. Eventually, Roy Rogers, or whatever his name was, scribbled on a pad, and went away happy

The damage was done. For one thing, nobody else had such memories, or nobody that he'd ever met. Nobody who would confess to them anyway.

The other memories were just much, much older: a glinting river in a white-bake desert. He wore sandals and bend down to take a long drink at the river. The helmet he wore when he fought bumped against his shoulders beside the wicker shield he carried across his back. The desert far too hot for fighting, but he knows that won't matter. He will come when he wants. I will be ready. That's all that matters.

Leshu.

The word runs through his mind over and over, though Al couldn't remember why any longer.

Leshu, Leshu –

Another: A high, thin land, cactus and rattlesnakes hiding under the hard stones. A weapon, like a sword, but made of sharp rock studded along the edges, a sword of a type, and quilted armor around his chest, good for keeping out the cold nights. Frost settled across the landscape every night. Behind him, days of walking away, a bright city on lake. Gardens and trees, wide, white streets, cream-colored pyramids that reach toward the sky, one for the sun, one for the moon. Ahead, twin smoking volcanoes, each snow-capped, despite the fire that glows from the cones at night.

Al remembered thinking: I'll reach the mountains by dark. He didn't like to fight at night, but he wouldn't have much choice. A trail wound between the mountains and he'd be waiting there, the worst possible place for me and the best for him. The trail past the mountains led to the city with the pyramids. He didn't dare lose; that was his clearest memory and the thought made him begin to run, hard as he could, up the rocky, cold trail, toward the two mountains with their smoking peaks.

Other memories drifted past, so distant he recalled them at odd times – just before he drifted to sleep, or when he saw a photograph of the rolling plains across Russia, or, during a visit to the university museum up the road fifty miles, when he glimpsed a little ivory statue of a running horse – not very impressive, no more than a tossed away thing, broken and dark-stained ivory, but Al couldn't leave it until Wheezel pulled him away.

He didn't try to bring them up, write the memories down, and look at them the way he would in chemistry class. He'd never tried, and the older he got, the more the memories crowded onto him. Some seemed so powerful, distant, and different that prying the lid off – Wheezel's phrase–wasn't worth it at all.

These were images, of places unlike anyone had every known, where the sky was tinged gold and glimmering, and the ground was tinged red and orange. And stars: he knew millions of stars, shimmering and brilliant, so hard they hurt his eyes, gleaming metallic colors, glittering white, gold, and blue.

Lumpy wheezed. The junkyard Dobermans guarding Mr. Schatz's Auto Purgatory nearby began howling. Black clouds were piling on the piney wood horizon. He didn't have to see them. He felt them in the air. Thunderclouds gathered almost every night this far south. But in the last few weeks the clouds were different. The thunder murmured and grumbled and, if he leaned toward the window, shut out everything else in his mind, and let his mind go back where it wanted, the thunder seemed to speak to him. Prepare yourself. Prepare yourself, it repeated.

For what?

Al realized that he was standing at his open window and waiting for the answer. He slammed the window shut. The junkyard dogs howled. A storm cloud broke overhead and pelted the old roof with a rattling drum roll of hailstones.

Al didn't have to be told. He already knew. He realized it, felt it, and it made his breath come in painful gasp.

Now

A single word: his word. Now

Al glanced around. The room was filled with blue light, and Lumpy was snoring mouth agape and nostril quivering. Al couldn't wait; it didn't want Lumpy, or Wheezel, or the little ones.

Al turned and ran over the old boards in his bare feet to the end of the hallway.

Nobody ever went up there; the narrow hallway, the servant's hallway Wheezel called it, wasn't safe. It was dusty and cloyed with spider webs. Al had been up there once in his life, when he was twelve and the first of his memories really began puzzling him. They were distant then. He'd made it all the way to a garret, the highest turret in the southeast corner, the one that, on that single clear bright day, he could just catch sight of the distant ocean.

Up the narrow staircase, wrench the door open and across the bare room the garret. Up high, in the small space with window in all directions he fell onto the floor.

A good place to begin a fight.

He didn't want to think that way; it just happened and the roughness of it came naturally to him. As if it fit.

Now

Al couldn't breathe. He seemed to be two people. He was two people, but nobody could be two people at once. He was one person: something was there and waiting to be discovered or waiting for him to discover it. His memories came up very strong, and worst of all, or best, of all, he let them surface. They were real, just as he always knew they were.

I should be afraid.

Losing his fear. That was the really dangerous thing. Fear kept sensible people from jumping out of airplanes with just a ripcord between them and being splattered. A thousand times it'd be just fine. Then there was number one thousand and one...

Not me.

He didn't know what had happened to him, or why he was chosen, if chosen was the right word. He didn't know the right word. Maybe nobody did; nobody he knew could tell him. If he confessed they'd stuff meds down his throat so his life would pass in a fog.

Not me.

He could still choose. He'd heard that little word over and over until he was sick of it. Therefore, he would choose.

Not me.

Al lay on the dry floor, looking up through the old window panes. The storm seemed to circle around the house. That couldn't be, of course. It just was, like the blue sky and A came before B. That was his world, sensible and even and not filled with memories of things that couldn't be.

And it wouldn't be.

Al felt something like peace, as if he'd stepped back from a ledge. A sensible thing; the right thing. That's what he needed to do. He could hear it now, from teachers, psychologist, and especially from Wheezel.

"Not me!" He said aloud and let the sound die in the big, empty room. The night was suddenly clear and peaceful and the hailstones were melting in the asphalt streets.

Al felt dizzy. He stood suddenly. A blue dawn was rising. He heard Wheezel banging around as she made breakfast just as she did every morning.

Al padded down the hallway, slipped in his room and climbed into his bed. Lumpy lay curled up into a tight ball. Al waited while the hot morning gathered outside. Wheezel pounded on the door five minutes late. That was all that was wrong with the world. Lumpy snorted and fell out of the bed. That much was normal. Everything was normal. Al stood and poked around for his clothes.

Everything's A-okay, he reminded himself. A-okay, nothing had happened, he wasn't crazy, the trees weren't waltzing down the street and the walls weren't talking back.

Wheezel whistled everyone down for breakfast. Al went last, and, as he shuffled down the hallway, combing his hair the way Wheezel insisted, the world dissolved.

Al found himself in a winter valley, deep and smooth with snow. As he watched, his breath steaming in the cold, a scruffy-looking white-haired man rode up the hill on a tired horse. The old man glanced up. His eyes were bright and alive. He nodded to Al. That's all he had to do. Al shivered. That's all it took. Al shivered so hard that he almost dropped his weapon.

In front everybody, Al tumbled down the full length of Wheezel's stairs.

Chapter 12

Two boys set out to have fun. Almost thirteen, their parents mumbled, better watch 'em, their parents warned each other. Theodore and Cody didn't want to disappoint. Their pitiful parental rented a place on Cornwall beach, a few miles from the real action over in Orrville. No laptops, no cable, no video games, no texting. You boys will have to make your own fun, they bragged, like we did back in the seventies.

The boys took it to heart. A mile beyond the last beach house, and among the dunes and scrub, lived an old man. He lived in a rusty little trailer back in the scrub woods and kept a kiosk where he sold weird stuff to the sunburned tourists who wandered down that far.

And the boys meant weird. Purple, gold and blue flags fluttered outside, each decorated with brilliant suns, glaring eyes, or scaly dragons. The boys stopped to figure him out. The old man slouched in a canvas beach chair, with sunglasses hiding his eyes and an old baseball cap on his head.

The boys sneaked up, Indian-style, through the sand. The man, whose back was too them, announced cheerily, "Good afternoon, Masters Teddy and Cody."

The boys stopped and glanced at each other and snickered. "How'd you know– Cody began, the less canny of the two.

"It's written all over your faces."

Teddy stepped up. "You sound like somebody's butler."

"He's a Brit," Cody explained, "You know, a redcoat."

"How'd you wind up here?" Teddy asked and maneuvered so he could study the old goat head-on.

"I just follow my instincts."

"That doesn't tell us much," Teddy challenged.

"That's all I've got for the moment."

"How long are you going to stay here?" Cody asked.

"Not much longer, I suspect."

"Got anything to eat?"

"I do. But sorry. Nothing you'd like."

Cody stepped closer. He was very big for his age. "How about letting us decide that?"

"You seem pretty well fed to me, boy."

Cody's face turned red. He stepped even closer. "I'm a growing boy. I need vitamins."

"A growing boy needs to remember his manners," The old man snapped. "I just heard Mildred call your name, child."

Cody blinked and stammered. "How'd you know my mother's name?"

"She's afraid you might have gotten yourself eaten by alligators."

Theodore tugged at Cody's arm. "He's right. I heard your mom and my mom talking about it. Anyway, how does he know that?"

Cody's face flushed. The old man's eyes turned grey as flint. Cody raised his beefy arm to give the old man a straight-armed shove. It didn't happen. Cody found himself doing a somersault in mid-air. Theodore took off down the beach.

Cody landed on his back. The force knocked out his breath. The old man turned and disappeared inside his tent. Cody scrambled to his feet and took off after Theodore and the two of them scampered home. Cody heard his inner voice crying, like two of the three little piglets, all the way home.

Of course, they came back the very next night. Revenge was everything. The boys went to sleep on time without complaining, which, of course, made their parents a little uneasy.

The boys counted the seconds till eleven fifty. Their parents had long since disappeared into their bedrooms. Theodore and Cody met by the swimming pool and slinked through the shadows down to the beach.

The old man never took anything down, not even the flags. They flapped idly in the off shore breeze. He'd closed the tent flap with pegs, no more than that. The boys did a lot of giggling and snickering. They couldn't help it. Cody carried a hammer he'd borrowed from a maintenance man's tool box.

They slipped into the tent. Just enough moonlight spilled inside for the boys to see rows and rows of strangely shaped, thick glass jars lining the shelves. Kind of like a doctor's office, but not – that's what Theodore thought, at least for a little while longer.

"Heck with this," Cody cussed, and fished out a little flashlight. The boys found themselves standing heavy boxes covered with strange writings. Bundles of odd feathers and thigh-bone flutes hung from the poles. Bizarre animal hides were tacked to the canvas walls.

Theodore gave a quiet whistle. "What about the goodies?"

"Close your cake hole."

Cody was near-sighted, though he'd never admit it for obvious reasons and passed the flashlight to Theodore. Cody squinted and peered at the jars. "Verrry interesting," he muttered. "Bingo!" He gave a muffled exclamation and wrestled down a big, dusty jar.

"Whatcha got?"

"I dunno. Olives." He sat the jar on a box and raised the hammer. "Or something, coming right up."

He giggled and brought the hammer down.

The jar exploded.

Oily brine splattered across the box and stained the sand. They boys saw, cried out, and jumped back. The olives weren't olives at all. They hopped, flipped and quivered on the box – eyeballs, liquid, blinking, some blue, some green, some golden, all of them slimy and angry as hornets.

The boys screamed and ran straight into the old scruffy man.

"Boys," he intoned in his deepest voice, "crime doesn't pay. How about joining me in a midnight snack?"

The boys ran howling far, far down the beach. The old man chuckled to himself and bent down to gingerly gather up the glass. The eyeballs, which he knew were really night crawlers from one of Jupiter's moons – he honestly couldn't remember which – went into another jar. He fed them properly and set them back on the shelf where they'd hibernate for another thousand years.

The boys had interrupted his sleep, and like most people who thought of themselves as old, he couldn't fall asleep again. He sat outside in the hot night while the high tide washed over the beach.

Merlin felt his bones ache. He rubbed his knees and tried to remember: How old ? What would be an honest answer? Thousands, thousands, he decided airily. It sounded worse than it was, though the last few centuries had been rather rough. His old friends – the Catabawa, the Tucucari, the Choctow, the Slinget – all had vanished like snow. Most died of disease, some were enslaved; other simply disappeared into the wilderness or hung around the edge of the towns that were chopped out of the forest.

Merlin couldn't prevent it. He had kept to the shrinking wilderness as best he could, until there was no more wild land, not in the forest, or the grasslands, or the mountains.

One day he simply walked into Denver, Colorado, a white man in leggings, long hair, and a quill-decorated deerskin jacket. He signed into the town hotel and announced to the more than mildly surprised guest that he would offer services as a scrivener, teacher of French, barrister, portrait painter, or spiritual adviser.

That evening he reappeared in borrowed coat and tails and began sketching the locals in charcoal. Murmurs of appreciations went through the Saturday night crowd. Before long he was busier, the wholly natural artist, than he needed to be.

He needed to stay busy. The world around him Hs begun to change. The wilderness disappeared, and farms, towns, roads, telegraph poles, railroad tracks appeared. The puffing, snorting, steaming, train engines than ran upon the tracks made him shiver and, more than anything else, reminded Merlin of the dragons that once ruled the sentient worlds.

Years and human lifetimes hurried past. Merlin wandered through the west, until, just before the First World War, he traveled back east and decided, just as a joke, to enter the stock market game and spent until the crash of '29 becoming a millionaire. Of course, he trimmed his hair, took to wearing suits, pronouncing 'bully' forcefully at every opportunity and preaching about the virtues of capitalism.. And smoking cigars; coughing fits hid his laughter whenever he was delivering one of his required philippics.

Two things happened. The market crashed and people began starving. He fell in love – he couldn't believe it either and for a while he thought he was dying. Her name: Marion and her beautiful violet eyes glowed and she was thirty-one when he found himself married. Merlin faced up to fact that he was nearly human by then and his mission had deserted him, or he'd deserted it; and then Merlin forgot how mortal people really are.

His wife died very suddenly.

Merlin's world collapsed. Merlin got rid of his money by throwing it from the window of his three-story mansion. Afterward he walked out of the front door.

Merlin hardened his heart as best he could and wandered the rails as a hobo for years. In Germany such an evil presence arose that Merlin though mortal combat with him was true mission, but

Corporal Hitler, bad as he was, Merlin realized, was mortal and all the worst that humanity could create. The whirlwind arose and passed and the world settled into an uneasy peace.

Merlin settled into his own uneasy truce. He spent the sixties in California lecturing at colleges and correcting some of the flaws in quantum theory, though, he soon realized, he was offering up ideas three hundred years too soon. Puny mankind, he shouted one spring day, do you really think this is all there is and that you are the only pig-headed beings in all of the creations !– then he stopped, chalk in hand, when he saw the looks his students were giving him.

I apologize to the swine genus, he mumbled, and hit the road again.

Puny mankind wasn't really the reason for his outburst. He knew something once more in the unreal, unexplained way a human somehow can foretell her death. Not why-- that was far beyond anything--- and that was all he needed to know.

His sense sharpened. He began practicing his old powers, even ones that he hadn't called on for a thousand years. He watched and waited. With each sunrise the feeling became a little stronger until he became resigned to it. Once again, he mumbled to himself, and journeyed where he thought he should be.

The knowledge wasn't precise; he would have to wait until the revelation was made. It had always worked that way before, but the landscape was so different then, people were so comparatively few, and they didn't seem anywhere nearly so suspicious. The present crop of humanity was likely to demand the secret of his special effects and, if he wasn't careful, he'd wind up with a Hollywood contract.

He wandered farther south, until, of all places, the instinct told him to settle on a beachfront near Orrville. He dabbled in real estate and ran a few mom-and-pop motels with the names Gulf Breezes, Palm Paradise, the Manta Ray and Coconut House. He sold out in the late nineties and waited for the millennium to change. His feelings were very strong, but still nothing happened.

But it was very, very close. He even saw signs: a red sun exploded into a super nova only few hundred lights years away and lit up the sky for months. A huge whale stranded itself off the beach. Merlin wandered down to do what he could. The animal wouldn't communicate with him and, instead, studied Merlin with a baleful, sad, all-knowing eye the size of a diner plate. Merlin rented a tugboat to pull it back to sea. Earthquakes shook the seafloor off the Gulf of Mexico and scared away the tourist for weeks.

By then Merlin had moved to the compound on the beach, complete with the rust-streaked trailer, awnings, a kiosk and all the special treats he'd collected for some time. A garage sale, he called it.

He didn't sell much. The market for pickled dinosaur eggs and yeti hair sweaters was surprisingly limited.

But he couldn't rest, not really. He lost weight and spent most of his time in the sun. He grew nut brown. The young adults and teens that stopped by made him nervous. The right one would never ask for it. The most innocent was always the one.

Merlin wasn't sure why, but that's the way it always ended. Maybe that's what made the contest even.

Or maybe, he reflected, he and the boy weren't always destined to win.

Besides, Merlin admitted to himself: he really was getting old. He couldn't understand the source. Wizards, he thought, never grew old, or morphed into anything except wizards. He always considered himself above time and tide. One day he began getting social security checks in the mail. How those people kept up with him he didn't know, but the two hundred thirty seven dollars and twenty cents was plain to see. He even began having breakfast with the boys - none of them younger than seventy-five- down at the Sunshine Biscuit Company and realized, in a way that made him shiver, that he fitted right in.

A thought occurred to him as he waited through the long, brilliant summer: he was all wrong. It could happen. Maybe the cycle was broken. Maybe there was something new under the sun. Maybe he had become into just a confused old man. Mordred lay in his tomb and would until the universe itself turned cold and his atoms disintegrated into everyone and everything else's atoms. That would serve him right and whatever it was that set the cycle of birth and life and death and good against evil - maybe that had given up, or disintegrated or whatever. One of the People he'd lived with for centuries earlier believed that the world was supported on the back of a great turtle. All around flowed an endless sea, the myth spoke. But his people lived on the Great Plains and no one had ever been closer than a month's travel to any ocean. They just knew; and maybe they were right, as right as anybody else. All was just the back of a turtle; as good as any other answer.

Still, Merlin focused as best he could and detected no sign, spoor, or hint that Mordred was about anywhere. The planet earth, and all its inhabitants, seemed, comparatively speaking, calm as a millpond.

Merlin rested in the shade of his awnings, digging his toes in the sand, and watching tourist inspect a unicorn horn. She snickered, but pulled out money to buy it.

"What kind of cow did this come from?" she asked, a girl barely old enough to vote.

"No cows involved. A golden unicorn product. Guaranteed," Merlin answered with a straight face and took the five dollars. "Don't leave it in the moonlight."

"Really now" she laughed. "Why's that?"

"Cause if you do, the first man you meet the next morning, why you'll fall madly in love with him."

"Madly?"

"Absolutely."

"You speak from experience?"

"Indeed I do."

She guffawed and hurried off.

Merlin, watching her go, sighed. If they'd just listen –

Well, they won't and never had, he reminded himself. Merlin settled back again and counted the cash in the till: eight dollars and twenty cents. The sun sank toward the west. Merlin watched a few people stroll by in the surf, splashing and letting the waves wash over their ankles. Peace and tranquility, if it ever was.

"After ten thousand years of righting wrongs and saving mankind, I am calling it quits," Merlin said aloud.

He said it aloud just to see what happened.

The words didn't make it farther than the hissing surf. Maybe a few seagulls heard, but they didn't seem bothered. Merlin sat quietly a long while. The earth didn't seem to hear. Maybe that's why, he told himself, I seem to be growing so white-haired and aching and wise beyond my years. People have come a long way. Maybe they can handle their own problems.

Merlin turned on his old-fashioned battery radio and listened to music. A light onshore breeze wafted. Every single thing he could see, or feel, or think about seemed at peace. Merlin's chin sank to his chest and he nodded into a deep, long afternoon's nap. Even wizards, he remembered mumbling to himself, need a rest.

Chapter 13

His parents just hated him. He couldn't think of any other reasons they would have given him such a name: Apollo. And the last name: Meatyard. His parents were hippies before they moved to the mountains of North Carolina in the late seventies and opened up a spiritual consulting business.

That didn't help their son. Call me App , he gruffed to everyone on first introductions. But son, his mother pleaded as she mixed organic yogurt, Apollo, the Greek god of poetry, beauty, truth and wisdom –

Their son still got beat up about it. His parents were college graduates. Apollo quit high school. That showed 'em, he groused to himself.

He got into the drilling game. The pay was good and you got to travel, he reminded himself – Arkansas, Mississippi, Tennessee, and L.A. (lower Alabama), places he otherwise would probably never see.

Once in a while he got a job close to home. That was Saturday; he didn't mind, because Saturday was overtime and he got time and a half. Besides, he didn't have anything planned. He hooked up the trailer and headed out by seven a.m. The rig included a wire mesh trailer, four hundred yards of stacked two inch pipe, a diesel engine to drive the drill, a fifteen- foot tall pipe tripod, and a diamond-bit drill, the business end of everything he did.

He drilled for finesse- -none of that deep and dirty oil-well drilling. He drilled a couple hundred yards beneath the soil and pulled out a long, clean core and delivered it to the engineers with their pocket protectors and calculators, who drank coffee, flirted with the secretaries, and scribbled little reports and declared this patch of ground and the other was suitable for constructing your basic butler building or a high school or septic tank or whatever.

Soil test engineering – not a lot of drama, but it paid the bills. His best friend ran a chicken farm. That was far too smelly and organic. The man fretted way, way too much about his feathered friends.

Saturday turned out to be a warm day in spring, with the fresh green buds popping out everywhere. App took the winding road off Turkey Mountain and drove a half hour towards the hick town of Frieda and the high mountains.

Enough people found Frieda attractive though, almost all old folks, retiring to their mountain chalets before the first coronary took them off. The old folks needed lots of water, though, and that meant another reservoir. The Teufel Area Water Commission engineers came up their version of a brilliant idea. Fifteen miles north of Frieda, a peak stuck out among the other smooth mountain tops. This peak was the weird sister; it rose high and ended in a rough half-peak, as if something had cut off the top third of the mountain and left it protruding like a jagged tooth. The idea: dig out the top of the mountain and fill it with water. Instant reservoir, stick in the pipes and run the supply straight downhill.

App got out his map. He'd heard of the place, but he'd never been there. He stopped to get a honey bun for lunch and asked around a coffee shop. Blank stares, until the crony woman at the counter wrinkled her nose at him.

"Killjoy Mountain?" she asked. "What business have you got there?"

"I'm just going to stick a little pin in her."

She shrugged and slid his honey bun into a paper sack. "You got no business whatsoever there."

App found his own way. He turned off the state road, took a county road, then a logging road. It wound its rutted way all the way to the top of the mountain. The road had been cut for pulpwood cutters to drive their rough trucks up to the flat top of mountain. The road was fresh mud and barely passable. App drove yard by yard, with his truck in low gear.

Despite the spring sunshine, he shivered. He hadn't seen another human being for a long while. His left-hand wheels dangled off the road half the time. App cussed the entire way up.

The road just ended on top of the mountain where the molar-shaped cut made a plateau a dozen acres wide. Stranger still: the soil was black and burned. The trees were twisted and dead. All the mountains for a thousand miles around grew thick, green woods.

Al got out of his truck slowly and kicked at the black earth. Somebody had goofed in a big way, Al decided, when they made this place -- or just dropped it here.

He glanced over his shoulder time and again. A grove of skeletal trees seemed to be beckoning to him, though he knew that was nonsense. On the ground were burned boulders, yellowish bitter weeds and colonies of thorn bushes. The low boulders reminded him, though he didn't want to think it, of the dead people strewn on a battlefield.

He listened.

He didn't want to listen. His ears pricked up even before he heard a sound: a low, calling voice, a long note that rose and fell; and then he heard the chill wind hiss through the trees.

"Yea!" App called out.

He hadn't meant to answer. He had an idea and called out loud as he could, "Come out, come out wherever you are!"

App snorted at his humor. The sky seemed a little brighter and reminded him where he was: on solid earth, the most reliable thing in the universe.

App waited anyway.

Absolute stillness.

App shrugged and started unloading. The iron pipes, as he tossed them, clanged.

He stirred. If you asked what it was like, he could answer: As you think. To be wrapped and bound in winding sheets as if dead, but not to be dead, but feel, to know, every second. Nine hundred and seventy-six years.

Mordred: my name means death, especially for them.

Merlin: the name made him crack his teeth. One of his kind, and the one who put him here.

Mordred groaned and writhed in his wrapping sheets.

Merlin: Traitor.

Traitors deserved death. Like this, Modred thought, but forever, forever, forever.

Modred knew, before the planet was consumed by fire or ice, that the cycle would repeat itself. If he didn't surrender and let himself be dissolve into nothing.

He heard the little man's truck grinding its way up the mountain. The other little men had come to cut the road, but when they appeared, Modred called for them too early and they ran away.

Modred listened to his footsteps: this one came alone.

He talked to himself, cursed, and grumbled at the machinery he began putting together. Modred listened to the clang of iron against iron. He didn't know what it was, but iron meant tools and tools meant digging.

Modred, remembering the last time, called for the little man very softly, just enough to let him know. The man didn't run away.

For the first time in a thousand years, Modred sang.

App hung the chains and tightened the last bolt and flipped the switch. The thumping, clattering and whining shattered the silence. He watched carefully for a little while, settled against the truck, and stuffed a wad of gum in his mouth.

For a little while everything went along swimmingly, as his father liked to say. Another sound rose up, over and through the road of the diesel generator. For a few long seconds he couldn't believe it; he'd never heard anything like the low, bass song. That's what it was: a song, just a few notes, over and over. It penetrated everything, though it seemed to come from beneath his feet. It thrummed through the air and through his skull.

App flipped a switch and killed the rig. The song lingered in the still air and died away. He froze. He thought about tossing the rig into the back of the truck and getting the heck out of Dodge. He'd have a lot of explaining to do about what exactly made him abandon a job. A man afraid of the woods; he'd have to leave town.

He toggled the switch. The generator roared and blew smoke. App ran it as hard as it would go. He pretended not to listen, but his ears listened anyway.

For a good ten minutes the drill whirled and dug deeper into the rock. App poured water into the hole to keep it lubricated. Steam shot straight up. App jumped back. The bore hole always got hot, but never enough to make another Old Faithful.

The rock beneath his feet cracked and began to split open. The ground for yards in all directions buckled and collapsed. The drill bit, freed from the earth, leapt up, sliced through the air and barely missed his skull. The generator, the derrick, and his truck disappeared into a huge black hole.

App ran.

His parents were wrong. Hell existed. He was about to be swallowed up. The ground under his feet crumbled. He fell into the blackness, and howled the entire way down.

Chapter 14

App lay on his back. Hell was a cave; its colors were black and blue. He blinked until his eyes focused. The blue came from the sky above his head. The blackness came from everywhere else.

App coughed and coughed. Hell stank like road kill. He rose on his elbows, and realized that he lay on a raft of sod that hand landed below rather bury him alive. The drill rig lay scattered nearby. His truck had crashed nearby, with its nose pointed down and the rear wheels resting on the lip of the sink hole.

He stood and tested his legs and arms. His ankle ached and tingled. App realized he stood near the floor of a dome-shaped cave that extended as far as he could see. He had no idea how much farther it went and wasn't about to find out. He turned and climbed a few feet, dragging left leg along. His truck made a perfectly good ladder.

The earth around him slid. He stumbled and rolled, over and over, all the way to the bottom of the cave. A stone coffin, lying broken on the smooth floor, stopped him.

Not good.

App used the side of the broken coffin to pull himself up. A shattered coffin lid lay on the floor.

Not good at all.

The hair on the back of his neck stood straight up.

App turned his head.

A man, not much more than a boy, appeared out of the dark. He was way too tall, deathly emaciated, with bright, yellowish, lozenge-shaped eyes sunk a long skull His hair was bristly, his fingers way too long and, when he opened his rubbery mouth, short, sharp teeth gleamed.

App didn't move. The boy, if that's all he was, studied him and gave a bitter grin. App felt he was being sized up for some purpose -- maybe for lunch. App closed his eyes then opened them wide, but nothing changed. He still lay on the floor of a dank cave and the stink filled his nostrils. His ankle throbbed. His truck, smashed at an angle, made the only way out. App cleared his throat. He didn't know what else to do. People said he had a way with strangers.

"Okay, so who stuck you down here?"

Why anyone would want to bury him alive in a cave--- that bothered App a little, too.

The boy growled some gibberish.

"You're not in trouble with the cops, are you?" App ventured.

It was thin, but App figured he needed a starting point. He pointed to the huge hole above them. "You go first and I'm right behind you."

Above, in the real world, thunder boomed and lighting crackled.

The boy stepped toward App, who wanted to run, as hard as fast as he ever had, but he couldn't. The boy's grin showed triumph. App wiggled as best he could, and swore to himself that he'd never hunt deer again. He prayed and prayed that the thing wasn't that hungry

The boy stopped an arm's length in front of App. The stench was terrible-- musty and corrupt, awful. He clasped App shoulders. App trembled and gulped. The boy spoke a long sentence to App's face, squeezed his shoulders so hard that App cried out, managed to break away and began scrambling up the truck as if it were a ladder.

App liked to pretend he wasn't sure what happened next. He had no explanation and, when the experts interrogated him later, he shrugged and shook his head.

Amnesia, he lamely explained.

The boy, or the thing, climbed out of the hole. App, despite his swelling ankle, hobbled right after.

Topside, a storm raged. Lighting attacked the earth – green, gold and blue- in a way App had never seen. The wind blew horizontal to the earth, sweeping dead trees along with it. App gripped the earth with both hands.

The boy, or the thing, stood against the wind and out stretched his arms as if he wanted it to happen-- and it did.

The storm doubled. The wind roared and screamed, scouring the plateau bare. The boy grabbed a pinewood stick and waved it toward the sky. The clouds roiled and, huge as they were, began following the motion of the boy's stick. The roiling became a swirling. It seemed that the entire sky was following the boy's stick. The swirling became furious, a monster in the sky, and focused itself into a huge eye that glowed orange to red to blue-white hot. The air stank of ozone.

The boy jumped high into the air and stabbed the stick into the earth. A tremendous bolt of lightning burst from the eye, vaporized the stick, and slammed deep into the mountain.

The earth shook from far, far below.

The ground shattered. The blast that followed reminded App of a whole airport of jet engines taking off at the same time. He tripped and fell and jammed his hands over his ears.

The earth buckled and collapsed. Lava, sparkling like a fountain, burst high into the air. The dry bush and wood burst into flames.

The boy danced in sheer joy. He sang. App could see his mouth move. He thought, over the roaring, the boy howled at him. "Once more! Once more!"

But that was all App could understand. A black funnel dipped from a cloud, struck the earth, bounced, drawing all the uprooted trees, thorn bushes, and even the rocks on the ground, into its maul.

The boy disappeared. App shielded his eyes as best he could, but the boy simply disappeared. All that just to end up this way, App remembered thinking. The funnel whirled and whirled and drew up into the greenish black clouds above.

App raised his head. He lay full on the ground, soaked like a rat. The winds died away. A patch of blue sky appeared.

The earth shook and split open even wider. Solid rock all round him splintered. A new roar erupted from the earth – a sharp, roaring whistle. The cave collapsed as more lava fountains burst into a geyser of red and black.

App grabbed a stick as a crutch and hobbled away for dear life. More and more and more lava plumes leapt from the earth. App forgot the pain in his ankle. Sometimes he tumbled down the hill, sometimes he rolled, but he kept moving as fast as he could away from the blossoming volcano.

He stumbled onto the asphalt county road. By then the entire top of the mountain roiled in flame. Beautiful fountains of deep red and yellow arched into the sky. Lava began cascading down the side of the hill, spilling into the dense, dry woods and setting them to fire instantly and everywhere.

The entire Sassafras Valley County volunteer fire department came careening up the road. The lead truck screeched to a stop. A singed man tumbled out of the woods. He struggled to his feet and hobbled to the first truck, waving a stick over his head. The company captain, Lewis McKennan, a used car salesman, jumped out of the truck. The singed man howled like a monkey and tried to run away. All five other volunteers were necessary to hold him down. His jaw worked, but words didn't come out.

The fire guys from the other trucks gathered around. The man raved and settled down to stare at his saviors with deep, black eyes. His chest heaved.

Otherwise, the volunteers didn't know what to do. The volcano that had been Killjoy Mountain roared and spumed. The woods were burning into cinders. Their biggest hose measure three inches around. Lewis got on the horn and called the US Forest Service, the Sheriff's office, the Highway patrol, the US army reserves, and the editor of the Sassafras Valley Democrat. Finally, he called his wife. "Put the dogs in the truck, honey," he yelled over the roaring mountain, "we're moving to Florida!"

In a little while the thrum of helicopters sounded – rescuer copter from the Forest Service, soon joined by dust-offs from the US Army, and swarms of news helicopters. All began circling the huge cone of fire.

An ambulance came for App. The medics wrapped him up and gave him a shot.

"Fools," he muttered to himself, "we're all fools."

He understood everything and as the world began to slip away in a druggy haze he knew something else: they'd learn it on their own.

Chapter 15

Merlin didn't keep a TV, a laptop, or cell phone. His Bakelite radio from 1962 ran out of batteries twice a week. He could learn new things, of course, but he liked to believe he didn't need them. It wasn't true and he knew that. Our faults are magnified, Merlin admitted to himself, as we get older.

If – if he'd had batteries for his radio (which he kept on the Met broadcast most of the time anyway), or a TV or a laptop with decent Internet connections Merlin would have heard about the first pyrotechnic explosion on the east coast of the USA in roughly sixty million years. It wasn't just unlikely; it was impossible, but, except for the flaming mountain top, no responsible person with a college degree would have given the idea a sideways glance. The mountain top, though, offered plenty of flaming evidence.

That night Merlin woke with a great gasp. He wasn't fully awake. He kicked open the trailer door and, before he knew why, found himself kneeling and trembling in the warm sand.

His first clue came from the moon. It rose out of the ocean, huge and pale. A shadow began to creep across the edge and, before long, consume the moon's bumpy face. A lunar eclipse, Merlin knew, but he suspected this one had never been predicted.

Merlin listened. He wasn't sure for a while. He paced up and down the beach, where a few late-night beach combers saw a knobby old man splashing ankle-deep through the surf, nose down, and muttering one word over and over.

Modred.

The beach combers kept their distance. Merlin couldn't have cared. Before this, he thought silently, I've always known.

Always.

No matter what form Mordred took or how he tried to hide, the signs had always been there. It'd be like trying to hide the Northern lights. Merlin's entire being had always known – head, heart and body. In the past he sometimes even broke into fever and splotches – not too dignified, but it true enough.

Why is the sign so weak? He was supposed to have an answer. He didn't. The moon lifted higher in the night sky. The shadow spread farther across the silver face, not a crescent shadow of the earth's orb, but the silhouette of a face.

A billion people witnessed the apparition. Explanations would come in the morning-- space dust.

Merlin knew. He stood on the warm beach as the tide rose. His heart pounded; his breath came in shallow gasp. Ten times I have done this, he reminded to himself, and always I have supposed I would see it a thousand times more.

This time was different. What he thought through the centuries was wrong. He was weaker in one way and smarter in another. Maybe, just maybe, things came to an end. Maybe this was his last time. That frightened him as much as anything else, the whispering thought and how the pieces seemed to fall in place.

Merlin shivered. The night seemed so beautiful. For a moment – for more than a moment – he wanted to be left alone. Peace meant everything to him now. But he was so human; he would stay with them forever, however long that would last. It didn't matter. Never surrender. Those were words he kept to himself.

"Never," he said aloud. "Not this time. Just like before."

People nearby glanced up at the old man clenching his fist as he stared at the shadow on the moon.

Suddenly the old man turned, his face set and eyes blazing and disappeared off the beach. He hurried off to his rusty trailer and strange tent set among the pines. One by one they shrugged and hurried back to their wives and husbands. What have I missed? They silently asked themselves.

They didn't sleep well that night. They didn't ask for it, either. They knew without wanting to know. That night they shivered just like the old man and stayed awake worrying about their children.

Chapter 16

Merlin kept a lime-green Chrysler Gremlin, a dish-shaped car from the seventies. He didn't want to attract attention. After he left the beach, Merlin dug out the keys, cranked it to make sure it'd start. It sputtered and came to life. A miracle, Merlin muttered to himself, and bumped around his trailer for the other props he'd need.

Ideas came to him clearly. He even heard a name in his head. Nowadays people were very careful about their names, so he put a great deal of faith into it.

Merlin tapped his chin as he put his plan together. He found a suit of clothes, ironed it smooth, trimmed his beard and a shined a set of black wing-tipped shoes. He did everything by hand, in part to get in character and partly to leave no trace of his presence.

He worked out a plan as he brushed his teeth. He found a tourist map and noted how to drive to Tintagle. The hamlet appeared on his old map as a little circle. The green of deserted pine forest spread all around the town from Orrville to Tallahassee.

By nine o'clock a warm day rose up in the pastel colors of the beach. The day filled Merlin with something like hope -- not exactly, but close. He dressed and locked the trailer and hung a CLOSED sign on the kiosk and wondered if he'd ever be back again. Probably not, he decided, but he never knew. He wouldn't mind staying there a long time, slipping into retirement. Morning biscuits with the boys couldn't be beat.

He climbed into the Gremlin, cranked it up, and pulled onto the road. He whistled 'Danny Boy' the entire way up.

A little later Merlin pulled into a dingy village with a red brick courthouse, a gas station, a few empty stores, a taxidermist's shop, and a grocery store. Merlin parked at the grocery store and went inside. He wore an expensive suit; the Gremlin's air conditioner blew lukewarm air. Merlin strode in mopping his face with an expensive handkerchief.

A tall boy behind the counter was bouncing a rubber ball on the counter and staring out the window.

"How's the basketball season, my man?" Merlin asked in his brightest tone.

"Round ball taint my thing."

Merlin lifted his eyebrows a little. Every willowy American boy he'd ever met got drafted into round ball sooner or later.

"Really?"

"Season's long gone, dude. This is summer."

"How silly of me. Can I ask another question?"

"Just one. I'm a busy man."

"I can see that. What does the young future of this great country do for fun around here?" Not 'entertainment,' Merlin noted to himself, 'fun.' He was proud of his command of the local language.

The tall boy wrinkled his forehead and sneered. "Do what?"

"What do you do for kicks?"

"Ride over to Orrville and beat up the freaks."

"Freaks? In this peace-loving paradise."

The tall boy gave Merlin an evil eye. "What do you care?"

"Actually, my man, I'm looking for someone."

"You a cop?"

"Heavens no. I'm – a relative. Let's leave it at that."

"Yea?"

"Yea."

"Who's the lucky dude?"

Merlin gave the skinny drink of a boy the name. The boy squinted a little harder and curled his lip into a sneer. "You got to be kidding."

"You have some solid knowledge, I take it."

The boy lifted his hand and pointed across the street. Merlin turned around. He faced gingerbread Victorian badly in need of a repainting. "You're talking about one of the throwaways."

"Throwaways?"

"Sure. Their mommies and daddies don't want 'em, so they get tossed over there. An old lady takes care of 'em."

"Orphans, you mean."

"I guess."

"So many thanks. Live long and prosper." Merlin turned to leave.

"Hey," the boy called.

"Yes?"

"What'd he do?"

"That remains to be seen."

Merlin stepped outside into the hot sun. He felt himself sweat. He knew he needed to move fast. Mordred, if he located the boy first, would catch the boy defenseless and totally unaware. That must never happen.

128

Merlin didn't like even to think about it. Usually, he liked to wait for some traditional sign that he'd arrived in the right place – St Elmo's fire skittering through a forest, a huge flight of ravens cawing and circling about the peasant hut wherein the boy lived, even a headless, free-floating apparition.

Across the street an electric bug zapper, a wire mesh bucket plugged into the wall, sizzled and exploded.

The boy stuck his head out the door. "You been foolin' with that?"

"It's not me."

"Squirrels," the boy sniffed. "Buck teeth and live wires just don't match, do they?"

"Evidently not."

The boy grimaced and disappeared. Merlin shrugged. I'll take what I can get, he thought to himself, and fished into his pocket for his brand-new cell phone.

Chapter 17

Wheezel got a peculiar phone call just before lunch. She was standing on the back porch, sneaking a cigarette while they boys were swimming at the local pool. A man, sounding very educated and very British, called to ask about Al. A relative, he claimed. Very distant, he explained, but, you know, there were obligations. After all these years, he sighed and asked for an appointment to speak to her and the boy.

Wheezel frowned. Adoption wasn't uncommon for the younger boys when the kids were cute as puppies. After a certain point they were just last year's merchandise.

Al and Lumpy (I mean Lawrence, she corrected herself mentally), a year or so before turning eighteen – the whole thing didn't make sense. The boys were pretty much grown. She smoked another cigarette to think about it. And the longer she thought, the less she liked it.

Her phone rang again. The bubbly social worker in Orrville, Ms. Candy Zucker, was especially loud. "Hello! And how are you, Cherish?'

Nobody ever used her first name, of course.

Wheezel grunted a hello.

"Honey, I'm bringing you an early Christmas. The boy – Al – this man's expressed an interest in taking the boy. His great uncle. Or great-great, I'm not sure about that."

"Who are we talking about?"

"Now isn't this a wonder. The old --I mean the elderly-- man is an honest-to-goodness doctor. Isn't that just peachy king?"

"Where's grandpa been hiding all these years?"

"Beats me. He's a proper Brit. Sounds so distinguished. Kinda like Sean Connery, sort of."

Wheezel lit another cigarette. "He's been thoroughly check out, I suppose."

Candy sighed. "He's retired. Took a little while for his records to appear, him being retired and all, but there you go."

"Goes where?"

Candy sighed again, longer this time. "Unless this man is some sort of freakin' alien, it sounds hunky doorey to me. Who knows? Maybe Al's going to inherit a castle or something."

"Or something."

"Point is, this boy's about to get a home."

Wheezel took a long, long drag off her Camel. "Yea," she said finally. "That's what we're talking about."

"What's done is done," Candy replied briskly, "We'll pay a visit today. Threeish?'

"Can't wait," Wheezel answered and, after she hung up, sat on her back porch long after she should have begun boiling spaghetti for lunch, drumming her fingers, with a hard knot of anxiety in her stomach. Maybe I can think of something, she repeated to herself, over and over.

She couldn't, though; she lit another Camel and waited for the boys to come streaming across the backyard with their towels and wet heads.

Chapter 18

The next few hours went by slowly. The boys, after they came home, she kept busy with KP duties, even the little ones. She couldn't bring herself to say anything to Al, not right away. They seemed to avoid each other. How could he know? Wheezel fretted, but he knows something.

Finally she couldn't wait any longer. He and Lumpy were wearing big straw hats and trimming the backyard shrubbery. Clack-clack –clack went the clippers. She sent Lumpy away with the little ones to go play ball down the street. The little boys looked at each other. They hadn't finished their chores. "And get rid of that darn hat!" she snapped on his way out.

Wheezel stepped into the sun and sidled close to Al. "You don't go anywhere. Do you have a moment?"

He glanced up and searched her eyes.

"The sewing room, what do you say?"

Al didn't say anything. He followed her silently. They sat in the little room off the living room. Here Wheezel brought the parents for their first viewing of their potential new joys of life. Just like the animal shelter, she sometimes chastised herself, but this time she felt even less comfortable. Al followed her with his eyes. She tried to talk. The right words wouldn't come. Finally she coughed and began, "Al, I have the best thing in the world to tell you."

The front doorbell rang. Wheezel glanced at her watch: two thirty. They were being ambushed. The doorbell rang again. Wheezel peeked out the living room curtain. A silver Ford waited on the driveway. A second car, a lime-green thing of the type she hadn't seen since disco days, was pulled up behind the Ford.

Two people waited on the porch. Al slipped up quietly beside her. "Who's that?"

"Miss Candygram and-"

Wheezel hurried to the front door and opened it. Candy stepped in, lipstick flashing and bracelets jangling. "Cherish, Id' like to present," as she breezed past, "Dr. Pendragon."

"Madam," he said. He stuck out his hand, American-style. Wheezel shook it. His clasp was dry and strong. He looked to be between sixty and seventy, not too tall, with a close-cropped white beard and leathery skin, someone who'd lived in the outdoors for years. That didn't jell with the expensive, well-tailored suit he wore, pricey enough, Wheezel automatically calculated, to keep her boys in black-eyed peas and ham for six months.

"I am honored," he continued.

"Sure thing," Wheezel replied with the tiniest possible smile. She glanced at his eyes. They were focused on the boy standing a few yards away. Dr. Pendragon's eyes gleamed with the deepest blue-green Wheezel had ever seen. The man was elderly, but, Wheezel decided, his eyes were absolutely ageless. She felt her face grow red.

"Let's have a seat, doctor," she mumbled and slipped to one side.

Dr. Pendragon didn't sit. He stood in the middle of the room and frowned at Al, who glanced at the other two adults for help.

Pendragon still didn't speak right away. Candy jiggled her bracelets. Wheezel frowned. The good doctor's trying to decide something, she though, but what? What's he going for?

Candy hopped up and jangled over to Al. She clapped a hand on Pendragon's shoulder and pulled Al by the arm until he stood directly in front of Pendragon.

"You two," she insisted, "stop behaving like perfect gentlemen. Al, this is Dr. Pendragon, your great uncle. Or something along those lines. Doctor, this is your grandnephew, or whatever."

Worse, Candy tried to push them together into a familial embrace. It didn't quite work. The two bounced off each other. Pendragon stepped back and brushed his suit. "Madam, if you please–."

He turned to Al. "I am very sorry." He caught himself. "Son-."

Wheezel stepped closer. "Maybe you two should just shake."

For a few seconds Wheezel was afraid Pendragon was going to bow to the boy. Al raised his hand. They shook.

Wheezel guided them to the couch. "Why don't you two get acquainted?"

She didn't manage to smile, however.

The two sat on the couch. Al stared straight ahead. Pendragon, if that was his real name, Wheezel decided, gazed through the living room window. Whatever's going down here, she thought, this man's no more that boy's blood than I am.

Al took a deep breath and turned to Pendragon. "So – turns out I'm a limey?"

"Pardon?" Pendragon turned his head to the boy.

"A Brit."

"It would seem."

"You're not thinking of taking me away from all this, are you?"

The adults looked at each other.

Wheezel coughed. "We were just getting to that."

Candy jangled and smiled as wide as she could and shook Al's shoulder. "He's going to be your - father."

Al didn't move. His mouth compressed into a thin line. He took a long few seconds to answer. "I know you from somewhere."

"Quite impossible," Pendragon muttered and turned pink.

"Okay, so where's your crib?"

"I think you're a little old for that."

"Where am I going to live?"

"Oh. That. I'll whip up something. Not too far away. How's that sound?"

Wheezel narrowed her eyes. "Whip up something?"

"Just a figure of speech, of course."

"Where'd do you say you practice?"

"I didn't. Practice. Hmm. Actually, I don't take patients anymore. I'm retired."

"What was your specialty?"

"Me? A little bit of everything. Psychiatry, I guess you'd say."

"A witchdoctor." Wheezel kept a little smile.

"Mercy no. A little more sophisticated than that."

"I hope."

"If only I could demonstrate. You'd be quite impressed, I think."

Pendragon and Wheezel exchanged stiff smiles. Candy sat up suddenly with a fresh rattle of bangles. "Let's get this show on the road! I know Al is chomping at the bit, ready to start his new life."

"He's got to collect his things--." Wheezel stammered.

"Well, let's get a move on." Candy turned to Pendragon. "I have an appointment today. My fiancé. Dinner. You know how that can be."

Nobody answered.

Wheezel hurried Al upstairs. She found an old suitcase of her mother's and helped Al toss all his clothes into it. She felt herself hurrying as fast as she could. Al asked her for a few minutes. He disappeared into the hall bathroom with his toothbrush and clothes. Wheezel, feeling she wasn't needed, returned downstairs. Pendragon had gone outside and waited on the porch. Candy swayed back and forth in a rocking chair beside him.

Wheezel found herself in the kitchen, slathering a peanut and jelly sandwich for Al to take along. She heard a footstep. Al stood in the doorway, wearing a hand-me-down coat and tie. The tie was polka dots of green and yellow. He smelled like shaving lotion.

Wheezel took a breath.

"Something wrong?"

She adjusted his tie.

"Wheez- I mean, Ma'am, is this for real?"

136

"I guess so."

"Guess?"

"Just sudden. That's the word. Life's like that sometimes." She forced herself to smile. "It's a great thing, don't you think?"

"That depends. What do you think this old coot really wants?"

Wheezel stepped back. She bit her lip. "Do you want me to get you out of this? I could try. That's all I can do"

He started to speak and stopped. "I have to do this."

Wheezel frowned. "You don't. I --."

"I do." He shrugged.

He turned back to the parlor. Wheezel wrapped up the sandwich and trailed behind. Al opened the front door and stood on the porch. He couldn't swallow. He didn't own anything in this house, not ever. He wasn't wanted, not in that special way, but, he thought to himself, that's all I've had for as long as I can remember, just what's exactly here. He turned to Pendragon. "Mind if I say something to Lump – Mr. Lance?"

Candy stood abruptly. "Gentlemen, time's wasting and I have that appointment." She squeezed Al's arm. "You'll be plenty close enough for visits, won't you?"

"That depends." Al looked to Pendragon. "How about a car-- Dad?"

Merlin blinked. "What would you want with that?"

Everyone else glanced at him as if he came from outer space. "Bother. Guess I could whip up something."

"There's that word again," Wheezel noted.

Candy took the two men and hurried them toward the steps. "Paperwork's done, so let's get this on the road, shall we?"

Wheezel took Merlin's arm. "Can I have a word with you?"

Candy glanced over, but pushed Al toward Merlin's green Gremlin. Wheezel cleared her throat and stepped close. He took half a step back.

"Where'd you say you're from?"

"Camden, just down –."

"I've lived around here my entire life and I've never heard of you."

"I'm a psychiatrist, madam, not a rock star."

"I might just drop by now and then."

"Call beforehand. We might do some traveling."

" Indeed. I suppose you're actually a Brit, aren't you?"

"Once upon a time." Merlin disengaged and slipped around Wheezel's left flank. "Lovely weather isn't it? Nice west wind."

"One more thing. Any harm comes to that boy and I'll skin you alive."

"Of that, madam, I have no doubt." He tipped his hat. "As you Yanks say, let's get this show on the road."

Candy waved to none in particular, climbed into her car and raced the engine. Merlin and the boy stepped into his car. The engine coughed and blue white smoke billowed. The gears clanked and slowly, carefully, stiffly, like one who isn't comfortable driving, Merlin backed into the road.

Candy roared out of the driveway, and, tires squealing, headed in the other direction.

Wheezel stood on the porch and fought the impulse to chase the saucer-shaped car down the road. I'm just being silly, she repeated to herself over and over. Silly old woman. Silly as can be. Silly, silly, silly, just like your Aunt Weizacker teased, you'll grown up to be so silly.

And she was right. Wheezel couldn't help herself. A boy with a great uncle who is a doctor for heaven's sake. College. A nice house he'll whip up. He'll whip up a car and decent clothes and gosh knows what else. Always knew the boy was smart. After all, he's just another boy.

Wheezel blinked back tears, and climbed the porch steps. Not another boy, the voice in her head repeated over and over again: It isn't right and it isn't over with. Not by a long shot.

The screen door slammed behind her.

Chapter 19

Merlin squinted as he drove. The road seemed to rush up to meet his eyes. Speed-besotted youngsters roared up to the car's bumper, honking and making impolite gestures, and swerving past him insanely. The temptation to turn them into wombats was almost overwhelming, but Merlin fought it off with great dignity every time.

After the twelfth car did the honking and swerving thing, Merlin noticed that the boy was clutching the dashboard.

"Something the matter?" Merlin inquired.

"You might speed it up a bit."

"Why do you say that?"

"This is a sixty miles an hour zone. You're doing fifteen."

Merlin glanced at the speedometer. "Sakes alive, we're just rocketing along."

"Maybe I should drive."

"Don't bother. It's my pleasure."

But the old man noticed that the boy had turned pale. Merlin shrugged and pulled over to the side of the road, just missing a semi-truck who insisted on hogging the other lane, as if he owned the exclusive rights. The boy stumbled out of the car gasping. "From now on I drive. Swear to it."

Merlin really didn't mind. The boy, as soon as his hands stopped shaking, pulled into the lane and they rocketed along.

Merlin shrugged. "Seems to know what you're doing."

"At least one of us does."

"The candor of youth."

"Youth wants to live another twenty-four hours, Dad."

Merlin shrugged and thought about what they boy called him: Dad, a solid word right out of the good old USA. Now that, he realized, was going to be different – profoundly different. This was his first American boy. Cowboys, football players and real he-men: John Wayne and Teddy Roosevelt. He'd known them all, but not with this degree of responsibility. Suppose, Merlin mused, Teddy R. had turned out to be his Arthur. Now that would be bully, absolutely bully. That would have been different. And disastrous, of course, but definitely 100 % different.

Different.

Just like today.

"What do you really want me to call you?" The boy asked but kept his eyes steadily on the road.

"Hmm? Oh, we'll get to that. It's going to take a little explaining. Your turn's coming up."

"The next turn is five miles down the road…Dad."

A turn appeared. The boy hit the brakes and swerved onto the road. "I swear I've never seen this road. She's got to be brand-spanking new."

"I promise."

They drove a few hundred yards. Merlin's dilapidated trailer appeared.

"Here we go," Merlin announced cheerily.

"Impressive."

"It's comfortable enough."

"Sorry, but I'm meaning it's a dump."

"Really now?"

"Really. Where's the place you were going to whip up?"

"Did I promise that?"

"It'll make the social workers, when they come by to check on you, very happy. In fact, they might require it."

"Tell me. What would you like?"

"Me? Four bedrooms on the top. Two of 'em would be mine. I've never had my own room, okay? Your basic living room for you old folks, a den with a big screen TV, a kitchen that takes care of itself. "

"What color shutters?"

"Heck. I don't care...orange."

"A bold choice."

"You're going to whip that up?"

Merlin shrugged and, as Al watched, he wandered away a few yards, clasp his hands and seemed to study the ground as if it would erupt under his feet. Al felt, deep inside, that Dad didn't need to be interrupted. Abruptly the old man shook his head and rubbed his elbows. "That ought to just about do it."

He strode down the narrow road and turned to Al. "Are we just going to stand there collecting flies?"

This coot's loony, Al thought to himself, though he tried to suppress it. Sometimes, he remembered Wheezel warning, the truth hurts.

Well, tomorrow she'd have to borrow the sheriff's car and come by to pick him up. Not so bad. Truth was, he was already getting homesick. Lumpy had never bunked in a room by himself.

And nobody, but nobody, Al swore to himself, was going to get his bunk.

The road they walked made a sharp curve. The bay washed on the sand a quarter mile away. Nestled among the low dunes and the sea oats, stood a beach house, two stories high, with every light blazing, and a roof, windows, whitewashed walls and, of all things, orange shutters.

Orange shutters.

Al stopped.

"Cat got you tongue?" Merlin mounted the low steps and opened the kitchen door.

The boy, though, wasn't moving.

"This doesn't please you?" Merlin asked politely.

"How....how...how...how. You gotta be a Houdini. Or something."

"Houdini? Clever man. The 'or something' – we're going to talk about that."

The boy stood stock-still another full half minute. Then, slowly, he lifted his feet and stepped gingerly toward the house. Even more gingerly he put his weight on each board as he took the steps one by one. Merlin held the door open.

"Well, hurry in and give us an opinion."

The house was filled with new furniture and shining floors. In the cupboard, Al found the dozens of cans of spaghetti and green beans; in the 'frige, twenty gallons of fresh milk.

"Well?" Merlin asked impatiently.

"You're some kind of magician."

"Why, thank you."

Al shook his head. "Something else is going on here."

"Quite so. We'll get to that."

"Sooner the better."

"Why don't you freshen up a bit and we'll have a nice little chat."

"Which is mine? Room, I mean."

"Upstairs somewhere. First dibs are yours."

Al began up the shiny new stairs. "You've never been in here, have you?"

"Can't say that I have. Seems nice, though."

Al nodded slowly and mounted the stairs. He felt as if he moved in a fog – not because everything wasn't real, but because everything was as hard-edged as it could be. He picked out a room on the far end. The bed and furniture were exact replicas of stuff he'd seen in an advertisement a few days before. He'd lingered over the photos, wondering if he'd ever have anything like that. In the closet, brand-new clothes, every piece of shirt and blue jeans and pair of shoes he'd fingered in Wally's Thread Barn and wished he could take home. Like the rich kids at school wore; those sorts of kids, the ones with parents named John and Sue, and brothers and sisters and a place in world. Those sorts of rich kids.

He lay on the bed a few minutes. He was afraid to think, especially about those unpleasant thoughts that bubbled up now and then – well, more than now and then. Shrinking Coach Marblehead down to a midget would be nice and drying up the brains of Wyllie Wanamaker, the class genius. Just to see the look on the face of his stage mother would be worth it.

Al chuckled as he imaged it in precise detail. He stopped, and sat up with a gasp.

"Don't mean it, don't mean it", he repeated aloud and held his hands over his ears. He took his hands off his ears and listened. The world seemed like he'd left it. He sat up on the bed; his mind wandered to school and to – he couldn't even think of her name. That would be bad luck; much worse, he'd make a fool of himself. Unless, of course, she'd glance at him now and then and think – just think, how darn good looking he could be and brave and cool. Not to mention smart. If she'd just notice those things. Maybe if he just wished about it…

Black haired and blue-eyed. Why she seemed so special he didn't know. She just was.

Sophie.

There. He thought of her name and imagined her face as clearly as he could. He wondered what she'd been doing all summer. Actually, he worried about what she'd been doing all summer. Her parents were pretty darn rich, definitely rich enough to buy her a car. That meant she could tool up and down the beach and give other boys a chance. Competition: and plenty of it.

Maybe if he just concentrated….sheer will-power…

Al sat up and wrinkled his brow. Positive images, Sophie big-eyed and melting in his arms. That was it. He let it be. Melting in his arms.

"Boy!" A sharp call came from downstairs. Pendragon clumped up the stairs. "Did you get lost? Any time today, boy."

Al jumped a foot off the bed. The old man poked his head around the corner. Al felt his face turn beet-red. "I was just thinking."

"Come downstairs, please and thank you."

Pendragon disappeared. Al rose slowly. Maybe, he thought as he took the steps down one at a time, I've actually hit the jackpot. Maybe he really was the old man's great-great nephew, though he knew the state would do almost anything to get rid of a tax burden. Not too many questions would be asked, either.

On the other hand, this whole house thing; and the mind reading – the orange shutters and such – told him something major was up and coming. Whoever pulled off that trick – well, they had to put a good deal of time and thought into the operation. Like Houdini promised: magic was just all smoke and mirrors, though sometimes the trick was complicated and the results seemed beyond all explanation. Still, that's all it was: smoke and mirrors and good for an old-fashioned laugh.

Well, Al mused, I could always use a good laugh, just like Wheezel insisted: we can all use a good laugh, even if it's at our expense now and then.

The old man wasn't downstairs. Al searched through the entire new house. I'm hungry he thought idly, nice to have hamburger, fries and a cherry coke.

On the shiny dining room table Al found a plate full of 'burgers and fries, cooked up exactly the way he liked them -- a little but burned around the edges-- waited, hot and steaming, beside a large cherry coke with fresh beads of sweat gathering on the glass.

Al shrugged. A good trick, don't know how they did it, but just a trick. He picked up the sinful platter of fat and cholesterol and went outside to eat on the deck. He sat in the pristine picnic table with its scent of fresh paint and watched the ocean turn deep purple in the twilight. He was starving and didn't ask questions. The answers would come. Sensible answers, but they'd come. The numbness was wearing off anyway. No more sleeping in a donated bed meant for a five year old with his legs hanging off the edge. No more stuffing a pillow over his head while Lumpy snored loud enough to set the blue-tick hounds next door howling. No more hand-me down clothes, no more looking like, as one of his teachers commented, Ferris Bueller, whoever that was.

Besides, Lumpy and Wheezel were what? – a dozen miles away-- and Al calculated, not without feeling a little bit guilty, that the old coot was good for a car, despite what he drove. Probably the first dollar he ever earned was still in the bank. Not that he'd try to break Pendragon's bank: an old Ford truck would be good enough, something with character and a little style.

Al ate peacefully for a minute or two before he spotted Pendragon a hundred yards away wading knee-deep through the rising surf. He held a white chum bucket in one hand and tossed the chum in sweeping half-circles a few yards ahead of his legs.

Al swallowed. Chum-- ground-up, rancid fish bits-- was good for just one thing: attracting every flesh-chomping shark from miles and miles away.

Al stood. The old man had lost his brains. Al figured he had zero time remaining before the first shark came up from the open ocean and chomped away the old man's kneecaps.

Al knocked over his cherry coke and vaulted over the desk railing into the sea oats. Soft in the head, the thought raced through his head as he struggled through the ankle-deep sand. That would explain everything... Didn't last long, did it?

Al sprinted the last hundred yards in a personally best record time. Pendragon tossed the empty chum bucket on the sand, gave Al a happy look, and reached to scratch two man-sized, torpedo shapes in the surf, one with each hand, the way he might play with a pair of cocker spaniels.

Except they weren't sweet and fuzzy.

They were sharks, seven feet long, turned over one their white bellies and lolling in the surf as scratched their tummies.

There was more.

Above him, came a peculiar whump whump, much like a canvas sail suddenly filling with air. A downward rush of air scattered the loose sand around. With it, a strange scent of dried leather, musk and burned sulfur.

Al glanced up. He saw, big as an airplane, its wings glittering emerald, its body ruby-red, its long head completely ebony, and its big eyes flashing gold, a dragon.

Nothing approximate or like or close to: an actual, living thing which twisted its long neck, gave a purling growl and snapped as it soared over his head, banked left and vanished into the piney woods.

Al sputtered. He heard himself yelling, "Up there! Up there! He jabbed with his finger. Yelling Fire! Fire! Or Bear! Bear! Or even Armadillo! Armadillo! made sense, but not Dragon! Dragon!

He sputtered until he blinked and realized that the evening sky was deep blue, salt-scented, and dragon-free.

The old man: he still stood in the surf rubbing the white bellies of his twin man-dismembering sharks.

"St. Olaf's shingles," the old man cheerfully noted, "you look like you've seen a ghost."

One of the sharks rolled over and considered Al with the coldest of eyes.

The old man, though, just scratched at their tummies, one for each hand.

Al sat down in the sand – hard. He heard himself sputtering. Somebody was sputtering anyway. Al grabbed his head and rocked back and forth just to hold in his brain which, he knew, was about to burst all on its own.

Merlin studied the boy. He knew he hadn't been minding his p's and q's lately; the dragon was his, a hold over pet from the good bad old days. A good creature, too, though it got lose now and then and caused all manner of problems with the local pilots and constabulary. Merlin patted the sharks.

"Home girls."

The girls rolled over, gave a little huff, and sped off with a splash of their tails.

Merlin washed out the chum bucket. The boy, however, didn't seem so good. His eyes were big as a bird's and his face pasty and his jaw seemed to have come unhinged.

Merlin sighed. "What's your problem, son?"

Al let out a huge breath. "You don't get out very much, do you?"

"Not recently."

149

"Help! I've been kidnapped by looney tunes!"

"We need to talk."

"At the very least."

"Come here, now, before you burst something."

Merlin beckoned. Al rose on shaking legs and somehow plodded with the old man back to the house.

"Mind the sandy feet," Merlin insisted and they stomped their feet on the door mat like everyone else.

Merlin led Al to the living room, with its beige walls and fireplace and knick knacks on the mantel. Well, that was what seemed to be there, if just for a few seconds. Al actually wasn't sure. The room seemed to be very beige and very normal, but when he blinked, the walls seemed to disappear and become dark and formless – not black, but deep, as if he could fall through them for years and years.

From outside the windows came the leathery flomp-flomp Al had heard a few minutes before. The iridescent green dragon darkened the windows. In a blink it was no bigger than a parakeet and flapping and tapping at the windows with its bony beak. Merlin raised the sash; the creature fluttered inside and snuggled onto Merlin's shoulder, making biscuits with its big clawed feet.

"He's just showing off," Merlin said.

"Got that. What's it eat?"

"Don't fret about that."

"Nothing like fingers or ears or eyeballs."

"Not if he likes you."

"Ah."

Merlin moved about the room, making motions as if he were opening curtains along the walls. "How much do you know about history, Al?"

"There's just too much to bother."

"What about your own history."

Al felt a lump in his throat. He swallowed. "Not a whole lot."

He actually meant to say nothing, but he couldn't. "Guess I'm about to learn," he whispered.

Merlin finished with his waving. All the light drained from the room. Al felt himself floating. It wasn't unpleasant. But he didn't know what was coming next.

"You dream, don't you?" Merlin asked.

The room filled with the peculiar darkness. Or, Al decided, the nothingness took over the room in all dimensions.

Merlin continued, "Everybody dreams. But some dreams are special. Much, much more than dreams."

Suddenly the space was filled with people from all manner of cultures -- Amazonian Indians, Russians, Inuit, Maori, Zulu, German, Han Chinese, on and on. Al felt as if he'd lived a lifetime with each of the people.

"To every time there is a season," Merlin said quietly. "A time to live."

The landscape was filled with armies on the march – ancient Egyptian, Assyrian, Samurai, Aztec, Napoleon's Grand Armee, columns of German Feldgrau, on and on they marched. Cemeteries for the war dead appeared next, landscapes of limestone and sculptures of angels.

"And a time to die," Merlin said quietly. "Then there is justice and injustice."

"I took civics last year," Al heard himself say.

"And glory. That happens, too."

Heroes came next, or the people Al had been taught to call heroes – Greek Hoplites, Boadicea, Saladin, Sir Francis Drake, Milton, George Washington, Lincoln, Crazy Horse, Churchill, Martin Luther King, on and on.

"Amazing, isn't it?" Merlin asked.

"Is there going to be a test," Al asked automatically.

"Always."

The other came next – Attila, Stalin, Hitler, Pol Pot, the destroyers with their hooded eyes and blank faces.

"Good and evil," Merlin sighed. "It never ends. Why doesn't all fall into chaos?"

"You're asking me?"

Al felt himself high in the air. The green folds of the high Appalachians appeared below. An entire mountain, blasted out to its core, burned and spilled, blighted the landscape.

Merlin took Al's arm. They spiraled downward, closer and closer. Al didn't want to get any closer. He felt, through his pounding heart, what he'd never really known before: a terrible fear. But Merlin's grip was like iron.

Al couldn't breathe. His throat seemed to close. They reached the mountain anyway. Al suddenly knew where he was - a tomb fashioned from a cave. The air was filled with a sickly-sweet stench. By the thin light Al saw broken stones and a wooden coffin. The coffin lay on its sides, splintered and broken open.

Merlin released his grip. "Not much is simple in our lives, but this is... It is simply evil." Merlin shook his head. "I thought I'd taken care of him. I should have known."

What the heck are you talking about? Al wanted to yell it loud as he could. Instead, he asked quietly, "I don't think I want to know."

"Too late. Your enemy. Your eternal enemy". Merlin leaned closer.

The look on his face was dark and angry. "You know him. You know him from your dreams, but they are much more than dreams. You've never just dreamed in your life. You know his name. Say it aloud."

Al backed away. "You're crazy."

"One of you appears every thousand years or so. Only one. And one of him. He's got a jump on us this time. He's already up and about, stalking the earth. He'll find you. You'll fight. As always. If he wins –

Al began backing away. He didn't know where he was, or even what world he was in. It's like falling off the face of the earth. But it's really simple. I'm crazy.

"I don't know anything!" Al called aloud.

He was lying. He knew it and, judging by Merlin's face, he knew it, too.

"Say his name," Merlin insisted quietly. "That's how it starts."

Al's sleep, for as long as he could remember, had been filled with those dreams, but they were much more than dreams.

153

Always.

"Mordred!" Al cried aloud.

He didn't want to say it. The sound echoed off the stone walls.

Merlin seemed to relax a little.

"His name means death," Al recited. "Why I am here? Again, I mean, if that's the truth."

"You are here because – because-- the thing I tried to do, I could not. All things seem to revolve like a wheel, this endless coming and going. I tried to interrupt the cycle, but it turns on and on anyway. Does that make sense?"

"Not to me."

"Questions from your world are all about how. This is about why. Does that make sense?"

Al blinked.

"Your people, not so long ago would understand. I mean those in the mud brick houses by the green reeds of the Tigris, or by the huge stone fortresses of Argos, under the Lion gate. You would revel in being chosen. Every man and woman in your village, clan or city would join the celebration with you. There wouldn't be any doubt. The last time, not so long ago, your own people in the villages outside of Londonium watched the Twelfth Legion withdraw from Britain, taking their Latin tongue and marble baths and good manners with them. Those abandoned prayed for their warrior and savior. The one chosen had no choice. Listen: this must be quite a shock."

Merlin stopped to stare at Al.

Al shook his head violently. "No. ..No...No...I've got it figured. I'm loony. So are you. I'm going to wake up at Green Acres, over at

154

Coosawatchee, the hospital where they send all the kids who need rubber rooms. I'll be shot full of wacko juice and then I'm going to be just fine. I'll have my own room back."

He squeezed his eyes shut.

"What are you doing?"

"Hoping for Kansas. You wouldn't understand."

"Don't try to calculate. Follow what you know. You know who you are. He frightens you and yet you have vanquished him. Only you. Always, always, you have found a way to win."

"Then why is he back?"

"I don't have an answer."

"I asked why. You can't keep your end of the bargain."

"It isn't just a bargain."

Al stopped.

"If you're not bargaining with me, what are you doing?"

"I am hoping."

Al didn't know how to answer. He didn't even know what to ask. I am playing a game with him, and not a very polite one. But that's how it's always been with me. Don't be like this, he heard Wheezel's voice lecturing and pleading with him: appreciate what you've got. And she would add under her breath: little though that may be.

You're right on both points, Al thought. Now look what you've got. I'm crazy, except I know I'm not. I know what I see and feel. No doubt. This is insane.

Well, that's what I've got.

"Where is he now?" Al asked.

155

"I wish I knew."

"Can't you pin it down a little? Make me an awesome hulk while you're at it."

"Power is a dangerous thing. I could do what you'd ask, but, to him, it would be like – what's the word? -- a spotlight--in the middle of the night."

"At least let's get out of here. I'm suffocating."

Light streamed into the huge room from a big hole in the roof. A ruined pick-up truck lay nose-buried on the littered floor. Its back wheels stuck up high on a mound of debris. Merlin and Al pulled themselves hand over hand until they reached open air.

"What exactly happened here?" Al asked.

"Destiny," Merlin shrugged.

We need to expand our vocabulary, Al thought, but didn't say it aloud.

Lava still oozed from the caldera blasted from the far side of the mountain. People in yellow HASMAT suits and gas mask swarmed over the far slope. Al felt the heat sear his face from a mile away. Helicopters flitted back and forth and filled the sky with hard whumps.

I'm crazy, Al thought, but so is the rest of the world. Not much comfort in that. Al had heard the hysterical news reports a few days earlier. Witness, the reports insisted, the first pyroclastic flow – volcano – to erupt east of the mighty Mississippi since the tyrannosaurus ruled the swampy bottom of Washington, D.C.

It couldn't happen, sputtered the geologist.

It's the end of the world, crowed evangelical types happily.

Everything is crazy, Al repeated to himself. After all, the skinny old man puttering around nervously a few yards away, look at what he's got me believing. Still, standing here puts things in perspective – a huge perspective, bigger than I could have ever imagined. Nothing at all makes sense anymore. All-in-all Al decided, you gotta stop asking how, just like he says. Ask why and wait and see. And hope.

He almost forgot about hope.

Merlin watched the boy pace back and forth, crunching the brittle lava cinders underneath his feet as he went nowhere.

But Merlin waited. This was always the worst time, even when the world wasn't so much a different beast. Something had changed, or maybe simply forgotten. Problem was, forgetting meant blindness. I am real; what is about to happen is real. Mordred is very real. People knew that once and, in just a flash, less than a thousand years, they forgot. For that reason alone the boy needs to be cheered on. Needs to feel that he is a prince among men, and that is all he was ever meant to be.

But this boy seemed so – unsure.

Lacking.

Merlin hated to admit it to himself. Where were the tree-trunk legs, the barrel chest, the neck and brain made of granite? After all, a warrior-prince didn't need much sense. Look at Achilles, great despite the flea-sized brain. But the confidence was there, even if nobody could stand him. After all, a warrior-prince was hardly out to win a popularity contest.

157

That, Merlin sighed to himself, sounded so un-American.

Al stopped. He studied the volcano and listened to the 'copters beat their way through the sky. "What does he look like, this other guy?"

" Thin and pale. Tall, though. He might play your basketball, if he had a better attitude."

"Except for the tall, that could be me."

"You'll know him, quicker than anyone else. He won't come quietly and he won't come alone."

The boy stood stock still.

"You expect me to do everything."

"That's because you can," Merlin said simply. Note, Merlin said to himself, I am pleading. The boy turned away and studied the metal dragonflies buzzing through the skies.

Chapter 20

Merlin considered having them take a bus. In the end, though, tired and fretting, he called up a few wisps of power and got them home. To Merlin that meant the beach house. The orphanage might be what the boy wanted, but Merlin had his own ideas. When they arrived, the sea had already swallowed the sun. The evening sky hung royal blue. The ocean rolled and hissed. The wind blew like banishes, coming from every direction.

Al, getting use to such things, found himself trudging through the sand behind the house. Time must have passed since they were gone. He didn't feel it, though. But time didn't seem to matter much to Merlin, or his type, whatever they are. Al knew a storm was coming. He knew that from having lived in the panhandle his entire life. Al glanced around. No Merlin, not just yet. A storm coming is and it's going to be a bad one.

Al shook his head. I'm getting use to this. Time travel, magicians,

People or whatever it is, living a thousand years, eternal combat with some evil genius, or maybe he's just a jerk – and look who the old man thinks you are –

Not that he's just an old man. I don't know what the heck he is.

Al realized he felt many things at once: confusion and exhaustion were just two of them. He wondered how many people knew what he knew. I couldn't have been the first, he thought. They kept it to themselves, though. That was the amazing part. How many carried this sort of knowledge in their heads, had their own wizards, who wanted to ruin their lives? Maybe they were many. They knew the secrets to just about everything, exactly the way he did. Count out all your physicist, astronomers, and scientist of any type, politicians, preachers, billionaires, and big people for whatever reason.

What I know, Al told himself, makes me want to stay pretty small, build a house with his own hands on a dry patch inland, some place with good shade trees, find someone to marry, and work Monday through Friday, and someday, somehow, someway, let his wife and kids knew what he knew. They had to know, especially the kids. Otherwise, they wouldn't know a single thing worth anything, the way he didn't know a single thing.

Till now.

Al climbed the steps and went into the house, mindful to shake the sand off his shoes. He walked into the living room. The house was empty. His footfall echoed off the walls. The living room walls were plain again, with a few plants near the windows and a TV staring at him from the wall.

The old man was there, standing by the wall. To Al he seemed a worried, elderly man, no more and no less. For a little while Merlin didn't say anything. Finally, Merlin asked, in a dry tone, "Taking up the task, it's got to be your choice. What say you? I've got to know now."

Al took a deep breath.

Abruptly he was tired and so much more.

It was impossible.

Everything was impossible.

The effort, even the thought of effort, left him breathless. Worse, he knew what was wrong and right. I know, he promised himself, I know what I care about.

I know what I am.

"Look. I got left at a gas station. A day old, stuffed behind the old tires. And I'm not even sure that's the right story...You've got the wrong one."

There, Al thought, it's done. His mouth felt dry.

"That's about it, then?"

Al shrugged.

"Then go! Leave!" the old man roared. "Blasted hurricanoes! I'll – I'll -."

Merlin sputtered.

The boy ran from the room. The kitchen door slammed.

Merlin let his shoulders slump; his heart sank, for the boy, for himself, and for everybody else.

Merlin dropped into a chair and waited for what seemed a long time. How does the human soul survive, he asked himself? Slowly, feeling aches in his joints, the magician rose and followed the boy outside.

He found the boy quickly and watched as Al climbed the low sand dunes. The beach road skirted the other side.

The boy held his ragged suitcase in his hand. Merlin's brain wanted him to run after the boy, grab him by the shoulders, turns him around and yell. But he didn't. He followed until Al reached the beach road.

Daylight was fading quickly. The colors everywhere were royal blue and purple. From a full mile away, where the beach road made a 90 degree turn, came the roar and high-pitched whine of a little sports car.

"A buzz bomb," Merlin muttered aloud, "that's all I need. Company."

The buzz bomb squealed around the elbow turn and headed up the straightaway toward Al. The driver swerved across both sides of the road. Gears clashed. The car went faster and faster. The headlight outlined Al and headed directly for the boy.

Merlin ran. He raised his hand ready to try a spell meant to deflect charging horses. The driver hit the brakes. Tires screeched and smoked. The rear end fishtailed. Al didn't blink. He stood motionless until the buzz bomb squealed to a stop. Al took one step and rested his foot on the bumper.

Merlin blinked. The freckled, carrot-topped boy, the one Al called Lumpy, sat in the driver's seat, seemingly happy enough and unaware of the damage he might have done to the lovely little fire-engine vehicle.

A passenger climbed out of the low seat and sat on the convertible's door: a lovely dark-haired girl with a heart-shaped face.

"How's family life?" Lumpy asked and nodded at the heaving, red-faced Merlin who'd sprinted the last hundred yards.

"There are issues," Al said.

"We just happened to be in the neighborhood," Lumpy said.

"Umm," Al said, "What about the wheels?"

"This old thing? She's a loaner. Borrowed for the shank of the evening."

"You know there's a law against shanking."

"Yea? Oh -- right here is Sophie. She's dying to meet you."

"Hi," Al said.

He swallowed.

"Hi," Sophie said.

"You two go to high school together. Remember Mr. Elmore's trig class?"

That's where you first met, though this is the first word you've ever said to each other. I guarantee."

Sophie smiled and didn't stop smiling. Lumpy glanced from Al to Sophie and back again. "You two need to shut up, hear me? Just shut up. Anyway. I've done the all the damage I can today. Hi Ho silver and away."

He crunched the gears into reverse and turned the buzz bomb around. He raced the engine and called over his shoulder. "The car's her old man's."

Tires squealed. Gears clashed again. Lumpy waved without turning around. But Sophie turned around. Her gaze followed Al, and, just before she disappeared, she waved goodbye.

Al didn't move. Merlin gave him a little time alone and walked closer quietly. "You have such nice friends."

"Who?"

"You. Such a nice boy. Very nice girl."

"You just don't know."

"I'm sure."

"No. Really. You don't."

Al picked up the suitcase and started down the road. Sunlight was almost gone. Merlin could barely make out the boy against the dark. He felt his pulse race and he realized he was holding his breath. Run

and grab the boy and shake some sense into him--
Merlin wanted to do it so badly that he trembled.

But he didn't. He couldn't do that, ever.

The last crescent of thin sunlight faded.

Al disappeared.

Merlin waited a little longer. A harsh wind
blew straight onshore; it seemed to carry the night
with it. Merlin shivered. Eventually he turned his
back and trudged through the ankle-deep sand.

People, he listened to himself say, think they're
going to live forever. But their lives end in a blink.
There's nothing more I can do. So this world, the
entire galaxy, really, falls under the sway of a
ruthless, eternal evil. Them's the breaks, you should
have looked before you leaped, ain't my problem.
Merlin repeated those homilies to himself as he
worked his way slowly back to the empty house, but
he knew in a little while, no matter what he did, his
heart would break.

A sand spur pricked his foot. He was barefoot,
not a big thing on the beach, but there were risk.
The pain made him furious. He hopped about on
one foot, cussing as he went, the last few yards
before he reached the porch steps. He dropped down
hard on the first step and dug at the bottom of his
sandy foot.

He wasn't alone.

Al sat on the top step hugging his knees. Merlin
forgot his foot. The boy suddenly looked to be what
he actually was: very young.

Neither said anything for a while. Al looked
down on the skinny old man with thinning hair
around his crown. After all I've seen today, you

would think he'd look like a damn movie star. You'd think.

Al heard a leathery flutter above his head. The green-gold dragon, now no bigger than a parakeet, extended his little claws, landed on Merlin's head, cocked its head and studied Al.

"Doesn't that hurt?" Al asked.

"You get used to it."

The creature climbed off Merlin's head and snuggled close to his neck.

Al began, "This enemy of mine, the one I don't know-- ."

"You know him."

"You aren't making this any easier."

"You've never hurt a fly, have you?"

"What's the supposed to mean?"

"Just a fact."

"You're going to change that?"

Merlin sighed. This one was at least smarter than the others. "It comes with the territory."

"How bad?"

"You'll be surprised how easy it'll become."

Al wanted to run. The night sky glowed blue-black. Over the Gulf of Mexico, where the ocean was black, deep, and ancient, a line of thunderstorms billowed. Lightning flickered yellow and blue.

"What if I sleep on it?"

"You know where your room is. Does it suit you?"

"It's fine. Don't...don't change anything."

"I hear you. I'm going to grab a little shut-eye myself. It's been a big day."

He stood and patted Al on the shoulder.

You're not just kidding, Al thought. He waited a few minutes before he went into the house. He carefully locked the door behind him, climbed the stairs and pushed open the door to his room. He looked upon the only room he'd every know, or a very exact replica – his old room in Wheezel's place, down to the two sagging beds, the toy knights lined up on the top of the third-hand dresser, the map of England pined to the wall, and the dusty cowboy lamp beside his bed. No Lumpy, of course, and none of Lump's snores.

Al shook his head. The old man didn't listen that well. Al lay down. Even the smells were just right, the scent of the U.S. army wool blanket and the smack-you-in-the face lemony of the cheap detergent Wheezel bought in twenty-pound boxes.

Something pecked and beat its wings against the window. Arthur yanked the sash open. Merlin's little dragon pet fluttered inside, mewing and keeling. It settled on the dresser, purled, and studied Al with its big eyes and made biscuits on the dresser. Its claws made deep scratches on the pinewood dresser.

"Okay, Okay," Al muttered. "You can stay. Just be careful with the stuff. I guess."

The creature mewed quietly, folded its leathery wings around its body, closed its eyes, tucked its head and began snoring with quick little sighs.

What am I going to tell my caseworker? Al thought. Or the national guard? Maybe I'll be on TV along with all the other crazies. If this were just one of those alien abduction things, life would be pretty darn simple.

Wait. Maybe it is.

Al sat up. The cat clock on the wall ticked off the seconds. Mr. Winkler, his history teacher, with his watery eyes -- he might understand. He let Al turn his homework late because, as he said, he "understood." Truthfully, though, Al decided, Winkler would probably be scared to death in a situation like this. That was the truth, and sometimes, as Wheezel put it, the truth hurt.

Okay – what about Wheezel? She'd narrow her narrow eyes and call his bluff. Then what? She wouldn't believe unless she was actually kicking Mr. Mordred herself. What about Lumpy? He wasn't sure he'd wish that on Lumpy, with his ears that stuck out at a fifty-five degree angle, as officially measured in third period math class. Lumpy, who ran when he walked, shoulders slumped forward so that he seemed ready to tip over at any second? The one with his big hands and flat feet that slapped the floor and who slept with covers pulled over his head and studied the faces of women on the street wondering, wondering, always wondering, are you the one who left me behind?

Sophie.

He caught himself thinking about her. He hadn't meant it. Got to keep this focused on a higher plane, he reminded himself. He saw in his mind's eyes the way she was just a little while ago.

Exactly.

She'd come to him. That seemed like a miracle. The idea just came to him. He'd never thought of anyone that way, though, he decided, he was plenty old enough. Some things came late, if they came at all. That was another thins Wheezle'd muttered under her breath, one of the lessons she meant to teach. She seemed to know everything, but she didn't know this. Not a chance. Nor did anyone in Tintagle Consolidated High, not a single one of the four hundred eighty-odd students, not the forty teachers and staff, nor anybody in Orrville, or anybody in the entire panhandle, not anybody in all of southern Alabama, or the USA, including territories, the English-speaking world, or the western hemisphere, or the planet earth, ever.

Al shivered.

Another feeling, like a dark, smoky ghost, seemed to pass through the walls and stand in the room. It wasn't like a mood they discussed in group therapy. This thing came from the outside. Al could swear to it. He knew what it was – the purest hate he'd ever known. Or felt. Or considered. Al knew what it intended to do. It had a soul, a life, a purpose, and he knew what that purpose was. I want what you have, it said.

Al slid out of bed.

He ran.

He ran downstairs, echoing through the house. He searched room to room, banging open doors as he went. The old man was gone. Al fumbled with the back door, jerked it open, thumped down the steps and ran through the sand down to the hard, smooth beach. The black ocean rolled and hissed. The beach curved to a point a few hundred yards past the house. Al found himself there. He faced the ocean; the salt water caught the starlight, what there was of it, and glittered.

He wasn't alone. Above, low in the sky, a brighter star appeared. It grew brighter and brighter and, Al realized quickly, headed directly for him.

He knew what it wasn't: a plane from the navy base fifty miles away --it was soundless; it wasn't a meteor -- he didn't hear thunder, and fire didn't trail behind it.

The light grew larger and larger, but it didn't seem to reflect off the ocean or the wisp of low clouds. Maybe I'm the only one who can see it. It's meant for me. Maybe it's meant to frighten me, Al thought, but I won't let it. I'm not going to cover my head and whimper and be tormented.

I've known enough fear in my time. Enough is enough. Come on. I'm waiting for you.

It plunged into the ocean with tremendous splash and a sizzling hiss.

Al waited and listened intensely. It emerged, a black, huge, devil-shaped, from the ocean a hundred yards out. Phosphorescent foam cascaded off the wings and off the barbed tail that churned the sea behind it.

It wasn't alone. On the body, the low hump between the wings and the head, a man, or a boy, appeared. He just stood there, pale, awfully so, with stringy hair and narrow shoulders. He wore simple white clothes, drenched, of course.

The creature glided softly to the shore and softly scared against the sand. Mass and weight, Al decided, to let me know I'm not dreaming. Mass and weight to let me know I should be afraid. Al realized his arms were shaking.

He seems a few years older than I am, Al though. The sea-rider's mouth was pressed into a thin line. His narrow eyes, deep in his head, seemed to have no color at all. The living dead, Al said to himself, real zombie stuff, except that's not it.

The man-boy stepped off his creature, harshly whistling a little tune in some ancient key as he went. At first he didn't seem to notice Al. He had landed about two hundred yards away. The boy pounded his fist in open palm, and paced back and forth, faster and faster, cursing in some language Al didn't recognize. Al hadn't watched anyone pitch a temper tantrum in a very long time. Wheezel wouldn't even allow that among the little ones.

Al refused to budge. The other one paced back and forth, faster and faster, more and more frustrated. He can't find me, Al thought. Long as I don't move. I thought these types could do anything we can do better. The old man's work was impressive enough. But in this case, the boy didn't seem to know what to do. I am invisible, Al decided, as long as I want to be. I have to reveal myself to him, if I want and only if I want. The choice, or the power, felt good.

Over his shoulder Al heard a familiar keeling. He glanced up. Small leathery wings beat in the air. Al crouched and tried to shoo the creature away. It didn't help. It dived and fluttered, mewing and keeling for all he was worth.

The boy on the beach glanced up. Al watched his face break into a terrible smile.

Al didn't flinch, at least not on the outside.

The tiny dragon hissed and dove for the protection of Arthur's shoulder. Where is the old man? Al asked himself. He knows everything else. What should I do?

Al stood stock-still.

Mordred didn't move.

Al stood. He didn't know why. He knew what he felt: burning anger, a need to strike now. The sounds of war roared in his ears. Finish it now. A hundred previous lives demanded it.

But what do I have? Bare hands. It's what he wants. End it now. That's exactly what would happen.

Their eyes met.

Al thought he knew evil. Modred's eyes were not large. They penetrated. They were empty and depthless.

Al stumbled. He will, Al knew, he will do it. Destroy everything of mine and enjoy it.

Abruptly he turned his back and ran as best he could through the soft dune sand. Merlin's little pet clung to his shoulder.

From behind him, Al heard a long, furious cackling cry of contempt intended for the sea, the sky, the entire world and everything in it.

Al glanced back. The giant manta-creature thrashed it tail furiously in the surf. Jagged streaks of color flashed over its body. Modred rode the creature high on the neck and guided out and up – out of the sea and high and higher into the night and ocean sky.

Al watched until it disappeared as a glimmer, in the sky. Long, long after Al still heard the other's bitter, hating laugh.

Al felt his chest heave.

He'd never know such fear. That's what it is, he told himself, fear. Fear for the best reason in the world.

He sank into the sand and stayed there. He didn't know how long. Maybe hours. Maybe years.

Eventually he made himself stand. He could barely do it. His legs wobbled like an old man's.

I can't do it. I might as well jump off a cliff. I can't. I can't except for the one thing.

One thing.

Except it's a biggie.

And he caught himself half-coughing, half-laughing at his own joke. Al wondered what they'd say, Lumpy, Wheezle, the little ones, the entire population of Tintangle Consolidated High...them, all of them, all the others. If they knew they'd die.

Lump, Wheezle, the little ones. Sophie.

If they knew, they'd –

They don't have a chance.

The house: Al stumbled and climbed the steps. A whole universe filled with magicians and creatures and thousand year-old villains and I have to climb the steps, Al complained to himself.

Merlin waited for him at the dining room table. The room was dark. He sat stiffly and drummed his fingers softly on the table top. "What did he say to you?"

"Not a word. You can pick them, know that?"

Merlin studied Al's face. He's trying to decide if I'm still with him, Al thought. He doesn't know; he doesn't know everything.

"Not a word." Al repeated.

"He let you get away. I'm surprised. Maybe it's arrogance. Maybe something else."

"That's encouraging."

"He's found you already. Usually there's time."

"Time?"

"To set up a defense, recruit retainers."

"Retainers?"

172

"Warriors."

"This is the twenty-first century."

"He's very creative."

"And plays well with others? Come on."

"Till he doesn't want to play anymore."

"He wants to play. How much time do I have?"

"A day or so. I guess."

"We need to find –retainers?"

"We'll do what we can do."

Al thought of the high school football team, but that didn't seem just a great idea. "What am I supposed to do next?"

"Get a good night's sleep."

"That'll be a trick."

"I'll stay up a while."

"There's something I want to do tomorrow. Have I got that much time?"

"What is it?"

"Just something a little something."

"No guarantees. We may need to get out of town pretty quick."

"Understood."

Merlin gave a stiff, worried smile. Hope just doesn't cut it, Al thought to himself, remembering Wheezel's words. He gave Merlin the same smile back. We're both cooked, and it's so bad neither of us can say it. Al grimaced inside.

"Good night," Merlin said.

"Same here."

Al climbed the stairs. He glanced at Merlin on the way up. The old man sat there, staring ahead and looking like a lost and fretting old man.

Chapter 21

But Al did sleep. He woke late, when the sun was high in the sky and sparkling off the sand and palm trees. The room was back the way he first saw it, bland, but comfortable. Maybe we are getting out of town pronto, Al thought, covering our tracks.

He hurried – a quick shower, clean clothes (they weren't changed, he noticed; no silver spaceman suits or anything), even a quick shave, just to look especially neat.

Downstairs, he found Merlin outside, studying the sky and drawing big symbols in the sand. Tourist who wandered this far up gave him the evil eye and kept their distance. Al approached and cleared his throat.

"How's things."

"Tight."

"Um – that little thing. Can I have an advance on my allowance and borrow the car?"

"Allowance?"

"Money to keep me out of trouble. Everybody does it."

"Sure. Hold on." Merlin dug in his pockets and dropped a few big coins in Al's outstretched hand. "How's that?"

"Nice. Spanish doubloons. Don't see many of these around."

"Problem?"

"How about a twenty or so?"

"Dollars?" Merlin glanced around, mumbled a few words, dug in his pocket and tossed Al thick roll of twenties. "Here we go."

Al swallowed. "Thanks...I guess."

"Don't mention it."

"I won't. What's my curfew?"

"Your what?'

"When I'm supposed to be home. It's another way of keeping me out of trouble."

Merlin snorted.

"How about... midnight."

"Yes. Midnight. Most definitely."

"Um...the keys?"

"In the car."

"See you around....Dad."

"My goodness."

But Al was gone.

Al drove into Orrville. There was a rundown coffee shop, painted chocolate brown with yellow trim: Mr. Jitters Fine Blends and Snacks. Al parked and peeked inside. He saw what he was hoping to see: Sophie, standing behind the counter, in the company Swiss miss outfit, complete with ruffled sleeves.

She glanced up and smiled. Al jumped, recovered, and pushed open the door. Sophie was handing a little boy a Galaxy Buster Fifty Ounce Triple Frappe. As Al approached a few nickels slid out of her hand and jangled on the marble counter. The little boy glanced back and forth, gathered up his nickels and hurried out.

Sophie kept smiling. Al wanted to smile, but he felt something like panic, too. He swallowed. "You work here?"

"Everybody knows that."

"I'm not everybody," Al said, not at all what he meant.

"I'll bet. And you're just in time."

"For what?"

"You must have ESP or something." Sophie nodded. Lumpy pushed open the front door and came inside, rusty bicycle and all.

"Surprise, surprise. Didn't I know you in another life?"

"What's he doing here?" Al asked Sophie.

"Civic duty. I'm a volunteer."

"A volunteer? In a coffee shop?"

"Sure. Nobody ever thought of that before. Where's the old coot?"

"Beats me."

"He loan you the wheels?"

"He did indeed."

Lumpy whistled. "Where's he getting his dough?"

"Magic."

"Must be nice."

"Not all the time."

Lumpy blinked. He leaned on the counter. "So what are we up to today?"

Sophie waited patiently. "The store room needs straightening. You know how Mr. Pinkerton is."

"No. How is he?"

"The store room."

"Looks okay to me."

Sophie sighed.

"Maybe I could check it out." Lumpy glanced over his shoulder and headed for the store room.

Sophie turned to Al. Sophie leaned forward on her elbows. "So what do you want to do?"

Al felt the sweat gathering under his shirt. "Huh?"

"I'm glad you came by."

"I just happened to be in the neighborhood. You know how that is."

"Sure."

"You do?"

Sophie pulled out a brand-new driver's license and slid it on the counter.

"We can use my Dad's car. I love calzone. I know they make you fat, but I don't care. You remember Cal Dewey? His parents run an Italian place on Holcomb road. Seven o'clock sound good to you?"

Al blinked.

"Haven't you ever been on a date before?"

He blinked again. "Sure. Lots of times."

"Good. I haven't."

The door jangled and a set of parents and six children under age ten swarmed through the store. Al retreated. He waved a last time to Sophie, who smiled back.

Al drove home very carefully not to get any speeding tickets and thrown into jail. At the beach house dinner was cooking itself on the stove, bubbling and whistling merrily. Otherwise the, the world seemed to be in good shape: the sky was blue, and no loathsome creatures were crawling up the beach. As usual, Merlin wasn't to be found until Al wandered out to the beach. Merlin was still drawing signs in the sand, studying and fretting, drawing and redrawing, frowning in concentration as sweat dripped of his off the end of his nose.

Al cleared his throat. "How's it going?"

"Strangely." He didn't look up, but frowned at what he was doing as if it were Calculus.

"How's the evening look? "

"Unsure."

Al took a breath. "Well, I've got plans."

"That's the understatement of the millennium."

"No. Little plans. Dinner."

"Dinner's on the stove. I told it to be ready in half an hour. But you know how crockery is."

"Not really... Just me and-- my friend --we need a few hours."

"Who'd you say?"

"Her name is Sophie... the one in the car. She's not always like that. Do you want to call her parents? I could borrow your cell phone, you know, if anything comes up."

Merlin frowned. "What did you say the name was?"

Al started to say, but Merlin seemed absorbed by his symbols in the sand. Suddenly he glanced up at Al. "Do you know what this means?"

"I get the car?"

"If you must," he intoned seriously, nose close to the sand.

Al felt dark clouds pass by. "It better get ready. It's getting late."

"Indeed," Merlin muttered.

Al hurried back to the house. He showered again, brushed his teeth twice, combed his hair three different ways, and studied the clothes in the closet. He changed clothes four times. The phone rang.

Sophie chatted happily on the other end. A change of plans; she was coming to pick him up. Her father insisted. He's such a worry wart, she explained. Al glanced out the window. The sports car sat in the driveway, its engine softly purling. Al took the stairs down three at a time. The pots on the stove gave him an annoyed hiss as he hurried past.

"Sorry, guys," he called after.

Outside, the weather, or more, had taken a step back. The sea was purple and black. White foam skittered off the wave tops. Draco chose that second to screech and flutter around his head. Al waved like a madman. Sophie sat in her father's car , still smiling. Al shoved open the kitchen door and tossed the angry creature inside.

Al took a deep breath. Sophie opened the car door for him. "I didn't know you had a parakeet."

"I don't."

"Well, you look nice. Most men don't know how to dress."

He felt his face grow warm. Pure dumb look, he knew, but couldn't say it. "Guess you've got it or you don't."

"Is the Holcomb place still okay with you?"

"Sure thing." Al shrugged, though hadn't been to a nice restaurant that required knife and forks since he was six and that was for Christmas. He didn't have pleasant memories.

Sophie ground the gears. "Oops. Dad hates that." She backed out onto the road. "Don't look so worried. I've been practicing." She lined up the wheels, ground the gears into forward and took off. "Come on. Smile. This is going to be fun."

Chapter 22

On the beach Merlin watched in his mind's eyes as Sophie speed away with his chosen one. In the darkening sky a phantasm sparked now and then, interpreted on earth, Merlin knew, as falling stars, meteors properly speaking, though the simple notion was closer to the truth. Science and dreams, he mused, both of you are wrong.

The summoned ones: Merlin guessed that would come next. The Word was utterly lost on the present crop of humans. Retainers couldn't be summoned under a giant oak tree, a promise of land, serfs, and a few little tricks, raising skeletons out of the earth to dance around, throw in a winged creature or two, that sort of thing. People were quite ready to believe. Forget that now. It'd get you a psychiatric evaluation and that's about it.

Those who were summoned would have to come from elsewhere. Merlin had ideas where Modred would have root around for them, but they were notoriously addle-brained and prone to run off screeching in all directions. They'd require a firm hand, strong displays of power and huge bribes to buy their loyalty. If you were evil to the bone, evil to the very marrow, evil a thousand generations back, they might be worth calling part of your camp.

I can't panic the boy, Merlin told himself, and he's risible enough as it is. The world he's lived in so far doesn't help. Maybe he doesn't value his world enough. That could happen; the will to win may not be there. Down deep, it's a choice and his world may not be mine. Or what I care about. Maybe that's it finally – what I care about.

An awful thing to realize, Merlin decided, maybe it's all about me finally. I've never been able to see any other path. Anyway, the boy will discover his way soon. The challenges would take shape, though with which players, and in what form, especially in this glittering, sleek mathematical world, Merlin confessed to himself, I simply did not know.

He paced faster. Now things were so much different anyway. People were so much more clever now, oh so much more clever. One little man with a truck and some sort of little drilling stick undid what should have lasted till the end of time.

All was chance, chance, ignorance – and innocence. Danger, danger, Will Robinson, Merlin chanted to himself, remembering an old television from the hippie era. That's right on the money. Danger, danger, danger above below and all around them both. And, as Merlin glance across the bay, toward Orrville, where the jeweled necklace of city lights glowed along the shore, the greatest danger for them, too.

The age of the prophet is long gone, Merlin admitted to himself. He wouldn't even try. How'd he explain it all to the FBI office in Tallahassee? Even the thought gave him a bitter chuckle.

His heart sank. I've never lost the fear, he told himself--the scent and taste of the battle -- no matter how many times he'd endured it. The hours just before were the worst: the dark hours of waiting and thinking and hoping. Maybe Mordred would make the first move. That was his way. If we only knew from where, when and where it would come.

From the corner of his eye, Merlin noticed, high in the heavens, a meteor cartwheeling through the atmosphere and throwing out a cascade of cyan and gold sparks. Closer to the earth it plunged into a tower cumulus cloud over the continental land behind him. . The interior of the cloud glowed and flickered as it were filled with lighting.

"First moves," Merlin whispered.

Chapter 23

A man or a boy in dirty white clothes hiked along the tarmac edge of Florida State Highway 91. Deputy Rachael Weiss, of the Sawgrass County Sheriff's Department, caught sight of him in her cruiser's headlights. They were on an empty stretch of dunes and seacoast between Orrville and Mitchell Air Force base. The Empty Quarter, everybody called it, the place where people wanted to be alone for good or, much more likely, nefarious reasons.

Anyway, Rachael knew, addicts did such things, stroll along oblivious to the sandspurs shredding their feet.

As she watched he wandered into middle of the road. That was probable cause.

Time to hear Mr. Clean's tale.

She shivered. The road seemed especially straight and empty tonight. Duty, she reminded herself, and checked her radio, Taser and weapon. Get control, she reminded herself. Don't you dare sweat.

She pulled the cruiser to the roadside thirty feet ahead of the boy. He didn't seem to take any notice of the police car blocking his way. Ninety-nine times out of hundred a meth head or any other of his ilk turned and ran like a rabbit. She reported her position, counted to five, and decided to request backup, just to be sure.

Mr. Clean kept coming as if she wasn't there. Rachael suddenly felt anger. She was being ignored; I should wait, she told herself, but I can't stand it.

She found her flashlight, cracked the cruiser's door and stepped out into the humid night.

She shined the flashlight directly into his face. He kept his eyes down. His blond ringlets, seemed precious enough, but when he finally looked up, ten steps away, all the sweetness dissolved.

Boy or bitter old man. Rachael asked herself. It doesn't make sense. His eyes glanced at her. The eyes –

Rachael stepped back. She gripped her nightstick. "Okay, friend stop exactly where you are."

He raised his hands and made a dismissing motion. His fingers were the longest she'd ever seen.

He kept coming. "It isn't necessary. And you're in my way."

She couldn't place his accent – British, but not quite; her grandfather had emigrated from the Warwickshire after the War so she knew a U.K. accent. This was – otherwise. The word ancient came to mind, though she didn't know why.

Another thing: a split second, a flash in her mind, as if she knew the man, if he was a man at all: no, something else. She didn't want to know and she did anyway.

Rachael raised the Taser and fired. The Taser pin struck the boy in his palm. She saw it. A surge of volts should have sent him crashing on the asphalt.

Instead, she was enveloped in fire and found herself tumbling through space.

But whose space and time she was never sure.

184

The two cruisers responding to her call found a full quarter mile of highway ripped up and the asphalt evaporated off the road.

"Cheezus", one of the deputies on scene hissed to the other. "What's gone on here?"

The second didn't answer for a few seconds. "Martians," he stated flatly.

Rachael's cruiser, melted along one side, turned up in a marsh half mile away. No Rachael. Fifty state troopers and deputies, bloodhounds, and a 'copter combed the dunes and empty seashore. Rachael turned up wandering along the road ten miles north of Jacksonville, unable or, some thought, unwilling to say how she got there. The distance from Orrville to Jacksonville: 410 miles.

By then, though, Orrville and the Sawgrass S.D. were quite seriously otherwise occupied.

Chapter 24

The Empress Mall didn't live up to its name. In the seventies it was shiny and new, the first mall in the entire panhandle. Even then it wasn't that much, just a long concrete building. An even shiner mall opened up closer to town and the Empress faded. Shabby dealers moved in, and sold shabby stuff – junk from sundry attics, used books, cheap pottery, and sad little dogs in rusty cages. The entire place reeked of fried food.

People still came, mostly the working poor looking for a bargain and something to do on Friday night. Otherwise, the Empress didn't cause much trouble. When the Sawgrass S.D. began getting crazy 911 calls, not one or two, but dozens and dozens of frantic calls from mothers with babies, retired postal workers and the like, the dispatchers already had their hands full with the missing Deputy Rachael.

What the citizens reported was crazy. There wasn't a better word for it:

An army of kids in Halloween costumes were attacking the mall. That was how the dispatchers summed it up, though they couldn't repeat what they actually heard -- stuff about ugly little creatures, hopping around, frothing and gnashing their big ugly yellow teeth, tearing up and down the aisles.

In forty years Sawgrass County Sheriff Parson Pettigrew had never heard such insanity. It's got to be LSD in the water, he decided, and sent half his

186

cruisers flying towards the mall. Calls filtered in about meteor showers lighting up the sky, too. That's the least of my worries, he decided, with a missing deputy, some sort of mass poising or some wacko gangland attack on the good citizens, even if they didn't bother to vote over in that neighborhood. Eight-one days until retirement. Yessirbob, he just wasn't going to think about that.

The cruisers, though, when they reported back, made him think about it.

Chapter 25

He loved to sing, when they would let him. Mordred reflected: maybe they were afraid the way the untalented always envied the gifted. Every sentient being knows petty envy.

So he, the anointed one, sang. He sang as he worked his way through a dark night after sending the woman in the baggy uniform on her way. He tromped alone through the palmetto and pinewoods like a common homo sapiens, just to get the feel for the slumming life.

He noted, with satisfaction, that rattlesnakes, some big around as his leg, slithered away as he approached. Mordred was proud of their fear. Being low life, they didn't understand what I mean, Mordred thought and pitied them: I am rebirth and renewal, even for the lowly. I shall take care of the lowly creatures. Maybe, he mused, I'll put them in charge. That would be interesting.

In the meantime, rebuilding needed to be done, he reminded himself. Rebuilding meant tearing down: serious destruction never set anything too far back. The fire, brimstone, earthquakes, and plagues, and slaughter that went with rebuilding would only disturb the unready.

Mordred felt his high mood suddenly evaporate. I am so seriously misunderstood, he groused to himself, and horribly so. Therefore, he reminded himself, I have so much to offer and I can never give up. Never surrender, never, never. Conviction is everything, and, beyond that, revenge against mine enemies, which were, of course, legion. And revenge tasted sweeter than all else.

Especially against the tottering wizard, whose tricks and cheating buried him: he felt every second of those suffocating, black, desperate years. I am an artist, he reminded himself, and feel things more deeply than anything on this planet. The old man forgot the one thing. Revenge was one its way. Fate, sweet, glorious, fate, always favored the oppressed and confounded the unjust.

Therefore, Modred told himself, I am free. Best of all, I have a plan, a thousand years in the weaving, and recited a million times at least.

The Plan wasn't complicated: simplicity and boldness were its fathers. Search for the flank, strike for the critical mass, and hit without pity or remorse.

First of all, he needed friends. Not friends in the common definition. He needed bodies, things to run interference.

They were already collecting; they filled the sky. They weren't pretty – far, far from it. He didn't like pretty things or people anyway. Making the pretty ugly was a pleasure.

Jin.

But nothing sentient had ever called a single Jin pleasant. Phrases like disgusting, vicious, double-crossing, slobbering, cheating, stinking, self-pitying cheats – that was closer to the truth. Once upon a time they'd polluted a hundred worlds, -- they were extraordinarily adaptable-- but thousands of generations of killing each other and astoundingly clogged arteries had reduced them to a remnant sulking on Jupiter's moons.

They sailed through the galaxies in hollowed-out obsidian meteor ships, a minimal technology that they'd robbed hundreds of thousands of solar years ago. The craft--- they looked more like shriveled-up sunflower seeds than anything else-- used gravity from huge bodies like Jupiter to slingshot their fleet toward earth.

Mordred's summons perked their interest right away. His reputation considerably preceded him. The deal included a promise of more loot than they'd ever imagine, and, even beyond that, a guarantee of the ultimate prize, that which no other sentient creature had ever won, though many, many, good and ten times as many very bad, had tried.

None had even gotten close. This time would be different, Mordred promised and his plan sounded like it might succeed. That was enough. They packed into their miserable little ships and set off for the pretty blue marble of the earth, sassy in its warmth and easy living. But that wouldn't be the prize; the blue marble was just an appetizer.

The sky above Orrville: that night it was crisscross with what seemed to be roman candles, sizzling through the clouds in the prettiest reds, oranges, blues and yellows. What was inside wasn't pretty, but at that exact time nobody knew that.

The learned quickly enough.

Mordred kept striding until he broke out of the woods. He faced a busy street. Mordred steeped onto the four-lane highway. Cars swerved, horns blaring, skidding and burning brakes, in an attempt to not strike the skinny drink of a man in grimy white clothes.

They missed him somehow. The man stepped onto a weedy parking lot and paused beneath a green neon sign that buzzed and crackled above his head: The Empress Mall, Where your dreams come true. Mordred hurried, not fast enough to break his stride and ruin his dignity, but enough to show that he could barely contain his excitement.

Inside the mall itself a handful of people hanging around the broken fountain noticed an "albino-type" (based on the police report) who appeared out of nowhere. He was barefoot; some women remembered his careless ringlets of hair. Describing his face was harder: men shrugged and called him a punk. Women frowned: good-looking like a movie star out of drug rehab one second and bitter and old in the next second. And the eyes: the eyes made them shudder.

A witness agreed roughly what happened, though they really didn't expect anyone to believe a word. But they agreed by and large, for what it was worth.

He strode to the old fountain, studied its green and scummy waters, seemed satisfied, and crossed a few yards to the Sandman's Perfumery, smashed the window with his fist and took a crystal bottle filled with what Sandman sold at his highest price-- a crystal vase of what claimed to be frankincense from the sacred gum tress of Ethiopia. Maybe Sandman was telling the truth: Mordred took it, held it to the light, and grinned.

He strode back to the fountain. Mr. Sandman, five feet two in his lifts, charged from his stockroom, sputtering and tomato-red in anger and waving his arms like a crazy man.

Modred glanced over his shoulder. Their eyes met. That's all it took. Sandman's face drained of color and he retreated, never daring to turn his back. By then a little crowd had gathered. Mordred nodded. Nobody wanted to interfere. "Top of the evening, one and all," he said. "Does anyone have a match?"

Somebody better have one – that was evidently the feeling. An old man held out an old-fashioned box.

"Just keep it," the old man muttered.

Mordred gave a courtly little bow. "You ladies and gentlemen will want to finish your shopping early today."

He winked to the crowd. Fire appeared. Some said it was the tips of his long fingers that actually burned. With his free hand his sprinkled the frankincense over the greenish water; it began swirling and bubbling and frothing. Abruptly, at the instant of the greatest froth, a column of fire erupted upward. "Pardon, folks," Mordred said. "There's hell to pay."

A column of fire, white and blue with heat, and roaring like a jet engine, burst through the roof of the mall and shot high into the heavens.

A bass rumbling began beneath the building. The foundation itself began trembling and crackling. Merchandise began to tumble from the shelves. Glass vases in Aphrodite's Apple burst in shards. Mannequins in Elmo's Threads and Notions waltzed across the floor.

People threw away their shopping bags, grabbed their children, and ran screaming for their lives.

192

The column of fire that erupted from the roof served as a beacon for the Jin. They were punctual if nothing else. Jin poured in from all directions, hobbling, sprinting and wallowing on flippers, hooves and gnarly feet and some turning cartwheels as they went. Their nut-shaped craft sizzled and tumbled through the sky. Some plowed into the ground, some rolled until they smashed against the walls of the Empress, and some broke apart in the sky and released a platoon of Jin who spiraled to the earth on outstretched gossamer wings.

Jin: graceful and elegant, a wonder of the universe – perish the thought. Jin: a huge variety of shape and form, ready to fill every grimy evolutionary niche – skinny, cockroach-like appendages, bleary and bug-eyed, pale eyed, howling and gnashing their sharp, crooked teeth- short, fat, thin, spindly, eggplant purple, cucumber-with-warts-green, squash yellow, rotten peach orange, or mottled like speckled butter beans – all these combinations were present and much more, whatever could churn the stomach of any other thinking being in the wide galaxy.

On and on they came, tumbling, rolling, clopping, appendages slapping against the asphalt, hopping, springing, dancing, each and every one howling and screeching with delight to be back in the fray.

Modred was correct: shopping was over for the night. Customers burst through the mall doors and collided with squirming Jin fighting to get inside. Jin howled. Citizens screamed. Sadly for the people, Jin lived for status, which meant the callous display of luxury goods, even the type found in the Empress.

Once inside, after tumbling, rolling and slobbering over citizens, the Jin leapt and rolled in ecstasy. Never could they imagine such a thing-spangled rows of fabrics, plastic flowers, toys for toddlers, running shoes, guitars, lawn mowers, cheap jewelry, air-brushed T-shirts, forty flavors of ice cream, roller skates, eye blush and cans of interior latex house paint of a hundred colors, every can good to the last drop – on and on it went, more delights than their peanut-sized thinking organs had ever imagined in the universe.

Mordred leaned against a pillar and jammed his hands in his pockets and watched. The Jin scrapped the shelves clean, wrapped their throats with feather boas, smeared puce makeup under their bleary eyes, jammed bunion toes into genuine imitation Italian leather loafers and stuffed their jowls with organic carrot muffins.

Mordred gave his host thirty minutes of fun, then raised a brass trumpet to his mouth and blew a long B flat.

Any hint of harmony and joy drove the Jin into berserk rages. Every toady form hidden behind a rack of summer wear, every leering, web-foot thing with its face jammed in a jar of peanut jar, twirled its head towards the hated sound, snarled, drooled and scampered toward the source.

The host thronged into the sizable food court, and, gashing their teeth, surrounded Mordred.

He refused to show the slightest fear. For one thing, it'd been instantly fatal. Mordred tossed the trumpet to the throng and let them crack their teeth

194

on it. The effect was enough. The host settled somewhat, muttering and chanting, while Mordred, sensing the time was right, raised his palms. Still, the host growled for five full more minutes until slowly, their emotions spent, they fell quiet.

"My children," Mordred began, "What creature lives by the moldy bones of their dead alone?"

Howls of denial.

"Is this enough for you? Are thee satisfied?"

Roars of denial and a mass slapping of appendages against the floor answered.

"But what you've seen tonight in this insignificant little rock whirling around a little pale sun – this is nothing. There is more, oh so much more – if you only might find a leader, one willing to sacrifice his youth, his health, yea, even unto his very life for your greatness. Greatness: yes – your courage, wit, beauty - not appreciated in so many corners of this galaxy. But they will learn. Yes, they shall. They learn reluctantly, but they will learn. They must be taught by needle-edge weapons wielded by creatures of ruthless determination, determined to transform the corrupt and inferior or destroy them in the attempt."

Mutters and slobbers.

Too many words, Mordred thought and paused.

He coughed. "There will be big fights and much killing of our enemies and the loot will pile up to the rafters – here –this high! And higher! And higher! I lead and thee follow!"

His hands were high above his head. The Jin host howled and cried and hooted with joy.

"All I have to offer thee is their blood, their sweat and their treasure!"

Mordred dug into his pockets and pulled out heaping handful of glittering colored jewels – cut glass, but Jin didn't know the difference. They dove pell-mell after the trinkets, snarling and biting. Mordred let them settle. After gorging and looting, the creatures loved to roll over and snooze. That couldn't happen. In a little while humans would appear from all directions carrying weapons and determined to get their property back, though, as Mordred knew, what they got back at this point they'd want to pile up and incinerate. Modred held up his hands again. The mass, still gibbering over the trinkets, settled.

"Now," he began again," what you can carry – keep. The rest is nothing. Our journey has just begun. We must move, swift and sure, great warriors swarming over this landscape. Moving is everything. We must move before the moon touches the sacred Tree.

The Jin, Mordred knew, had no idea what he meant. I do, Mordred thought, suddenly filled with anxiety. Mordred grabbed a long, golden curtain rod to serve as a staff, jumped to the floor and lead the squirming mass as it poured out of the double doors, even the ones marked Emergency Exit Only.

The Jin, thousands strong, formed up into a huge, ungainly column, hurry fast as it collectively could, with Mordred at the head. He covered the ground in long strides. He knew exactly where he was going: through the scrub forest and toward the true place high on the mountain of the moon, which didn't quite exist. It would shortly. And for one night it would be the most important and wondrous place in the galaxy.

Chapter 26

Dewey's Restaurant, on a slow night, seemed more what it was: a drab small town place. Alberto Pisano, age eighty-four, didn't care. His granddaughters, who took an Anglo name, kept the place going. He loved to play the accordion and that was that. On that special Tuesday night, when so many legends were born, a couple of kids showed up, awkward and gawking at each other.

Alberto grabbed the squeeze box and, before the youngsters got a chance to order, he was in their face, pushing the bellows back and forth. Promptly he lost himself in the music of Verdi.

Al, far too polite to ask an old man to please shut up, managed a conversation by leaning so close to Sophie that their faces almost touched. She didn't seem to mind.

Sophie ordered her calzone. Al ordered spaghetti, the only thing on the menu he really recognized. He didn't want to end up with a plateful of snails. Wheezel served spaghetti at least three times a week, but, Al confessed to himself, eating wasn't the point of all this at all.

He rolled his spaghetti on his fork and took tiny bites and sneaked glances at Sophie. He'd never seen anyone so beautiful. The thought seemed to be the most natural thing in the universe. He looked down to hide it and snipped off another few strands of spaghetti.

Sophie ate away. "You know, at this rate, you're going to be here till next Thursday. Don't you like it?"

Al put his fork down. "I'm not too hungry."

"We can get you a doggie bag."

"I don't have a dog."

"It's just an expression. It means you're going to take it home and eat it for a midnight snack."

"I know that."

"I didn't mean --." She glanced up with a big frown and caught Alberto's eyes in the wrong way. Alberto ended the last chords of Aida and shuffled away.

Al watched him go. "What was he trying to prove?"

"He was just trying to set the mood. I think he was sweet."

"Yea. That's what I meant."

Sophie smiled as if she understood something he didn't. "So: What about college? Where are you going?"

"What about it?" He answered quickly.

"I just mean – to my parents it's the most important thing in the universe." She stopped as she remembered Al's situation. This time she blushed. "I mean for them. Nobody asked me. I might just bum around a while."

"Don't be a bum. It's not all it's cut out to be."

He sounded so much older; he wasn't joking. Sophie touched his hand. "That's not how anybody thinks of you."

Al knew that wasn't the exact truth. A nagging anxiety had settled in his chest for the last hour. Anxiety and fear and expectation – the strangest feeling, the fear that a terrible thing was about to happen and an even greater hope that it was about to happen anyway. He didn't want the feeling, but it was there and it was the truth.

He took a deep breath and looked up, not at Sophie, not even at the yellow wall across the room.

Sophie had read about epilepsy; the boy she, without reason or cause that she could see, simply stared straight ahead and left the world. A thousand-yard stare, her father, who was in the army, would call it. Sophie sat up straight. Her heart began beating hard in her throat. What should I do? She asked herself the question quickly.

Just as quickly, Al blinked and stood straight, so quickly that his chair hit the floor. He started for the door and, at the last moment, seemed to remember that she was there.

"I've got to get some air."

He hurried out. Sophie dug through her purse and tossed down some bills and followed after him. The Pisano girls, mother and daughter, gave her a sympathetic glance on her way out. No, no, you don't understand, she wanted to cry out, but she didn't have time.

Her first real date, and the first time she'd been allowed to take her father's mid-life crises love out on her own; and she was going out with a boy nobody seemed to like, and she had no idea why, and out of the blue he goes blank on her, and charges out the door.

Need some air? Maybe it's my mother's perfume she thought fleetingly, stuff she got from Jamaica. I knew I shouldn't, but it was too late. I'll never live through the night, Sophie groaned to herself.

Al stopped at the edge of the gravel parking lot. He faced the woods to the north. He didn't turn around, though she called his name three times.

She waited. She guessed other girls would have stormed away and let him walk home.

But this wasn't like that at all. She wasn't sure what it was. She felt fear and more. She wanted to stay; she wanted to see what was going to happen. Even if someone dragged me away, she thought, I would come back.

Al faced upward as if he expected something to come over the horizon.

"Al" Sophie said firmly, and stepped closer so that he had to look at her. "You can talk to me."

"I will not be what he wants me to be."

"Good. I guess."

He turned around suddenly. His mouth was pressed into a thin line. "How could I have missed it? It makes so much sense. It's all so clear."

"If you say so. I'm just going to ask this once and don't get offended: Are you taking something for this condition?"

She frowned; she wasn't sure how that came across.

"It's way gone. Do you feel it?"

"I'm not sure what I feel. Confused, yes. I feel that. And more, but I don't know what it means."

"He really doesn't want me. I just stand in his way. It's all he's ever wanted -- Merlin and everything he is."

"Who?"

"It's time for you to leave now."

"I beg your pardon."

She was surprised how angry she became. She grabbed Al by the arm.

"Get in the car." She pulled him along as if she meant it. "You need help. I don't know what to do, but I know who does."

She didn't tell him more. Sophie pushed Al into the car, and climbed into the front seat, and started the car. She downshifted – for the first time she got it exactly right – and headed for the state highway.

She wasn't exactly sure how to get to Tintangle on her own. She found it anyway; it didn't take long to get to nowhere, a shabby square with a tall flag pole and the peeling, gingerbread orphanage house on one side.

She pulled up to the curb and killed engine. Lumpy was sitting on the porch with a half dozen little ones clustered around his knees and leading them in a song.

"Ninety-nine bottles of beer on the wall, take one down, and pass it around," Lumpy warbled.

"Hold on a sec," she ordered Al. Maybe he understands something sensible, she thought, but my main concern is getting in and out before the ugly lady who owned the place catches us.

Kidnapping – could you kidnap somebody in the same grade? Sophie asked herself. Just if he refused to go, she decided. Then what? She didn't know. She stepped on the porch and gave the little chicks here best Omega Young Ladies Society smile. "We grown-ups need to talk just a minute. Do you mind?" She grabbed Lumpy by the arm and pulled him across the yard.

He glanced at Al and whistled. "Family life not agreeing with you, boss? I kinda had my doubts."

Al suddenly sat up straight. "Take her and both of you get out here. Run. Hide. Everybody hide."

Lumpy sighed. "Where to exactly, Captain? I've got thirty-four dollars and twelve cents to my name. How far is that going to get us?"

Sophie pushed Lumpy into the back seat and slid into the driver's seat. "You two chat. We've got to be somewhere."

She didn't know how she knew what to do. Her parents were big on her following her inner voice. Usually the voices didn't have much to say. Suddenly they had plenty to say.

Besides they weren't voices; they were feelings telling her what to do. She was frightened; she knew it sounded like one of those how I met your mother or father stories her parents like to tell at Christmas parties. It was real and that was the most frightening of all.

Sophie drove northwest out of Tintangle, zooming up a county road that, as far as she knew, didn't go anywhere.

They topped a low rise and saw, filling a huge wedge of the northern sky, a roiling, green-black thunderstorm.

Lumpy leaned forward. "Maybe we should put up the top."

Lumpy cleared his throat, but it was a lost cause. The lovebirds didn't seem to hear. They faced straight ahead, eyes big, chins up, a regal and scent-sniffing pose, he decided.

"Okay," he mumbled aloud, "We'll just get soaked."

But his stomach was tied in a knot. He hadn't the slightest idea what was going on. All along, since the first day he met Al, he knew something wasn't exactly right about the boy. Al was – the word just didn't exist. But I'm here, he though, and I'm not going to bail out of this sports car driven by two crazy people. Maybe I'm crazy, too. That's not it…Maybe we're the last three uncrazy people in the whole darn galaxy and I have no idea why I just thought that.

Ahead, emerging from the storm, he saw the mountain coming toward them.

Chapter 27

Merlin ran. An old man with thin legs, wearing khaki shorts and a purple Grateful Dead T-shirt ran flat-out down the middle of an asphalt county road. His chest heaved and the few vehicles that passed took him for just another silly old snowbird jogging his heart to death 'cause he ran the New York Marathon in 1972.

It was getting dark and only the reflective silver tape on his shoes kept the occasional traffic -- mostly thundering county dump trucks heading for the landfill-- from flattening him.

I've lost. Merlin accused his soul with every pounding stride. His lungs felt as though they were afire. I can't go much farther, unless I use my skills and I can't do that.

So he ran. His goal – five impossible miles away, where the moon was rising and soon would silhouette the Tree, exactly where the storm was turning and twisting and ripping up the earth and pummeling the ground with purple lightning. Storms destroyed; this one, Merlin feared, would build.

Despite all his years he'd never witnessed what was about to happen. Never, never had it gone this far. The Trees -- a few marked that place on this earth. I don't know them all. One for each continent, Merlin thought frantically. Had to be. Had to be. How to approach them, how to capture them – this must be the way. The only way. How did he learn it? Get the power? It shouldn't be. Never, never. He was after all –

Modred. Maybe I have under estimated him. Clearly you have, he accused silently. How else could he get this close? What are you going to do now? You can't even get there before he does. That can't happen. What can I do? One bit of power and I'll shine like a beacon. He'll end it then. Maybe I can save the boy. If I am hidden, run like a ghost, just a little longer. How much farther? Four miles. I can do it. Yes I can.

He stumbled and fell flat on the road.

A rusted pickup truck sat in the weeds by the road. FOR SALE a crayon-scrawled sign said in the windows.

A sweating old man pounded on Mrs. Wilson's door and paid her in gold coins.

Gold.

They were heavy like gold should be and old. The truck was worth about one hundred bucks; he got the keys and a quarter tank of gas. She offered a couple of mongrel puppies from the barn out back, too, but he took off. She stood on her porch, and watched the truck grind its way up the road toward one of the worst storms she'd seen in a very long time.

The truck thumped along. Merlin pushed the gas pedal to the floor. The engine wheezed. Forty miles an hour. Just a few more miles, just a few more, Merlin prayed under his breath, fully realizing he was praying to steel and oil and torn seat covers.

So be it.

Merlin set his jaw and stomped the gas pedal. The truck lurched and the surviving three cylinders raced to double nickels.

Emerging from the greenish swirl of the storm, Merlin saw the mountain, black and seething, swelling up from the woods.

Lava bubbled up from the granite mantel. The pine wood flamed and the fire brilliantly illuminated the landscape.

Merlin saw them by that flickering light: Jin by thousands, hopping like fleas, gibbering, trailing every manner of spangled dress, jewelry, shoes, hats, cutlery, watches , crates of lemons, barbeque grills, electric can openers, scented insect spray, floor lamps, bouquets of carnations from the floral shops, push lawnmowers and much, much more.

At their head, Merlin saw, wearing a blue Union Army overcoat from the Halloween costume shop, the tall and thin and striding

Mordred.

Merlin nearly wrecked. Merlin couldn't avert his eyes from the boy's pale face. He seems so much older now, Merlin thought. Where once was petulance I see determination and vengeance.

Merlin abandoned the truck and took off on foot through the pine woods. The smoke burned his eyes. He thought as he ran: the mountain will be finished soon and then I need to summon the boy.

Merlin's thoughts raced ahead: Once I summon the boy, Mordred will be warned. In the past, a summoning took place on a high Tor, a high hill, with the entire community spread along the flanks. The boy was a hero then. He still may be, Merlin thought, though nobody may ever know it –

Down the road came the gear-grinding of a high-performance sports car. The little car swerved past with young, dark-haired Sophie driving, and Al, eyes big as fried eggs. The car whizzed past Merlin with millimeters to spare. The red-haired boy, Lumpy, sat stuffed in the back seat, knees almost to his ears.

Sophie slammed on the brakes. The car slid to a stop. Merlin hopped into the back seat and pushed Lumpy aside.

"By the ghost of Balazar – drive!" Merlin roared.

He attempted to grab the steering wheel from Sophie, who pushed the old man away.

"What's going on!" she cried out just as loud. "Who are you? What are you?"

It didn't seem unreasonable; an hour ago her biggest concern was how to eat a calzone like a lady. Now she was racing down some back road toward a volcano rising out of the panhandle and, she knew perfectly well, that hadn't happened in her lifetime.

"The lecture comes later! Pedal to metal!"

She jammed the gas and the car lurched forward and down the narrow dirt road, past the ring of burning woods and, suddenly, the road ended.

It stopped at the slope of a huge mountain. Sophie hit the brakes. Her father's pride and joy slithered and crash into a ditch.

The old man, spry as a goat, hopped over her shoulder and hit the ground. He tried to pull Al from the front seat.

Sophie glanced over. Al wasn't the same at all. His mouth was pressed into a think line. His eyes caught the firelight. He leapt out of the car and after the old man. Together they began climbing the mountain slope.

Lumpy watched Sophie jump out the driver's seat and toss the keys on the leather seat. She reached the steep slope. Al and the old coot were already yards ahead. The mountain rumbled and shook and spilled more black streams of mud and lava cascaded down the slope.

A geyser of lava erupted directly ahead, sprouting an arch of fire.

Lumpy moved faster than he ever had in his life. The lava welled up and buried the car. The metal crumpled like cellophane.

He glanced up. The three others were almost out of sight. Lumpy ran after hard as he could. Behind him, gas tanks exploded and incinerated what was left.

As Sophie climbed she still tried to understand. The mountain seemed to be made of cinders and mud and lava, exactly like the volcanoes she'd read about. But reading didn't prepare her for the heat that burned the soles of her shoes and hands when she stumbled and grabbed a handful of sizzling rock.

All was unreal. But she knew Al was real and her burned hands and feet were real and, maybe, the strange, intense little man. She followed him; she struggled to keep up. She followed because he was dragging Al along. She glanced down; Lumpy was following, too, though she wished he hadn't, and she had no idea what else he would have done.

The old man kept climbing, pulling Al up higher and higher. I'm in some sort of dream time, she thought frantically. But why do I feel that I should be here? That's the scariest thing of all.

She climbed faster.

Merlin felt the heat burn his lungs. His human body was spent and burned and exhausted. He felt surprise about how much pain he felt. Part of their charm, he repeated to himself, and gritted his teeth and pulled poor body along.

In a few minutes he realized something downright strange. I am pushing myself just to keep up with the boy. A good thing, an excellent thing, Merlin said to himself. Look: he's ten yards ahead, roaring for the fight.

Al topped the summit first. Merlin scrambled; he didn't want Al to face what would be there alone. Not yet anyway. That would be unthinkable. Eventually it would have to be, but not in the first encounter. No one could survive those seconds untutored.

The summit made a mesa a quarter mile wide. The sky above glowed green and yellow and orange.

Merlin, sweating and cinder-covered, stood on his shaky legs and squinted. He could barely see through the acrid mist. On a small rise at the very edge of the mesa, an oak tree clung to the summit. The bark was singed and peeled. The gnarled limbs ended in long, fragile fingers.

Merlin's heart beat in his throat. He couldn't find the boy. Merlin struggled to breath. A wild wind swept over the mesa and green lightning flickered and thunder crashed.

Merlin felt himself toppling backwards. Someone grabbed him.

"You stay here, okay?"

The young girl was telling him what to do. The red-haired boy was holding him up his other side.

Merlin jerked away. "I can take care of myself!"

I sound like a spoiled child, he told himself. He bent his head down and hurried forward. "Whatever you do, don't fail me!"

I don't even know who I'm admonishing, he told himself, but kept going against the wind and snapping lightning.

Merlin caught sight of Al. He was bent forward and struggling against the sudden wind. Merlin knew where he was going, even if the boy didn't. But the boy was doing what he must do. Even I am afraid for him, Merlin thought, but he keeps going. He knows nothing; he has no training. Look at him, he repeated to himself, and he is so weak and unready. I wish, Merlin wanted to call out to everyone, I had this much courage.

"But courage will us get you so far," Merlin muttered.

Merlin grabbed a splintered pine limb to use as a staff. Al suddenly stopped and stared. Merlin caught up and stood beside him. In the shallow valley between them and the tree an army waited in ambush.

The Jin, still eating or dragging prom dresses, garden tools, fruitcakes, pastas strainers, jeans, barbeque forks, stuffed toys and frozen pizzas, milled around the tree.

Merlin let out his breath. He thought the Jin had been exterminated, though he heard something about a last stand on Jupiter's moon. They were stupid and greedy enough to follow anyone who offered them war and loot and a chance to inflict pain.

Sophie and the skinny one reached Merlin's side.

They stared.

"I know, I know," Merlin muttered. "What you see here is what you get. Whatever you do, don't look them in the eye or sing."

"I'll stifle myself." the red haired boy muttered.

"Who's that for?" Sophie whispered and pointed to the burned tree.

Merlin said carefully, "We'll see in a very short time."

"I'm dreaming, right?" Sophie asked. Her voice was shaky.

"We're always dreaming," Merlin answered.

"That's not quite an answer," Sophie replied; her voice was still shaking.

"What am I doing in your dream?" Lumpy asked. "I never remember my dreams."

"You'll remember this one," Sophie retorted.

You're exactly right, Merlin thought silently. All was up to the boy. I can do some things for him. I can try to see things objectively; but reason tells me we will lose. Finally, after centuries of fighting and death and rebirth, the game is done. It's likely Mordred shall win. Persistence: maybe that's all it was, an endless beating at the walls of the castle until they cracked. All the plans I've tried, all my skills, all my being wise and clever.

Mordred, defeated so many times, must be terribly strong now. That would explain everything.

"What about the tree thing?" Sophie asked.

Merlin blinked. "A door of sorts."

"To where? Sophie asked.

"It's better experienced, thought let us hope it won't come to that."

"Come to what" Sophie asked. "Be concrete."

Merlin leaned close and spoke loudly against the wind. "Your Milky Way is a beautiful and filled with wonders. This blue planet is one. Your galaxy has a center, a place of origin for all life. This tree marks how to get there, transcending space and time."

"Oh." Sophie swallowed. "

You understand a little more now, Merlin thought. But you don't understand one thing: Behold the one responsible for the catastrophe you are about to witness: me.

Chapter 28

Al walked slowly. The things surrounding him stank like no other funk he'd ever known. They were mottled, bubbling, seething, wheezing and hissing. Some, he could tell by the horn-yellow eyes, wanted to rip him into pieces; others, he could tell by their sly, slow looks, would just take their time.

He set his eyes straight ahead and shouldered his way through the crowd. I can't believe I am doing this, he thought. Al felt claws and nails pluck at his clothes and tug at his hands. He refused to flinch. He kept his eye on the gnarled tree. Almost nothing could be less impressive, but Al felt himself drawn to it.

Modred stood on the lowest limb. As Al pushed his way through the last of the Jin, he stood straight and faced Al directly.

Al could see that Modred didn't carry a weapon. Al studied his face in a way he'd never studied anything before. Who was he? What did he really want? Al thought he knew the simplest answers, but no more.

The Jin became still. From the corner of his eye Al watched Merlin and Sophie slip closer. Sophie started forward. Merlin held her arm firmly and spoke into her ear. She stopped, though clearly didn't want to.

Al stopped a few yards away from Modred. He seems not much older than I am, if age has anything to do with it Al thought.

"So you're it," Mordred sneered.

"I'm what exactly?"

"Beats me, too. What are you? So far I'm not impressed."

The Jin hooted and jeered.

Mordred sighed and sat on the limb. "So, little man, what would you be wanting with me?"

I know the answer, Al realized.

"I'm here to stop you."

"What have I ever done to you? I'm just an enterprising individual. What I've got, I've earned on my own. Go ahead. Share the secret. How do you plan to stop me? You don't have the foggiest about where I'm going, little man."

"Want to bet." Al lied, and glanced at the old man.

"You've already lost. Your old friend isn't going to tell you. Anyway, father time over there is getting weak. I don't think he picked out the right one after all. If your parents didn't love you, what are you worth?"

Black anger surged up from inside. He knows exactly what he's doing, Al thought: Wait. Wait it out.

The Jin mocked and hooted twice as loud.

Al felt as though his head was about to burst. His vision tinged with red. A Jin ripped a limb from the tree and tossed at Al's feet.

He picked it up. He didn't want to grab it and feel how well it felt in his hand-- how much it will feel like a club. I have a weapon now, he though without wanting to think it at all: it's the best feeling in the world.

Mordred spat in Al's face.

Al charged, without a plan or skill.

Mordred waited till the right second and hit Al squarely in the head.

Al reeled. Pain exploded, yellow and red.

"A day late and a dollar short," Mordred called out to everybody.

Al lay on the ground. Mordred hopped down from the tree and bent over him. "And you don't even know who I am."

Al's mouth was filled with cinders. He spat them out. "My enemy."

"Unto death. Meaning yours."

Al sat up on one elbow.

The clouds above them billowed and roiled. A banshee wind roared across the mesa. Clouds descended with the wind. Green and gold lighting crashed. Directly above, a golden disk, hundreds of yards across, appeared in the clouds. Its golden light grew stronger and stronger. Al shielded his eyes. He tried to stand. He'd never been so hurt in his life, not physically anyway. The world seemed to whirl.

Mordred mounted the tree. Behind the tree Al saw a true abyss, a seemingly endless fall.

Mordred climbed to the top of the tree. The tree cracked and began leaning into the abyss.

The Jin jumped howled and scrambled for the tree.

Suddenly they stopped. Al glanced up. Merlin stood at the base of the tree, swinging a club. Jin fell away left and right. Suddenly Merlin wasn't alone: Sophie and Lumpy stood beside him, swinging clubs, and throwing rocks like Wheezle never allowed them to do.

The Jin retreated, hissing and seething.

"Now!" Merlin roared.

Al felt Sophie and Lumpy drag him away from the tree. They made a perimeter of three. Al shook himself and managed to stand. The tree, with Modred still swaying on the highest branches, began splintering. Its roots ripped from the earth.

The tree groaned and slowly, then much more quickly, fell toward the abyss. Mordred held onto the branches and focused his lozenge-shaped eyes squarely on Al.

Modred was laughing. Lightning exploded against the last roots holding the tree to earth. The trunk gave a last great crack.

And vanished.

Lumpy felt his face burn; the pain distracted him for a few seconds, that and the sheer fun of chucking rocks rights in those ugly faces. He got a number of good hits, too; then Merlin grabbed him. They retreated and let the things or whatever they were, rush past. The weird boy climbed the tree like a monkey and wouldn't come down. Behind it, something that looked deeper than the Grand Canyon. The wind screamed. The tree, with the boy clinging to it, ripped from the ground and tumbled away. The boy was laughing.

The old man grabbed Al's hand and howled a war-cry of his own and dove after the tree. Sophie didn't hesitate. She grabbed Al's hand and the three of them followed the tree into the abyss.

Just like that.

The last and craziest part happened next. Lumpy, the only one with any common sense, heard himself give his own howl and jumped for Sophie's hand. He got it, too, a good firm grip. The four of

216

them, like a string of fish on a line, tumbled into the scariest, deepest dark he'd ever imagined.

Al howled. Lumpy heard his own voice yelling and the sickening feeling in his stomach, the dread of the final bone-splattering crump against the rocks down there somewhere.

It didn't happen.

In the last few seconds of light from above, Lumpy saw that the air was filled with Jin who'd followed their leader off the cliff. They made twirling, whirling, squealing mass.

That was his last earthly image. Seconds and the dark took over. Lumpy thought the yelling was his own. He wasn't sure. Quickly somebody stopped crying. The quiet was worse. Wind whistled in his ears. As he watched he changed and his friends changed and the old man changed and he was absolutely, definitely sure he was finally and without doubt, dead.

Chapter 29

Al didn't know why he did it-- grab the old man's head and jump off a cliff. There is trust and something more; and yet he would have jumped on his own. The old man made sure it would happen.

Al wasn't at all completely sure what happened next. The journey began with the tumbling through the dark night air, followed by your classic free fall, end over end, sideways, and upside down.

The scruffy tree tumbled along with them. The noise nearby was tremendous, the screaming and yelling from his friends and the squealing from creatures above and below. Al seemed to be watching his body twist and turn. The tree fascinated one part of his brain; it turned on its long axis, slowly, majestically. For a few seconds Al didn't catch the scary part: he shouldn't be able to see the thing. Everything else was howling and screaming, but it was all sound. The tree glowed, bluish purple, brighter and brighter.

Even that wasn't the right word. It changed. Metamorphosis, Al thought, the first time he'd had a chance to use the ten dollar word. The air around him began to glow brighter, then darker. He had an idea – imagine what it would be like to tumble through the mirror hanging from your wall.

The tug of gravity was gone. That was perhaps the scariest part. Gravity had been his companion since before birth. It wasn't weightlessness either, which would be the opposite of gravity. This was -- something else.

The huge tree glowed and began to sizzle and riots of color ran over its surface, like a huge squid underneath the sea. Then, with a distinct snap the entire tree disappeared.

But I'm left behind, Al thought. That's exactly it. I am still traveling, though how and why I haven't the foggiest.

Seconds or years or decades-- Al didn't know how much time past. He had no other ideas except that was going somewhere and he was still living and thinking.

Gravity was back. The world around him grew lighter. Suddenly a sky arched overhead. The dark sky was filled with brilliant stars, many, many more than he'd ever seen before.

He glanced down, now that there was a down and saw, turning majestically, large planet green where there were seas and light green on the island continents, dun-colored in the plains, and glittering ice toward the poles.

Al caught sight of Lumpy and Sophie to his right and left, Sophie closer and trying to keep abreast.

The dark green-blue of the ocean filled the horizon. Al took a deep breath and oxygen filled his lungs. Al couldn't get enough of it. He saw that his friends were gulping as well. Al felt deliriously overjoyed, even if they were skydiving without so much as a handkerchief to slow them down.

The huge ocean grew bigger and bigger by the half-second. What he'd read was true; the sensation of falling wasn't there. He felt himself watching everything with a strange detachment. His heart was pounding, but even his heart seemed to belong to someone else. This is the way it's going to end, he thought, not what I expected. Hardly.

The ocean resolved into sparkling waves. Just beneath the waves, huge tear drop-shaped creatures swam along lazily, a pod of a dozen or so, mottled pearl-grey and white. They were huge, each big as a city bus.

He wondered what they would think, when three alien creatures -- he guessed Merlin would save himself -- splashed into their world. Al didn't think they'd be pleased. Anyway, Al thought, for the three of us it'll be over in a millisecond.

Al shut his eyes.

Someone tugged his sleeve. Merlin tumbled past, yelling something over and over again. He didn't seem calm at all. Bad form, Al thought, to disturb the others like this.

At the time it seemed a reasonable. Merlin spread his arms and legs to catch as much as air as he could. As Al watched, Merlin slowed and flashed past. Al understood instantly. Merlin was slowing down; he, Al, was falling past. Sophie and Lumpy imitated Merlin and, suddenly, they flashed past as if they'd been attached to a huge rubber band.

The ocean was close. Al spread his legs and arms like the others and, suddenly slowed, the others seemed to catch up with him.

Merlin splashed down first. A spout rose up. As Al watched, Sophie and Lumpy hit the ocean, though not quite so elegant.

Arthur rolled up in a cannonball and hit hard. The sea was warm, then cool as he sank deeper. He unfolded his legs and, as he did, found himself in a luminescent world of blues and greens. A few yards away a huge eye, big as a dinner plate, considered him balefully. It was intelligent and embedded in the head one of the huge creatures he'd seen a few seconds before.

Al shot up through the surface, gasping. Sophie, Lumpy and a beaming Merlin, obviously very pleased about something, sat atop one of the huge creatures.

"Decided to take a dip?" Merlin called. He and Sophie extended their arms. Al, dripping, pulled himself up and sat on the creature's broad back. It skin felt like warm, thick rubber.

Merlin cleared his throat. "On the way down I just couldn't recall that incantation for deflecting gravity. It doesn't always work anyway. So we had to just to do it the old-fashioned way."

"Kinda fun," Sophie said and began squeezing the water out of her hair.

"Kinda," Lumpy wasn't smiling.

Al stood. He felt the firm ripple of muscles through the skin of the huge creature beneath his feet. "Is this thing hungry?"

"They're always hungry, but just for this ocean's version of asparagus. Rather like plankton back on earth."

Lumpy's voice cracked. "Back where?"

"On Earth. That's what the man said," Sophie answered.

"How right is she?" Lumpy asked Merlin.

"Don't fret. We're save enough. For now."

"Let me put it this way. If somebody wanted to drive to Kansas - how long would that take?"

Merlin sighed. "About a hundred million years. Give or take."

Lumpy turned pale.

"Come now. Take a breath. Smell the roses." Merlin took a deep breath and let it out. "The oxygen level here is twice that on earth. No cars, no plastics, and no oil. Just billions of years of wholesome organic growth."

Lumpy coughed. "I didn't bring my allergy medicine."

"What is this place?" Sophie asked. Politely.

"Your distant ancestors, before they let themselves be blinded, could tell you. In the ancient Greek language this was known as the Omphalmous, the navel, the center, of the galaxy." Merlin paused. "I'm going to say quite a bit. Just listen and accept what I say…This is the starting point, the origins of all life in the galaxy. All life began here and was transported, though in simple forms, to the other planets, the other wanders, that could support life. The number of such planets is legion. Our earth is one and, we think, of course, the very best."

"This is Eden," Sophie said quietly, "That's what you're saying."

"That would be correct. A garden – yes, it is a garden, but so much more." He added, seemingly for himself. "That is why it must be saved."

"What a minute," Al said," we're talking a few billion light years from Kansas – I mean home – to here. How? The short version, please. "

"Billions of light years, true. But just in three dimensions. What about crossing dimensions, the way you might cross a shallow stream?"

"What about it?" Lumpy narrowed his eyes.

"It can be complicated," Merlin answered.

Sophie said. "At least. Why are we here?"

"A hundred thousand bio-planets still exist in this galaxy alone. We lost one last year to a supernova explosion, but accidents happen."

"Evidently," Lumpy spoke up.

"Disturb the web of life here and there will be no more life, no for future planets as they are formed and cool. The fish in the sea, the pears that ripen in the fall, the white clouds of birds. All gone."

"So there are thirty-nine thousand nine hundred and ninety-nine rocks with little green men on them are whirling around out there?" Lumpy asked, irritated.

"Not a single one is green," Merlin snorted. "Though many aren't what you'd call pretty."

"You said something about other dimensions?" Sophie asked.

Merlin didn't answer right away. Then: "Dimensions – here they intersect. At no other place. Only here."

"Is that how we got here?" Sophie asked.

"We skated along the edge. Yes."

"Been here before, I take it?" Al asked.

"This was the first stopping point. I was a visitor. Maybe intruder is the better word. All happened a long time ago. There were others, sticking our noses where we had no business."

"Who might the others be?" Al asked, frowning.

Merlin shrugged. "You cannot understand. For now"

Lumpy stood. "Nobody knows anything. So where's the beach?"

Merlin squinted toward the horizon and pointed. "Why, right over there."

"You look like that Christopher Columbus guy." Lumpy grumbled.

"I'll take that as a compliment." Merlin answered.

"What happens after we storm the beach?" Al asked quietly.

"That remains to be seen."

"Not a lot of definite answers."

"That's why they call it an adventure," Merlin answered. And all depends on you anyway he thought and kept his smile.

Chapter 30

The huge creature, with its stubby legs and obliging nature, pulled himself onto the beach so that his guest landed with dry feet. Their clothes were drying by then. The three younger people looked around cautiously. Merlin thanked their creature by patting its flank. The creature turned its bus-sized bulk around and slide into the warm sea.

As far as the three younger people could tell, they might be home – almost. The forest that began beyond the yellow sand seemed to consist of huge oaks, except that the bark was smooth and big, rainbow-colored flowers covered the branches. The sky was cloudless and a deeper blue than back home. Birds-- creatures that were more like lizards than birds-- glided from limb to limb and hissed through the teeth that lined their sharp beaks.

A narrow dirt road lead from the beach and curved inland. Ruts marked where carts had used the road. Lacking carts, they walked for hours past fields filled with tall plants burdened with a heavy grain. Some fields grew a wild profusion of brilliant flowers.

Until late afternoon they traveled through a deep forest.

"Something's watching us," Lumpy shivered.

Merlin craned his neck to see. "It's just the trees. They're nosey and grumpy. Don't approach them with an axe and you're fine."

Lumpy sighed. "Somebody want to make a note of that?"

The fields spread out, the forest thinned and, eventually, as they worked their way to the top of a steep rise, the fortress appeared.

In the late afternoon sunshine the fortress walls, a hundred feet high and built of a translucent stone, glittered in the light. Colored tiles decorated the huge gate directly ahead. Tiles decorated the roofs of stone barracks and storehouses behind the walls.

"This is a dream." Sophie said quietly.

"The source of all your dreams? Maybe so." Merlin answered. "Be proud. You may be the first living human beings to visit this place. Likely you will be the very last."

Merlin led them across a bridge that spanned a rushing river that served as the castle moat. They stopped in front of the ancient and huge gate.

"Shouldn't we knock?" Sophie asked.

"That would be very impolite. We'll be recognized in time. This world – and you will soon see this – is protected by a band of fierce warriors. We dare not offend them."

The huge gate began to groan and slowly, ever so slowly, lowered. Merlin straightened his shoulders and led them into a huge courtyard.

It was empty, though; weeds sprouted here and there. Al noticed that ornaments were faded, the tile roofs were cracked and moss grew on the castle walls.

"Everybody out to lunch?" Lumpy asked.

Merlin frowned. "Apparently. Let's move along."

He herded the younger ones through a stone doorway to a large hall.

That doorway was unguarded. Merlin stopped, frowned even deeper, and glanced around. He cleared his throat and rubbed his elbows. "Let us continue."

They entered a wide hallway. Spider webs decorated the corners. At the end of the hall an embossed and heavy door stopped them.

A warrior blocked the door.

He was a dumpy little man-like creature, with a big red nose and bow legs. He wore a rusty breastplate and dingy pointed shoes. His shoes had holes in them. The four knew about the holes in the shoes because the man was sleeping – snoring, actually, and blubbering for all he was worth, snuggled into a carved wooden chair dragged in front of the door clearly for that purpose.

"This is a trick, right?" Lumpy asked loudly.

Merlin sighed and stepped close enough to poke the man with his walking staff. The guard gave a great snort, bolted upright, and came to attention.

Or he would have, had he not tripped over his spear.

"Halt! Who goes there!" he cried as he untangled himself.

"The old and innocent... Luckily." Merlin growled.

"How'd you get past the sentries on the walls?"

"What sentries?" Sophie asked.

"And you would be who, child?" The sentry peered closely and stuck out his nose as he did.

"May we see the commander, friend?" Merlin asked.

"And who would you be, strangers?"

"A wizard," Merlin answered and straightened his spine. "Now: what is your name, friend?"

"I am called Igat, son of Ebert, who was son of Ungart the Unready. I am master of the watch and all living things therein."

Lumpy snickered.

Igat furrowed his brow. "Did you say wizard?"

"Indeed I did."

Igat jerked open the door and slammed it behind him. A few seconds later he opened the door a crack and stuck his nose out. "Enter, if you must. Leave your pride and weapons on the other side of this door."

The young ones snickered. Merlin sighed when he heard their snickers. Things change, he told himself, after a few ten thousands of years and clearly not to our advantage.

He sighed larger still and led his little band through the door.

The hall they entered was huge. The walls were festooned with old and rusting weapons – varieties of spears, swords, halberds, javelins, axes, maces, and spiked clubs. Statues of scowling warriors looked down from wall niches. A problem, Al noted: the statues were faded like old ivory and missed fingers and toes. The weapons, every one, were rusty.

Chairs lined the walls, but the hall was empty. From the high rafters came a familiar cacophony of cooing and squeaking. A flock of purple, red, green and gold sisters and brothers of Merlin's little Draco dove and whirled among the rafters.

Draco squawked from a pocket inside Merlin's tunic, dug his way out of his master's clothes and flittered off to wheel and soar high among the rafters.

A heavy dark purple curtain concealed the last fourth of the huge hall. From behind it came the thump and rumbling of many hobnail boots. A pallid, middle-aged man peaked out from behind the curtain and disappeared when he was noticed, double-quick. They four heard the urgent whispering of elderly and middle-aged men: They're here already! Why weren't we warned? I sees 'em!

The confusion swelled into a hubbub. Next came a great rattling and banging of metal and a clatter of steel against steel. The great purple tapestry parted. A bedraggled procession emerged – half a hundred or so knights filed solemnly into the room and lined up in front of the high-backed chairs lined against the wall.

It was Merlin noted dourly, a procession of rusted armor, dull weapons and tunics pulled tightly over bulging bellies. There were white, scraggly beards, palsied hands and generally a gathering of decidedly grumpy older men. Just like me, Merlin admitted to himself, even more dourly

The parting of the tapestry revealed an impressive throne of polished stone. After the appropriate pause, the commander appeared from behind the curtain. He made a stately walk toward his throne. He wore splendid, embossed silver armor and a deep-blue tunic, perfect and noble for a man thirty years younger. His eyes, Merlin noted, looked bloodshot and puffy and bleary. His gait was frankly a little unsteady. In other words, the commander had already had a few.

The commander stumbled only once climbing to sit upon the throne. He nodded to the multitude after a long pause. The knights, with much scraping of chairs, and hoarse coughing, sat in their chairs.

The commander stared for a few moments. His eyelids fluttered and shut. He snored lightly. Merlin cleared his throat – several times. The commander's eyelids fluttered and finally opened. "Where's the bizard? I mean, where's the wizard?"

Igat gave the quartet of visitors a shove forward.

"They're right here, your munificence."

The commander twitched. "A wizard? Where is this real born to the Outremer wizard? Wizards have long since forgotten about us poor guardians. He must want something." He leaned forward. "What is it that the wizard wants?"

Merlin stepped forward and spoke in his clearest voice. "You are all in mortal danger!"

The commander started. The edges of his mouth twitched, and then erupted into laughter.

Merlin's face turned tomato red.

But the laughter, once cued, spread. Soon the hall echoed with laughter from puffy faces that had seen much better days.

Merlin took a threatening step forward. Al grabbed his arm. Merlin, restrained by the boy, set his jaw and waited it out. The commander eventually gave a few final cackles and wiped his eyes. "And who exactly is coming to get us? Be precise."

"Mordred, whose name means...you know what it means," Merlin said.

The laughter stopped.

The commander smoothed his moustache. "Gone these thousands of years. Dead and buried, I am sure."

"Buried once. I know. I buried him."

"You didn't finish the job?"

"I...I considered the job finished," Merlin stammered.

"How did a great wizard such as you manage to drop the ball?"

"I have no real answer. He lives. That much I know. I swear to it."

"Too bad. Let's get to the point. What's that got to do with us exactly?"

Merlin cleared his throat. "He is here."

"You mean on this planet? Now wouldn't we know something about that?"

More snickers.

Merlin glanced around the room. "If I might suggest..."

"Bother, bother. We'll send out some patrols."

Groans and muted protest arose from rheumy throats.

"I insist that you start soon."

"Duly noted." The commander peered down his long nose. "Any volunteers?"

Silence...for a long count.

Igat shuffled forward. "Master your lordship sir..."

"Bravo," the commander exclaimed. "Right off the bat."

"Your greatness!" Igat stammered. "I was meaning only to ask about buns for breakfast tomorrow. Anyhow, I can't abandon me post."

Igat glared at Merlin.

"You are relieved. First light tomorrow, up and at 'em."

"But your wonderfulness!"

"I applaud you nobility. Case dismissed. Everybody back to... whatever it was you were doing. I believe it is tea time."

The warriors broke ranks with a clattering of armor and dragging of weapons across stone floors.

The commander kept his rigid smile till the room emptied. His smile promptly vanished. To Al he suddenly seemed years older. He beckoned to Merlin. "Old man, if what you say is the slightest bit true, then somebody is in for a fight to the bitter end. If that Mordred thing made it that far. Not that that has ever, ever happened."

Merlin leaned forward. "I brought the boy. There is hope."

The commander glanced over Merlin's shoulder to Al, who was fidgeting with a hangnail.

"He's much tougher than he looks," Merlin added.

"Ah-ha," the commander noted. "I guess we can keep up appearances for the time being."

"I don't think we have time."

"We have a little. If what you say is true. And I will discuss this with my most trusted advisors as soon as they have their naps. You and your young friends will want to freshen up, I'm sure. You certainly could use it."

Merlin gave a little bow.

The commander nodded to Igat. "Show them to the dormitory. It's the least we can do, considering the plague you've brought us."

232

They followed the shuffling, snuffling, grumbling Igat deep into the castle keep, up musty stone corridors and around and around stone steps until Igat rattled the iron keys he pulled from his tunic. "Now gents and your ladyship, this is the best a body could do on short notice."

Igat pointed a key at each of the three doors on the hallway. "You lads get this one, the young lady the next and Mr. Wizard, the last but not the least."

He rattled the key in each door and led his charges into airy, big rooms crowded with expensive tapestries, paintings and ornately carved furniture.

Merlin studied his room briefly. "Give me a few minutes shut eye, if you all please." With that he closed his door.

Sophie studied her room. "Mind if I freshen up?" Al and Lumpy hurried into the hallway and she shut her door.

The younger boys shrugged and turned to their room. Lumpy bounced on a bed a few times and turned to Al. "What do you think your highness?"

"It'll do," Al shrugged. He wandered to the open window and looked onto the open woodlands below. Igat hurried over to Al and bared the window with his crooked arm. "You boys keep to your rooms tonight. If what you say is true, there's trouble among us. " His gaze searched the younger one's faces. "Long as we got that straight. Sleep well and don't let the bed bugs bite. That's just a saying, y'know."

The crooked little man bowed, closed the door behind him and could be heard whistling as he shuffled down the hall.

"What about room service?" Lumpy asked and searched the tops of the marble tables.

"There's fruit in the bowls," Al said and picked up what seemed to be a kiwi fruit the size of a cantaloupe.

Lumpy frowned. "I want cow."

"I wouldn't count on it," Al answered.

Lumpy paced back and forth. Al stared at the little door. Lumpy checked all the cabinets and, when that was done, threw up his hands in exasperation. "There's got to be a deli or something around here. These people have got to eat."

A little side door opened and Sophie stepped into the room. She wore a long dress of pale silk material.

The boys stopped and blinked.

"What?" she asked.

Lumpy and Al glanced at each other, and then glanced away.

"Nothing," Al said.

"Oh, yea. Nothing,' Lumpy said.

Sophie turned away, confused. When she turned back Al was standing in front of the window, staring at the evening landscape. Lumpy wandered over and stood beside him.

They've been sharing space for a long time, she thought. Should I even go over there? Interfere?

Al turned around. "Feeling solitary?"

Sophie felt herself blush. Lumpy retreated. Sophie stood beside Al.

She thought he might have appreciated the dress. Instead, he seemed uncomfortable.

Sophie waited. Al blinked and seemed to notice her for the first time.

234

He tried to smile. "Don't suppose you want a second date?"

She laughed quietly. "What's up for act two?"

"First of all, feeling bad about getting you two involved."

Sophie wished she could say it was all her fault. It wasn't, of course.

"We don't know how it's going to end," she managed.

"Okay. So what do you make of all this?"

Sophie felt her heart beat faster. What does he want to hear?

"It's a dream," she said.

Lame.

Al frowned. "Have other people known all this? Magic--where did all that come from?

Sophie shrugged. "Imagination? Fear? Hope, maybe?"

Al shook his head. "There's more than that. What people dream—don't they believe that?"

Sophie frowned this time. "It's not the same thing."

"Than what?"

"I don't know what you've been through."

"Meaning I could be crazy. You've got to think something is wrong."

"Wrong isn't the word."

Al was quiet. Sophie couldn't understand his expression. I'm trying to offer you something myself, she wanted to say, if only the idea we aren't victims.

"You two still don't belong here," Al said.

"Maybe," she said slowly, "you're wrong. We do belong. You need us."

Sophie didn't hear the door open. Merlin appeared at her left hand.

"He does. I think he knows it." Merlin looked at Al, who didn't answer.

"You two know so much already. Let me confirm it. All this about your friend being born again and again, all to fight implacable, inevitable evil--you don't want to believe. But it's simple and true." He seemed to think for a moment. "Just a few generations ago you wouldn't resist. Your senses, your reason-- those you would distrust. You'd know where to find truth--in your dreams. They told you who you were and who you would become. But how does it work? I can give you part of it. More may come later. I am guilty. Arthur: I created the spirit. The powers didn't like such a task. After much trial and error and disappointment I succeeded-- to a point. Arthur is mortal, my first failing. When one Arthur passes the spirit assumes another life. Who is chosen I don't know right away. When Mordred, who never dies, begins another of his schemes I go searching. The sword and the stone ceremony –that marks things, doesn't it?" He glanced out the window. "Your last question: why can't I do away with this Mordred myself? Or he with me? Why this back and forth? Because we are equals—that's why. Because equals care forbidden from killing each other. It is the law. Our law, the most ancient of laws. I can't explain it now. Later, perhaps. You wouldn't understand now."

"Are you sure?" Sophie asked.

Merlin didn't seem to hear.

Lumpy sat quietly, mouth agape, his eyes curious and afraid. Al listened, though he seemed to be staring out the window, too. Sophie was frowning, trying to understand.

"So what do we do next?" Lumpy asked suddenly.

Merlin stood and brushed lint from his robe. "Why follow the first rule before a great contest: get a good night's sleep." He opened the hallway door and paused. "I always do."

The friends, of course, didn't.

Chapter 31

The huge pale sun glided above the green horizon a few centimeters at a time. Her light filled a huge, misty field outside the castle walls with a cool light. A heavy mist clung to the hollows.

A little group of bleary-eyed people – Lumpy, Sophie, and Al - shuffled through the ankle-high grass to the center of the field, uncertain what to do next.

Clanking sounded through the fog. Igat approached the three friends through the mist. He carried a load of leather bridles, leather bags, and dragged along his rusty sword.

Merlin followed close behind, wearing a splendid wizard's uniform of emerald and gold. He strode along with a polished staff. He'd trimmed his beard and projected a cheery face. "Lady and gentlemen, today you travel like kings! Better than kings!"

Lumpy nudged Al. "Mine's going to be silver, five in the floor, and take unleaded."

"Don't count on it," Sophie warned.

"That's the spirit." Igat grumbled loudly.

He dumped what he was carrying near the three friends, stuck his fingers in his mouth, and gave a truly ear-splitting whistle. He scanned the sky. "I hopes they hain't gotten fat, young ones. I hate it when they've let themselves go. When they get fat-- that makes 'em slow and sassy."

Through the fog came an earth-trembling rumble. Big muscular Equus-like animals --

hundreds and hundreds of them -- thundered over the low rise. Perish the thought, Al thought, that they were fat: they were ready. Their almond-shaped, golden eyes flashed. They tossed their long necks and ripped at the ground with the double claws on their four feet. Their hides were deep and burnished and covered with short fur. Some were deep chestnut colored; some were pure white, some speckled black and white, some were striped; some were shining ebony black. All were huge – Al guessed they weighed a ton apiece – and ran fast as the wind.

Griffins, Sophie thought and thought she'd never seen anything more beautiful, not on earth. But then we're not on earth, she reminded herself. That explains it. They are powerful and sinewy and graceful and seemed to skim the ground. I'm in love.

The heard topped a rise not too far away. They kept coming. Sophie glanced around nervously. Al slipped closer and fumbled for her hand. She let him hold her hand, but, thoroughly annoyed, stepped forward so that she stood by his side.

Lumpy slipped behind his friends. "Okay. I've got your backs."

The heard didn't stop. Igat stood a few yards away, seemingly unconcerned. He fumbled inside his tunic and produced a knobby stone pipe, lit it, and grumbled as the stuff in the bowl flared and burned. A cloud of sweet-smelling reddish smoke drifted across the field.

The creatures still didn't stop. They disappeared into the nearest low valley and reappeared, thundering and shaking the earth, atop the nearest rise. Al and Sophie closed together. Sophie caught herself squeezing her eyes against the inevitable trampling.

It didn't happen. The animals, lightning quick, every one of them, shied to one side or the other and, one by one, slowed and spread over the field. Their sides heaved as they rested and took in the rich, oxygen-filled air. They studied the three friends and softly whistled now and then and sniffed the air. They trotted away, waited, and carefully kept their distance. Some deigned to take a mouthful of grass, but clearly that wasn't what they wanted.

Igat bustled up and thrust a fist-sized lump of amber-colored substance into each of the friend's hands. Merlin wandered over. Igat handed a lump to him and turned to the younger people. "Listen up. The stuff in your sweaty palms – first thing, don't lick it. You won't stop chewing on it. It's for them creatures. They can't live without it, even if it means they gotta work to get it."

"Ambrosia," Sophie ventured.

Igat shrugged. "I always called it stuff, but if it makes you happy."

The animals sniffed the air, determined the location of the stuff- the ambrosia – and charged across open field.

This time even Merlin instinctively huddled with the younger ones.

"Wait for it...wait for it!" Igat called as the mass of animals charged closer and closer. At the last second, the animals parted, streamed around the little group and stood close, whining, whistling, pawing at the ground with their sharp claws and rolling their golden eyes.

Igat tried not to appear impressed. "What you've got here is the chance to make a friend for life. Feed 'em this garly stuff and they're yours for life."

The animals snorted and whistled. They seemed almost driven to distraction, yet struggled to remember their training and manners. They held back, but just barely

"Very well, lady and gentlemen," Igat called, "chose your mounts!"

The boys glanced at each other. Sophie charged forth, patting an animal here, stroking a short muzzle here, and searching for something in one of the animals that didn't seem readily apparent to the boys.

"Hurry along, lads," Igat admonished, "before one of 'em takes off an arm.

The boys moved fast. A milk white mare grabbed Lumpy's ambrosia from his hand and swallowed it in a single gulp and immediately began purring loudly deep in her throat. She nuzzled Lumpy's arm and left his shoulder joint intact.

Al wandered to the outskirts of the heard. He spotted a reddish-colored, spindly animal with a scruffy hide and a suspicious glance in his big eyes. Al approached him carefully. "Nobody seems to want you. Seems familiar. "

Al took the ambrosia from his pocket. The animal gave dumfounded stare. Al kept coming. The creature, when he was certain that he was the chosen one, gave a self-satisfied yawp and a growling purr. He tossed his head and shuffled forward, his knobby head held high. He snatched the ambrosia from Al's proffering hand and smacked loudly as he chewed it with ill-spaced teeth.

"Bet you'll try harder," Al said and patted the creature's muzzle. "At least, that's my hope. It never exactly worked for me, but you never know."

The creature didn't answer. He smacked and swallowed and studied Al with the happiest, most contented wall-eyed stare Al thought he'd ever seen. Sophie wandered over. Her sleek, startling attractive animal followed obediently behind. "Meet Athena, after the ancient Greek god of wisdom and bravery."

"Gottcha," Al smiled stiffly.

Lumpy approached trailed by a huge animal with sharp teeth, and a fiery, especially disagreeable countenance. "Folks, this is Cuddles, named after my cat. If I had ever had a cat…anyway, may I present – Cuddles."

"Right on," Al said with a stiff smile.

"What about you choice?" Sophie asked and frowned as she studied the animal. "Lots of potential here."

Al cleared his throat. "His name – Brick. As in wall. Tough and stubborn."

"Interesting," Sophie said politely.

Igat hurried through, tossing the bridles over each animal's long neck. He turned to the three friends. "Up you go, unless you want to be running along behind, and I hardly don't recommend that."

Sophie mounted first. She settled easily high on the animal's neck and beamed. "Wonderful!" she called down. "I'm going to love this. Nothing to it."

242

"Come along, ladies," Igat chided the two boys. "Surely you two gents know how to ride."

The boys coughed. "Lots of times," they mumbled and glanced at the ground.

"One, two..." Al called out. Up they leapt – and promptly tumbled off the other side.

Igat howled with glee. Even Merlin, magnificently mounted on a huge, purple-black animal, suppressed a chuckle.

Al felt his face burn. Lumpy spat the grass out of his mouth. They didn't look at each other and tried again. They tried three times before they crouched in the resting place just behind the long neck where a rider could clasp the animal with the knees.

Igat bid the new riders put their animals through a moderately fast run across the field. Back and forth they went. "Now," Igat called as they passed, "the rules are just two, really. Always take off into the wind and never, ever let go."

"Take off?" Lumpy frowned. "Take off what?"

"That explains it," Sophie whispered to herself

Along her animal's flank she felt what seemed to be a strong, flexible tendon that ran from she sat to the animal's last rib. She turned and ran her hand along a deep crease below the tendon. "Imagine that," she whispered. "I didn't even dream of this..."

I gat gave an ear-splitting whistle. The mounts not chosen turned away as one, thundered over the nearest rise, and disappeared.

Igat help up two fingers. "Five knots out of the borealis, don't you think wizard?"

"That would be my guess," Merlin answered.

"Then let us grab some sky," Igat called and slipped easily onto his mount. He slapped its flank hard and bent low as it charged across the open field.

Merlin slapped his animal. Lumpy raised his hand. His Cuddles took off on its own. Sophie, head up and eyes bright, whistled to her mare and off it went, striding long-legged across the field to reach the others.

Al gave his animal a hard kick in the ribs. It responded by nipping at Al's kneecaps and growling deep in its throat. "Hey!" Al yelled, "Anymore of that and you're on restriction!"

The animal took off, pumping its long legs, sucking in its breath, and bounding toward the three riders already charging far ahead.

Faster and faster they strode-- the long-limbed creatures, with limber spines and bodies that seemed to elongate as they dug their claws into the ground.

At first the three friends clung onto their animals for dear life. But as their animals gained speed, the riders seemed to gain confidence. They learned to lean low to the animal's neck and how to clasp just behind the forward shoulder blades, an easy space for their knees.

And suddenly, at the crest of the hill, the creatures unfolded their wings.

The effect was instant. The animals rose effortlessly into the air. The ride became clean and silky-smooth under a cushion of air.

Higher and higher they soared, spiraling steadily upward. At first the three friends felt fear, but only for a few minutes. They learned to clasp even harder with their knees and follow the natural balance of the creature they rode.

Like riding a roller coaster, Al thought. And it's more than just riding. Maybe he though quickly, I'll never have to leave this place.

The animals responded to their rider's slightest pressure from their knees, legs and shifting of weight. Leaning forward told the animals to soar; a hard lean in either direction produced a stomach-churning dive.

Merlin studied his charges carefully. Their doubt, as he was sure it would, turned to whoops of joy. They are young, he told himself, but not too young. Maybe I've done exactly the right thing.

Up and up they soared, higher and higher above the green landscape and past towering cloud castles.

Sophie took the lead. She'd ridden her grandmother's animals back home. She shifted her weight well forward and, with her hair streaming behind her, put her animal through all sorts of acrobatic delights – steep turns, heart-racing climbs and heart-racing dives.

The boys were not to be outdone. They watched and learned and, when they were all brave enough, they leaned forward as far as they possibly could. They carried out the most dangerous exercises possible – half rolls, corkscrew turns, barrel rolls, full loops, loops within loops, and, just to see if they could, even outside loops.

And they could. They could do anything and knew it; their eyes shown, they called to each other, and even made up songs about it and sang the way they did as little children.

Merlin and Igat watched from a safe distance above. "They don't seem a bit different than the way I was," Igat half-smiled, "Course I mean quite a few years ago."

"Quite a few," Merlin answered quietly, "if only we knew."

Merlin let the young ones soar and play through the plumes of clouds and open air as long as he could. Steadily they moved forward. Merlin kept an eye on the landscape as it unrolled below.

After another half an hour, a range of serrated, ice-covered mountains appeared on the horizon. "Like soldiers," Merlin muttered to himself and called to Igat, "Better round them up! We've got business now."

Igat whistled and waved. The three friends turned their mounts and, as if they'd been riding all their lives, drew up in a line beside Merlin, whose face now looked so plainly serious.

Al glanced down and shivered; sentinel mountains waited below, immense, lonely and deep.

Igat called out, "Wizard, if your bogey man is anywhere, it's down there! What do you say?"

"Great minds," Merlin answered and put his mount into a steep dive.

They descended together until they were parallel with the highest frozen peaks. Gradually they descended even farther, past the walls of immense, aquamarine glaciers and thundering waterfalls, higher and bigger than any they'd ever seen on earth.

Merlin led them yet lower. They glided to where the air became warm and humid. Huge canyons miles and miles long appeared. Emerald rivers frothed down the canyon floors. Everywhere, even on the steep mountain sides, and clinging to the canyon sides, grew dense, tropical forest of huge trees with fat leaves colored purple and vermillion. Flowers, all the colors of the rainbow, and the size of umbrellas, decorated everywhere. Thick vines entwined; dark tunnels seemed to snake through the crowns of the trees.

The forest was absolutely still.

"Better be friends," Igat insisted, "Let's not be shy."

The mounts slowly beat their wings. All remained quiet until, from the black of the deepest canyons they heard a weird symphony of cat-call, whines and trills.

The friends flew even closer together. The canyon they followed narrowed from a half mile wide to a quarter mile and began to twist and turn along its course.

The riders formed a single file. Igat took the front and Merlin the rear. To Al , even Merlin seemed nervous. Igat turned and whispered loudly enough for everyone to hear, "I never liked this place."

From a few hundred yards below, an outburst of keeling and big-animal screeching erupted. The cacophony echoed off the canyon walls. Vermillion-colored trees clinging to a wide ledge shook. Huge leaves trembled and branches crackled.

A coven of leathery dragons, each one a deep, azure blue and the size of an airliner, shivered the trees a last time and took flight from their nest in the strongest limbs.

The coven called back and forth, angry at being disturbed from their afternoon siesta. Each animal spread their transparent delta-shaped wings and soared on the updrafts to inspect the intruders.

"Posh," Igat snorted as if he believed it," they're just showing off."

The creatures formed up, a half dozen on each side and eyed the interlopers and nipped at their mounts just to see what would happen.

The taste testing wasn't at all appreciated by the mounts. They hissed and shied away. At the last second, evidently satisfied, the coven broke away as one, executed a sharp turn, and glided back to their aery among the trees.

"That went better than expected," Igat sighed.

The canyon steadily widened and ended at a horseshoe-shaped waterfall, Al guessed, more than ten miles long and a mile high. Clouds of spray billowed up and the river that ran from the lake of the falls cascaded emerald green.

Merlin studied the three friends. They were quiet and seemed too overawed to speak. I don't want to overdo it, Merlin reminded himself: if only I could ease them in, but there is no time for that.

Merlin urged his mount closer to the three. "What you've got here -- don't you know, clever ones? Surely you do."

"Home is pretty far away," Sophie replied politely.

"The crater of souls," Merlin said.

"Crater?" Lumpy frowned.

"Look there." Merlin swept his arm toward the jagged peaks on the near horizon." It's all around us now. These hills make a perfect circle. This is a place of peace and beauty."

" How big?" Lumpy asked.

"A hundred miles wide."

Lumpy whistled. " Crater? As in meteor? That must have been one big splat."

Merlin laughed; the boy was right, of course. Merlin spurred his mount ahead and led the group high above the waterfall and to the other side of the jagged peaks.

The landscape changed from dense forest into rich meadows and smooth hills and large meadows of wild flowers glowing gold, lemon-orange, scarlet and royal purple.

"Delicious," Sophie remarked. "Good enough to eat."

"Like jelly beans," Lumpy added.

"What's this jelly beans?" Igat asked.

"Like ambrosia," Lumpy answered. "Kinda."

Merlin hung back and listened to his animal as it softly beat its long wings.

He was not relaxed. He kept his peace and listened and watched and listened.

The landscape gradually became rougher with low hills and open patches of rough rock.

After a full hour's flying the first of the ruins appeared.

Lumpy saw them first, called out, and pointed below. Sophie and Al glanced down and, surprised, leaned far to peer over their animals' neck.

The ruin stretched across one hill and shallow valley after another. They must have been very old; the different colored stones that made up the walls, the three-sided pyramids, the octagon palaces (the word that the friends used automatically), and the wide street pavers were cracked and crumbled. It seemed, Al noted to himself, that they'd caught the city, or the cities, halfway before they crumbled into dust.

Al closed his eyes and felt his brain spin. Worse, he felt more, except that it wasn't a feeling; it was a knowing that seemed to come from the tips of his fingers. Since he'd met the old man on his broomstick (okay, not fair, Al reminded himself), this way of knowing without knowing how was a confusing part of everyday life.

Like now, Al thought, and this was a big one.

His brain spun faster and faster. The ground seemed to want him.

Sophie cried out.

Al sat upright. "I'm okay! I'm okay!" he called out to everyone.

Merlin swooped down to catch Al. Igat hovered close by. "Steady, steady, young mister," Igat warned. "Remember the first law!"

"What have you got to tell us?" Merlin asked quietly as he could.

Al shivered. "I don't know, as usual. What place is this?"

Igat shrugged. "Who knows? It's always been here and always will be."

Merlin leaned close to Al. "How close is he?"

Al didn't answer right away. "Not far. Don't you feel it?"

"Not as well as you," Merlin muttered and suddenly led them downward.

The animals flared their wings and landed with soft clumps. They landed near a large gate to the city. At ground level the ruins seemed a confused complex of temples, palaces, paved streets and needle-thin obelisk. Wild flowers covered the ruins. Gnarled trees sprouted from the terraces and split the stones.

Lumpy shivered. "Is anyone at home?"

"Only the long, long dead," Igat answered.

"Who's watching this place?" Al asked.

"It's never needed guarding before," Igat insisted.

"Let's be careful, careful," Merlin said and held Al's arm.

"I can take care of myself," Al pulled his arm away and, before anyone else could react, ran straight through the keystone-shaped city gate decorated stone carvings of reptilian creatures.

Sophie ran after. Lumpy glanced around a few seconds and followed. The three friends cast a few backwards glances, but kept going.

"Mind what I said!" Merlin called out automatically.

I might as well be talking to a wall, Merlin thought, and watched the three disappear into the city of the dead. I

Igat wandered closer. "You're going to let them go just like that?"

"Do I have a choice?"

"That's the way you're going to work it?"

"How else are we to find him first?"

Igat rubbed his lower back. "I aches...I've passed my entire life without this much trouble. Now this."

"I'm very sorry about that."

Igat glanced over. The old wizard sounded sincere and sad. Seems as is the wizard and his troubles could have stayed home a few more centuries, but evidently not, Igat sighed to himself. He wandered away, and stretched out on the grass. His dug in his pockets and chewed on a few crumbs of ambrosia. "Problem is," he pronounced aloud," you people let your imaginations run wild…dangerous thing, imagination."

Merlin didn't defend himself. He wandered away and studied the ruins.

Igat shrugged. Imagination, he praised himself silently, that's darn clever, don't you think? He agreed with himself one more time, and as he studied the roiling clouds on the horizon, worked himself into an afternoon nap.

Chapter 32

Al ran down an ancient thoroughfare that led arrow-straight deeper into the city. His mind created questions: How big is this place? Who built and why? It's huge. Everything stone is carved and polished, every inch of it, till it gleamed, or it shined a long, long time ago. Anyway, it's amazing. Everything's so complicated, so wonderful and so dangerous.

He shivered. I'm not sick. I know I'm not. But I can barely stand it. I'm quivering inside. What's going on? I'm going to find out. Maybe that's the answer. I'm just going to find out on my own.

"How's it going, fleet feet?" Lumpy asked. His face was red and he was sweating.

"I'm scared to death," Al answered.

Sophie gave Al a hard glance.

"He's like that all the time," Lumpy said loudly.

Al broke away and ran pell-mell down one wide street after another.

Suddenly he turned and began scrambling up ancient stairs that led to the top of one of the many pyramids.

Sophie followed him with every step. Lumpy, puffing and huffing, trotted behind.

The climb up the steep stairs quickly became long and hard. They sweated and gasp for breath. They reached the summit, a flat square about thirty feet on all sides, and sat down hard. No one spoke for a few minutes. Al finally sat upright and listened. Lumpy, after he'd gotten his breath, began tossing pebbles off the summit.

Sophie looked long at Al's face.

"Don't do that," Lumpy huffed," you'll just encourage him."

Al suddenly focused on some point among the high, silent ruins. Suddenly he turned and began scrambling and sliding down the steep steps they'd just climbed.

Sophie and Lumpy glanced at each other and launched themselves onto the steps. The ancient blue stone that covered the pyramid shattered and cascaded down the steep slopes.

Al ran as he would never stop. His friends sweated to keep up. They ran and ran, farther and faster than they ever imagined they could.

"I can't do this," Lumpy finally gasp.

"Sure you can," Sophie sputtered, though she didn't seem much better.

"How's he doing this?" Lumpy managed.

"Inspiration," Sophie managed through her clenched teeth.

Al disappeared around a pyramid. Sophie and Lumpy followed and found themselves facing a weedy courtyard.

Sophie stopped. The courtyard was simply huge, paved in green flagstones that, a very long time ago, must have gleamed in the sun. She caught her breath and began walking quietly across the space. It must be thirty acres wide, she thought. And look – seven sides, a heptagon, I think it's called.

"The topless towers of Ilium," Sophie said to Lumpy, who was following a few yards behind.

"The what?" Lumpy managed to ask. He tottered along, doubled up and holding his stomach.

"Nothing," Sophie said and frowned. "Where's he got to?"

"I think I'm going to lose my cookies," Lumpy groaned. "I think we'd better head back now."

"Not yet. Something's going on. Don't you feel it?"

"I know what I feel," Lumpy said, put his fingers into his mouth and gave a shrill, ear-splitting whistle. The echo bounced through the ruins. When the echo faded, Sophie stood still and listened. She heard a quiet return whistle and spotted Al standing a few hundred yards away doing exactly what she'd been doing - standing stock-still and listening.

She listened again; she heard a strange rattling and scraping cacophony coming from close by. The sound seemed to come from a dozen places all at once.

Sophie wrinkled her nose. "What's that smell?"

"Don't look at me." Lumpy called back.

Al was climbing the broken wall that enclosed the courtyard. Sophie hurried and began climbing with him.

"What are we after?" she asked. I'm so loud, she thought.

The sound came again, louder this time, a scrabbling and scraping against the rough rock. It was louder and seemed to surround the courtyard.

The hair on the back of her neck rose.

Al stood on top of the wall. He kept his frowning, puzzled look. Sophie pulled herself up and stood a few yards away. Being high up isn't such a bad idea, Sophie decided. Feels safer –

Lumpy howled. He alternated between howling and screaming. He came running, legs pumping, and eyes wide.

They came behind him.

Jin.

They were grown-up, larger, with bigger claws, gnashing teeth, some with vestigial tails and brighter, Technicolor hides.

They were hundreds. They were thousands. They swarmed over the streets, the courtyard, and the pyramids. They scurried, scampered, and hop-frogged along. Lumpy kept just ahead of the mass and made a frantic beeline for the only safe place— a space beside Sophie and Lumpy.

But Lumpy was losing the race. He scooped up rocks from the littered courtyard and let the creatures sniping at his heels have it. One screeched and fell; dozen tripped over the creature's body as it fell and gave Lumpy the seconds he needed. He leapt from the plaza to the top of the wall in one bound.

All three leapt off the wall and used the few seconds that the Jin needed to clamber over the wall to run, just run, tired as they were. A hundred yard dash, Al though: How can I do this? Those things behind me, that's how, ready to slice us into sushi. I can't do this. But I can. Look at me. Look at us. I can. I can.

Until he fell.

Chapter 33

Igat was snoring. He snored while Merlin paced nearby.

Merlin stopped. With a gust of wind from the city came a revolting, musty, old-leather stink.

A chill ran down Merlin's spine, all the way to his toes. Then followed the scratching, clacking cacophony of the many Jin attacking from three directions.

Igat sat bolt upright. He grabbed his rusty sword and cried out, "The Mounts!" The mounts wheeled and galloped toward his voice.

The Jin army broke from the ruins, covering every inch of stone surface, howling for victory.

Merlin glimpsed Sophie and Lumpy dragging Al as best they could. They made it through the ruined gate, but the Jin, pouring in from both flanks, surrounded them. Igat and Merlin jumped onto their mounts and charged, one hand pulling the mounts for the younger ones and the other flailing away at the Jin.

"Wizard!" Igat thundered, "Now is your time!"

"Too dangerous!" Merlin called back

Igat cut swathes with his sword. Festering claws ripped at his mount's wings and gnashed at Igat's sensitive bare feet. "Wizard," he cried again, "I beg you to reconsider!"

Al watched the Jin close the lane between the three and Merlin. The two old people seemed to be buried by Jin warriors. A dozen knobby, hairy clawed arms tore at Merlin's beard and slashed at his mount's legs. Merlin's face turned scarlet; he chanted a spell.

Clouds boiled up out of the dry sky, and swirled into a vicious, black tornado that tore into the Jin army, whorled the masses into the funnel and scattered the remains over the landscape. The vortex even dragged Al and his friends along the ground. Al managed to grab onto Igat's ankle, Sophie onto Al's legs, and Lumpy onto Sophie's foot. For a few seconds they made a chain that bounced along the ground.

The vortex dissolved. That was enough. The three younger, considerably bruised, climbed onto their mounts. The creatures spread their wings and pulled for the sky, sweating their coats dark and puffing from their wide nostrils as they climbed into the open air.

Gradually the ruins fell farther and farther below; they seemed to be a huge puzzle tossed on the ground and swarming with black ants.

Merlin flew closer to his charges.

"Counting fingers and toes," he lamely joked. He saw plenty of bruises, and torn clothes. And pale, frightened faces. Merlin expected that; the first fight for your life doesn't go away easily.

Igat felt his ribs aching. Once he relished a good fight. Now his sword arm felt as if it might fall off and he wanted, more than anything, to quaff down a deep mug of sweet brew and snore in his own soft bed.

"What have you done?" He groaned to Merlin.

"If you want me to apologize – you have it, as far as I am responsible."

Igat leaned closer. "You can send these children back where they came from, can't you wizard? You wizards can do anything, correct?"

"You must have misunderstood. I make no such claim. I'm a very simple being, actually. It's all about fate."

"Fate," Igat grumbled, "I'd love to get my hands on that one."

"Let's not blame what we don't understand," Merlin answered and thought to himself, I have to tell the truth now and then.

They flew quietly a few more minutes. Merlin took stock of things: Mordred has been located, or at least his Myrmidons. No prince, especially the dark sort, amount to anything without their mindless hoards. On the negative side, those creatures seem to thrive in this world. But then every living thing thrives here. Even the young ones showed their strength just by surviving the day. Even Lumpy's skin was clearing up, though Merlin would never mention it.

The waterfall and deep canyons appeared again. The descent into the canyons went easily. Merlin took the top and rightmost position where he could keep an eye on their most vulnerable spot.

The tall cloud castles still sailed along. Merlin continuously glanced over his shoulder.

They appeared first as black specks that dove from one cloud bank to another.

Merlin called out the alarm. Igat turned his mount and climbed to meet the threat. Merlin cried out and followed. The younger ones milled about in confusion. Merlin bellowed, "Scatter and fly for your lives!"

But they hesitated. Merlin called over his shoulder, "We'll catch up!"

The black specs appeared suddenly from the nearest cloud. They weren't specks by that time. Merlin guessed they were fifty or more, Jin for sure, with claws and something he'd never seen before – glider wings. Igat glanced at Merlin, "Now's your time, wizard!"

"Can you think of anything else to say?"

"No harm in asking!" Igat called back and aimed his spear at the nearest creature. Then the Jin were among them, screeching and screaming and slashing with their scimitar claws.

Merlin made up a bow and quiver of razor-tipped arrows. With a skill that impressed Igat , he skewed six Jin before they flew ten yards closer. Merlin nodded and Igat found a bow his hands and a quiver of arrows on his back. "A woman's weapon!" Igat called back.

Jin swarmed from every direction. But Igat drew his first arrow and scored his first kill – then another and another. He didn't need to aim very exactly; there were too many targets.

The younger ones didn't do as Merlin ordered. They wheeled around to join the fight. Igat's cry of warning died in his throat. The fighting became too close for the arrows. They slashed and stabbed with swords.

They fought in the air with all the advantage that their intelligent, lithe mounts brought. Merlin glimpsed Al slashing with his weapon as if he was meant for war. The red-haired boy did well. The girl closed up to fight beside Al and slashed a wing cleanly off an especially huge, hissing Jin. It

260

squawked, spouted yellow fluid, and spiral toward the ground.

Igat and Merlin closed with the younger ones and formed a flying ring, each protecting the tail of the one in front. Slashing and jabbing and even using the bows kept the Jin away. The Jin are slower and pea-brained, Merlin noted. Our problem is endurance. We have no chance to rest. Exhaustion is already making us weak. We're fighting for minutes now. Surrender isn't even thinkable.

A claw cut the air a few centimeters above Merlin's head. Merlin struck back, but he could barely lift his arm. Al took a shallow slash across his shoulder. It only cut fabric – this time. I've violated the first rule of warfare, Merlin reproached: never do the same things twice. I led us back by the same path we took getting here. How could I make such a stupid mistake?

"Wizard!" Igat roared. "Any suggestions?"

"For what?" Merlin roared back.

"What do you think?"

I get it, Merlin thought: you want something wonderful and righteous. Magic of course. Every living creature dreams, cajoles, prays, and insist on magic.

Merlin muttered aloud. A ring of shielding opaque cloud collected around Merlin and his friends. It hung in the air a few seconds and dissolved. Igat and the younger ones stared at Merlin. Fear showed clearly on each face.

Merlin held his breath. A stripling might go around getting red-faced and puffing and snorting and seeing his work disappear in a huge smoke ring. I am becoming a child again.

By then, as with all aerial combat, the fight had drifted toward the ground. Merlin saw that they'd reached the canyons of the blue dragons.

The tumult raised the huge creature's interest. They keeled, waking each other from their afternoon sleep, unfolded their wings, and sailed out on the afternoon updrafts.

The fight confused them. The Jin, Merlin realized, were new to the dragon's world and maybe even seemed trivial. But one especially foul-tempered Jin, clenching his teeth in blood fury, collided with an old female dragon. Rather than whimper and wisely dive away the Jin slashed at the alpha female with its long claws.

The wound drew blood. The great dragon bellowed in rage. Her call of pain and anger roused the entire coven. Every creature, Merlin estimated, weighed a thousand pounds. The big trees and dense forest along the canyons shook as dragon after dragon rose into the air. They were dozens, then hundreds. It's the entire species, Merlin realized, keeling, trumpeting, roaring, and filling the air.

They attacked. The battle erupted between the azure dragons and the black-winged Jin. Merlin whistled and rounded up his little squadron of friends and led them toward the concealing clouds. "Children," he called, don't let us hang around to enjoy this!"

Merlin glanced over his shoulder anyway.

It wasn't a battle, not really. The dragons, working in teams, snapped up the Jin as if they were summer mosquitoes, a bit here, a mouthful here.

And it didn't take long. A few forlorn Jin screeched, a few dragons snapped their last mouthfuls and the skies were quiet again. The clouds floated along peacefully.

The alpha females sailed up and studied Merlin's little squadron with peaceful eyes.

"Many, many thanks," Merlin called. The dragons purled, turned on their huge wings, and banked away.

Igat exhaled a long sigh. "Wizard, that dragon trick was just the thing."

"Don't thank me. Really." Merlin coughed/

Chapter 34

Modred stood among stone ruins and studied a pool of black water from a decayed fountain. The Jin packed the floor around him, cringing and wailing.

"Shut your whimpering," Mordred snapped. "Your cousins taught you a lesson. Eagerness and stupidity. Makes a good politician, but a dead warrior."

The Jin muttered in confusion.

"Give it a long think," Mordred sighed. "I know that's not going to happen, but I tried." Mordred sat closer to the pool and dipped one finger into the water. A scene appeared: Al and Merlin flying on their mounts with their friends just behind.

Mordred tapped his chin. "The next time it'll be my turn. As it should be and will be. You've told me what I need to know, old man. You can't help yourself. Justice: you want it as much as I." He stood suddenly and threw a rock into the pool. The images shattered.

Chapter 35

Igat found that putting his life in mortal danger again woke his instincts. I am leading the old Wizard, who doesn't seem to be good for much and his apprentices low and very fast, skimming the treetops, toward the castle and safety. Low and fast means we couldn't be ambushed from below. In any case, it's worked, Igat noted; we are everyone returned. How long has it been since somebody from this castle returned from a patrol, weapons blooded and sweating from a fight?

As they landed, a squire known as Pickering waddled as a fast as he could along the battlements. With a supreme effort he lifted a twenty-pound hammer and struck the sun-shaped warning tocsin.

The gong, unpolished for generations, reverberated with a dark bass tone through the sleepy courtyard and castle apartments, where comfortable warriors snoozed through their after-luncheon nap.

The long-forgotten sound ended afternoon siestas everywhere. The courtyard began filling with grumpy warriors, some rubbing their aching backs, some still in their stocking feet. All were thoroughly irritated. Many yelled impolite phrases at the poor Chickering. Stones were chucked in his direction. Pickering hid behind the huge disc of metal and screeched back invectives of his own.

As the corps assembled in the hot sun, an event brought everyone to a stop: the commander appeared in his glittering state armor. None could ever recall seeing his highness in the high dress. It meant one thing -- war.

The commander cleared his throat and clapped his hands. "Now! Now! Let's not blame poor Pickering. I gave the order to disturb your slumber, badly needed though it may be."

He paused. His eyes swept the faces assembled on the courtyard. "Gentlemen, I am afraid something has come up." He cleared his throat again. "It means fighting. And plenty of it. Nothing pretty, either."

After the initial shock -- and a few faintings -- the corps adjourned to the dusty Hall of Heroes. The room was mainly used for storage.

The assembled corps' mood remained serious. Merlin appeared from a side door and studied resentful faces that turned in his direction. What trouble did you bring us wizard? Merlin knew they were thinking. He stepped forward anyway. "Gentlemen and warriors, for warriors you are, each and every one. Not bakers, bricklayers, house painters, woodcarvers, or even poets. You are skilled with the long sword, the lance, the spear, the bow, clubs, rocks, even your bare hands. Skilled to seek out, engage and destroy the enemies of this most scared of places, this wellspring of goodness, light, and truth in this galaxy. That is what this place is, the glittering jewel in the firmament."

A skinny warrior raised his hand.

"Yes?" Merlin asked

"What's a firmament?"

"The night sky."

"Why didn't you just say so?"

Another warrior raised his hand. "What are we up against? For most of us- well, it's been a while."

"A very, very long time," red-nosed axe man called out. Others echoed with a Hear! Hear!

Merlin's face grew deeply serious. At first he couldn't speak.

"Mordred," he finally said. "Many of you might not know the name. All began on Earth"

"Earth?" someone asked.

"Small place with big oceans."

"Our oceans are better," another voice insisted.

"Yes, yes," Merlin continued. "That's not the point, really. Mordred is a wizard similar like me, only -- different. He possesses power, strength, cunning, and endless, ruthless, killing ambition. But small fires can cause great conflagrations. Mordred is here to strike that match."

"Who does he think he is?" someone angrily called out.

"We will show him won't we?" Merlin shook his fist in the air. "But I will be honest. We are hopelessly outnumbered by his blood thirsty host led by a foe of implacable evil who, if he destroys us individually, will rip the universe that we know from its foundations." Merlin paused to catch his breath. "However, we are not perturbed, are we?"

Silence.

A low murmur swept the hall. A stooped warrior stood. "Pardon your wizardship, but some of us see the need for a second opinion."

Merlin glanced around the room. Seated in each of the tall Chairs of Glory were great warriors of generations ago. Now, Merlin realized in despair, they were tense and confused and worse, just plain old.

Igat suddenly bounded up from his chair and drew his sword and jabbed it deep into the refreshment table before him. "If any of you sons of lily-livered newts don't believe the Wizard here -- then, then-- well, use your eyeballs!"

The blade showed fresh nicks and gouges. Gore stained the metal.

The audience grew very quiet.

The commander, who'd been filing his nails, put down the file and studied the room. He blinked a few times a sign, from those who knew him, that meant that he didn't what to do.

"We need a plan," he announced evenly as he could. "Any takers?"

Merlin let the confused muttering and eyeballing run through the room. He stepped forward.

"That's the easy part." Merlin grabbed Al by the shoulders and pushed the surprised boy to the front. "Here is your leader."

Silence-- stunned silence.

Then -- gales of belly laughter. Al's face turned scarlet. After the laughter died away Merlin stepped forward once again. "You gentlemen will want proof, I'm guessing. Very, very well."

He studied Al long and hard until the boy squirmed. Merlin suddenly whirled around. "I demand the test! Show me the sword!"

Again--silence. Even the smirks of contempt vanished. Merlin looked over an audience of disbelieving, puffy and myopic eyes.

"Wizard, your joke has gone far enough," the commander growled.

Merlin raised his arm and pointed his long finger directly at Al. "That boy is our slim and only chance."

Al felt sweat trickle down his back.

The commander cleared his throat. "Let's be creative. Any care to offer reasonable ideas at this point, no matter how loony they may seem right off the bat? Going once, going twice–."

Chapter 36

All great and very ancient places, filled with warrens and dungeons a-plenty, largely forgotten, and moldy, spider-webbed and populated by gruesome creatures lurking in the subterranean world, have the same charm. That was the intrigue of the great castle keep, a place designed to survive desperate sieges, horrific assaults and hand-to--hand combat last stands. The commander didn't find it very intriguing, though, and meant for the last fifty years to have the whole place redone as a spa, but he'd never gotten around to it.

Instead, he found himself leading half-dozen torch-bearing guards into the very bowels of the place. Behind the guards Merlin, Sophie, Lumpy and a very self –conscious Al crowded together for comfort and security. Down, down and down, they went, through the first great cellar, through a great iron-bound door and down yet again through dank passages hewn through solid rock. Eventually the stone walls ran with chill water and the guards imaged they could hear the shrieks from the demons of the underworld.

Finally the dank tunnel ended at the heaviest, most iron-bound door Al had ever seen. "What's on the other side?" Al asked thickly. Whatever, Al thought, it means trouble for me.

"The archives, Merlin answered. "That's so, isn't it commander?"

"Indeed it is," the commander answered. He banged on the door with this iron mace.

"Somebody lives down here?" Lumped squeaked.

"That's what they say. We send his provisions down six months at a time." The commander banged yet harder against the bound iron. "He's gone a bit deaf I understand. Among other things."

An eye hole on the door suddenly slid open. A single red-rimmed eye glared through it.

The commander gave a nod. "Greetings. We have visitors, Herr Doctor Mister Lanois."

"Do you have an appointment?" The face who owned the eye demanded tartly.

"I'm afraid not," the commander sighed.

The peephole was slammed shut. The commander turned to Merlin. "I was afraid he might need a little persuasion."

He nodded. Three of the bodyguards wrenched a log support from the wall behind them. The commander nodded. The three warriors slammed the battering ram against the ancient door. Bam! Bam! Bam! The door's hinges gave way and the door collapsed inward with a hollow Boom!

Dr. Lanois, the archivist, stood in the doorway. His plum-colored academic rob hung around his emaciated frame. His nostrils flared. He raised his arms out to block the entrance. "Foul barbarians! Take me if you must, but spare my treasures!"

Everyone flowed around him and occupied a huge stone room. Four wide and seemingly endless hallways radiated from the main floor. Al gawked at the floor-to-ceiling shelves packed with manuscripts, illuminated and plain, scrolls, maps, paintings, sculptures, printed books and cases of

271

jewels, every form of treasure any person could imagine, except for money itself.

Merlin inspected a papyrus roll. "The lost plays of Sophocles. Lost from earth anyway. Mind if I borrow them for a little while?"

"Don't be insane," Lanois sniffed.

"That's not what we're here for anyway," Merlin said. "Do you know what it is?"

Lanois turned pale, looked away, and sniffed.

"I see you do," Merlin said. "Point out the armory."

"You're making a huge mistake." Lanois frowned. "Therefore you'll have to make it on your own."

The bodyguards rushed to the shelves. Fragile, priceless things crashed to the floor.

Lanois squeezed his eyes shut.

Lanois' face turned pale as milk.

"Now," Merlin said, steadily as he could," The armory thing."

Lanois turned to his desk, pulled out a map copied on parchment and thrust it to Merlin.

The party followed Merlin through one hallway after another and down another flight of ancient, slippery stairs. Another heavy door blocked their way. Merlin motioned for Al to come forward. Al stepped up, feeling every eye on his back. He stared at the heavy door bound in heavy iron.

"What do you want me to do with it?"

"Try it," Merlin said quietly.

Al felt his heart beat faster. "What good is that going to do?"

"Maybe it'll know you."

"How much sense does that make?" Al felt his hands sweat. He glanced over his shoulder.

Nobody moved. Al realized he couldn't run away. His hands trembled. He reached for the handle and pulled.

The doorway slipped open as if it had been oiled yesterday.

"Not so bad, was it?" Merlin smiled and let his tense shoulders drop.

Al stepped inside. The others tried to follow. Merlin held out his arm.

Al took a few unwilling steps forward. He craned his neck. This room alone is as big as all of Tintangle put together, Al decided. And it's cut from solid rock. Nobody around here does anything halfway.

The shelves hewn into the walls held swords of all types, spears, clubs, maces, shields, helmets of metal and armor of all imaginable forms and sizes.

A thin layer of dust covered everything. How long has this stuff been here? Al asked himself. Since before the Beatles broke up, he decided, and then some. But there was more – much more.

He turned to Merlin. "It's here, isn't it?"

"You tell me," Merlin answered.

Al motioned for Sophie and Lumpy to follow.

Al hurried ahead. Sophie pulled Lumpy along. They carried one smoky torch and Al another; the ceilings grew lower and lower the farther they searched. Al paused now and then, but always passed on. The tunnels became smaller and smaller. Dust deadened their footfalls.

Al reached the end of a tunnel. He stopped at a niche carved deeply into the wall. Spider webs decorated the entrance. Deep enough, Al decided, for spiders. I hate spiders. I hate, hate, hate, hate…hate…spiders.

He stuck his hands under his armpits to stop the trembling, took a breath and reached inside the niche.

"Please, please," he mumbled aloud," No spiders."

Something fuzzy and alive brushed his fingers. Al jerked his hand back. Inside something squealed and scurried away.

Al let his heart calmed down. Very slowly he reached inside again. I'd never done this a few days ago. Wheezle would never let me. Or maybe, all considering, she insist. Come on boy, he imagined her poking him in the ribs, get on with it. You just think you can't. Maybe this is your one big chance.

Al's finger touched a scabbard wrapped in a silky cloth. He closed his hand around it.

No poisonous spiders, but Al suddenly let it go and jerked his hand away.

I know, he realized. I don't know how, but I do. If I step back and pretend I haven't been here things will fall apart.

But there's always a way back. Even if the old man isn't pointing that out I can always go back. For the first time, I don't have to do something.

I don't.

For the first time I don't.

What if I don't?

Al heard the others calling to each other. Some seemed close; some seemed far away. All sounded confused and angry. He listened to them as they ripped weapons and equipment from the walls. They don't know where to look he told himself.

I do.

I know everything. This time. But what's the saying? The bloom is off the rose. Even if I lie he'll know. What will he think? Time to go home, he'll sigh and he'll understand in a second: I, Merlin, was all wrong.

Time to give it up.

He'll turn his back. Not your fault, he'll say. I dragged you into this and you weren't the one. So very sorry.

He might be right, Al thought.

Maybe I'm not.

Too bad.

He reached inside.

His hands closed around the scabbard. It wasn't too big or too heavy. He lifted it into the light.

He saw a scabbard of embossed leather wrapped in ancient silk. The hilt was plain metal; the grip was no more than corded leather. The simple blade didn't seem ferocious. A good sword, Al thought, and that's it.

He stood and whistled. Everyone came running. The warriors, Al noted, kept their distance. Merlin seemed quiet and calm. Al held up the sword to him. "Do you want to look it over?"

"Me?" Merlin pretended to be surprised. "What do I know?"

Sophie and Lumpy appeared. His face was red and his eyes were watering. He sneezed and blew his nose. "It's the dust an' the mold."

"We need to get him out of here," Sophie said. She studied the sword in Al's hands. "That's it?

That's what all the fuss is over." She slipped closer. "It's beautiful. Can I hold it?"

Merlin stepped closer and said firmly, "Let our friend do his job."

Sophie began to protest, but stopped. "Let's get out of here," she said quietly.

Merlin leaned closer. "Don't be hurt. Don't you remember the story?"

Chapter 37

The old wizard didn't give them a minute. Not even time for biscuits and a good brew, the commander grumbled silently. Mordred, he thought suddenly and felt cold. He is the prince of chaos and disorder and the end of all things, if he gets his way. At the very minimum. His type was supposed to be banished and kept at a very, very long distance. That's what the wizard's job was, wasn't it? Let Mister Mordred create havoc on his little speck on the cosmic map. No real harm done.

And this whole situation is entirely the wizard's fault. Clearly he's a bungler way out of his game. He's dragged a few innocent children into the mix – that's just sad. Somebody needs to put an end to this. That's going to be me, of course. The ceremony with the sword is the real business. The tottering old fool and his sad boy are about to suffer some serious humiliation, but maybe the young one will eventually get over it. The old man that will be another matter. At his age they're so frail. After I'll just assume my proper place and pick up the pieces.

The wizard, hurrying ahead, led the little procession to a broad meadow by the sunrise gate. The wizard, on the way back, had sent one of the guards ahead to request the entire corps to assemble at the meadow. They already lounged in the long grass, pennants limp around the poles.

The commander frowned even deeper. Not only did the wizard insist on disturbing everybody, but the fool's confidence seemed boundless. He took the sword from the boy, held it above his head, and paraded the weapon in front of the line of warriors.

The troop muttered and glanced at each other. They knew what the ceremony meant. They just never expected to witness it. Down deep, no matter what words were used, the ceremony meant one thing: trouble.

Merlin paraded the sword a little while longer. He nodded and the trumpeters blew a rousing, is somewhat ragged, fanfare.

Merlin promptly broke up his little procession, gathered up the young friends and led them behind a nearby grove of trees. Once out of sight, Merlin became as tense and crabby as Al had ever witnessed.

"Boy," he groused at Al, "you know this is everything."

He drew the sword from its scabbard. Sophie stepped closer. The blade, somehow, now gleamed and reflected the faces of the people who watched it.

"Do you know its name?" Merlin asked.

"Excalibur," Sophie said quickly.

"I was going to say that," Al swallowed.

"Do you know what comes next?" Merlin asked. He didn't wait for an answer. He turned to one of the large boulders half-buried in the ground nearby.

Merlin raised the sword point as high as he could and plunged the blade into the rock. There was a blue flash and a resounded crash.

Al shut his eyes and, when he opened them saw the sword plunged into the rock almost to its hilt. Merlin was rubbing his hands as if they were burned. "Do you young ones know the story of the sword? It's as old as these hills and any other."

Lumpy glanced at Al. "What story?"

Merlin sighed. "The details don't matter. Boy, all you need to do, when I give you the signal, is pull this sword from this stone."

Lumpy blinked. "Won't he need help? I'm thinking a welding torch. Unless there's a trick."

Lumpy grabbed the hilt and pulled hard as he could. He tried over and over again. Merlin simply watched. Lumpy glanced over his shoulder, got no encouragement, and gave up.

"Quite so," Merlin said clearly.

Al frowned. "I'm supposed to do that?"

"Right. Just snatch this sword right out of this silly old stone."

"And then–."

"You're hailed as the king and then you'll lead us to final victory," Merlin said quickly.

"Me?"

"No doubt."

"What do you mean no doubt? I've got plenty of doubts."

"What could you possibly mean?" Merlin asked innocently.

"Is this an elective?"

Merlin let his shoulders sag. "Nobody can make you. In fact, you have to believe in yourself."

Al paused and honestly seemed to think about it. My heart, Merlin thought, is sinking.

"Has anyone just walked away?"

"it is possible. The results wouldn't be pretty.

"But he who runs away--." Al began.

279

"Lives to run away another day," Merlin said softly.

The commander stuck his head around the screen. "What's the hold up here?"

"Give us a little," Merlin answered.

"It's well past afternoon biscuit time," The commander grumped.

"How sad," Merlin said. "Very sad."

"Nothing a few biscuits wouldn't fix," the commander said and disappeared.

"A few biscuits," Merlin muttered and turned to Al. "Now is show time, son." He turned to Sophie. "See that he gets to it, will you?"

Merlin pulled Lumpy along with him and disappeared to the far side of the screen.

The trumpet sounded a fanfare.

Sophie watched Al carefully. He knew it. He turned away from a little so he couldn't see her eyes. She slipped her arms around his waist. "You can do this. I always knew you were different."

Al couldn't answer. She rested her head on his shoulder. He couldn't breathe, but decided he'd be perfectly happy suffocating. Instead he heard himself say gruffly, "That's easy for you to say."

It wasn't what he wanted to say at all.

She turned away angrily. "Isn't such a big thing, is it?" She grabbed the sword and pulled.

The blade slid halfway out of the stone.

Al stopped. Sophie released the hilt as if it scalded her hand. The blade slipped back into the rock.

They stared at each other.

In the middle of the field Merlin raised his arms. The trumpets sounded again. The curtain dropped. Al suddenly faced the entire corps drawn up in a wide semicircle.

Merlin cleared his throat. "Gentlemen and warriors! You are called here to witness the right and most ancient of trials. Each of you knows how the trial is carried out. The one who pulls out the sword from this stone leads us, each and every one, into battle. Not just any skirmish, but in this case, the greatest of battles. The one we cannot gainsay; the one we cannot lose. If he can prove himself, we are bound to him so long as each of us shall live."

A giant of a flabby man suddenly stood. "Who is this pipsqueak?"

Al felt every eye on him.

"Wizard," the huge man continued, "We know you not from Adam's housecat."

Murmurs swept over the field.

"How'd we know that the sword is not greased?" The obese one demanded." How about a real man gives it a try?"

"Try what?" Merlin pretended to be coy.

"If I yank that butter knife out of that rock, then everybody's got to call me your munificence and do whatever twattle comes to my mind. Correct?"

"I would say so." Merlin stroked his chin.

"Any objection if I give her a heave-ho, then?"

Merlin glanced around. "Why, no. Not at all."

The big fellow's nose grew red. He pushed his way through the crowd. "Goodwood's the name," he told Merlin. "But then everybody knows that."

"Charmed," Merlin muttered.

Goodwood strode to the rock. Ragged cheers followed. Goodwood pumped his biceps and grabbed the sword's protruding hilt.

He pulled --and pulled and pulled. And pulled again-- right-handed, left-handed, both hands at once until his face grew tomato-colored. Merlin tapped his chin and didn't say anything.

Finally the commander stepped up and waved Goodowood away. "You're dismissed. We're all going to die of old age out here."

Goodwood hung his head and slipped away, serenaded by catcalls. The commander turned to Merlin. "Surely you're ready."

Merlin nodded to Al, whose hands trembled noticeably.

"Easy, son," Merlin muttered.

Al felt his face drain of its blood. He reached for the hilt. His hand barely covered it.

He pulled.

Nothing.

Al tried again.

Nothing.

"I said--," Merlin began testily.

"I heard." Al hissed.

He turned to his right. Sophie was watching. She nodded to him and said something Al couldn't understand.

Al turned back, grasped the hilt with both hands and pulled the sword from the stone.

The blade glittered in the sun.

The warriors sat silently and blinked.

"Well", the commander sighed for everybody. "Well, well. How do we explain this?"

"I don't think it needs explaining," Merlin said.

The commander drummed his fingers against his ceremonial spear. The corps waited. A light breeze stirred the rodent-chewed banners. The commander whistled a little hunting tune, drew his own sword and held it above his head. He roared in a way Al had never heard: "Warriors! Salute our prince! Our leader in war! Vanquish our foes! Never, never surrender!"

Cheers erupted from every throat. Merlin took a step back. The sudden enthusiasm astounded him. Merlin heard himself cheering.

Al watched their faces. The cheers, and the light in their eyes, he decided, were real. He felt as though he'd left his body. From the corner of his eye he watched his friends yelling and waving their swords as if nothing else in the universe mattered.

Sophie: he couldn't keep his eyes from her. She seems to cheer louder than anybody else, Al thought. How am I going to live up to that? She doesn't understand. There's something else I know, pure and simple: fear.

Chapter 38

The commander and Merlin cobbled together a quick ceremony. Al was directed to take his place on a rock that served as his throne. Al clutched the all-important sword and quickly he learned how heavy holding a sword upright could be.

Each warrior came marching through the grass to give a quick nod of fealty to their new prince.

The truth was, of course, that Al didn't look the slightest as if he were ready to slay multitudes of the enemy. But Merlin, as he watched the frumpy warriors go through the head-bobbing, reminded himself, appearances aren't everything.

Sophie and Lumpy flanked Al, who'd asked for them to be there. Lumpy gave a little counter-bow to each older man and mumbled, "You're excused" as they passed. Sophie seemed ready to burst with pride and, before the ceremony ended, actually held Excalibur when Al's arm finally gave out.

All went well, all things considered, say for one incident which took place just as the ceremony ended.

A copse of gnarled trees fringed the ceremony site. A handful of the warriors stood guard and scanned the horizon and the sky; after all, war had been declared for all practical effects. As the last man to swear fealty – the commander himself – gave his slightest nod, a guard a few hundred yards away suddenly leapt up, his head bobbing up and down as he search one of the grand trees nearby. The man drew his bow and aimed it at the crown high above the ground. He held his breath a half-second and let the arrow fly.

The arrow struck home. From the treetop came a death-screech. A body crashed through limbs and hit the earth with a sickening thud.

The corps glanced at each other in alarm, broke ranks and formed a circle around the thing. It was a Jin with wide leather wings and huge, lemur-like eyes. .

Al kneeled and studied it. Within its dying eyes Al saw –he was sure of it – the face of someone watching him. The lens of the eyes distorted the face, but Al knew it: Mordred.

Gradually the creature's eyes lost their luster and life. The body became still. The image of Mordred faded away. The creature's eyes became like black stones.

"Petulant little brat," the commander said aloud. "Not you, of course," he said to Al, "the other one. You two aren't related, are you? Forget it. Perish the thought."

The commander stood and gave the creature a little kick. "Is this the sort of thing we face?"

"I haven't seen this exact type before. There are plenty more. More variety than you'll find of apples," Merlin said

"I know what apples are," the commander answered. "How many can we expect to face?"

"Legions," Merlin said simply.

"They can be beaten," Al heard himself say.

"I should hope so," the commander said. "That's the whole idea. I certainly can use some cakes and drink. Especially the latter."

"We should leave today," Al said. He knew he had to speak. "Before they grow stronger."

Merlin glanced up. "What do you know?"

"Look at this one. It's a new type. Look how strong and big it is. They're bigger than they were at home, don't you think?"

"Oh, bother," the commander said, "More trouble."

"We'll need to force them to come for us. Otherwise they'll just stay away until they get so strong nothing can stop them." Al felt Merlin watch him as he spoke. "You'll need a plan. And, fealty or not, you'll have to convince the others in their hearts that they need to follow you."

The commander brushed his moustache. "Very noble. However, my men need a good night's sleep and a chance to tidy up."

"Then soon they might sleep in their graves," Al said.

"Yes," the commander finally answered, "that could be. But they've been to war once upon a time."

"Then they should know." Al said.

"They know," the commander said, "and so shall you."

Al thought that all the bowing and scraping meant instant obedience. Guess not, he told himself. He cleared his throat. "Tomorrow morning. Everybody should be up at sunrise. Not a minute later."

What would Wheezle have done? Al asked himself. Storm into each room and yank the covers off. That wasn't very likely. "Okay. Tomorrow. An hour after sunrise, everybody assembled right here. Just like today. Then we're off."

"Very good," the commander said, "off to where?"

Al cringed inside. "I'll have more on that tomorrow."

The commander winked at Merlin. "Speak to your man, will you?" Then, to Al. "Permission for cakes and ale."

"What? Yea, sure. Everybody chow down." Al said automatically and hoped the commander couldn't see the red flush rising up his neck. The commander gave a little salute and strolled away.

Merlin felt a pang of guilt. His boy's clumsiness didn't bother him. He'd seen it before. The guilt came before the actual fighting. I know what will happen, Merlin thought, and by the time it's over, the boy will be someone else completely. The important thing -- he learns to stand firm. Maybe he will and maybe he won't. That's the problem with the young, Merlin sighed inwardly. Everything is in the future, not now, when it needs to be.

A watched the warriors break ranks and spread out over the grass. They began unbuckling their heavy armor and untying their thick leather jerkins. Each warrior carried a clumsy armload of body armor, shield, buckler, a short spear, helmet, and a sword. The trudged across the field and toward their castle apartments with the painted shutters, pots of flowers and wash billowing gently in the breeze.

"They've got all the heart in this world," Merlin said. "Don't doubt that."

Al blinked. Can he actually read my mind? Or maybe my face just tells everything.

Sophie stepped close to Al. "What's the other one like? The one we're going to fight"

"Mordred," Merlin answered strongly," is smart enough to get others to fight for him. One you see that he's coming for you, act instantly. He's closing in for the kill. That's what he likes best – the kill when you're down. Trickery and lying and worse – he'll use that. Guarantee. Don't expect mercy. Don't give offer it. Not once, no matter what."

"Mama," Lumpy blurted.

The commander appeared at Al's elbow. "Well, let's break the ice. An informal conference. Nothing extravagant. We'll have a chat at my place for dinner. You'll hear the dinner gong, and then feel free to come by. In the meantime I intend to take a nap."

The commander bowed and strolled away.

Al turned to Merlin. "What am I supposed to say?"

"Use your native intelligence. I'm going to have a nap myself." Merlin answered.

He yawned and strolled away.

Is this a test? Al thought. If so, I haven't got the study guide.

Lumpy and Sophie appeared. They climbed the stairs to their rooms. He wasn't sure, but it seemed that his friends were hanging back a little. That bothered him as much as anything else.

But almost as soon as he hit the bed he felt himself drowsing away. "Let me close eyes just a sec," he said aloud.

His head whirled. He vaguely remembered leaning back. He didn't rest, though. He dreamed the way he'd dreamed as far back as he could remember.

He heard a gong sound for dinner. He sat up suddenly. Sophie and Lumpy stood by the bed staring at him.

Al swung his feet off the bed. "What about a little privacy?"

"You were acting weird." Lumpy frowned. "Your eyes were twitching and you were trembling a little."

Al felt his face turn red. "I didn't drool, did I?"

"No worse than usual," Lumpy answered.

A knock sounded on the door. Al made a point to walk steadily to the door. Merlin stood there and beckoned for him. They didn't speak on the way over. They hurried.

The commander occupied big rooms on the highest level of the castle keep. He opened the door himself and led his guest to a large room that overlooked the shallow valley filled with flowering trees.

Dinner was already there. Al didn't want to eat. He nibbled to be polite. The commander seemed to eat all he wanted. Al noticed that Merlin ate slowly and very little. Finally the commander wiped his hands and pushed his plate away. "Shall we begin? Good. May I start things off? No use being too polite. First and lastly, we don't dare fight here. This is a palace, not a fortress. Too many gates broach the walls and the towers are simply living quarters, complete with windows in the walls. We have beautiful views and streams nearby and fertile land. The wars were done when this place was planned. Bivouacking in the cold fields and scratching fleas grows old very quickly, I promise."

Merlin nodded. "Agreed."

"Absolutely," Al said suddenly.

The commander glanced at the other two. "That didn't take long."

He looked sideways at Merlin.

Al sat up straight. "The other place: The fortress. The ruins I mean. They're far away, but it's our best option."

"Makes sense to me," the commander interjected. "Take the fight away from our fields and our wives and children. Draw them off and fight on ground of our own choosing. That's the spirit."

"Tomorrow morning, then?" Merlin asked.

"Bother these early mornings and all," the commander said. "But we don't our nasty little friends to trap us here. It'll hurry things if we set out tomorrow, but so be it. I keep saying that, don't I?"

He rose from his chair. "At first light, up and at 'em. Just like the old days. Well, not exactly, but you get my meaning. I wish you a good night's rest. I certainly intend to enjoy one."

The two older men walked slowly toward the door. Al followed, waiting for something eternal and memorable to be said. The commander clapped them on their shoulders and escorted them to the hallway.

That was all.

Merlin shuffled along, chin down, lost in thought. Al stayed close to his elbow. "So how did I do?"

"Absolutely fine"

Merlin hurried ahead and refused to talk. I deserve more, Al thought, but I'm not going to get it. Instead, he frowned, kept his chin down like Merlin, and tried to think about the next day: Nothing back home matches what's in my head. It's all mine, though and always has been. Why? What's different? Maybe everybody has such dreams and just keeps quiet about it. No. That couldn't be. They'd be locked up.

A terrible thought came to Al. How do I know, when we leave the palace and take off for la-la land that Mordred will follow? What if he doesn't? What will happen to their homes and their wives and their children? I'll be responsible.

But Merlin didn't stop me, he reminded himself. He knows all about it. He knows what Mordred wants now, truly and forever.

Al felt the old sword bumping against his leg.

I get it, he thought. It's so easy. He wants:

Me.

Chapter 39

The next day came cheerful, all golden and blue. Even the air smelled sweet. But the courtyard was crowded and busy.

The warriors were up before sunrise, piling their wares of war in the courtyard. Warriors sorted, polished, and oiled and sharpened their accoutrements. First came the swords, shined, ground to razor-sharp; then bows and arrows for some, bound and readied for traveling. Spears, maces, and daggers and spiked clubs followed, according to each warrior's choice. Each one got a polishing and sharpening from the grindstones that threw so many sparks that courtyard seemed to be a scene for celebration.

Mail shirts and armor were laid out and polished. Leather jerkins meant to soften the heavy armor's weight got such a deep oiling that the entire courtyard smelled of seed-oil. Pennants were unfurled. Even they'd been washed, pressed, and the rodent-holes mended.

In the full morning light the entire corps, every warrior still able to obey the call, formed a double column and marched through the beautiful rose gate and out to war. The regimental band escorted the column with drums and pipes. All one thousand and ten warriors gathered on the green grass field and spread out. The band filled the air with patriotic tunes. Each man carried a fresh lump of ambrosia.

In a few minutes the distant sky was flecked with the shapes of the wide-winged mounts. As they drew closer, every color of the breed appeared, pure black or white, steel-blue, ochre, satin grey, mottled, and roan. They circled first, the glided downward by the dozens, flaring their leathery wings, and skimming over the earth until their claws lightly clipped the ground.

The warriors gathered up their mounts and, most surprisingly, in full battle gear swung onto the backs of the animals with a minimum of stumbling and a crashing of armor.

The mounts clawed at the earth and hissed. The commander nodded. Each warrior patted his mount. The creatures charged into the wind. The field filled with the whoosh of strong wings beating against the morning air. One by one, then in two and threes, then by the dozens, the mounts and their riders lifted into the morning sky.

The commander saluted Al as he and the last of the corps rose into the sky. Merlin, Sophie, and Lumpy, the last to leave, rose into the sky on the same mounts that had carried them before.

Al watched the corps circle in the air. His mount softly hissed and let Al scratch its neck.

The corps formed into ragged v-shaped formations, each V protecting the flank of the one below it. Merlin led them high into the air and, with Al conspicuously in the foremost place, guided the four to a station above and ahead of the entire corps.

They made a line of four. Sophie glanced in Al's direction now and then. Lumpy craned his neck above and behind, the direction from which they'd been ambushed before.

At first Al felt self-conscious about Sophie's glances. That didn't last long. The situation was real: the air was filled with mounts and heavily-armed warriors. The very first duty of a leader, Al realized, wasn't courage; that came later. The first duty was to use the strongest weapon.

Al realized that he and his friends had strayed ahead of everybody else. Sophie was frowning, as if she was trying to take in everything. Lumpy was frowning, too, and glanced over his shoulder again and again.

And so they flew for hours until the sun sank lower into the sky.

A dense cloud bank eventually appeared. High, steel-blue craggy mountains appeared .The problem: the mountains rose up much higher than the corps was flying.

Great, Al thought, I've almost led my entire army into a mountainside. He glanced all around, keeping his nose up as if he had planned this all along. What next?

He didn't have an answer.

Sophie waved and pointed toward the ground. Al glanced down. In front of folded foothills the ruins of the city- fortress appeared. Crumbling towers poked above the walls. Seven-sided pyramids filled the city spaces. The tangle of vines produced huge blooms that spangled the landscape with vermilion, saffron yellow, royal purple, and tropical blues.

Al turned his mount downward into a tight spiral. As he drew closer he realized what didn't seem important before -- the walls were badly broken and tumbled down. An earthquake, Al thought, or terrible battle lifetimes ago.

Merlin took his place behind Al. His friends flew on each side. The fight, Merlin thought, will make them even closer. They'll be friends of the sword; it's the saddest thing of all that humans found their greatest courage in the worst of conditions. And this fight, when it comes, will not be pretend. The desperation will be real and the fear and the panic.

Who is the victim? Who is the slayer? Speak.

Who said that? Merlin wrinkled his brow. Grey-bearded old Sophocles, Merlin recalled, who lived so long that Merlin, when they were nodding acquaintances in Athens, thought I actually might be a demi-god. Despite the wars Sophocles died in his sleep at ninety years old.

The challenge is happening again, Merlin thought. History makes a circle. How many times have I thought that over the centuries? Here I am, no matter how hard I tried to prevent it. But this time the winner will own everything, even the stars in the sky. For the losers-- there is no word for it. I know it and so do the paunchy gentlemen a little airsick from their first time on their mounts since they were young themselves.

Al gave his mount a hard nudge and pulled far ahead of everyone else. The commander drew close to Merlin. "We don't know what's waiting down there. What's your boy doing?"

"Showing some backbone."

My stomach is in knots, Merlin thought, but I can't possibly humiliate him in front of everybody at his first decision. If I do he'll be worth nothing.

Al's mount flared and landed gently. Al stepped down and studied what he saw surrounding him. He felt the deep stillness in the mute pyramids with their hard green stone and the empty, vast streets.

Everything, Al decided, seemed to be built for grandeur alone.

His mount softly whistled and scraped with his clawed feet. Al's ears pricked up as he tried to hear a frightening scratching and growling.

Dried leaves skittered along in the breeze. Tiny animals scratched here and there.

"Nobody's home," he announced. The sound of his voice echoed from one pyramid to another.

Shadows flitted across the roads and stones. Al glanced up. The entire corps circled above, waiting to for his signal.

He waved his sword. They came quickly. Soon they were everywhere, filling the streets and the plazas.

Al decided he needed to be seen. He took a place on a little hill on one side of the plaza. The commander drew close on his mount and nodded. "We await your orders."

Al felt every eye turned to him. He cleared his throat and spoke as grandly as he could. "How about lunch?"

The commander gave a little salute. "Exactly what I was thinking."

A warrior trotted his mount forward. "Your munificence – I hear there's an opening for an orderly," Igat bobbed his head

"Hard service. But so ordered." Al agreed, very pleased inside.

Igat leaned forward. "Did I hear some mention of a lunch? How about a nap to go along with it?"

And he yawned.

Merlin, who'd been listening, cleared his throat. "May I suggest a guard?"

"Right," Al said. "Call out the captain of the guard. Two men take their place on these three closest pyramids or whatever you call them and two on that wall."

"Who is the captain of the guard?" Igat asked. "I'll go fetch the poor fool."

"I'm speaking to him," Al said.

Igat sighed mightily and turned his mount away. "War is hell," he muttered.

"Would you like to take the tour?" Merlin asked.

"I was about to say that." Al answered quickly.

The city was far too vast for a complete tour. Only one section mattered. Al saw that right away. Where Al had them land formed an island in the center of a huge lake. Three stone causeways led into the central city. The low hills on the far side of the lake were lightly forested and seemed otherwise empty.

Al studied the landscape and thought to himself, I see everything differently now. Look at the hills and the thin woods. They might provide cover -- for someone else.

"How will we know when they're close?" He asked suddenly.

"By the smell," Merlin answered.

"What if the wind is blowing the wrong way? And these hills will hide them till we only have a few minutes. Then they'll be on us."

"True," said the commander said, "but once they're knocking on the front door--." He pointed to the causeways. "Just three ways in. Perhaps five or six of their kind can shoulder their way abreast, wouldn't you say?"

"Four if they've been feeding regularly," Merlin answered.

"This lake and these bridges are our only chance," Al said quietly.

"Let's look on the bright side," Merlin said evenly.

"Wait. Can't they swim? I mean rafts or the like – anything that floats. Wouldn't that do the trick for them?"

The commander slid off his mount and heaved a small log into the lake. It floated peacefully a few seconds. The surface exploded into froth. The stick disappeared. It bobbed to the surface chewed and shredded. A half dozen pale faces hovered just beneath the surface. They floated quietly little while and sank away.

"They are so touchy," the commander sighed.

"They what?" Al began. "Or what? Which is it?"

"Their ancestors took up life by the lake when this was a living place. The lake became theirs as they spent more and more time beneath it. Gradually, very gradually, they became -- different. But then they've had plenty of time. The lake is their protection now that the city is dead."

Al frowned. "Okay. Who killed the city? Who lived here? I thought this world was paradise and that's all there is to it."

The commander glanced at Merlin. "Wizard, I never liked turning over rocks."

Merlin thought for a long moment and turned to Al. "What do you know?"

"Me?" Al asked, his voice rising. "You keep asking me. How would I know anything?"

"Maybe you just don't recognize it."

"Get real."

"Very well. I will get real, though I want your promise that you'll have use your imagination and just accept. Cities never appear by accident. There's always a purpose: for trade, or, in the oldest way, because the place is sacred. They, the long-gone ancestors of the warriors you see today, banded together and, over hundreds of lifetimes, built this place. Eventually they had a falling out. Clans became tribes within the city and tribes became bitter enemies. They fought one great battle. The survivors, horrified at what they'd done, agreed to abandon the city. Each tribe went its own way. Over time they forgot what their ancestors knew."

"Forgot what? You said something about sacred."

"I don't know. Not really." Merlin looked away.

Why is he not telling me the truth? Al thought. I didn't think he was able to do that.

"All that matters is this fight," Merlin said.

"Sure thing," Al said as evenly as he could. He felt his anger and fear rising. "How's that going to go?"

Al turned away.

Merlin watched him go. He wanted to grab the boy and shake him. But I can't, he told himself. I'm not in control anymore. It's never gone this far. This

299

is the end, one way or the other. It's so simple and after all this time. I never thought --

The commander clapped his hand on Merlin's shoulder. "Wizard, you look like one who's swallowed a toad."

"No doubt," Merlin said quietly.

Merlin gave the boy some time and quietly re-joined him. The tour took the rest of the afternoon. A fight like the one that's coming, Merlin reminded himself, leaves no second chances. They are legion and we are few. We have strengths: determination, grit, and the fact that our backs are to the wall. We also have old joints, paunchy stomachs and stringy arms that haven't struck a blow since--.

Advantages, he repeated to himself. Think advantages. We have the boy, an incalculable help, provided that I haven't made a mistake. Merlin shivered at the thought.

Merlin and the commander offered one suggestion after another. They pointed out where the warriors should be stationed to stand and fight. The corps, Al learned, was divided into families of fifty, then clans of 150 and tribes of 300. The remaining 150 served as officers, messengers, and the band.

"Defending the causeways," the commander lectured, "is everything. We've offered our suggestions. Now, deliver your orders."

They'd arrived back at the courtyard. The warriors lounged in the open spaces, drinking and stoking campfires. Many faces turned to study him. Al felt every gaze. The commander and Merlin prodded him forward. Al glanced behind; the two old men blocked him way. The only way out, Al decided, was up.

He coughed and cleared his throat. "Tell you what we're going to do, people–."

I sound like, Al thought, my gym teachers. He paused and began again. "You don't know me. I don't know why I was chosen for this job, but I am. We're going to divide into four companies, one to block each causeway and cover the walls between. One company will be held in reserve for whatever may come up. The commander tells me you have done this before, so it shouldn't be new to you. Just to me. We are few and they are many, but we are stronger, braver, and much more intelligent and, I am sure, we stink much less."

There was light laughter. Al felt himself relax a little. "I suspect they'll come soon, probably at first light. That's about all there is now. I know you love a long speech, but that's all I have."

There was light applause. My voice, Al noted, only cracked twice.

The warriors stood and began to take their places. A great deal of clanking of armor, spears, swords, helmets followed, along with quiet joking.

Al watched the corps take their places for battle. He felt his heart sink. The territory they had to defend seemed so wide and the warriors seemed so few. Al glanced at Merlin and the commander. Their chins were up; they were smiling and chatting. Don't they see? Al fretted silently and realized, that yes, they did see. He forced himself to smile and hold up his chin. The first rule of a leader, he decided, was not to show your fear or doubts. It's not exactly lying, but it is something else.

"Where would you like to set up your headquarters?" Merlin asked.

Beats me, Al thought, but already I know that wouldn't be the thing to say.

"May I suggest?" Merlin asked. He nodded toward the south causeway, the closest place to where they stood. "It's the first place they'll reach if they come directly across those hills. If they're not extremely ambitious and climb the bluffs behind us."

"Lots of if's," Al noted.

Merlin shrugged. "It's war."

"Okay. It's good enough for me."

The commander, who'd been listening, turned away and issued his orders. Al wandered and watched the warriors arrange themselves along the walls facing the south causeway. Without being told they'd already decided which small squads would defend particular few yards of the wall. The line, Al noted, was anchored at both ends by two steep pyramids. As Al watched the warriors began to tear up the ancient stones from the streets and stack the walls even higher.

Everyone seemed very busy. Nobody seemed to need him at the moment, Al decided, but he felt that every eye was following him. As he walked past the wall, men from the working parties would at least give him a quick nod. What else am I supposed to do? He tried to imagine what would happen and what it would be like. The one thing I know-- once again-- is that we are far too few. I need five times more. Ten times more would be even better. A child could see it. But I don't have what I need here and I never will.

The warriors worked quickly. They stacked rough pile of stones walls higher and higher until they joined to the steep walls of the pyramid. By late afternoon their work was done. Al studied the place that Merlin had chosen - suggested - for his headquarters. There, Al guessed, I'll stand wise and noble, with banner flying high, just like the stories I read about in history books: Henry the Fifth at Agincourt, Wellington at Waterloo, and Thomas at Chickamauga.

A little procession followed Al as he made his inspection: Merlin, Igat, Sophie, and Lumpy stood behind while Al climbed the little mound, and firmly planted his banner. The commander appeared and ordered that a fire be built for boiling dinner and brewing up his cordial

The commander took over the fire and began preparing edibles he'd taken from his knapsack.

"Do you young ones know what season it is? It's the season of the Quicellus- a fuzzy, juicy fruit, sweetest thing you've ever tasted, ready right off the bush and a delight to the senses. Usually their ripening is celebrated with a huge banquet. Everybody wears maroon. The feast and the party would have usually started tomorrow at sunset. Instead, tomorrow we'll be up to our armpits in muck."

"Sorry about that," Lumpy mumbled.

"Peace and quiet," the commander sighed. "It couldn't last forever."

"You had a few years," Sophie answered.

"A few more years wouldn't have hurt anybody," the commander said. "At least it'll be over quickly, one way or the other."

Nobody replied. The huge, pale sun, so much bigger and cooler than Sol, was already descending behind the horizon.

Lumpy shivered. "In the dark – how do you know they'll find us?"

"I'm sure he's kept an eye on us," Merlin said. "Whither we go he's sure to follow."

"Like a bad penny," Lumpy said.

"Maybe he'll just starve us out," Sophie said. "Or what if we aren't where we need to be? Maybe he'll go in the other direction."

"We're right where we need to be," Al insisted.

"I hope you're right," Sophie said.

I promise, Al thought.

The kettle on the fire whistled. The commander clapped his hands. "I made a tea from the first of this year's crop. Aren't you lucky? There is enough for everybody."

He puttered around the campfire, pouring steaming drinks into stone mugs. He looks just like somebody's butler, Al groaned inwardly.

The commander handed out the mugs. Everyone smiled politely. "Glories to the season!" the commander beamed. "A good long, guzzle. Come on now, it's the custom."

Al tried. The concoction tasked like a mix of old cantaloupe and fender rust. Everyone else did their best to smile.

Along the wall, where the warriors camped, cooking fires glowed. The warriors were quiet, though now and then Al heard low laughter.

Merlin wandered away from the campsite. Al quietly followed and together they pretended to inspect a far section of the wall.

"When will they come?" Al asked.

"Tomorrow. No earlier, I think. The landscape is rough and in any case he'll have to offer his creatures much more than blood, sweat, and tears. They have tender feet and big stomachs and short attention spans. But you know that."

"What will it be like?"

"It will be chaos."

"What if I can't take it?"

"You'll want to run. But you won't."

"You know that?"

"Yes, I do."

"I don't."

Al turned his face away. He needs a little time, Merlin thought. Then we'll see. I've given all the hope I can. Each of them, each of my Arthurs, have been so independent, so unalike.

The quiet lasted only a few more minutes. A lone guard atop the highest pyramid began whistling, lit a torch, waved it over his head till it was fully aflame, and threw it down the pyramid steps. Orange sparks showered down.

Alarm.

Al ran back to Merlin, eyes wide. The warriors rolled out of their blankets and scrambled for the protection of the wall. Metal clanged against metal. Swords were drawn and spears were lifted into the sky. Warriors crouched against the barriers and tried to peer through the gloom.

"What's the matter?" Al asked. His voice cracked.

"I suspect we have visitors."

"You said we had until tomorrow."

"Perhaps I was wrong."

305

The commander, breathless and still buckling on his sword, hurried to Merlin. "The mounts: I thought we had until tomorrow -."

"So I've heard," Merlin growled. "Well, let's do what we have to."

The commander turned and called for Igat. The stout warrior came running and puffing. The commander whispered urgently in his ear and pointed to the huge herd of agitated mounts. Igat waded among the milling, terrified creatures, blowing a shrill whistle was he went. The mounts shook themselves and, with a great snorting and clawing, began spreading their wings, and charged across the narrow field. They rose into the sky by the dozens, then hundreds, and soon the entire herd wheeled into the evening sky and flew toward the horizon.

"What are you doing?" Al demanded.

"If they're slaughtered here, we'll have no way out at all."

Merlin began climbing the cracked stone of the closest pyramid. Al followed; they scrambled up as fast as they could and let lose avalanches of stone.

At the summit Al saw what he hadn't understood. On the low ridges that surrounded much of the lake thousands of wavering pinpricks of light outlined the crest. Torches, Al decided, but how could there be so many? As he watched, the pinpricks of light seemed to cascade down the ridge and filled the plain in front of the lake.

Al glanced at Merlin's face.

"What's going on," he asked quietly.

"They're here. I guess they were on our heels from the start."

The warm pinpricks of light spread until they covered the hill and the entire valley. It's like a celebration, Al though, and it'd be beautiful if I didn't know what it means.

Merlin climbed down the pyramid slope. Al hurried after him. By the time they reached the ground the flickering torches crowded the shoreline. Al watched hundreds of warriors drew out their bows and strung them with double-strong twine. Each warrior carried a quiver packed with arrows longer than their arms. They climbed the flanks of the pyramids and took their post that looked down on the causeways and the field in front of the walls. A killing ground, Al thought and wondered where he'd heard the phrase before.

The commander appeared. His jaw was set and his eyes were narrowed. He'd already drawn his sharp, oiled, shining sword. He turned to Merlin. "How's there get to be so many?"

"Everybody wants to know," Merlin said, "Perhaps the trick of the dragon teeth; an old trick: Bury a bone or a finger or whatever body piece is not critical and by the next moonlight a new body emerges from the ground."

"I guess he doesn't care that many of his are missing a finger or an eyeball or a brain or two. Still, I don't like the odds," The commander said. He pointed with his sword at a place on the wall. "Anyway. I have my place. It feels most fortunate."

Igat, carrying a diamond-shaped banner, appeared behind the commander. He called to Al. "You greatnesses, you don't mind if I keep him out of trouble, do you?"

"We expect it," Al said.

Igat hurried away and planted the banner beside the commander. A ragged cheer came from the barricade.

Merlin turned to Al. "Are you ready?"

"Am I what?"

"At this point we are waiting for your orders."

"You can't do this to me," Al heard himself hiss. His teeth were suddenly chattering.

"Just something simple. That's best," Merlin said quietly.

Al thought: My legs are weak. I'll let it carry me along. I just hope nobody's taking a picture.

He turned and called out in his loudest voice, "Let them come to us. We'll be the rock. They'll smash against us!"

What have I done? Al thought. He realized his was holding the sword, Excalibur, in the air. Thin cheers swept around the perimeter. At least, Al noted, nobody is running away.

Merlin waited until had Al passed and followed him back to his place on the low hill. Al nodded to Sophie and Lumpy.

Merlin though that Lumpy simply seemed nervous – what he should feel. Sophie seemed otherwise; everything about her seemed so different. Her mouth was set in a firm line. Her eyes were bright. She'd found an old sword that she'd shined and sharpened and kept in a leather scabbard. There's no precedent, Merlin thought, but there it is. My boy can't get along without her.

At the very least.

"We can't stay back here," Al said. His teeth chattered as he said it. "How about the wall? Anybody with me?"

Sophie pulled Lumpy along. Merlin followed as Al picked a place on the center of the line and stepped up the wall. His young friends stood on either side. The warriors, all old enough to be his father and grandfathers, cheered again, but this time the cheers were loud and they went around all the barricades.

Merlin saw that the boy's face was pale, but there was a little smile and he let his hand rest on the hilt of his sword. I don't know if it's sincere, Merlin thought, but at least he's learning. After the cheering died down, each group of warriors unfurled their own banners and marked where they would fight.

The warriors fell silent and watched the seemingly endless gathering of torches on the far shore. Each pinprick of light meant an enemy. The torches spread across the hills as far as they could see.

Al watched quietly for a few minutes. He turned to Merlin. "Are they going to come now?"

"Maybe." Merlin said, "But a night attack will play into our hands. We have prepared fields of fire and their battalions will fumble about in the dark. Know your enemy. These creatures are less an army and more a mob. An army fights and dies for each other. Each of these creatures only fights for itself."

"Still," Al said quietly, "looks like somebody kicked open an ant hill."

"We know what we have to do. What Mordred has to work with-- let's see what he does with it."

"Guess we'll know PDQ," Sophie said.

The pinpricks of light began to thicken at the edge of the lake. Disorganized ranks pushed into the ranks of those ahead. Ragged line after ragged line compressed into the lake shore, each creature marked by its smoky orange torch. The dusk was filled with the swish of their rough legs brushing through the high grass.

The old man's right, Al decided. This is just a mob. I wish they weren't so many. They'll be like a tsunami when they hit. They don't need brains or courage. All they need is a direction.

The Jin gathered and gathered until the torches, pressed so closely together, ceased bobbing.

From the hills came a long, wavering call - a single note held for an impossibly long time. Merlin knew the Jin communicated on their battlefields through chants and songs.

The soloist's call faded away. Other Jin in the valley answered with a rumbling chant. The chanting grew and grew. Hundreds became thousands and thousands. The valley filled with a low, rumbling song. As the song faded regiments of Jin higher on the hills began chanting, taunting, one another.

The taunts filled the valley. Merlin felt the anger build in his heart. What about that, he thought, music that poisons.

Al clenched his fist. Blood pounded in his neck. I want it to start now. I don't care. I want to fight. His right hand clenched the hilt of his sword.

The terrible music continued. Eventually the warriors tried to rest at the barriers. They couldn't, of course, but they tried. Al couldn't rest at all. He'd never felt more awake; he knew he should try to rest, but he felt he couldn't never rest again.

Whump!

The Jin pounded their hoofs against the ground. Whump!

The entire army, covering the hill and the valley, took one step forward. A furious rattling began. To Al it sounded like hailstones smashing into a metal roof. Instead, Al realized, the Jin were pounding their weapons against their shields, their armor, and against each other.

Cacophony Al thought: one of Merlin's ten − dollar words. It meant noise and worse. The cacophony grew louder and louder until some warriors put down their weapons and covered their ears. All began to group into nervous groups. Lumpy and Sophie stepped back, though they had no place to go.

Then -- silence. Maybe, Al marveled, all these creatures actually share a single mind. Maybe they're part of one huge melon head, a meat-and-bone Internet.

The pinpricks of light began to wink out by the hundreds, then by the thousands.

The warriors seemed to be swallowed up in the dark. But Al noticed that the sky to his left was glowing saffron. Dawn was coming. Nights weren't that long on this place, Al remembered. He took a deep breath. The night made fear much worse. Of course, maybe Mordred thought the same way.

Al stared across the barrier. Shadows still covered the lower slopes. A light fog drifted over the tops of the hills.

A single Jin voice called out a single, wavering note.

Whump!

The earth shook.

311

Ha!
Their voices resounded against the lake.
Ha!
And with that they swarmed off the hills.

Chapter 40

The mass flowed downhill. Al saw Jin crushed shoulder to shoulder as they crowded onto the causeways.

And the causeways Al though, lead to me.

He realized he couldn't move. He'd read about fear in adventure stories, but this fear was real. He couldn't breathe.

Sophie, close on his right, drew her sword. He glanced at her face; that broke his fear enough for Al to draw his sword. His arm trembled. The sword felt slippery. I'm going to drop it, Al thought frantically. He fumbled for the leather loop below the grip and wrapped the rawhide around his wrist.

He glanced at Sophie again. He felt a flash of anger that she'd managed to put herself in such danger. He tried to push her away. He didn't think about it. He acted and she pushed back -- hard.

Al regained his balance before he fell off the wall. Lumpy, just to make matters worse, worked close to Al's left-hand side. He carried a hooked spear. His Adam's apple bobbed up and down and he clenched his teeth. He wouldn't even play volleyball back home, Al thought. What's next?

The dark mass of Jin grew resolved into creatures with arms, legs and trunks, and fearsomely ugly heads. White spray burst upward as the first ranks crashed into the green water of the lake. Other ranks collided with the first and the mixed the closed ranks together –all the ugly varieties of Jin, twisting, turning, gashing, yelping, shrilling, howling, and hooting. A third, fourth, and fifth rank collided with the first. On and on it went; rank, after rank, until it seemed that the lake would fill up.

The morning light spread over the lake and hills. Al saw that the Jin, who didn't seem to swim much at all, weren't thrashing in the deep water alone. Al remembered playing Marco Polo in the city pool. The big kids pulled the little ones under until the little ones screamed and choked and Wheezle made everyone stop before Somebody Got Killed. This time the big ones were the pale lake creatures with their clawed hands and big, translucent eyes.

They slipped powerfully through the water. To Al it seemed that Dolphins and human were fused into one creature. They fought to keep their world. Jin disappeared, gibbering, squeaking and shrieking. They vanished by platoons, then by the companies. The warriors on either side of Al laughed.

The confused hoard of Jin behind flowed toward their only safe route--the narrow causeways that led straight to the barriers. They turned quickly, Al thought, like a flock of birds.

The causeways filled. A dozen crowded where there was space for one. They still came, shoving their way onto the safety of the causeway. The barrier shed Jin bodies by the hundreds and hundreds. But even more came and, beyond that, more and more.

Al watched the warriors close by clutch their weapons. He guessed they had less than a minute before the tsunami struck their barricades. Al glanced around and realized someone was missing.

"Where is he?" he called.

Sophie glanced around and shrugged. "He's old. What can he do for us?"

Al felt a pang in his chest. Why would he leave me now? Am I completely wrong about him? What do I do now?

The front ranks of the Jin howled and fell upon the friends.

The warriors answered with their own roar. The first crash of metal weapons against Al never forgot: a deafening clang. Al roared with the rest of the warriors. He brought his sword down. A creature squealed and fell back. Another appeared in his face. Al struck again. It disappeared. Al struck again and again.

Almost as suddenly as they came the Jin tide ebbed away. Al suddenly felt too exhausted to lift his sword. He slumped by the barricade and listened to the breathing of the warriors around him. He shivered and felt the world, bad as it was, come back to him.

Sophie.

She stood close enough to touch. She was sweating with pools under her arms and rivulets running down her face. She stared ahead, as if her eyes were focused far ahead. She's hasn't come back, Al thought. His slipped his arms around her shoulders. He did before he could stop himself. She felt so soft, even her shoulders. She pressed his face against his.

Al felt as though the entire universe was watching them. But he realized that the rest of the world paid no attention at all. Some warriors were wounded; more than a few. Friends bandaged their wounds carried them to the rear where an open-air hospital waited by the ruins.

Al glanced at Lumpy. His face glowed strawberry-red. He was sweating even worse than Sophie. A bead of sweat dripped off the tip of his nose. He still gripped the heavy spear.

Al glanced at the field in front of the barricades. The field was once decorated with red and white flowers. Now it was littered with motionless Jin bodies. Some had fallen in groups; some lay alone, as if they'd been dropped from high above. The Jin farther away lay contorted with throwing spears or long arrows stuck from their heavy bodies.

Al glanced up. Dozens of warriors with their bows and long arrows still crouched along the steep sides of the pyramid. Each archer had stuck his arrows feathers by his right hand for easy grabbing. Al realized noticed that most of their arrows were gone; the arrow shafts spangled the field below. Closest to the barricade, the Jin dead reached halfway up the walls.

Al felt numb; tragedy, nobility, even sadness, were gone. Not that the Jin were people, he reminded himself, or even close to us. Not that they wouldn't do the same thing to Merlin, Sophie, Lumpy, the commander, Igat, or the rest of warriors. To them, we're vermin.

Al shivered. How could repulsive things like these not see how much better we are? Look what its cost them. Look what we've seen today: we're dozen times better than they are. They just came at us, straight on, just the way we wanted them to do.

316

But they are so very, very many, he reminded himself and we aren't.

A sergeant elbowed past Al and jumped onto the far side of the barricade. Slide was more like it; he landed on a pile of Jin before he found his feet. More warriors followed. Each carried a spear with the point bent into a hook. The squad worked quickly, hooking the Jin dead and dragging them away from the barricade. They piled the dead along one side of the field.

"Nice and tidy," the sergeant called out.

The warriors laughed.

"Heads up!" A lookout at the top of the pyramid bellowed. The sergeant wrenched his spear free and climbed over the barricade. The other warriors scrambled after him. In an instant they were ready.

The star above made the day warm; its light shone down golden-orange. The water of the lake glittered and sparkled where rafts of drowned Jin floated. The low hills turned dark with Jin. This time they banged drums and blew trumpets. The noise was tremendous, a wall of sound.

They came on in the same way, spilling onto the causeway, shedding Jin as they went. This time Al saw gangs of Jin launching logs bound into crude rafts. A dozen Jin climbed onto each raft. They paddled with the weapons, limbs, or even their clawed hands.

The rafts filled the shoreline. Al couldn't count them all. The lake people rose up from the lake. Jin clubbed at the pale heads. The rafts were crude, but heavy and strong. The lake people couldn't flip them. They tried again and again. The lake was being reduced to a moat.

Al felt his heart sink. The first rafts jammed against the island. Jin, hundreds at a time, began to swarm up the bank. Freed from the causeway, the Jin advanced as a solid mass. They struck the barricade from all sides at once.

The fight grew even more desperate. Al couldn't imagine such a thing was possible. The warriors thrust, parried, hacked scythed, and bashed. But to Al it seemed that five crowded against the barrier for each one that fell.

The archers on the pyramid did all they could. Jin tumbled by the dozens. The rain of long arrows slowed and stopped. Al glanced up; the archer's quivers were empty. They threw down their bows, grabbed their swords, and slid down the pyramids to join their friends.

Slowly the warriors were being wrenched free from the barrier. A warrior fighting three Jin at once would take a step back. A Jin squeezed through the rent in the barrier. Most of the Jin survived only a little while, but others came immediately afterward, and more followed them; and more after that.

The warrior's line at the barricade disintegrated. The warriors sweating in their thick armor mixed with the Jin. Here and there a warrior fell. Sometimes his friends carried him away with a bleeding head or smashed arm or leg. Others lay still. Jin struggled and swarmed over the barrier

Al felt a hand grab his shoulder. He whirled around. The commander, his armor bashed and his face bleeding, leaned close to Al. "Call our people back!"

"Where can we go!" Al shouted to be heard.

The commander pointed to a stone courtyard that enclosed a pyramid. A few warriors were already breaking open the ancient wooden gate leading to the inner sanctum.

"How do I get them there!" Al yelled as loud as he could.

Igat stepped up with the largest hunting trumpet that Al had ever seen. "Retreat and reassemble. He knows the tune." The commander yelled in Al's ear.

"Do it!" Al yelled at the top of his voice.

Igat raised the horn and puffed out his stomach. His face turned scarlet, but the triplet came out loud enough to make Al jump. The warriors began a steady retreat, shoulder to shoulder, slashing and stabbing as they went.

At first the retreat went well enough. But one warrior stumbled and a handful of Jin penetrated the line.

Al saw the effect: panic. A section of the line collapsed. The Jin poured over the barricades, and attacked from everywhere – ahead, on both flanks, and even from behind.

"By your leave!" the commander called to Al. He ran to re-join his warriors. Too late, Al thought, too late. Armor, helmets, shields, even standards were thrown into the dirt.

Some warriors fled together; some took off alone, but they all fled. Al thought frantically: What do I do? What now?

Sophie grabbed his arm and pulled him toward the courtyard. The last few warriors rounded up Al, Sophie and Lumpy. They began a fighting retreat. The Jin flowed around and beyond them, intent, Al saw, on trapping as many warriors as they could on the wrong side of the pyramid gate.

Al fought facing the gate. More warriors began passing through the broken-open gate to the inner courtyard. They scrambled to the top of the walls and bashed the Jin attackers with stones ripped from the wall.

A crescent of warriors fought to keep the gate open for the last stragglers which, Al realized, meant his little group. "There!" Al bellowed, as loud as he ever had. "There! Not much farther!"

The warriors glanced up. If they didn't understand, they do now, Al realized. I see it in their faces. And they're looking to me. What do we do next?

Al grabbed Sophie and Lumpy and ran – not a jog, or a lope, but head-on, hard as he could as he pulled along Sophie who pulled Lumpy.

The Jin pressed closer from three directions. Only the warriors at the extreme edge of their formation found the space to slash and stab. Al grabbed Sophie and tried to push her toward the gate. She jerked away, furious.

Old Man, Al thought frantically, look what you've done. No, not me. So where are you?

They were close. The high gates stood only a few dozen yards away. But as Al watched the formation of warriors fighting in front of the gate crumbled. The survivors pulled their wounded through the gate. The gate, besieged by the crush of Jin bodies, slowly and steadily closed.

Al stopped. Sophie still stood by him, fighting and sweating. Lumpy stood on the other side, wild-eyed, gritting his teeth and slashing with his spear.

They hadn't left me, Al told himself. Look what it's going to cost them. I've failed them; that is the very worst of all.

And then sky began falling.

Chapter 41

Al felt a breeze against his face. It stirred the dust and came from directly above. He glanced up. Huge shapes were crisscrossing the sun. They were so many that they almost blocked the light. The battlefield seemed to be in twilight. The breeze became a strong wind that kicked up enough dust to blind warriors and Jin alike.

Al got a face full of grit. He rubbed his eyes and squinted at the sky again. The great blue dragons filled the sky, more, with their gigantic size and billowing, translucent wings, than he imagined could ever exist. They whirled and swooped in the sky; they were stacked dozens high. Each creature carried a boulder tucked in its claws. The dragons formed long lines, folded their wings and dove steeply. At the last second each creature unfolded its wings. Each opened with a tremendous crack.

That made the instant's warning. The talons released and boulders tumbled out of the sky.

Each dragon's aim was very deliberate. Their release point couldn't have been more than a few hundred feet above their targets-- the s packed mass of Jin below. The ton-heavy boulders didn't explode. Quantity, speed of delivery, and accuracy made up for it. First there came the snap and crack of the dragon's wings and then the thud of a huge boulder slamming into the earth.

The stone didn't just ram into the earth. The Jin swarmed in a panic to the right or left; the boulders thudded down and shook the ground with each blow. The dragons kept the eyes focused. Jin, by the dozens and hundreds, got in the way anyway.

A flight of dragons glided above the lakeshore filled with Jin rafts --- and their frantically splashing Jin owners-- and released.

Huge geysers erupted from the cold water. What was the formula for force? Al asked himself. Force times mass. Majestic plumes rose up, math or not, consisting of an unequal mix of green water, shattered logs, and Jin.

The warriors crouched and waited. Al watched the azure dragons wheel high in the sky and return quickly with their claws filled.

The Jin didn't just retreat. They panicked; they gibbered, howled, and blubbered. They skittered and scampered toward the causeway and the reasonable safety on the far side. The Jin streamed under the walls of the enclosure where the warriors had retreated for safety. The warriors jabbed with their long hooked spears to keep the mob moving, and, if they hesitated, the Jin were jabbed in their crusty knees, spindly legs, and grape-sized toes.

How long did the bombarding last? Al wasn't sure. The dragons filled the sky as they wheeled, dipped, attacked and soared. Finally, Al decided, how long didn't matter. There's just one fact: we are saved.

Eventually the last keeling dragon turned on its wing and soared away. Huge boulders littered the landscape. Some lay piled up in haphazard cairns. Everywhere, awfully evident where the boulders had bounced once or twice, laid mangled and flattened Jin.

The warriors at the walls slowly stood. Al looked at his friends. The field in front of the walls was empty, except for the pattern of giant boulders that began a hundred yards away.

Lumpy blinked. "Talk about road kill."

"We owe somebody," Sophie said quietly.

Al glanced up and spotted Merlin's silhouette slowly walking along the parapet.

Sophie frowned at the low hills on the far side of lake. The Jin still teemed on the slopes. They were even pressing very cautiously closer toward the lake's edge and the boulder-smashed causeways.

"Let's get out here," Al said.

Once inside the perimeter, the warriors, with a great deal of groaning and shoulder muscle, pushed the heavy gates shut. A work party began piling up rock and paving stones high against the doors.

Al didn't stay in the courtyard to watch. He found Merlin standing on the top of a pyramid in the center of the courtyard.

Al climbed the steep steps. A stone house topped the pyramid. The walls were open on all sides. It wasn't a bad view, Al decided -- not so much now, but once upon a time. He wished he and Sophie could see it the way he imagined it must have been. Nobody else would be around to bother them. They'd just have time to talk. It wasn't too much to ask.

Al took a last step and stood on the top of the pyramid.

"Always take the high road, son." Merlin's voice sounded close by. He found Merlin standing in the shade outside the stone house.

"Where'd you go?" Al blurted.

He glanced away; he didn't mean to sound so angry.

"What's it matter? I had a little way to go. I kept my mount tucked away. I wasn't sure it would work. I didn't want to make promises I couldn't keep. That's something I've learned the hard way."

"I guess I owe you an apology."

"For what? Thinking bad thoughts?"

"For saving our skins."

"Wasn't that something? I wasn't sure I could make them understand. Pidgin dragon. Their grandmothers those were the ones I had to convince. Our fight is your fight, I swore. They bought it."

"Great timing. We were almost done. " Al felt his knees shake.

"But it turned out well enough."

They were quiet. Al studied the causeway and the battleground on their side of the lake. On the hills, all the way down to the lake shore, the Jin were still gathering and milling around. They're terrified the sky is going to start falling again, Al decided. He turned to Merlin. "Can we count on them again?"

"Not a chance. They're busy moving their young high into the mountains."

"I guess that says it all."

"So it seems," Merlin said

That's it? Al thought. He spoke quietly to Merlin. "But why here? It's close. Close, close, close. That's all I know. That's nothing. If you know, tell me now."

Merlin turned away.

Al let his shoulders drop. He accused himself: Do you have to get hit in the head? Get ready to get dropped. Didn't he say it? It's never gotten this far before. First back home at the miserable little tree and now…look what you've done to his beautiful planet. And the warriors…look where you've got them.

Do you blame him?

Merlin turned back and said. "However, we have our immediate goal: surviving. Whoever wins will have all the time in this world to complete his search."

"How --." Al had to take a breath. "How will we survive? They're going to hit us again. And again. Over and over again. That's going to be the end of us."

"Possibly not."

Al frowned. "Possibly. That's not as good as maybe. Just hear me out. You've got powers. The mumbo jumbo. The magic. We need help. Not later. Now. I'll never ask again. Not even to fix a lottery ticket. I swear."

Merlin simply tapped his check with his right hand. Finally he gave a long sigh. "It just isn't possible."

Al swallowed. "Talk about desperation here. Give me one good reason."

"It isn't about one reason."

"Then what is it about? How about defeat and death?"

Merlin, the magus to kings, emperors, and prime ministers, shook his head.

Al felt as though he'd been hit in the chest. He took a deep breath to control his anger.

"Defeat and death," he repeated and weighed each word.

326

"Some things are worse."

Al felt the energy, even the anger, drain from his body. The old man sat carelessly in the warm sun. Maybe he just doesn't get it, Al thought desperately. What's the word school counselors used? Empathize. Or maybe I'll just pitch a fit.

Instead Al forced himself to say evenly, "What would that be for instance?"

Merlin smiled.

Al decided it was the saddest smile he had ever seen.

Al found his voice. "Without some sort of help we don't stand a chance."

Merlin didn't answer. Al had almost given up when the old man said, "Maybe that's just how it's supposed to be."

Al didn't have an answer. No answer seemed possible. What am I supposed to do now?

Merlin stood and said, "Let's re-join the world."

They climbed down.

At the perimeter wall Sophie and Lumpy waited. Lumpy clutched his heavy spear. His eyes were bright. "Some kind of bug stomping," he said loudly, though his voice sounded more than a little strained.

"How about an encore?" Sophie asked. "Tomorrow would be great."

"Obligations are paid," Merlin answered quietly.

Sophie searched his face. "Do you see what's still out there?"

Merlin shook his head. "Indeed I do."

Sophie turned to Al. "He's joking, right? I don't care about this fate stuff. You can help us, can't you?"

I'm begging, Sophie thought. Listen to me. He's got to understand.

Instead Merlin shook his head again.

Sophie stepped back.

Al watched her face. What can I tell her? Anything hopeful would be a lie. She could tell I was lying and then she'd hate me always.

Al turned away.

The commander, with dented armor and bandaged head, stepped close. He carried a soot-blackened can, dumped some sticks on the ground, and got a hot fire going.

"Time for a victory celebration. That means a brew. Where you people come from-- you can't possibly know the joy. Mot in the open air." He dipped a cup into the brew, held it under his nose and steaming or not, took a long drink.

"Life is good," he muttered. He held up another cup. "Any takers?"

The younger ones murmured polite refusals. Merlin accepted a steaming cup. The commander poured himself a second. "No reason we can't enjoy life while we have it."

Merlin smiled, but his eyes followed Al as the boy wandered away and stood alone. Look how lonely he is, Merlin accused himself. He always ends up like this: alone and tormented. But it's very different this time. We're standing here, not back on the warm, green earth. That's the way the story has always been till now, a drama the way people like such things. I didn't tell him the other thing: fate is

328

not all. There is simple, dyed-in-the wool personal failure. If I were young, crazy young, that would be my concern.

In his mind Merlin retraced the events back on earth. Did I hurry too much? I was tired and angry. I've become so much like them that I always think anything is possible. Muddle hope with a little imagination and cocky self-confidence, no matter what you've experience before, and you have one, upright, breathing human person. Help me, but I am afraid I am just about one of them. But I don't think it's made any difference. I am blind. I was blind then and I blind now.

Merlin took a long, bitter, scalding drink.

Chapter 42

Sophie watched Al wander away. He rested his hand on the pommel of the stained sword hanging from his belt and began to tour the line of warriors. All were exhausted, but they lifted their heads when Al approached. Al said something encouraging and they answered back with the same polite nothings.

Look at him, Sophie thought: he reminds me of my Dad after he lost his first business. Leave your father alone, Mother warned me, but that was just money and personal pride. This is so much more -- this is what it must mean to have the whole world on your shoulders. A few days ago I just wanted him to take me out. He didn't know anything. I didn't either. A milkshake and a nap aren't going to fix things. Sorry, Mother. If somehow I even get back. I don't know what to do---but wait: that isn't exactly right. There's always an answer. A voice inside will tell me what to do. They promised me.

The commander dipped his mug into the bubbling concoction and drew out a third cup and slurped noisily.

"A simple, pure joy," he beamed.

Sophie managed a half-smile for him. What about tomorrow?, she asked herself. Fear felt like a stone in her stomach. Even the commander -- all he can do is smile.

Sophie slipped away. Al was already wandering in her direction. He studied the ground. Not a great sign, Sophie decided. Not even a good one. The commander is pretending nothing is going to happen. What about what my stomach is telling me? Al: he's finished with his walk. He can't give me anything more. I know why: it's called the truth.

Al scraped the ground with his boot. I can't call it the earth, he reminded himself, as he scraped the bluish surface. It can't call it earth for a good reason. But it is home in one way. Here is a planet shaped like a ball, pretty much, and we have a sun, even if it too big and pale; and trees of some type or another, a sky, grass, animals (okay: add dragons) people, some of them quite funny, and fortresses and enemies and war.

Just like home.

A little bit anyway.

Al kicked at the ground. The Jin-- when the returned they'll come on like a flood. We were saved today, but not by what we did. I can hope-- maybe tomorrow the ground will split open and the swallow them. It's just unlikely.

Think.

Tomorrow and tomorrow and tomorrow – tomorrow is everything. You've only got one thing you can do:

Think.

The mounts: maybe Igor or Merlin can call them back. But how'd that work? Could they land in our perimeter? How many abreast? Three or four. Ten or fifteen might land at a time. Give it five minutes to get fifteen of our people lifted out. Total time: a couple of hours. That doesn't include the wounded. All during that time I would be pulling warriors off the walls. Who would be last? It wouldn't matter: the walls would be overrun long before that. How many could I get away? A few hundred. Save a few – that's better than nothing.

Suddenly Al felt cold. How would I pick? The wounded would slow everyone down. I don't think they'd leave their wounded. Maybe I could save just a few, enough to live and tell the story. Of course, that would include Sophie and Lumpy. Maybe they could get home and tell the story. Somebody's got to return home and warn our people. That's the reason they'd be the first out.

I can't think like that.

Al took a deep breath. The air, even now, smells like cinnamon. . The night sky -- it's more purple than black. It's never really dark. This close to the center of the galaxy too many stars glow close together to let the night stay very dark.

Think.

The families at the fortress – what will happen to them? They won't stand a chance. Mordred will deal with them when and how he wants.

The place: the talisman.

Mordred will have all the time in universe to find it. He will, eventually. In many ways, it couldn't be easier. We lose everything. That isn't complicated at all.

Al glanced up and realized that he'd wandered to the edge of the perimeter. He turned around and returned to the camp. He slowed his walk to appear calm. There were no fires. No one made a sound. Each warrior – those unwounded anyway – slept at his place in the wall, wrapped in a blanket, with his personal weapons close by.

Al felt a warm hand on his shoulder. Sophie stood beside him. "Got you a present." She held up a stone cup of steaming mat.

Al wrinkled his nose. He took a sip, despite the smell. At least it was hot and, somehow, almost tasty. He wasn't sure how to describe it, but he was alive to drink it.

"A penny for your thoughts," Sophie said.

"Hmmm?"

"My Dad says it whenever he wants to pry."

"You're prying?"

"I hope so. How bad is it?"

"Not that bad."

"That's not even close. Everybody else is scared to death."

"I'm working on it," Al lied.

He couldn't look into Sophie's face. He turned to look at the camp; the commander still poked at his cooking fire as if that were the most important thing in the world. Lumpy sat on an ancient stone, propped upright by his spear and snoring.

The commander stepped away from his fire. "We await your orders."

"I don't have any. Not yet." Al saw Merlin close by and grabbed the old man's shoulder. "I need your help."

They walked away from the fire. Al waited till he thought they stood a safe distance away. He turned to Merlin. "I'm out of places to turn. I don't want to play fair. What can you do for me?"

"For you alone?"

"You know what I mean?"

"I'm afraid I do."

"I know you're dead set against it --but I'll take anything. A blinding fog, a snowstorm, a plague of grasshoppers – on their side, of course. Maybe I'm just being crazy."

"Crazy isn't the word. But the answer is the same."

Al felt his face grow red. "Is this what you brought me here to do?"

"I didn't exactly bring you here. Things just happened."

"I've seen what you can do. Just some small thing."

Merlin shook his head.

"At least tell me why."

"You'll learn. It wouldn't make sense now."

Al clenched his jaw. Count slowly now, he demanded of himself, just like Wheezle insisted under these circumstances.

Al turned and walked away a few steps. He glanced back to see Merlin looking at the ground. He doesn't seem to know who I am anymore, Al fumed. Maybe he's under some sort of spell.

Maybe Mordred has gotten to him.

Maybe he's just old.

Merlin strolled closer and gave Al a pat on his arm and returned to the warm circle of the campfire. He sat on a rock by the snoring Lumpy and stared into the fire.

The flames began to die. The circle of light faded. The commander put down his spoon.

"Breakfast for tomorrow," he announced cheerily, shook out his thick blanket, leaned his back against another big stone, and wrapped himself up.

A chill wind blew from the lake and carried with it the scent of the Jin armies on the other side of the lake. Al shivered, imaging what the countryside would look like in the morning. Should I sleep? he asked himself. I don't want to sleep. I want to hold onto every second. Why doesn't everyone think like me? But I don't need to think this way. I need to stay awake and come up with answers. One idea didn't work. Okay. Tried A, now let's try B. Al turned away from the fire and walked away. The crunching of his footsteps sounded very loud.

Maybe's he's just getting old.

Al realized he was staring at the ground.

Maybe Merlin is the weaker. Once they were equals, but not anymore. Maybe, if they engaged in an out-and-out mutual war Merlin knows he'd lose. And, of course, every living thing on the planet would be friend or disintegrated, say for those two. Would that bother Mordred? Only if he didn't know that the old man is --old. Mordred can't take the chance to find out. Now think: Mordred will follow me. I don't know why. Unless I do and don't know it. Maybe I have my own powers, some even Merlin doesn't know. He created me or my fate anyway, but not everything.

Maybe I can just do something. Maybe I don't fully understand why I'm going to do it. I know it's going to happen. It's a journey to a place. Like it is for everyone. That's what I know and all I need to know.

He returned as quietly as he could.

I'm going to need a little time to rest.

He studied where his friends had ended up sleeping, each propped against the remains of a stone wall. Sophie was the nearest. Her legs were curled and she was frowning. Sometimes she sighed, and sniffed and stirred, but she didn't open her eyes. Al sat beside her and closed his eyes.

I'll need time. I don't have much. That's all I've been doing since we got here -- buying time. Maybe we should have just gotten it over with early, but that's not how it works. We'll fight like demons for just another minute.

Al felt his heart pound. From now on I don't want to waste a second. I'd love to have every second I've wasted in my life. I'd love to be home, wake up in the morning to Wheezel's bossing and griping and have her morning waffles. She cooked like a lunchroom lady. It'd still be delicious. I'd always turn in my homework. I'd be nice to everyone, even the football players and I'd be especially nice to Wheezle, for everything she did for all of us –

Sophie.

How'd I get her involved? That wasn't my intention. She followed me. That's everything, I know. I want her here, but I don't. I wish she was home, waiting. I know that isn't what she wants; it's what I want.

The night suddenly turned colder. Al began shivering. The twin moons rose from their opposite sides of the sky.

Al found a scrap paper and scratched out a note for Merlin using a graphite pencil he'd found in his pocket. He folded the letter, quietly stood, and slipped the folded scrap into Merlin's robe.

The old man didn't move. Neither did anyone else. The sky began to lighten. Al slipped away and began to climb the wall that had saved them yesterday. He picked his way through the awful mess and litter of the battlefield. He stopped: on the far side of the lake, a big, two-legged Jin rider splashed to the edge of the lake.

Its passenger--Mordred.

Al crouched and waited. Mordred's head was bare. He wore no armor at all. He led the creature to the nearest causeway and, after glancing left and right, crossed the bridge.

Modred alone: why? What's important to him? He forced his mount to pick its way across the carnage on the causeway. Look how nervous he is, Al thought: Watch him glance around. Is he trying to count how many of us are still alive?

I know what he wants.

Mordred stopped and swept his eyes across the field.

I won't flinch Al promised himself and felt his hands tremble anyway.

Mordred settled back on his mount. He turned away and let it splash back over the causeway until they rode on the dry ground of the low hills.

Al turned away. He climbed off the wall and back to the shadows. He took a thick blanket and enough ambrosia for a few days, and a broken spear blade. He wrapped up the ambrosia and spear into a blanket, tied up the blanket at both ends, and carried it across his shoulder. The old sword Excalibur he strapped across his back.

He climbed the wall behind the pyramids. Just behind the wall, high, crumbling cliffs rose and formed a deep U. The Jin couldn't attack for that direction; if they could, Al realized, we wouldn't have lasted ten minutes.

The rising sun showed a wall of narrow ledges, gullies and thickets of tough flowering vines. Al studied the cliffs as long as he could. I've never climbed anything worse than a flight of stairs, he told himself. He studied the way up from one angle, then the other: it didn't help. The cliffs still looked as dizzyingly high as the steeple on Tintangle courthouse square.

Never look down. Al had heard that about climbing more than once. He'd watched a TV program about climbing thousand-foot cliffs in the Rockies. Keep three points on the cliff face, the narrator demanded, and know your equipment. Be sure to take training from a certified instructor and never climb alone.

Well, Al sighed to himself, three for zero is consistent, at least.

He stepped up to a ledge that cut deep into the cliff face. One foot up, then the other, grab with the free hand and pull-pull-pull. Push upward with the other leg. Repeat with the other leg and the other hand. Work steadily upward, like a sand crab gone vertical.

The process worked well enough as long as the cliff bowed inward and Al could scrabble for handholds on the crumbling rock. TV lessons never mentioned exhaustion. Al had never thought of gravity as a terrible thing, at least not until then.

The second lesson was true enough-- never look down.

338

He kept his head up and facing the blessed top of the cliff that never seemed to be getting any closer. After an hour or so he guessed he'd made it halfway up. But the next dozen yards were over harder stone and the handholds were much tougher to find. The vines didn't grow there either. The rock felt hard and sharp; flaking mineral chips got into his eyes.

Al managed an especially scary up-and-over crawl and found himself weakly balanced on a ledge little wider than his feet. Above, another outcropping protruded like a fat nose. He glanced in all directions. Here's something they didn't cover, he thought; I can't climb up, down, or sideways. Maybe if I had a few hundred yards of rope and lots of jangling climbing gear and a partner. Maybe I'd have a chance then – not much of a chance, but more than I have now, which is zilch.

Mordred won't be able to find me. Isn't that sweet? Neither will anyone else. And I did it all myself.

He took three very deep breaths and leapt for the tip of the nose.

He dug his fingers into crumbling shale and kicked as hard as he ever had. His legs flayed in empty air. His fingers began to slide down the rock. He kicked and kicked and glanced down despite himself and saw the long tumble down and squeezed his eyes shut.

It tickled his nose. His eyes popped open.

He stared at the frayed end of a rope. Someone at the top of the cliff wiggled it so that the frayed bits tickled his nose.

Al yelled a few words he knew he shouldn't have and, blinded by the rope jangling in his face, let go of the nose and grabbed for the rope.

His right hand caught empty air. The left one closed around rough fibers. He grabbed with both hands and held on so hard that his fingers bled. He felt tremendous weight as his body swung in the open air.

At that instant someone above yanked the rope- - hard. Al bounced up the cliff.

He bounced over the lip. The tumble knocked out his breath. Al lay on the rock and tried to breathe as the world faded in and out. He heard feet padding close.

Sophie dropped to her knees and grabbed his head. Lumpy appeared in his sight.

"Like a duck hit on the head," Lumpy answered.

I'm not quacking, Al thought. He clenched his jaw, spat out a few loose pebbles and demanded, as best he could, "Who yanked the rope?"

He felt his friends lift him and propped him against a rock. Rocks, he groaned inwardly. The world whirled and whirled until it gradually came into focus. Merlin, Sophie, and Lumpy were each frowning and staring into his face.

"What are you doing? Al began, "I mean, how'd would find – "

Lumpy nodded toward Merlin.

"Why didn't you take rope with you, son?" Merlin asked quietly.

"Rope? Who knew?" Al glanced at Merlin. "You didn't read my note?"

"Indeed I did. But there were no takers."

"Couldn't you make them?"

"I'm afraid not."

"What am I supposed to do now?"

Sophie sat beside Merlin. She took Al's hands. "Feeling better?" she asked sweetly.

Al blinked and felt himself begin to blush. Suddenly Sophie grabbed Al's little right-hand finger and bent it back as far as she could. Al howled. She let him flop for a few long seconds before she let go and starred in his watering eyes. "Know what that was all about?"

"You've gone loony." Al moaned.

She threw his hands down. "You don't do this to people who ...you just don't ."

Lumpy blushed. Merlin coughed.

Sophie stood with her back to everyone and began coiling rope. "Did you even know where you were headed?" she asked, not even bothering to turn around. .

Al glanced at Merlin, who shrugged. "Better answer."

Al stood and pointed. "That way."

Sophie, without a word, struck out alone. Lumpy glanced at Al and Merlin, and, when they didn't move, hurried after Sophie.

Al called out," You're headed the wrong way!"

He pointed a few degrees to the south where it didn't seem they'd want to go – toward twin, looming, smoking black volcanoes that dominated the jumbled horizon of mountains.

Lumpy stopped. Sophie headed where Al pointed. She called over her shoulder, "That's more like it!"

Al, and Lumpy and Merlin looked at each other. Merlin shrugged. Al managed to get to his feet and hobbled as fast as he could down the rough trail toward the rumbling mountains.

Chapter 43

Al didn't speak for a long time. He kept his head down and drove ahead as best he could. The landscape rolled steadily upward. The forage and flowers grew only ankle-high. The flowers were beautifully white and blue; here and there they past families of twisted trees with leaves as big as umbrellas.

The sky turned bright and warm. Sophie, who stayed in the front, turned her head once to ask where exactly they were. Merlin began to answer that he had no idea when black, whirling shapes caught his eye.

The specks quickly resolved into hissing, midnight-black flying Jin with especially large, gawking, all-seeing eyes. Sophie and Lumpy and Merlin ducked beneath of a stand of the big-leaved trees. Lumpy began stringing a short bow he carried across his back.

Al, though, scrambled up a pile of boulders and stood high for all to see. He faced the valley they'd just left.

The winged Jin didn't attack. Five whirled around Al's head, just out swatting range, screeching and hissing in delight that they'd found their prey. Lumpy finished stringing his bow and crept closer for a clear shot. Merlin grabbed Lumpy's arm.

"Hold off," Merlin growled.

The Jin keeled and spat and hissed a few more times around Al's head, turned on their leathery wings and glided away.

Al didn't move. Sophie hurried from under cover and climbed the rocks to stand beside him. Al's focused on the smoky horizon of the valley and the lake.

"What's the problem?" Sophie asked.

Al paid no attention. Maybe, Sophie thought, he's finally lost his marbles. It's bound to happen. My mother thought it happened to my father a long time ago. Sophie pulled at his arm. "I'm going to help you now. Easy does it."

Al felt the tug on his arm. He yanked his arm away. I'm standing in two places at the same time, he thought. It can be done, because I just experienced it. My eyes are following the midnight Jin as they swirl down into the valley and the hills on the far side of the lake.

Mordred: he's wearing black armor and a blood-red cape so that all would know him. Behind him, his great army spread out as far as anyone can see. They're milling about, waiting to be told what to do, but Mordred doesn't seem to care. The Jin that circled my head are circling him as well. He's looking up and using their eyes to gaze directly into mine.

I won't look away. He's smiling, but it is poison. He knows where I am. He can't help it.

Mordred whips his mount into a rage and rides it back and forth. He raised his sword and called to the countless creatures behind him. The winged Jin turned quick as a shadow. Their screeching echoed across the valley and up the cliffs and over the rough fall of boulders where Al and Sophie stood.

Sophie shaded her eyes with her hand. She saw the Jin host darkened the shallow valley and the low hills below them. Rather than swarm across the lake and the causeways and overwhelm the thin line of the warriors, the Jin attacked the low cliffs farther from the lake. There cliffs rose gently, much different than the one near the causeways. A cloud of choking red dust boiled up; the army began scurrying up the lowest reaches.

Lumpy and Merlin climbed the boulders.

"What's the plan?" Lumpy asked. "Where do we hide?"

"I don't think that's the idea at all," Sophie answered.

"I suggest that we get the heck out of Dodge," Merlin said.

He didn't need to explain. The dust cloud topped the cliff. Al glanced over his shoulder. He guessed the cliff was an hour's walk away. And the Jin weren't walking. They were coming fast. How could they? Al asked himself. How could they come so fast?

The friends jumped to the ground and ran. They ran for their lives. Every piece of unnecessary equipment they tossed away -- a helmet, Lumpy's bow-and-arrow, their water gourds, and coils of rope -- all went into the brush.

The cawing, gliding Jin circled overhead again. For the first few miles they easily followed Al and his friends. The grass, never more than waist high, offered no place to hide.

Al didn't look back. Neither did anyone else. They knew what hurried a few miles behind. Al listened. He couldn't help it: he heard the huff and puff and heavy footfalls of his friends.

Gradually they began to spread out. Sophie took the lead. Al remembered she'd run track at school and now her running showed it. Lumpy disappeared behind him. In a little while Al only heard his own feet pounding the ground. What about the old man? Al worried. How's he going to do this? My lungs are burning--

Somebody behind Al crashed through the dry brush. Al stopped and turned. Lumpy lay on the ground. His face was strawberry pink and strangely white around his mouth. "That's it for me," he gasped.

Al glanced up. Sophie appeared at his elbow. Sweat dripped from her chin. Merlin stumbled close. The old man trembled. He bent forward and rested his hands against his knees.

"They're very close and angry ," the old man managed.

"Don't care" Lumpy gasp.

"I'm not kidding," Al rasp and wished they'd kept just one last swallow of water.

Lumpy pushed himself off the ground. "I'm not doing this. Just remember that."

He began a pitifully slow trot down the trail. One by one the others followed him.

Nobody knows where I'm going, Al thought. But I know...listen to me: I sound like Ms. Filtzer, my graduation coach. You'd be proud of me if you were here and didn't die of fright first. But then I don't know exactly where I'm going. I don't. This will be the end for all of us. Maybe this is the way it's supposed to be. I can't think that way. But why else would am I able to think it?

Al was still fretting when the landscape dropped away. Sophie, ahead again, whistled. Now, closer to the mountain slopes, steep canyons cut into the prairie. Fast streams, gushing off the mountain slopes, had carved steep arroyos into the hard earth. But unlike the prairie, the canyon had let dense stands of big-leaved trees grow.

Sophie disappeared into a canyon first. Al followed. Lumpy and Merlin crashed into the foliage behind him. Huge leaves made a green-yellow shade; stream purled through the narrow valley floor. No one spoke. They took long drinks with their faces in the water.

Al rolled over onto his back and squinted at the sky. The flying Jin began crying sharply to each other and crisscrossing the sky.

"Not too much farther," Al said a little too loudly. "I think we're about to lose our friends upstairs."

"Maybe for a little while," Sophie answered.

Merlin washed his face. "Maybe we can gain a little time. Sometimes that's all it takes."

Al glanced at Merlin. The old man seems happy with that thought, Al thought, but look how frail he looks. What if he doesn't make it? Can he die like the rest of us? If so, what do we do then?

Al cleared his throat. "There's a lot of real estate out there. Maybe we can get off the trail and hide out for a few days. Maybe they'll get lost. Literally"

"Looks like they're about a zillion. How are they going to just get lost?" Sophie asked.

"I bet they're no more than a hundred thousand," Lumpy replied nervously.

"I stand by my guess," Sophie sniffed.

"Hiding. It's not bad plan," Merlin said quietly.

Al glanced at his friends. Look how slowly we move. Look how tired we are. Hiding may be the only way. I can't decide right now. Let me worry about one more thing. "What do you think happened with our people? Do you think all of those things are after just us?"

"The fields were empty," Merlin said, "I left instructions in your name. The commander was to call in the mounts and get out of there. Return to their fortress, prepare for the worst but keep hoping of course."

Al swallowed. "What did you tell them about me? Do they think-- "

"Nobody questioned."

They stood, gathering what little they still carried. The water made us a little stronger, Al told himself, but we're pretty much done for. They aren't going to make it much farther.

Neither am I.

Al looked toward the two volcanoes and closed his eyes. Think, he repeated to himself over and over. He began to feel something. I'm not sure what, or where it's coming from. Maybe I'm just desperate. But we've come an incredibly long way. Something has to be right and fair. But I know it's more than just a notion and it's there.

Between the volcanoes Al saw a low cliff, and below the cliff, not more than a mile away, a narrow valley.

There, he told himself.

"Hurry," Al commanded, "Just a little more."

Merlin leaned forward. "Now are you sure? I don't think we'll have another chance. They're too close now."

Al glanced at Merlin sharply.

"It's there."

The path wasn't easy; the roots and trees slowed them. Al listened as he climbed steadily, but the flying Jin seemed to have given up. Now and then he thought he might have heard a frantic cawing, but he wasn't sure. If they don't know, then Mordred doesn't know either. These mountains go on for hundreds of miles. He won't know anything unless I show him.

Eventually Al saw the high cliffs a few hundred yards away colored in swirls of grey and black. Al realized he was looking the entrance to a huge cave.

His heart pounded.

Sophie and Lumpy waited. Al tried to make his voice sound steady. "It's going to be dangerous just crossing between here and there. Eyes in the sky and all."

The field was open to the hot sun and overgrown with vines that seemed ready to trip them. They didn't run. Al remembered reading that predators' eyes naturally followed quick movement. They moved steadily and glanced over their shoulders every few seconds.

They reached the end of the field. They stood quietly at the entrance; it felt cool and dry, not dank at all. The entrance was sandy and smooth.

Sophie rested her hand against the rock. "Look here. Caves back home are usually made when water dissolves limestone. The results are pretty ragged. But this is wall has been deliberately cut. And from the inside out."

A studied the wall. He decided Sophie was right. Long cuts ran in parallel lines along the stone walls. Sophie brushed her foot along the sandy ground. "Easy on the traveling shoes. Smooth and easy, a path big enough for an army."

"Or something just plain big," Lumpy observed. He squinted deep into the cave and walked a few yards farther into the darkness. "I think somebody left a light on."

"What are you talking about?" Sophie asked.

"Look yourself. Way down there."

Al tried to let his eyes adjust to the dark. He felt Merlin's eyes on his back.

Sophie elbowed past Al. "There is a light. Maybe it's not too far." Sophie tugged at Al's arm. "You and me."

Al felt his heart even beat faster. "No way."

She narrowed her eyes. "What do you mean?"

"I mean we don't know – I mean somebody needs to be in charge back here." Al glanced at Merlin, who was looking the other way. He thought of a bright idea. "I travel faster by myself."

But Sophie had already turned away and stood rocking on her heels in the bright sun.

"Keep an eye on her," Al muttered to Lumpy, who wasn't listening.

He turned and disappeared deeper into the cave. He'd always hated caves. This cave was much like the other, just much larger, with the feeling that tons and tons of rock were smashing in from all sides. Then, too, there was the deep, deep, dead silence. But there were differences, too. The floor remained even and sandy, the walls smooth.

Al stepped softly. The farther he went, the more carefully he padded along. The darkness gathered; the light from the entrance, large as it was, gradually faded.

Al began using his hands to grope along the wall. After another few minutes he blinked: the heavy felt boots he'd borrowed from the warriors were covered with a fine layer of glittering dust – and the dust glowed like jewels. The cave began to curve away from the entrance and suddenly became dusky-dark.

A sighing sound came from directly ahead. A reddish-orange glowed from glittering veins in the rock. By then the sighing became a little louder, a wistful, even mourning sound.

A different sound came from behind Al, but it was very distant and he wasn't sure if it was just his imagination: a crashing that died quickly. Al considered turning around, but thought: If I leave now I may never come back.

He heard a third sound, the rush of cascading water. It wasn't threatening; suddenly, Al, just as he let out a breath, stood there.

A cathedral.

Al had only seen photos of the immense churches and their aspiring lines of stone that reached skyward. The roof soared as high as Al could see in the quiet light. Ten, fifteen stories high, he decided. The veins of glowing rock swirled higher and higher. Al guessed the floor of the cathedral covered two acres, as big as the town where he'd lived all his life. The floor was sand, about an inch deep and smooth and untouched, Al imagined, as long as there have been people, or dinosaurs or bugs swimming in the ancient seas. "Crazy," Al whispered aloud just to hear his voice, "just like everything else around here."

The sound of the cascading water came across clearly. At first Al couldn't see the source; the thin light from the rocks didn't penetrate very far. He began to trace the sound as best he could. He kept constantly to his right and counted a hundred steps as he padded ahead.

He glanced up and for a few seconds forgot his fear. He saw the source of the splashing: a curtain of water, shimmering as it tumbled into a pool some thirty yards wide. Al guessed it was water; it was liquid at least, and shimmered with every color he could imagine

Al felt his hands clench; he didn't understand why and decided that a forgotten part of his mind was reacting to what it saw. The feelings, a mixture of fear and hope, flooded his mind. What am I going to see? What do I already know?

And why?

A chest-high stone wall surrounded the pool. Al peered over the edge.

At first he didn't understand what he saw. The liquid swirled into the pool as it cascaded from the waterfall. But the pool had no outlet. The liquid thundered into the pool and vanished. He closed his eyes, counted to ten, and looked closer. He studied what he saw for a long time. I know where it goes now, he thought: It falls as rain.

Al peered through the shallow pool; where he would expect to see rock he saw a bluish-green sky, complete with thin clouds. Below the sky, he saw a landscape of rolling hills and scattered clumps of silvery trees.

Another world, Al told himself, if I'm not being made to see things. And I'm not. I know that much. What do I know about this place?

He watched the world slowly revolve below and, as he did, the tension and fear he'd know dissolved. Back home, sometimes he and the others had been carried off to churches for soul-saving: A gift to be simple, A gift to be free -- Al remembered the words to one song he actually liked. Now they were the right words. Free, he thought, to go where and be what? An answer came back: Here and be who you've always been.

I don't want to leave, he thought. I'm this close. I've never had an answer till now. I don't know what to.

But that isn't true. I know exactly what to do.

He climbed on top of the wall. He stood for long seconds, a man on a ledge.

He closed his eyes.

He leaned forward.

Very easy to do –

Someone called him.

--From very far away. So far it could be his imagination. From the distant entrance to the cave came a heavy clattering and animal snarling and crying out. Al knew very well who was calling out his name. He jumped to the ground and ran. His feet left deep funnels in the sand. Faster, he demanded from his heart and lungs, but he seemed to be standing still. He didn't cry out; that would be wasting breath. He ran and he ran and ran until he hoped his heart would burst.

354

Chapter 44

He knew an instant before he saw.

They were quiet as Al emerged from the cave. Al saw everything all at once. The detachment of mounted Jinn, fifty or so, rested in the thin shade of the trees. Lumpy and Sophie sat on a blanket, unbound.

Behind them -- Mordred. He stood, one leg propped on the low crook of a tree trunk, a crimson cloak still around his shoulders. His death's head uniform of midnight black and silver was dusty. Mordred's hair was sweat-matted. But look, Al thought; he isn't looking at me.

Al stopped. Merlin: where? Maybe he got away. But Al shivered and followed Mordred's line of sight. At the edge of the clearing Al saw a dark purple blanket covering a long form.

Al looked to his friends. They stared ahead and far away. Al forced himself to make the dozen steps. He barely managed it; the ground seemed to shift beneath his feet.

Merlin's face was barely covered. Look, Al told himself, he's so small and frail. How did he get to be so small? What's cheated him? But it's done. Al whispered aloud: It's done; it's done, done, done.

The world seemed unreal. Al felt that his entire body was numb. Somebody slipped close by and stood by Al's left shoulder.

"You failed," Mordred whispered.

Al turned to face Mordred. Al had never stood so close to the other one; eyes reddish and watery, a joyless and tired face.

"You killed him," Al said simply.

Sophie didn't leave their blanket. "They came over the hill. They didn't make a sound. If they had we'd --."

"Done what?" Mordred sneered.

"They grabbed everybody that quick. The old man tried to run, but they grabbed him. He went down. Limp. Like a rag doll. That's it"

Al shook his head to clear his mind and turned back to Mordred. "Let the other two go back where we came from. You've got everything you want."

Mordred made a mocking frown. "Really?" He leaned closer. "Did the old coot trust you with anything? Anything really special? No? You don't want to share? Well, then, I promise you it's barely begun."

"I want to bury him," Al said.

"Hold on now. Doesn't he look beautiful? Just waiting for a kiss from those that yet love him."

Al stood stock-still.

"Even I was surprised how easy he gave up. All I really had to do was wish it and it happened. See? Life is worth living, if you give it long enough. The wonderful thing, the longer he spent with your kind, the weaker he got. If he'd just remembered who he was I'd had real fight on my hands. But that's not how it went. His choice. Nobody made him weak. I am the one who defeated him. Therefore, I must be made happy. If I am to control myself."

"Whatever you want," Al said.

"That's the spirit. All I want from you – just accompany me inside this miserable hole in the ground. I know what you saw on the other end."

"It's just a cave."

Mordred shivered. "No. It can be a tomb. I know more than you. There are terrible risks, but wonderful rewards at the end."

"I said-- ."

Mordred's face suddenly brightened. Al shivered and asked himself: How could anyone go from such pale fear to crazy happiness so fast? It's like turning a light on and off.

"A beautiful day isn't it?" Mordred asked and squinted at the copper sky. "Nothing could be better."

Mordred lifted his nose slightly and took in the entire scene. He doesn't really even see us, Al decided.

Al realized he was clenching his fist over and over again. I'll make you pay; he thought it over and over and caught himself staring at Mordred's thin back. No, no, he warned himself, I've got to go slowly and understand. Watch and wait. Wait till he's forgotten about you, if just for seconds.

Mordred turned his gaze to the cave. He took a deep breath. What's he afraid of? Al thought. I'm going to find out. First we've got to get him started.

Al stepped closer to Mordred and began to unbuckle the leather scabbard that held Excalibur.

Al said, "This yours now."

Mordred grabbed for his own long, glittering sword.

Al said, "I just don't think I can handle the responsibility anymore."

"Liar!" Mordred hissed.

Mordred turned toward Sophie and Lumpy. His face was contorted with anger.

What did I do? Al thought frantically. He let Excalibur slide back into its sheath.

"However you want it," Al said loudly. "Okay by me."

Mordred's face began to relax. "Okay. An awful American word. I won't hold it against you this time."

Mordred grabbed Al's shoulders, turned him toward the cave and gave Al a hard shove.

"What about your smelly friends?" Al asked. "Am I supposed to trust them?"

"They're harmless. For a little while." Mordred turned and spoke in sharp sentence sharply to the Jin drowsing under the shade. Abruptly they sat up, confused, and retreated a few yards from Sophie and Lumpy.

Mordred gave Al another hard shove. "How many times do I have to tell you?"

Al felt the hair on the back of his neck rise and headed where he least wanted to be -- deeper and deeper into the cave.

358

Chapter 45

Mordred chanted and sang to himself. He's scared to death, Al thought. What's back here that frightens someone like him?

Al hurried just to make Mordred as uncomfortable as possible. The closer they got to the rock cathedral and the pool, the faster Al hurried. Mordred's breath become louder and shallow. Maybe he's no stronger than I am, he thought. Maybe he doesn't really know how to use that sword.

They arrived. Now the pool glowed with blues and reds and yellows and greens Mordred's face completely focused on the pool. His eyes gleamed.

"You did well," Mordred purred.

He studied the world turning majestically far below.

"Whatever that was," Al answered. He fixed his eyes on the back of Mordred's neck.

He whirled around to face Al. "How did you resist its call?"

"Don't know what you mean," Al lied.

Mordred began pacing along the wall. He kept his eyes on the pool. "Do you know why I let you-- ."

"Let me live?"

Mordred gave a weird, triangular grin. "So right! At the Tree I let you run around like a madman. I knew you were the right one. Old Merlin could do one thing -- winnow out the one and true prince!"

He turned and opened his arms out wide to embrace Al, who stepped away. Mordred swept past Al and began pacing and speaking quickly. "Your kind has lost so much to you science, your technology. No one has any idea where to go or what to do." He stopped. "And you? They don't love you. You've been forgotten. An orphan true and deep. How does that make you feel?"

Al turned away.

Mordred stepped closer. "But the calling. Can you deny it? A place you belong. Home. At endless, endless last."

Mordred's left hand -- he was left-handed--- reach toward his sword hilt. He stared into Al's face. "Why did they only call for you? I hear the call. But it's no more than an echo. Old Merlin gone. Don't you think he wanted to leave you? Who's left? You and me." Mordred took a deep breath. "However, you have done your duty. You have led me here. You can rest now."

Mordred stared full into Al's face. He followed Mordred's hand. It grasped the and pulled the blade free with a quick sssh of metal against leather.

Al whirled around, drawing Excalibur as he did. His sword blocked Mordred's heavier blade as he chopped down, again and again. Mordred's fury drove Al against the low wall. Al's sword arm already felt weak. He'd learned that sword fights actually didn't last long.

Somebody died quickly.

From the corner of his eye Al caught a blur: Sophie and Lumpy sprinting across the sand.

Mordred gasp. Al heard the sound exactly and lunged. Mordred knocked Excalibur aside. Lumpy,

360

his head low, tackled Mordred. Sophie hit around his knees. Mordred's sword flew from his hand and whirled into the pool

Lumpy was thrown through the air. He hit the ground with a brutal whoosh from his lungs. Sophie rolled across sand and tumbled against him. They struggled to untangle and stand. Al still held Excalibur. Mordred glanced once at Al, and fell over the wall.

Sophie managed to stand. She saw Al glance in her direction once. He didn't seem to see her at all. He sheathed Excalibur and, quick as Mordred and jumped over the wall.

She reached wall. She didn't understand what she saw below -- a world, even unlike the one where she stood. As she watched the sky, if that's all it was, became more opaque, even distant, as it began to fade and vanish.

Sophie climbed onto the wall.

Lumpy struggled to his feet. He opened his mouth to protest. From inside the tunnel, and very close by, came the snarling and trumpeting of Jin in full charge.

Lumpy hopped onto the wall. "I thought you said they wouldn't come this far!"

"So shoot me!" Sophie yelled.

The mob of Jin, howling and slobbering, erupted into the huge room.

Lumpy jumped.

Sophie went right after. She felt herself falling – at first. She spread her arms wide and let the air flow around. The sky below disappeared. That wasn't the right idea. It ceased to exist. A new feeling took over. She glanced down. Her fingers

began to dissolve. Her hands went next, then her
arms and legs. Her chest went last. She tried to cry
out, but even that was gone.

Chapter 46

She knew she was there. A quicksilver glimmer surrounded her. She suddenly felt all of her nerve endings came alive in the same instant.

Her lungs gasp. She felt herself tumbling down a steep embankment. She felt a solid thump and realized she was lying on her back.

She wasn't alone either. She heard Lump's voice crying out before he came cartwheeling down the slope. He landed all legs and arms with a solid second thump.

They lay on their backs for a few seconds. Lumpy saw that Sophie was squinting at the sky. Lumpy did the same. He saw streaks of purple, blue, green and orange, roiling and swirling, where he expected something like an earthly blue.

Storm warning. The thought came to Lumpy automatically. He pushed up on his elbows.

Sophie gasped.

Lumpy glanced skyward. A huge moon sailed through the angry sky. A roaring shook the ground. The sphere began to disintegrate, pulled apart like cotton candy, into long streams of dust and rock. A banshee howling replaced the bass rumbling. Rather than fall toward the ground, the remains twisted into what seemed to be thousand mile long tendrils. Up and up they flowed, higher and higher into the atmosphere until they disappeared.

"That makes me nervous," Lumpy finally said

"Very peculiar," Sophie answered, but that was all.

They stood slowly, testing their arms and legs for fractures and gashes. They silently studied the landscape. They saw a long valley formed by two lines of parallel, weathered hills. The hills ran about three miles apart. Trees, or some version of them, grew in the valley and along the low slopes, not thickly enough to make a forest, but enough to give shade.

The air was warm, dry, and Sophie, noticed as she took a deep breath, oxygen-rich. The tree-cousins rose up on scaly bark and spread out with curling limbs. The leaves, short and broad, a little like gingko leaves, Sophie noted, bloomed more yellow than green. Low plants, deep yellow, blues, and orange, grew from a burned soil.

Sophie wrenched away a fist-sized fragment from the ground. She pounded it apart against the boulder. The sound echoed against the nearest slopes.

"Shhh! You'll wake something up," Lumpy hissed.

"I don't think so."

"Really now?"

"Really. This isn't sedimentary rock. This is metamorphic, once upon a time. I've never seen anything like it. All I can guess is that it's old. The hills – they're crumbling, too, just like this rock. Look at this."

Sophie hopped off the boulder and began pushing over rocks half-buried in the ground.

Lumpy frowned. "Something's going to come out of those rocks and sting the fire out of you."

"What? Like termites or centipedes or beetles and spiders? She pushed over a last boulder and stood up. "I've got nothing. I mean, actually, we've got nothing." Sophie rubbed her nose with the back of her hand. "I don't know…"

"I do. I've got the creeps, big time."

Sophie shivered. The boy is right, she thought, but I can't say exactly why. The air is good – great, actually – but that's always meant no people back home. And this is like home, but not quite. I shouldn't be surprised. Nothing should surprise me anymore. What'd we learn in biology? Evolution only has so many solutions to making life. Fifty species evolved eyes, minimum. At least this place is alive. At least we're alive. I should count our blessings. At least we're-- .

The sky roared again. A fleet of meteors sizzled through the highest quadrant of the sky and bounced back into the outer space.

"Cloudy with a chance of getting your brains bashed out," Lumpy fumed. He stood and brushed off his pants. "Got to find the man. Where do you think he's hiding?" He glanced over his shoulder. "Nobody that way." He kicked at the ground. "Look like a path going uphill. Maybe this goes somewhere. Whatch say?"

Sophie shrugged. She had no idea. They began hiking quickly uphill. She spoke quickly, as if she was talking to herself. "Look at things. Why are we here? We found this place. How likely is that? We're trailing after Mr. Al once again. Don't you think that maybe there's something bigger than us involved here? Maybe some huge plan?"

"I just want to get home," Lumpy answered. "And there's no good reason to go this way. I'm just going."

"What else have we got?"

Lumpy felt a chill. Sophie didn't seem sure either and she was sure about ninety-nine percent of everything. Anyway, Wheezle had always been suspicious of hope. Go for the thing you can get your hands on, she warned. But hope's all we've got, he told himself. Besides, these two heroes depend on yours truly. They're both flighty. No common sense.

"I am a rock," he muttered.

"What?" Sophie interjected.

Lumpy felt his face grow red. "I didn't say anything."

"You were mumbling."

Lumpy looked down and hurried ahead.

The landscape continued to rise slowly. The path wandered on and on as far as she could see. Whoever owns this place likes to hike, Sophie decided. I see no evidence of horses or animals of any kind. No wheels or wagons either.

Nothing.

Let's consider what's not here one more time: insects of any kinds, creatures in the sky, nothing else on the ground -- nothing reptilian or mammalian or any cousin of any sort.

There should be. There's plenty of oxygen in the air and warm temperatures. Somebody made this path a long, long time ago. They've got to be like us to make paths. Still, I see no sign of war or fire and earthquakes. Everything is just-- still. The plants aren't doing well either. They're stunted and dry. In another few years they'll dry up and blow away.

Everything.

Lumpy had rushed ahead. There wasn't a reason that Sophie could see, just a sudden burst of energy typical, she reminded herself, of boys this age. He sprinted almost to the top of the hill, a steep rise. He looked breathless and waved to Sophie. As he reached the top of the rise he stopped. By then he saw what waited on the far side of the hill. He didn't move. Sophie called his name. He sat on the ground.

Sophie ran as hard as she could. She reached the top of the rise and saw what waited. She didn't speak either. She sat on the ground beside Lumpy and closed her eyes, thinking over and over: What do I do now?

Chapter 47

It was a city. A very big city, like the Los Angles she remembered seeing as a kid from the hills above the valley. It was that big – with one big difference. This was a city of colors, buildings rising up in thin spires that gleamed as if even their walls were made of jewels – emeralds, rubies, yellow diamonds, and sapphires. She saw hundreds of spires that ended at seashore miles away.

Another thing: complete silence.

"We're cooked. We'll never find him in that haystack" Lumpy moaned.

"Are you kidding? Where else do you think he'd go? Sleep out in the cold?" She halfway believed it herself. She pulled Lumpy's hand. "Come on. I've got some ideas."

Lumpy got to his feet. "Like that's never happened."

Sophie admitted to herself that she hadn't a clue where to start looking for Al. Close to the city the roads seemed to be made of porcelain, or something like it. They were smooth like glass and curved among the buildings.

But she didn't see any signs telling what the buildings were for. The colors made the interiors opaque; she didn't see any doors either.

Nothing moved. Nothing living anyway. Couldn't be, Sophie decided, as she studied their feet. A very thin layer of dust lay on the porcelain. In fact, it covered everything.

"There you go," Sophie said. "We've got it now."

She pointed at the dust. "Anything that comes along is going leave a sign."

She pointed the tracks they were leaving in the dust. "Except they'll be ahead of us."

Lumpy frowned. "And great for anything that wants to follow us."

"I don't think we need to worry about that," Sophie said quietly.

They hiked silently for a long time. Sophie noticed, but didn't speak aloud about it: here and there she saw other building, smaller and crudely made compared to the spires. Some were fairly well made, a few stories high, build of cut stone and roofed with tiles. They seemed ancient, too and because they were built of cruder materials, they were much more broken down. They were fewer – many fewer than the spires. But here and there were even cruder places, tossed together, made of stones robbed from the bigger buildings. Shacks, Sophie thought, and that's being polite. Somebody, it seemed to her, didn't care anymore.

Or remember.

She saw the first footprint. Lumpy saw it at the same second – a track on the thin dust.

Lumpy grabbed her arm and jumped up and down. Sophie stuck her hand over his mouth, which reduced his enthusiasm. She let him go slowly.

"What!" He demanded.

Sophie grabbed him by the scruff and pointed at the footprints.

"What's the problem here?" She whispered fiercely.

Lumpy frowned. "Whoever made these prints is barefoot and has six toes. Live with a guy all your life and you never notice those things."

Sophie opened her mouth to tell him what they were going to do. But a storm began ripping through the sky. Strictly speaking, Sophie saw right away, it wasn't the sky, but the meteors that burned as they cascaded downward.

They struck the city. They struck at random, all sorts of different sizes. They struck with shrieks and roars. The spires, unbelievably tough, took the blows, most of the time, and shattered the meteors into exploding fire bombs.

The street around Sophie and Lumpy suddenly blazed. Thousands of meteor fragments, sizzling, skittering and flaming, filled the air. Sophie grabbed Lumpy, who grabbed her and together they fell onto the street. Lumpy tried to protect her with his lanky body. That made Sophie furious. She pushed him away. That didn't help. A big skinny, grey hand, with the longest and ugliest fingers she'd ever seen, grabbed her by the hair and dragged her over the smooth road. She cried out. Another hand grabbed Lumpy by the foot and pulled him along.

Sledded Sophie thought, as they got slithered across the road. She saw an equally ugly foot, almost as skinny and long as the hand, pry open what seemed to be a manhole and knock the cover aside.

The skinny man threw them down the hole. A rabbit hole, Sophie thought as they tumbled. They struck a slide, long as an old-fashioned amusement ride back home. They were dumped unceremoniously into a tunnel big enough for a

370

subway. A blue-green light glowed from the walls and ceilings.

The skinny man came sliding down the chute and rolled onto the floor. He scrambled to his feet. He was skinny to emaciated, with bulbous eyes, a carrot nose, and a grizzled, short beard. His huge feet and hands they'd already seen.

He wore faded clothes crudely woven and roughly sewn together.

"Merlin?" Lumpy squinted.

Sophie frowned. Lumpy was right. The similarities were there, except this would be an even more run-down model.

The lights flashed in sequence. The grey man -- Sophie didn't know what else to call him -- grabbed their hands and pulled them farther down the tunnel to a circle-shaped room. He shoved Lumpy and Sophie into the circle.

The lights changed colors and pattern in sequence as if, Sophie decided, they were communicating to each other. The grey man, nervous with excitement, perched on the edge of the edge of the circle.

"What's your problem?" Lumpy said loudly.

The grey man jumped up. The circle filled with light. A bluish haze filled the air.

Lumpy turned to Sophie. "What's next? Do I keep talking?"

"Keep talking," the grey man repeated.

"About what?" Sophie asked, though she was pretty sure.

"About what. Keep talking," The grey man repeated.

"Okay. We're going to sit now." She pulled Lumpy down to sit beside her and spoke to the grey man. "Did I ever tell you about my grandparents, who came from Romanian? Of course I didn't. In the fourth grade everyone thought I was a vampire. I convinced myself, so I stayed awake for a week straight…"

Sophie went through her life story, as best she could remember it, and she had a good memory. Lumpy glanced at her as if she was crazy. She spoke for half an hour. The grey man didn't move. He stared directly at her, seemingly entranced. Eventually she poked Lumpy in the ribs. "Now it's my friend's turn."

Lumpy cleared his throat. "What does he want to hear?"

Sophie poked him a little harder. "Anything."

"It's not polite to talk about yourself."

Sophie pinched him.

Lumpy jumped and began. Once started he went, as Sophie noted, he took off a mile a minute. Lots of vocabulary and everyday expressions. It'd help if he didn't swallow so much, though.

He didn't stop for an hour, Sophie guessed. The grey man finally raised his hand. "That's quite enough, friends."

Lumpy whispered to Sophie. "He's been holding out on us."

Sophie shook her head. "He's been to school." She looked up to the grey man. "Isn't that right?"

"You're right on the money, sister." He seemed pleased with himself and spoke in a musical voice.

"You say he just learned American ? That quick? I failed Spanish three times."

372

"With help," Sophie said. She nodded toward the bluish light that surrounded them. "Think: we learn how to throw a baseball in a few minutes, learn a song after a single time on the radio. Maybe someone else similar us but not exactly the same...with the right software, if that's what it is, can pick up a language pronto. That's what this entire space is for."

"We can ask him anything?" Lumpy frowned.

"Fire away," The grey man answered.

"What's your name?" Lumpy asked.

The grey man looked away. "Failure to launch. Once upon a time maybe I had a handle, but I can't bring it up."

"Didn't you have parents? A social worker? Somebody?"

"Long gone."

"Where'd everybody go?" Lumpy asked. "Are they hiding out somewhere?"

The grey man looked down. "Gone west...Bought the farm."

"All at once?" Lumpy asked. "Was it the water?"

"Don't be funny," Sophie grumbled.

"It's how I deal with anxiety," Lumpy grumbled back.

Sophie said carefully, "It happened over a very long time, didn't it? Fewer and fewer of your type each generation. Maybe you are among the last."

"Last of the many," the grey man said quietly.

"We need to know more. A lot more. We have...friends... here. Who built this place? How can we use what they knew to find them? We need help. Before...you know what I mean."

The grey man hung his head. Suddenly his head jerked up and, bright- eyed, he hopped into the circle, grabbed Sophie and Lumpy by the arm and pulled them along a short distance to another wide room with low ceilings. The lights in ever changing colors and patterns followed their path.

"Have a sit," he insisted. "Sorry. No snacks on this flight."

They sat on the cool floor. Balls of light appeared – seven at a time, Sophie counted – gathered above their heads, whirled around and around, and shifted a few yards away. The light combined and whirled faster and faster until they formed a vortex. A shape began to appear. The vortex dissolved and in its place, a woman appeared, perfectly formed with gleaming teeth, a lime-green dress and a necklace of pearls. She opened her eyes – the only imperfection, Sophie noted; they were deep golden.

"I am your docent." Her voice was smooth and alto.

"Our what?" Lumpy frowned.

"Our guide." Sophie answered.

"That had to come out of your head," Lumpy sighed. He raised his hand. "Are those pearls real?"

Sophie rolled her eyes. "Ignore him."

"You are equals," The docent purred.

"She's a genius." Lumpy beamed.

Sophie stood. "Nothing's perfect...we have important questions. One: where are we?"

"Of course," the docent answered. "Anticipated."

She stood and soundlessly crossed the floor. She made small motions with her hands and arms.

The lights all around responded. Shapes appeared that filled the space around them, translucent and sparkling. Sophie began to walk within it. "A star map," she whispered.

There were, she realized, at least three dimensions. The bright speckles of light were galaxies, she discovered, and could explore them in seemingly endless detail. She stopped. "Something's wrong. No – I mean different."

The docent smiled. "You are ready to know."

"Birds and the bees," Lumpy sighed.

"You insist on knowing. That is why you created me."

"You are afraid. I will inform you directly."

The map began to show other star maps, just a few seconds for each. And each was different, sometimes only a little, but some seemed violent, and filled with storms.

"The stars number trillions in each universe."

"Each," Sophie marveled.

"As there are trillions of stars, so there are universes."

"Multiple universes? We suspected that back home." Her eyes were bright. She explored the miniature galaxies and suddenly stopped. "It's where we are now. Another universe."

She stopped and studied the wall for a long moment. Finally she looked at Lumpy.

He shrugged. "So? What else can go wrong?"

Sophie turned to their docent. "Let me tell explain it."

Sophie imitated the docent, manipulating the map and moving among the galaxies. The galaxies gleamed and twisted into new shapes again and again.

"What's the problem?" Lumpy asked.

"No problem," Sophie replied. "It's just history."

"I don't see little men riding around and waving swords."

"You won't. This is the other history."

The galaxies began to fall apart and meet in a common center. In seconds they formed a tiny point of light so brilliant that Lumpy shielded his eyes.

"Everything has a start. Common sense isn't wrong for once." Sophie said.

The pinpoint of light exploded. A sphere of translucent colors spread outward and became a breath-taking shower of tiny stars which, in turn, swirled into galaxies as they had before."

"But with a beginning--." She said quietly.

"Comes an end," Lumpy answered even quieter.

The galaxies slowly, then much more quickly, rushed toward the center. The pinpoint – less than a pinpoint – burned as brilliantly as before.

"How would somebody know that's happening? The comets and such would rain down, and they'd feel earthquakes and no telling what else. But they'd know. And they'd hide in rabbit holes …like this. Do you think I didn't notice? It's common sense. And heaven knows I've got plenty of that." Lumpy looked at his hands. "How much longer have we got?"

"It is imminent," The docent answered. She never lost her smile.

"Okay. Is there a reason we got picked for the honors?"

"Do you actually need an answer?" The docent asked.

"It would help." Lumpy said.

"I don't understand. How would that help?"

"It just doesn't translate well," Sophie insisted. "Unless why could tell us how and maybe we could do something about it."

"and then we'd get home," Lumpy added.

"Impossible," The docent answered.

Sophie narrowed her eyes. "We'll see about that. How about plan B?

Lumpy raised his fist. "Right on. Whatever that might be."

Sophie turned to the grey man. "Okay. What about the other one- -the one who looks like me and got here first. We need to find him. To do that answer a few questions: He belongs here doesn't he? What does he want?"

The grey man blinked. "What everyone wants?"

Sophie turned to the docent, who began manipulating the map so quickly that Sophie couldn't follow her. The map filled the room. Galaxies appeared and rushed past. Soon only two galaxies remained; one elliptical, the other a spiral. They drifted toward each other and, as they watched, collided.

They exploded with such ferocity that Sophie gasped. A quick snap, more like a welder's torch, burst from the new epicenter. The map whirled and vanished.

Darkness remained for seconds. A tiny, brilliant arch appeared above. Sophie barely found time to register it before another explosion nearly blinded her. Another orb gleaming with a thousand colors blossomed outward. A shower of pinpoints of light swarmed outward as they'd just seen. Islands of stars gathered and sped outward. Sophie stepped into the map. She selected one galaxy that seemed to be heading directly for. She expanded the map until that galaxy filled the room.

From one of the spiral galaxy's arms she selected a medium yellow star with eight planets. Lumpy stood and stepped into the map. A warm aquamarine planet appeared, flecked with swirling clouds.

"I want to go home," Lumpy said quietly. "What have they done with it?"

"They created it," Sophie answered quickly . "Not deliberately. Do you get what we just saw?"

Lumpy hated when she got excited. She got there quickly, waving her arms as if she was conducting an orchestra, eyes big as eggs. "There's a theory -- guess it isn't just a theory anymore -- that something never comes from nothing. What if some event in a universe already existing triggers what we're seeing now? It wouldn't take much to make another universe. Just the right conditions. Maybe the cores of two galaxies collide, exactly we just saw. Maybe it begins with two stars, or even a few atoms. I don't know the exact details."

"Aw snap," Lumpy muttered.

"Don't you get it? This is the answer to how everything we know began." She took a breath. "This explains how we were able to travel through the Intersect. Because where we are now is the parent of everything we know back home."

She stopped and folded her arms.

"So how do we get home?" Lumpy asked.

Sophie sighed. "Same way we got here. I guess."

"It's important. Don't you think? Especially since where we are now is doing its best to explode."

"Implode."

"Whatever. Why don't you ask Miss Perfection while we've got the chance?"

The docent smiled. "It may be difficult. It is the end of days."

"Try us," Lumpy frowned," we're at the end of things, too."

The docent glanced at the map. The city appeared, now as it must have been, filled with colors and people, or a version of people, simply dressed, and hurrying with definite purpose in every direction.

"Anybody ever take a vacation?" Lumpy asked. "Or the other big one: Where are they all hiding?"

"First, you need to understand their knowing...you word science, is too small. Knowing brings all things together, the living and unliving, what you call philosophy, the past and future. But most of all, it is about what is right – what must be done."

"Must?" Sophie asked. "Anyway, you mean the Intersect."

"Yes. Once unveiled, it brought about a crisis. You place, your universe, existed as a child of our universe. There were obligations. First of all, we searched for life. Yours was young. There wasn't much life to choose."

The map moved forward in time quickly and settled on a galaxy Sophie recognized instantly: The Milky Way. The map focused until it found the aquamarine earth again.

"What are they about to do to it?" Lumpy grumbled.

"All that could be done," The docent answered.

The map disappeared. Thirteen men and women, each wearing a plain uniform, appeared. To Sophie they seemed healthy and, honestly, arrogant younger adults. They stood in a ceremony.

The scene changed: a large clear water spring appeared. A wood surrounded half the pond and meadows the rest. The woods, Sophie realized, were healthier versions of the trees she'd seen outside the city.

The thirteen stood at the edge of the spring. Each stepped toward the spring and, as they stepped into the water, vanished.

Shimmered away, Sophie thought, fascinated.

Fifth in the line, his beard trimmed exactly so and dark sable, stood Merlin as a young man, with his cheekbones and perfect teeth, flashing eyes and his chin held high.

"Their duty and all?" Sophie asked.

"They intended to teach you well."

Springs and ponds on earth appeared. Some were water sources on brilliantly green oases, some limestone ponds in jungles, and another a rocky pool in dark woods.

The map narrated again. Each of those who passed through the Intersect appeared at a spring. A little group of people waited near the water's edge. They wore a mix of hides and roughly woven cloth. Tattoos decorated their faces and bodies. They carried light, long spears. Their clothing matched the climate, fewer for the dry desert, heavy layers for the snowy woods, something in between for grasslands.

The Voyagers, Sophie decided to name them, quietly, with smiles and open hands, approached each of their little groups of people. But the men stepped forward to protect their children.

"Teach them what? How to dress better? What were we doing so wrong back then?" Lumpy asked.

"Everything," Sophie muttered.

"Most of all, there was our knowing. A gift for eternity. There was resistance. To be expected.

A series of images followed: Docents, still smiling grimly, demonstrating their powers. Sophie bit her lip. Maybe, she thought, because I'm used to it now, but these are just tricks.

Trees blossomed in a winter landscape and suddenly bent with a burden of summer fruit. A cliff above a desert valley broke apart. A tower of cold, clear water gushed from the exposed rock. Fire erupted from a field. A docent with an especially smug smile - Merlin - rolled the flames into a circle and whirled it high into the sky.

"What'd he do " Lumpy burst out, "to get so old?" He thought for a few seconds. "I mean, sixty, seventy years, that's all we get. I mean…this was when? I don't want even to think how long ago. A hundred thousand years…so I guess he wins." He frowned and took a breath. "And these powers…Why? How?"

The docent kept her smile.

"I've got an idea." Sophie said quickly.

"Surprise, surprise," Lumpy sighed.

"Okay," Sophie continued, "We didn't fall here. Not exactly." She swept her arm through the air. "Don't look at it directly. See the colors? We didn't fall. We didn't go anywhere. But in another way we've gone farther than anyone ever has before."

Lumpy cocked his head.

"The colors tell you. We – you and I - don't exactly match this place, this everything." She leaned a little closer. "We crossed dimensions. Added dimensions. We couldn't possibly subtract. Our eyes detect the extra dimensions here. Our brains try to figure them. But they can't." She turned to the docent. "How am I doing?"

The docent said, "Largely correct."

"So the powers – much of it is just smoke and mirrors. One thing builds on another. But not all. The part we have reason to fear. Causing mountains to erupt into fire. Mixing up time and space, and cause and effect. What went wrong?"

The docent lost her smile.

Images cascaded around Sophie and Lumpy. They drew closer together. The images carried all three dimensions they knew, complete with the sounds and scents.

The voyagers wore jaguar skins, ermine, polished armor, killing weapons and other symbols, tattoos, uniforms, and killing weapons of those who ruled and commanded. They were knights, Rittern, Chevalier, chiefs, prophets, and shamen.

Chaos.

Warriors and war. Spears, shields, swords, stone-edge and metal, and axes. They heard the screams of animals and people.

Images moved forward in earth-time. A red sun shone on medieval battlefields, and a cacophony of crashing long swords, lances, and pikes. Men fought in leather and armor.

Images created an eighteenth century battlefield. Armies wheeled in precise lines across green fields, brilliant uniforms of green, scarlet, blue, and white. Musket fire crashed: clouds of dirty grey stinking smoke roiled across the fields. Shrieks of the lost echoed into the dust-red sky. Blood flowed into streams and tainted the ponds.

The tempo speeded up. Ragged men in butternut and grey fought men in union blue, battles over landscapes Sophie knew. The American civil war passed. Faster and faster the tempo flowed: a troglodyte's battlefield of mud, man-dug caves, trenches, and blasted forest and towns. Steel cannons, set wheel to wheel, fired barrages that mocked summer lightning and burst as terrible, huge flowers in the muddy fields.

The worst was saved for last: Feldgrau and dragon panzers churned over Russian plains. Winged metal dragons filled and divided the sky, screaming as they dived toward the earth. Black flack burst among them. Dragons exploded and tumbled from the sky and spiraled toward the flaming pyre-cities below.

"Stop!" Sophie cried and covered her ears with her hands.

Lumpy pulled her away.

"We get the idea," he said.

Quiet and darkness again. Blue light returned. Lumpy felt Sophie's shoulder's shake. He let her go and realized that his shoulders were shaking.

"Do you?" the docent asked.

Sophie took a deep breath. "Intruding into another universe …all for the good of those on the other side. Didn't work, did it?"

"Clearly not," the docent said.

"Clearly," Sophie muttered.

The thirteen appeared again, quickly, in the uniform, armor and weapons of Roman consuls, Chinese warlords, Hittite emperors, Aztec priest, Feldgrau Generalen, whatever symbol and clothing carried the meaning of the leaders of great and terrible armies.

Time moved forward. Fewer travelers appeared with each cycle, though the uniforms and armies were more recent. Tombs appeared, some gleaming marble, some carved wooden sarcophagi, some mounds of dirt on a dry battlefield.

Two remained. The first was a skinny and scruffy old man in an ink-blue cloak and a rusty mail shirt. A wooden palisaded fort protected the hill behind him.

Afterward, a boy-warrior in full black embossed armor appeared. A vast mounted army filled the valley all around him.

Sophie frowned. "The other eleven… we couldn't get rid of them. Not a chance. They had to destroy each other. And they did."

She glanced at Lumpy.

"See? We did it to them: we corrupted them. They became us, not the other way around. We were too much…not too good…just too much. It's

384

too much, too strong…too sweet…the evil…it's so simple. You and your kind never had a chance."

The docent's face froze.

"That's just about everything," Lumpy sighed.

"You think?" Sophie frowned.

"What? Me think? You do that for everybody." Lumpy retorted.

The docent began to grow more transparent.

Sophie jumped up. "Wait!"

The docent grew lighter still.

"The one we call Al - I mean Arthur! Where do we find him? What have you done with him!"

She glanced at Lumpy. Her eyes were frantic. Lumpy watched the docent give a last smile and dissolve.

"What'd we do wrong?" Lumpy asked.

Sophie didn't answer. She hung her head. Lumpy didn't know what to do. He felt his heart pound. "Look – maybe, just maybe, we've got something. They stick together. I mean where one goes, there's the other--."

Sophie shook her head.

"Listen now--." Lumpy began and head his voice shake. "He's not going to leave us." Lumpy felt a knot in his chest grow harder and harder. "He wouldn't. I know it. "

"No," Sophie answered and sat down.

The pale man dangled his skinny legs over the ledge behind them. "Somebody's not happy."

Sophie glared.

He leaned close to Sophie. "You two are strangers. Your friend isn't. The other one, the one with death on his mind – I wish he was, indeed I do. I know what you want."

He whispered in Sophie's ear. Her eyes grew bright. She blushed and showed her freckles. The pale man took off down the long hallway. Sophie jumped onto the walkway and ran after him.

Lumpy climbed onto the walkway. He heard the pale man's feet slapping and Sophie's heavy warrior's boot thudding against the walkway. He struggled to keep up, even as they climbed onto the street and Lumpy decided he'd been forgotten already.

Chapter 48

Lumpy felt his own boots pound against the road. The hard surface didn't last long. Cracks appeared until the road was no more than a wide path of crumbling gravel.

By the then they were outside of the city. They ran through open, dry and empty countryside exactly like all the landscape Lumpy had seen since they'd arrived. Eventually even Sophie slowed. Lumpy kept his bearing; they were traveling northwest and climbing steadily into the high hills that surrounded most of the city.

He couldn't see anything special about the landscape. Lumpy didn't question the pale man. After the second hour, though, his legs ached. Even the pale man's head began to hang down. Maybe, Lumpy fretted, he's leading us into an ambush. Then what?

Lumpy let the thought bounce around in his head without doing anything about it. He glanced to his right; the first stone caught his eye. It stood just off the path they followed at the top of a ridge.

He understood what it was. They were everywhere back home, or something like them: a gravestone.

The stone had been buried deep in the ground and roughly chiseled into a rectangle about his height. A face had been carved into the rough surface.

The face, Lumpy decided-- that was another matter. The detail was impressive. He'd recognize who it was instantly. The expression showed the most pathetic longing Lumpy though he'd ever seen. For what? Lumpy asked himself and didn't have time to find an answer. The three reached the top of the next ridge. They faced a wide, bowl-shaped valley ringed by low hills. The soil was dark and dry. Nothing grew or lived there. The valley was crowded with the stone carvings like the stone at the top of the ridge.

Lumpy couldn't begin to guess how many. They were thousands, and they covered every square meter of ground. Each stone was carved differently; each face was unique.

At the center of the valley stone post and lintels made a series of concentric circles. The outer circles were clearly of newer grey and white stone. The circles closer to the center grew increasingly dark and age-streaked.

The pale man trembled. Sophie stepped closer to him. "Why are you afraid?"

"You've got no business here."

"Why can't we visit your dead?"

The pale man shook his head. "Dead doesn't mean anything."

Lumpy stepped up from the other side. "What gives you the idea somebody else might be here?"

The pale man turned away and started down the path. Lumpy turned to Sophie. "How can he know?"

But Sophie's eyes were following the pale man. She started down the hill without looking at Lumpy at all.

Chapter 49

Sophie wasn't sure. Actually, she didn't know at all. She couldn't say anything to Lumpy because she knew, as her mother often informed her, she was a second-rate liar.

So they passed seemingly endless numbers of the gravestones. Sophie didn't want to call them gravestones; they seemed to be more a celebration of each life. Celebration wasn't exactly right, either; they seemed a memorial, a way of freezing each life in stone. Like the concentric circles, the stones closer to the center appeared older and older, darker and deeply weathered. Even the all-important faces -- the portraits -- were almost worn away.

How long would that take? Sophie asked herself. Maybe a hundred thousand years back home. Maybe a lot more. No, she warned herself, that couldn't be.

They passed through the first stone circle. The construction was simple, huge stone blocks cut exactly so and buried deep in the ground. Lintels topped the post, each slightly curved so that they eventually formed a circle several miles in circumference. Carved into the post were all sorts of symbols. Got to be an alphabet of some sort, Sophie decided. Beside the symbols were carving of mysterious of animals and plants and some things in between.

The pale man strode ahead. Sophie and Lumpy managed to stay close, though it wasn't easy. The next ring, about a quarter mile farther, was worn darker still. Between the two rings they passed a courtyard filled with memorials decorated with more symbols and thousands of carved handprints. Signatures, Sophie thought, proof that I was here and that I was alive.

At the next and older ring the memorial were fewer. She counted four more rings ahead.

"Seven," she said to no one in particular.

The pale man eventually slowed. His attention focused a few hundred yards ahead.

The last ring rose a half mile away. The pale man startled. Sophie watched the pulse in his neck throb. She took his arm. "What do you know?"

Lumpy tugged on Sophie's arm. "Is he up there? I don't get that feeling. Why would Al want to be here? Everybody's already dead."

The pale man took off. Sophie barely had time to jump out of the way. He's going, Sophie decided quickly, in a blind panic, the way we did when the Jin almost trapped us. He's never been so afraid. But he's running toward, not away.

Sophie ran. Lumpy ran, too. Their feet crunched the loose gravel.

The stones of the last ring were deeply sunk into the earth. The tablets so near the center lacked symbols --except for the handprints like those on the younger stones.

The pale man slowed and stopped.

Look how big his eyes are, Sophie thought, he doesn't know how to hide his fear. Maybe he's never been afraid before. But he's been alone on this world for so long that's all he must know.

The pale man moved quietly ahead. He held out his skinny arm to keep Sophie and Lumpy behind him.

Beyond the last ring Sophie saw seven causeways, each about a quarter mile long and wide enough for a dozen people, all leading like spokes on a wheel to a temple, or something like it, in the center.

The temple wasn't much, a quartet of big stones planted haphazardly in the ancient ground; clearly these smooth-worn and age-darkened stones were the oldest of the very old.

Below the causeways they saw simple beauty. The causeways served as bridges; a wide spring bubbled between the oblong island of the temple and last of the rings. The water glimmered deep, translucent emerald.

The pale man saw him first. Sophie knew because his eyes got bigger than ever. He stumbled as he tried to run away. But he caught himself and let Sophie help him stand.

The temple stones enclosed an area big enough, Sophie guessed, for the old Hilltop Home yard. The ground was dark and bare.

He stood by the center in ragged clothes.

Mordred.

His cape was gone, his hair was matted and his boots were scarred. His left hand rested on a sword.

He gave a poisonous smile.

Lumpy startled. The pale man began backing away. Sophie slipped her arms around the others. "Too late," she whispered, "he's seen you and you, and me."

She wanted to close her eyes. Mordred, a few hundred yards away across an ancient bridge, seemed almost relaxed. Sophie could feel Lumpy's tense back. His left hand instinctively searched for a sword. The pale man's eye grew even bigger. He whirled around, shoving Sophie one way and Lumpy the other, and ran.

Lumpy wasn't sure what happened. Never turn your back on Mordred; he knew that much. He heard a crackling snap. A python, an electric bolt, struck out toward the three.

The writhing python wrapped around Sophie, Lumpy and the pale man. Sophie felt herself tumbling over and over. The power carried its own fear; it wasn't muscular or gravity, but much stronger, wild, and able, she feared in those seconds, of jerking her to pieces.

Another snap. The python vanished. The three lay heaped together. They slowly untangled and swayed as they stood.

Mordred leaned against a stone ten feet away. "Rough trip over to see me?" he clucked. "I don't understand your dog faces. Look how far we've come together. I knew it'd end exactly here." He stamped his foot. "At the end of so many things. Of course, for someone it is all about beginnings. Not for everybody. For you three it'll be over very quickly. I promise."

Lumpy watched Sophie glance to her left and right without moving her head. She glanced at Lumpy and stepped sideways. Lumpy understood and did the same. Now they outflanked Mordred slightly. Lumpy spotted a sharp-edged stone a few feet to his right.

"Of course," Mordred sighed," you did it to yourself. Nobody asked you along."

"What have you done with him?" Sophie managed.

"What's the name? Albert? Al? The excuse for Arthur? I didn't have to do anything. I can't find him anywhere. Checked your tweets? Maybe he's gone to the water. Around here that means that he's gone home. He can do that. What's that tell you about loyalty-- or more."

Lumpy watched Sophie's face darken. He lies. She's got to understand that he lies.

The sky, quiet for a while, gave a shattering boom.

Modred winced and ducked.

"You've used your powers here," Sophie said.

Mordred fiddled with a piece of parchment he'd taken from his shirt.

"What you received was just a tap. It could have been so much worse."

"Merlin was always afraid to use his powers. At least this far out."

"That's what he always was. Afraid."

The sky flashed gold and green.

"Remarkable." Mordred muttered. He folded the parchment. With a finger snap he set it aflame. It fluttered to the ground and burned to ash. "Too bad you never knew what it all meant. I'll educate you just so you'll appreciate it before you have to -- go."

"We've been informed," Sophie answered.

Mordred nodded toward the pale man. "By what? A docent from somebody's dusty memories? They omit the really juicy parts. To whit: around you -- a graveyard. After all, the body eventually fails, doesn't it? The tak, the soul as you call it, sleeps. It sleeps within each of these stones. That's why each is so unique. And they've slept for untold eons, waiting, waiting. Someone needs to bring them back. Someone special."

Silence.

Mordred frowned. "Who do you think that will have to be?"

Near the center of the temple stood an oblong boulder. It didn't seem special, except for its tremendous age. Mordred searched inside a clef in the boulder. He withdrew a dagger with a green stone handle and a black stone blade. It was simply carved, but the stone edge glittered razor sharp.

The pale man took a sudden breath. Mordred turned toward him and held out the knife. "Why the fear?"

He turned to Sophie and Lumpy. "Everything he and his kind ever lost shall be returned. He understands, because he was properly instructed." He placed the tip of the blade against the pale man's ribs. "We have no hearts like yours, but we have our souls. The souls trapped in these stones beg to be released. But who is going to be the prime mover? I mean the one who plunges the blade into his body, melds his soul and body into one tak. For the weak it would mean death, but for the strongest it means rebirth for him and for millions upon millions of others."

Mordred touched the knife point to his chest. "Of course, those who are saved owe absolute fealty to he who releases them."

"It's going to be a very short life," Sophie retorted, "if they hang around here."

Mordred smiled bitterly. "We will go to the water together. We will emerge where I began. Where I will them to be. A people reborn--."

"A slave army," Sophie said quietly. "Millions and millions, as you say."

"But you've already got army." Lumpy interrupted.

"Slugs and worms." Mordred answered. "Besides, to be adored by your own kind, to rule them with an iron hand-- what more is there? Your kind taught me. I owe you that."

He stared so intensely into Sophie's face that she glanced away. His face suddenly seemed withered.

The sky roared and burned. The ground quivered. The lintels swayed. Mordred rolled the stone dagger in his hand. "You failed if you meant to distract me." He held the dagger to his chest. "So quick and my soul shall fill the universe and save all."

"What," Lumpy said loudly," if it's just all just a story."

Everybody looked at him.

But the ground shook again. The stone rings began collapsing. Lumpy glanced to his left and as he did caught sight of someone sprinting across the nearest causeway.

Al.

I mean Arthur.

Whatever he is now.

He carried the sword Excalibur in his right hand.

Lumpy blinked. From the causeway to his right he witnessed a ghost, thin and pasty, like the pale man. He wore the same ragged khaki and green clothes in which he'd died.

His eyes blazed.

So much for death, Lumpy thought.

Mordred glanced frantically left and right. Surrounded, Lumpy thought triumphantly.

Mordred plunged the dagger into his chest.

Al stopped. Mordred collapsed. Merlin cried aloud. Merlin never reached Mordred. He stopped a dozen yards away.

Mordred rose from the ground. He extracted the dagger. Merlin backed away. The stone graves glowed from within in beautiful colors. The colors swirled until they focused into single shapes, one for each stone. The shapes began to transform into heads, trunks, arms, and legs.

Al--Arthur--attacked. Mordred turned to meet him. Sophie snatched a rock from the ground and rushed forward. Merlin cried out and charged. Al reached Mordred first, then Sophie, the hammer stone in her hand, and Merlin last, all seconds apart.

Modred raised his sword. Fire, or lightning--Lumpy didn't know what--crackled around the blade and coursed through Mordred.

Mordred slammed the sword down. A crest of flame shot outward and filled the air all around. Al and Sophie tumble over and over until they were raised above the ground and suspended in a shimmering, diamond-clear space.

The pale man attacked. Mordred slashed his sword and just as quickly the pale man was struck, swirled, and hung in the diamond space exactly like the other two.

"You!" Lumpy roared at Merlin. It seemed as if he was watching someone else. "Do it! Now!"

Merlin—

Retreated.

Lumpy howled and charged toward Merlin. But he couldn't reach Merlin on a straight line; he sprinted along the edge of the circle.

Lumpy saw red. He intended to ring the scrawny old man's neck until he sang his incantations and called up dragons or dinosaurs or wombats to save them.

Things don't work out like you hope, Whizzle warned him over and over. He tumbled, end over end, as the ground under his feet split into huge puzzle pieces and rose up and down. Thundering, roaring, sizzling and crashing rang in his head as he rolled over the ground.

Chapter 50

Mordred wanted to sing. I could sing my victory song, he told himself. Instead all what is mine will sing it with me. I witness them growing from shades to the living all around me. Their lives will have purpose. I shall give it to them. An island of stars in another universe shall fall under my vision.

Unbelievable.

Insurmountable.

Mordred glanced at the three bodies suspended above his head. To his left, the old Merlin sat on the ground, unmoving, a pile of rags. Maybe he's finally dead, Mordred mused. After all, he is no more than a shell and mostly human now. Anyway, that's what they do best: they die.

Halfway up the horizon Mordred saw what he'd never saw before -- a darkening center of the sky surrounded by a crown of swirling and sparkling stars.

I understand, Mordred told himself, as I must. It is the eye of the beast. I am looking on the singularity. All things that begin will end. Soon the galaxies will be drawn into the soul and all will be reborn as another universe is born in the next explosion. All shall begin again.

What about me?

Now, he chastised himself, time to bring my new warriors down to the water. Time--there is no time.

Mordred turned toward the closest and oldest stones. The warriors there were almost reborn, arms and legs and trunks and faces and eyes so close to being opened. They were doing nicely, he noted, and most of all they would be ready to do what they are told.

Mordred heard a moan. From the corner of his eye he watched Merlin struggle to his feet.

Chapter 51

But Merlin did nothing.

Mordred threw a rock at the old man. "Happy?" he called.

"It's done," Merlin croaked.

"Close. You and yours will be remaining here. I have other rows to hoe." Mordred snickered. He squinted at the old man's face. Such pity on it, he thought. Mordred's heart began to beat faster. Pity? For whom?

Sophie could still see. She watched what emerged from the crumbling ground. There were seven, one for each spoke of the wheel. They were giants, a head taller than her father. She couldn't focus on them; they seemed blurry, without sharp boundaries between themselves and the air.

She couldn't force herself to think much beyond that. Mordred still held her in the clear cocoon coffin. She watched the giants rise out of the ground and she didn't care what they were or what they meant. She tried but she couldn't. She glanced at her hand and realized she could see through it. I'm dissolving, she told herself, like everything else in this place

Then a surprise: the giants, now completely emerged, grey-black, focused on Mordred. They surrounded him. Stalked him, Sophie thought. On Mordred's face, she saw an awful fear. If I weren't so tired I would be enjoying it, Sophie thought. Look at him; he's always been so afraid and now it's so clear.

Mordred fought back. She watched as he tried his power. But the explosions evaporated against the seven who surrounded him. They drew closer and closer until Mordred couldn't run in any direction.

A loud pop hurt Sophie's ears. She hit the ground hard. She lay on the heaving cracking ground, free from her cocoon. I'm solid again, she realized, because I hurt that much. She rolled and scrambled to her feet.

Chapter 52

Lumpy watched his friend fall like ripe apples and smack against the ground. Not that much good solid ground remained, he told himself. Even the sky flickered crimson and yellow and gave off sorts of strange howlings. Everybody else is crazy, he told himself as he tried to stand. Mordred is over there screaming and begging, surrounded by these brownish blue-black things. Now Merlin has his face in mine yelling: Down to the water! Down to the water!

I don't get it. The pale guy does. He grabs Sophie and me and begins dragging us toward the well. Sophie breaks away and sprints for Arthur -- I mean Al. He isn't moving. This whole place is cracked like an egg dropped on the floor. The ground is wrenching and groaning, worse than the sky. The sky is filled with silver streaks. There's an eye up there now, so bright that it burns my eyes.

Mordred: somehow he breaks away from those things that surround him. He runs toward us, begging and crying.

Al goes after him anyway. They fight with their fist, but not like kids. Merlin is yelling to the pale man. They both grab Sophie. She yells back terrible things I bet she meant at that exact moment. But it's two against one and they throw her into the well.

Al saw what happened to Sophie. He turns away and Mordred slams his head with a balled fist. But Merlin grabs Mordred and pins his elbows. The pale man, while Al isn't watching, makes a running leap and tackles Al. Together they disappear into the well.

It's just me.

And Merlin and Modred.

And the end of everything.

I hear Merlin cry out what I don't believe. It'll die with me.

The maul above me grows huge. The sky is black and silver and swirling and the ground is dissolving. Merlin yells at me. I make my quivering legs run. I stumble over the ledge into the well. I hit head first. I remember the splash. The falling, like always, came next.

Except it isn't falling. I'm swimming again and about to drown. I swim upward. My head breaks into air. It's the pool in the cavern, where we'd just missed the Jin, except that it's quiet and cool now. The pale man, Sophie and Al are climbing onto the wall.

No Merlin.

We sat in the wall a long time and tried to breath. The water in the pool swirled, turned a brilliant blue and slowly the light from deep below died. Then it seemed to be just a pool of clear and cool water. From all I could tell that was all it ever had been.

Nobody said anything. Al stared at the water. The pale man sobbed. Sophie watched Al carefully. After a little while she took Al's bruised arm and led him across the sandy floor and began to hike out of the cave.

Chapter 53

They emerged into a green sunset. The landscape was quiet and empty. At the entrance of the cave, where they'd been ambushed, the blanket that had covered Merlin's body remained. The tracks of the Jin and their mounts in the dust had disappeared.

Sophie lifted the blanket. It disintegrated. Sophie turned to Lumpy. "What day is it?"

Lumpy shrugged. "Our Tuesday."

"So we were gone about three days."

"Sure."

Al, who'd been quiet for a long time, glanced at the blanket. "No way."

The pale man sniffed the ground. "It's sweet enough. Just ground now."

"The evidence tells me it's been...quite a bit longer," Sophie sniffed.

There wasn't much discussion about it. They'd already decided what to do, return to the jeweled fort where the commander and warriors still held out.

That was the hope, of course. When they left, a war was still being fought and they were losing. In any case, from there they could figure out some way home. That was the best bet anyway. If not – they didn't speak about it. But that was the likely outcome. They didn't have the old man. Merlin : nobody said his name but they felt the emptiness.

They used what they'd learned. They kept to the forest and other good cover and crossed open spaces at a run. They didn't dare try to summon the mounts. They had no more ambrosia and, much worse, a squadron of mounts sailing skyward would mark their location to every enemy on the planet.

They lived on the wild fruits they could find, though most were bitter and shriveled so late in the season. The slow and careful journey took six days. On the fifth day they arrived at the old causeway battlefield. The stone debris of the battle had been neatly stacked. The dead were buried underneath mounds.

There was no explanation. They hid in the forest that night. The fort stood a day's hike ahead. No one felt like talking much that night. What they found there would determine the rest of their lives, however long that might be.

They left early and reached the fort in the early dawn. The walls were intact; the main gate was down. They slipped, one by one, close to the walls. All was very quiet and nothing seemed to be moving about.

A huge brass gong boomed.

The friends hurried back to the edge of the forest. They couldn't see over the walls, of course. They listened as companies of warriors woke, filled the courtyard they couldn't see and shuffled back and forth.

Al and Sophie stared at each other. The warriors never marched about in bare feet. Sophie leaned close to Al and whispered, "How about the east corner? We can watch the parade ground from there. That'll tell us something."

She didn't want to say what the something was. They kept close to the woods and where they had a full of the field.

Al stared quietly at the boulder where he'd first drawn Excalibur from the stone. He still carried the sword, for all the good it had done him, or Lumpy, or Sophie, or the pale man. They weren't part of his problem in the first place. More than likely they were trapped with him. Forget home. He couldn't say it. They'd figure it out on there on soon enough.

And the old man.

He had a name. He gave everything for you.

"Merlin," he whispered.

A trumpet sounded and, marching in neat company squares, the field began to fill with Jin.

None of the friends spoke. They saw six companies of Jin in scarlet and yellow uniforms; those that could wore shiny boots. More wore sandals or went barefoot if their feet were that bulbous.

But they were Jin, several hundred strong, which meant that the castle held thousands more; and that meant that they infested the fields, woods and shores, the entire land that belonged to the commander and his warriors.

"Maybe they got away," Lumpy whispered.

Nobody answered. Al and Lumpy looked at the ground. Sophie sniffled and rubbed her nose. The pale man turned even paler.

They lost their concentration. That explains what happened next: They were surrounded. A detachment of Jin wearing imperial blue, appeared from the behind the woods and encircled them.

Al slowly reached for Excalibur. Sophie stayed his hand. She kept her eyes on the tallest Jin, ugly enough to be in charge.

The detachment simply stood there. They were unarmed. They kept their eyes on the horizon like well-trained soldiers. The Jin sergeant in charge spoke "Do you gents and ladyness wish a brew?"

Granted, his accent was like listening to gravel in a cement mixer. The four stared. The sergeant waited patiently. The Jin in the field received hoes, rakes, axes and pruning shears.

The Jin still waited.

"Make mine black," Sophie said loudly.

Lumpy cleared his throat. "Ditto."

The pale man raised his hand. "Yo."

All the eyes and eye-like appendages turned to Al. He glances around very carefully and said, "Yea, and make it strong."

The Jin, so released, bustled away.

The friends didn't move. "What did we just see?" Sophie asked aloud.

Someone cleared his throat nearby – a normal throat. "My word, look what the fates have dragged in!"

The commander stood a dozen yards away. Behind him stood an entourage of sub-commanders, including a beaming, and much thinner, Igat.

"With your permission!" Igat beamed. The commander nodded and Igat trundled across the field as fast as his bowed legs would let him. Igat tried to embrace everyone at once. There were tears -- Sophie despite herself, Igat unashamed, Lumpy got red eyes and the pale man because everyone seemed so happy.

Al hung back, even as Igat lifted him from the ground with a bear hug. The commander happily shook hands all around and hugged no one, of course, but his eyes were bright and his cheeks flushed.

The two groups paused and stared at each other. No one knew where to begin. The questions were too many and too enormous. The commander broke the ice. "Well, you lads – and lady – have certainly given us a wonderful what about it. Most wonderful, especially considering all the years you have been missing. What is it? Two? Three? Your old rooms still await you, I am sure. We shall all meet in three hours for a repast." He glanced at the pale man. "Even your new friend."

Lumpy frowned. "Two years? More like two days."

"We shall cover that, won't we?" the commander insisted politely." Now -- off with you!"

The sub-commanders gave four cheers as Igat led the friends away. As she passed the commander, the commander tugged at her elbow. "The wizard?"

Sophie shook her head. The commander glanced down. He glanced up quickly for everyone's benefit. "No dawdling! The gong shall sound soon!"

Chapter 54

The gong boomed exactly three hours later at the end of a peaceful gold-and-red afternoon. They found their rooms exactly as they'd left them, though now cleaned until everything shined. Nobody spoke much during their free time. Sophie closed her door, lay on the giant princess bed, and fell into a troubled sleep. What she thought she heard in the last seconds in the other place, the other universe, as it disintegrated, haunted her.

Al and Lumpy dozed on their imperial beds. The pale man insisted on curling up and snoring on the carpet.

Igat appeared as soon as the gong sounded. He hurried them along. "Two years! Two years! You young ones have missed more business around since – since ever!"

The dinner was held in the commander's private suite. Only the friends, the pale man, and Igat were present --and two Jin servants.

Sophie and Al glanced at each other as the Jin, decked out in royal blue, their hair tufts slicked back, served. They were spotlessly clean and even carried a scent of blooming things. The iced appetizer came first, along with especially pungent -- even over powering -- mugs of mat.

The commander's eyes gleamed. "Our friends behind you have mastered the art. It is distilled, hardly brewed." He smiled at his guest and took a long slurp. "I am sure you have a few questions...We had little to do with the change initially. After you three -- and the wizard -- vanished, their armies acted most oddly. They ceased their hostilities. It was really much more than that. The simply began wandering about. We guessed why: this other fellow, this Mordred, was nowhere to be found."

"We found him," Sophie said.

""We figured that. We could only hope for you. But in only a few days we found that our mortal enemies had become a hundred thousand starving and bellowing refugees. We knew why: this Modred was their brain and he had removed himself. They were suddenly, to the ogre, quite helpless."

Al shook his head. "How can you be sure?"

"Now, now. Do you fear that they're awaiting the chance to cut our throats, that sort of thing? We put our best minds to the task. They affirmed what we suspected: these creatures, once abandoned by their powerful and ruthless leader, were wholly without food, purpose, or souls."

"My heart bleeds," Al said.

"I shan't take offense. That was our attitude till they came begging. Our best minds proposed that we utilize them."

"Slaves?" Sophie asked.

"No, no, no. Every Jack man of them is free to leave-- take to the hills, so to say. But we all get along here, don't we? We have so much work to do-- our fields, castles, homes, roads, arts, industries, both manual and high, all need to be attended. Every soul has a place, a purpose, dignity, medical care, and as you can tell, quite a bit of personal cleanliness."

"What about a hundred years from now?" Sophie asked.

"That time will have to take care of itself," The commander answered quietly. "It's your turn to illuminate me...if you wish to even talk about it."

There was silence.

"Maybe some other time," the commander said gently." We shall move along --."

"He didn't make it," Al said suddenly.

Everyone remained quiet a few moments.

"Very, very sorry to learn that," the commander said.

"He sacrificed himself for us," Sophie added.

"No one is surprised," the commander said. "But if it's painful to remember, perhaps later."

Sophie shook her head. "There won't be another time. Tomorrow we're going home one way or another. Nobody here will ever know what he did for us. Everyone who owes him something is going to talk." She nodded toward Lumpy, the pale man and, finally, Al, who shifted in his chair. Excalibur scraped against the floor.

Sophie rubbed her thumb over her left hand as she did when she was especially nervous. She nodded toward Al. "I thought he'd never speak to me. Merlin made that possible. He did, didn't he? Even if that wasn't the most important thing for him. But he let it happen. He let me follow. If he hadn't I wouldn't know what I know today. And I wouldn't have-."

She stopped and felt her face burn. At least here they believe me. Once I am home I can never tell the story again.

She looked at Lumpy.

He cleared his throat loudly a few times and said simply, "I never thought I'd fight in a war. I did and I survived. I never want to go through it again. He saved our lives a dozen times. I mean he saved our lives from day one till -- till now."

He looked down.

The pale man swallowed. His Adam's apple bobbed up and down. "I just want to say, though I am still learning the lingo, that he was totally righteous. Is that the right notion? Look now-- I remember two people caring for me when I was a wee lad. I barely recall their faces. They've been gone a long, long time. Then Mordred arrived, and Al, my friend, and I didn't know what to make of them. But Mordred was all fear and hate. That was easy to figure." He turned to Al. "You were otherwise. Then you disappeared. But you came back. The wizard...I knew him. He was one of mine. But so was the one filled with fear and hate. But they're gone now. All gone...there's just me... And the wizard was brave."

He glanced at the table.

Everyone waited for Al.

He wouldn't look at anyone. "I suppose I better tell something about myself first. I don't have that much to forget. First thing I remember is wandering down an asphalt road. Maybe I was four or so. I don't know how I got there, or why. I am Al. I am, or I was, Arthur, too. Either way, I know who I am now. I know what I want and what I should do." He glanced around the table. "He gave me that. He knew what it would cost him and he carried it out anyway. That's everything. And I will never forget him. That's everything, too." He turned to the

412

commander. "We're at an end here. Everything has a beginning and an end."

"Maybe it's all just a circle," the commander said quietly.

"Either way, we want to go home now," Al said.

"You're very welcome to stay here forever. I speak for every soul on this world!" Igat burst out

The commander said, "You are exactly correct. But these young ones have the friends and their families fretting about them."

"You can do that for us, can't you?" Sophie asked. Get us home?"

"We shall put our best people on it," the commander answered cheerily.

The commander rose. The party ended. The friends were exhausted anyway. I gat led them up the winding stairs to their rooms. Warm mat waited for them. They'd learned to appreciate its benefits and drank it to the dregs.

Chapter 55

Igat didn't come for them till the day was bright and warm. A trio of accessories-- the official title for the Jin now--served them a dry crust and marmalade breakfast. "It's what," Igat explained, we call a traveling ration."

He led his friends down the stairs and through the hall of heroes. The hall was burnished and uncomfortably neat. Fluttering among the rafters a covey of draco-creatures hissed. Merlin's green and crimson Draco spiraled down and landed on Al's shoulder. He pecked at Al's ear. Al cried out and swatted the creature away.

It squawked and fluttered high among the rafters and hissed at the people below.

"Guess we aren't what he wants," Lumpy said.

Igat led them through the hall outside to the huge field where they'd first watched the mounts come to earth. They were back; the field was crowded with mounts, snorting and clawing the ground. A warrior, dressed in his parade best, stood beside each mount and held a lump of ambrosia in his hand.

The commander in golden armor strode to the friends and shook hands all around. "As you can tell, our best minds came up with some ideas. I have high hopes."

"Lady and gents," I gat said, "please follow me. It's going to be simple. Nothing you haven't done before."

414

The regimental band, now made completely of former Jin, struck up a lively tune.

The friends found that their old mounts waited for them at the head of the formation. Igat distributed a handful of ambrosia. The mount purled and nuzzled as their old connections were re-made.

Igat rode a few yards ahead of the friends and thus took point for the entire corps. The four formed a line behind Igat.

"Young ones," he called behind him, "stick close and do exactly as I say."

The friends climbed onto their mounts. Igat gave the call and began the galloping run across the huge field. Igat's mount spread her wings and rose into the air. The friends followed. Behind them, flight after flight soared into the air until the sky was filled. The mounts – ebony, roan, milky white, and mottled – shone in the sun.

The formation climbed to several thousand feet, wheeled toward the sun, and after a short time, passed over the ocean.

Igat leaned far to one side and intensely studied the clear air below. He pulled his mount in a circle; the friends followed, one after another. The commander drew close. Igat nodded emphatically and pointed toward the ocean. The commander nodded back and called to the friends, "Good fortune to you forever!"

He turned his mount away and soared back to his place.

The entire corps began a majestic wheeling beyond the circle that Igat and the friends made.

Igat motioned for the friends to fly as close as they could. He jabbed his finger toward the air below.

Sophie peered down. That was all she could see-- air and, far below, the whitecaps of the emerald ocean. She squinted and looked again. Now the air didn't seem quite that clear. Directly below, maybe five hundred feet, she noticed an almost transparent whirling vortex.

Igat called out, "Friends, this is it! Your way home! Just the way you got here! Just the other direction."

Lumpy groaned loudly.

"It comes and goes! Here a while, gone a thousand years! Mind your aim!"

The friends looked at each other.

The vortex began drifting away.

"Dawdling won't do!" Igat bellowed.

Al and Sophie looked at each other. They pulled their legs from the stirrups-- and jumped.

Lumpy, howling, jumped, eyes squeezed shut. The pale man, eyes big as eggs, tumbled away last.

Igat peered over his mount. Their collective aim seemed good. The vortex swallowed each. Abruptly they were gone.

"Another time!" Igat called after. His heart ached. He took a deep, deep breath and turned his mount to join the rest of the cheering warriors.

Chapter 56

At least once a week Lake Chittatocheebee got cleaned of alligators. Fifteen miles east of Tintangle, wide, olive-colored and shallow, Lake Chigger (as it was locally known) hosted the performance of the Amazing Mermaids and Aqua Devils on every Saturday, April through September.

That special June day nobody understood how the mermaids or the aqua devils managed it. At the climax of the show, Mr. Poseidon, aloof in a huge kite drawn behind a candy-apple speed boat, was already roaring toward the Pyramid of Perdition, six hale fellows stacked in a wobbly V and bouncing along a few hundred yards ahead.

At the precise second, Poseidon, gliding closer and still closer, was to release himself from the kite and crown the pyramid.

It worked none times out of ten.

On June 9, however, there were particular problems. Four skydivers spun out of the low clouds. Just like that. The first of the individuals, a young man grabbed Poseidon's ankles. A girl tumbled past and grabbed the first interloper's leg, followed by a skinny red-haired fellow. Finally, certainly not least, an albino grabbed the last available ankle.

The top two of the Perdition Pyramid grabbed for whatever ankles was they could latch onto. A game effort; it didn't quite work. Bodies splashed every which a way. The confused audiences cheered and gasped. Management called the sheriff about the malicious skydivers.

"Could you repeat that?" The dispatcher begged.

The fantastic four were fished from the lake, dripping and clothed in strange cult grab. Identities weren't difficult for the younger three: two runaways from the Hilltop Home and the promising daughter of a local businessman. They'd vanished on a disturbed night two years ago. Despite APBs, posters, Internet postings galore, and a TV episode, nobody knew anything. The fourth, a peculiar big-eyed, loose limbed individual pale as clabbered milk, seemed some sort of guru.

They refused to divulge the name of the pilot who transported them, or if individuals had forced them out of the plane. No parachutes were found.

"Optical illusion," the girl insisted.

Two years gone: by then they were all of legal age, though just. Sheriff Ed Eggly, accustomed to the really puzzling after the last few years, threw up his hands. Except for some questionable trespassing, he didn't figure he needed to get involved.

"Everybody," he sighed aloud, "let's go home."

The girl went home to Mom and Dad, who tearful with joy, whisk Sophie away before any one asked questions.

Rumors spread anyway that the three had been hiding out in some wacko commune near Mt. Rainer. That explained their guru friend, who never asked for anything and didn't even seem to know what a dollar bill was.

The boys went back to Wheezle. She consented to take in the lost lambs, though, according to state regulations, they weren't lambs anymore. Wheezle wasn't to receive a dime's support either. She took them anyway, even the guru, who never seemed to understand how pitiful he was.

The two boys went back to their rooms. The guru got a little space in the garret, which seemed to delight him unreasonably. That and cinnamon cookies.

Wheezle understood that the boys were changed -- sunburned and thin, more confident, and yet tired. But they didn't seem physically a day older.

They found part-time jobs, Lumpy and the guru (who settled on Joe Smith Jr. as a moniker) with a car parts dealer. Al worked a series of jobs, unable to settle on anything.

Both boys worked to finish high school on-line. Al saved his money and bought an old car. Sophie was accepted to an early admissions program at State, forty miles east where, everyone was sure, she would accomplish amazing things.

Al disappeared every weekend.

Wheezle lets things go generally. Finally she decided she had a right; neither boy ever hinted where they'd gone, or why. That kept her up at night the most: Didn't I give them everything? Wasn't that enough?

A long while after her return she stopped Al in the hallway. It was Friday; he was heading out the door with his suitcase for his weekend visit.

"We need to talk," she frowned.

"Sure. We'll get right on that."

He smiled and edged past. In a few moments his car coughed as it started downstairs.

Wheezle stood stock still.

They had their talk eventually. It wasn't till months later, in June, the day after the boys had finally finished their GED course. Lumpy and Mr. Smith had taken the little ones to the Tintangle pool. The house was wholly quiet and empty. The boy, now nineteen or thereabouts (nobody really knew, she realized) sat reading in the living room. She studied the top of his head peaking above the chair. She cleared her throat and strode forward.

Al closed his book.

"Time to talk. Don't you think so?"

Al managed a polite smile. "I want to thank you for all you've done."

She coughed a little and swallowed. "You're quite welcome."

"We'll be getting out of your hair pretty quick. Even Mr. – Smith."

She waited.

"I'm heading over to state. A college kid. Imagine that."

"I can, yes."

"Lumpy and Joe, too Well, Joe intends to work. Lumpy wants to get into the business game."

"Very good."

A pause.

"Sophie and I will be getting married next spring."

Wheezle closed her eyes. "Congratulations."

She wanted to say much more.

"Do you know what Sophie's studying? Astronomy. Guess I'll be hitched to a college prof."

"You two will be very happy." Wheezle managed and took a deep breath.

"Not quite sure what I'm going to do."

"You've got time. So much time. It may not seem so now, but you do."

She wiped her eyes. "Oh, listen to me. I sound like my mother."

Wheezle imaged her mother's face as she lectured to the ten year-old Wheezle. What can't money buy? Love? I'm not sure about that. Time. Try to buy that.

"Account closed," Wheezle said aloud.

"How's that?"

"Nothing. Can I ask you something? You don't have to answer, seeing that it's all done. But first a little background. The good doctor...the night and you and Lumpy disappeared, all heck broke loose here. Volcanoes, comets in the sky, hoodlums in Halloween mask smashing up the mall-- did you ever hear anything about that?"

Al swallowed. "Not much."

"That night your good doctor also flew the coop. Puff! Right off the face of the earth. I got somebody to go through the state records again. Guess what? No medical or driver's license, no phone or utilities, credit cards, no police records either. Isn't that very peculiar?"

"Depends."

"What-- what did he do with you, Al? And Lumpy and that girl? Is he the one who led you three astray? Rumor has it that you were all held by some cult up in Idaho. Is that true?"

"Not exactly."

"Montana?"

"Not even warm."

Wheezle gave a huge sigh. "I've got to know. You can understand that, can't you?"

Al stirred in his chair. Wheezle was sure he intended to walk away.

He didn't. "Maybe you don't want to know."

"Try me."

"Trying isn't going to be good enough."

Al hesitated. Wheezle realized she was holding her breath. Al looked down and began to speak. He spoke straight through. Now and then he glanced up at Wheezle's face, which went from puzzlement to deeper puzzlement to being truly confounded. But Al found he could speak about it.

And then he was done. He stopped and drank a little of the lemonade on the table. He leaned back. "That's just the way it was. Unless we three dreamed the same thing. And that would be a real trick."

"At least you're all home," Wheezle croaked.

"I warned you."

"No. You're here and that's all that matters."

Al felt his stomach churn; suddenly, he realized, I want the world to know. They've got the evidence all around them. That's just for starters. But wait, he told himself, it's always accused them eyeball to eyeball.

He glanced through the tall windows. Downtown Tintangle was there: the red-brick courthouse and a dozen, low concrete block buildings. A few folks, heads down, hurried through the rising heat.

Al looked back to Wheezle. "Maybe that's it. Maybe we were dreaming. It could happen."

Wheezle grabbed a Kleenex and dabbed her eyes. "At least - ."

"Right."

They looked at each other.

Wheezle's phone jangled.

"Lo!" She answered loudly. She listened a few seconds and stood quickly. "Lawrence and Mr. Smith and the little boys are ready for lunch. How about you take the van and gather them up? It's too hot to walk. I'll get the spaghetti." She hurried toward the kitchen and turned around. "No dawdling, please and thank you! I'm almost done here." She reached the kitchen and started singing.

Al scooped up the van keys.

That, he told himself, is that.

Chapter 57

Wheezle managed to retire in time for the wedding. The nuptials happened a full seven years after her conversation with Al. The event was scheduled three weeks after Sophie, now Dr. Sophie Bruening, received her Ph.D. in Astrophysics and Al Niemann, M.A. defended his thesis on American native mythology. The location: beneath gnarled live oaks outside Tallahassee, the site of the state university, and where the two had lived most of those years.

Wheezle was proud of herself. She only cried a few times. The bustling wedding planner pulled Al aside, "Where's the mother?"

"Right here.' Al answered and took Wheezle's hand. She lost it then, if just for a while.

"The father?" the planner fretted.

"Deceased," Al answered gruffly.

The sun was golden; the bird's chirped and flitted overhead. Say for Lumpy, the best man (of course) and the unique Mr. Smith Wheezle didn't know anyone. The shady space was filled with graduate students, professors, and all of Sophie's family. Dancing and loud music followed. Wheezle remained until dark before excusing herself and driving back to Tintangle.

That night she slept alone in the rambling Victorian she'd bought forty years before. The next day she put the Hilltop Home up for sale. The old place went in three days. Wheezle bought a huge straw hat, a folding canvas chair, a box of books, and a condo in Orrville that weekend.

On Monday she grabbed a book and trudged through the sand to a spot on the beach with her hat and the canvas chair. The book, The Last of Mohicans, didn't hold her. She drowsed and finally fell into a deep, blue-black sleep. She found herself in the middle of the wacky world Al had conjured up years before. She saw flying horses and dragons and monsters of all sorts and men in armor. She traveled among the stars and far, far beyond.

She awoke gasping.

The sun had set; the beach was empty. A fitful wind blew onshore. Clouds, yellow and red, were billowing up from the sea.

For a few seconds she didn't know who or where she was. She took a deep breath and slowly exhaled. The world came back. She was shivering. Her mind wouldn't let her alone. Someone seemed to be speaking to her.

Wheezle stood suddenly. The wind grabbed her big hat. She tossed the book into a bag and snatched up the canvas chair. She struggled across the cooling sand. The voice stopped her.

--The boy never lied to you in his life.

She shook her head hard as she could.

--He couldn't get away with it. You knew every time he tried.

--Always.

"Always," she whispered.

Chapter 58

Lawrence ("Lumpy") and his partner, Mr. Bob Smith (Perfection Auto Parts, Inc.), after a long day filming TV spots for the Labor Day Lumpalooza, got the news first.

A homecoming: Drs. Al and Sophie Nieman had accepted posts with the Gulfstream College near Orrville. That was in the Orrville Democrat. Al sent a text the same day. Fifteen years of upstate winters: 'nough said.

You finally get the idea, Lumpy answered. As he typed he felt someone looking over his shoulder. He whistled nervously for a few minutes, finally picked up the phone and called Al.

"Frostbite finally curl your toes?" Lumpy asked. He managed to chuckle, though he didn't feel like it.

"It isn't helping. Sophie's Dad isn't doing too well. The usual reasons are lining up."

"We'd just about given up."

"You know what they say."

"No, I don't."

"You can't go home again."

"Who says?"

"A writer from a long time ago."

"Did he ever go home?"

"Sure, after he died."

"There you go."

A pause.

"Still there?" Lumpy asked.

"Sure. How's things?"

"Fandarntastic. How's the kids?"

"Getting too big."

Pause.

"How's your sleeping?" Lumpy blurted.

"I don't get it."

"You know, dreams and such."

"No, I don't know."

"Maybe I just need a glass of warm milk."

Another pause.

They hadn't talked about that Past in years. They just didn't.

Lumpy hurried. "Look – I don't want to cause trouble. It's just the dreams. I wasn't special like you. Look. The way I look at it we were kids once. Crazy things happened. They're done. We were just kids. It's not coming back, no sir. I don't care what dreams wake me up in the middle of the night." Lumpy stopped, breathless. "Are those dreams bothering you? They're not the reason you're coming back, is it?"

Lumpy listened for a reply. He didn't hear one. He said quietly enough, "He's gone...the old man. You and I are sure of that."

"I don't know what you're talking about," Al answered.

Lumpy let a few seconds pass. "Sure. Now-- want me to help you find a house?"

Chapter 59

Al wanted the help, of course. By then he and Sophie had two daughters, Ariel, age six, and Miranda, age eight. Both looked just like their mother. Lumpy picked out a half dozen houses to show on the east side or Orrville, the lonely side of town, but a place with memorable 'scapes of sea and sky. They couple selected an older two-storied craftsman property on the edge of the city limits.

On moving day Lumpy, Mr. Smith, Sophie's mother, and even Wheezle came to help. By lunchtime the movers had left boxes stacked in every room. The day was warm and breezy and bright. Al and Sophie threw open all the doors and windows.

In the girl's room Sophie and her mother, Beatrice, unpacked boxes. Beatrice had things to say; she waited till she and her daughter were alone. Sophie had seemed too quiet all day. Downstairs her daughters shrieked and clattered.

"Sophie," her mother ventured, "is everything--proper?"

"What do you mean?"

"I mean this: do you really want to be here?"

Sophie paused. "Of course I do. This place has character."

Sophie returned to the boxes. Beatrice watched her daughter carefully. She had hoped that Sophie would take the bait. Her daughter had never discussed, under any circumstances, That Time.

Sophie opened a big box. "Towels? Why, yes they are."

"Sophie," Beatrice blurted out," Two years!"

Sophie inspected the towels. "Didn't seem that long."

"Don't you think you owe me?"

Sophie studied a threadbare beach towel with a huge sunflower on it. Beatrice slumped where she sat.

Al yelled from downstairs, something about a couch. Sophie hurried away. Beatrice waited till she thought she had regained her composure and followed. She watched her daughter and her husband manhandle a dreadfully ugly couch through the front door.

The girls squealed and got in the way. Sophie took charge, Beatrice noted, because she always considered herself smarter than everyone else. Beatrice considered interfering, but decided they were having way too much fun.

Then the old lady, Al's foster mother or whatever, appeared, gathered up the girls, and ushered them to the front porch. Well, Beatrice mused, she's certainly had plenty of experience. Forty years of taking care of waifs everybody else tossed into the cold.

A few minutes later Al hurried outside and stood close in conference with Mr. Lawrence and the Hungarian fellow, Mr. Smith. Al quickly rushed back into the house and talked quietly with his wife. Sophie stuck her head around the corner and called to Beatrice, "We're going to the beach!"

No explanation followed. Mine is not to reason why, Beatrice sighed. She wandered to the open front porch. Al and his two friends were already ahead. Sophie, her hair up and her face pink from the heat, hurried behind, pulling the girls along.

The wind blew onshore; the air smelled like the ocean.

"Watch out for storms!" Beatrice called. She realized she wasn't alone. Wheezle sat in a wicker chair on the porch.

"What's the plan?" Beatrice asked.

"Evidently we're not supposed to know," Wheezle answered.

"Nothing new there." Beatrice agreed and shaded her eyes as she looked seaward. "They just took off on a hike. What's with that? Doesn't look like just a stroll either. Look at them go."

Blue-black clouds quickly began to mottle the sky. Green lightning snapped soundlessly out at sea. The women glanced at each other.

"Children out in this weather," Beatrice fretted.

The little group was already far ahead. Al was the first, then Mr. Lawrence and Mr. Smith. Sophie and the two girls brought up the rear.

Beatrice tapped her fingers against the porch railing. "Heaven knows what they're up to."

"At least," Wheezle replied.

Beatrice glanced at the old woman. Wheezle seemed to be elsewhere. A penny for your thoughts, Beatrice thought. Bu she didn't say it.

"Manners, manners," Beatrice whispered to herself and turned to Wheezle. "Coffee time. May I bring you a cup?"

Wheezle didn't seem to hear. Anyway, she didn't answer. Beatrice turned away and crossed through the open front doors into the living room.

"Nobody ever tells me anything," she sighed. She went straight to the kitchen and began scrabbling through the boxes for the coffee maker.

Chapter 60

Sophie glanced at her husband. He wasn't glancing back. His chin was up; he didn't seem to realize how fast he was going. They'd already hurried past the public beach. They were heading, quick as they could go, toward the isolated inlet farther east.

Sophie recognized the dunes and the scrubby pines. On the other side of the dunes would be a sandy road that ran parallel to the ocean. Her father's poor car and Lumpy-- this was the place she'd first met Al. And, sure enough, to their right, barely out of the dunes, she spotted the house where Al and Merlin lived for one night or so. No other houses stood nearby. It was deserted with windows for eyes and a wide door for a mouth.

Miranda tugged at her mother's hand. "Where's he heading. Dad, I mean. Does he know?"

"We're going to find out," Sophie whispered loudly.

For the last year Sophie had been coming across her husband, more than a few times, alone in the backyard in his pajamas. A foot of fresh snow didn't matter. And he was always watching the night sky.

Problem was, Sophie told herself, that they never spoke of back then. How could we? She reminded herself. What's left? Look at my teaching load and the children. And then there's my research. And he's got about the same thing, though its social science.

432

Then they moved back home. Al made everything seem sensible-- your parents down there, the great weather. Don't you just feel it? He'd put it that way over and over. After all, she decided, he was half right. My folks aren't getting any younger. I'd love for my children to grow up near the sea. Except --

"Done, done, done," she said aloud.

Her husband and Lumpy and Mr. Smith were far ahead by then. They splashed through the edge of the surf. They looked like boys again.

Sophie tried to see farther down the beach. Salt spray speckled her glasses. She pulled the girls along fast.

"Mom," Ariel complained.

But now Sophie's chin was up. Along the curve of the beach, hard to judge at that distance, but there at the edge of the surf she saw something.

Miranda squeezed her mother's hand. "Mother, what's going on?" she whispered fiercely.

Abruptly Miranda twisted free from her mother's hand. She sprinted ahead. Ariel cried out and twisted her mother's arm.

Sophie tried to hold on. She couldn't. The youngest broke free and went calling after her sister. They were barefoot and so fast. How could they be so fast? Sophie asked herself frantically.

"Ariel! Miranda!" Sophie threw off her shoes and ran and felt the sand give way underneath her feet.

Al let their children catch up. He held out his hands. His children, squealing with delight, grabbed his hands.

Sophie stopped when she could see it clearly, by then a few hundred yards ahead, close enough to know what it was.

"Always," she said. There isn't anything I can do, she thought, and took off her glasses. The salt air stung her eyes.

"Always," she repeated quietly.

Chapter 61

Al: A child's hand in each of mine. The onshore wind is stinging my eyes. What to do? I've got a little time. I can see ahead, but my eyes aren't good like they used to be. Maybe it's a fisherman. Come on. Turn around. Sophie told me it was a dream, so nothing is there. The thing is -- what's it mean for the children? Maybe nothing at all. It'll just be a dream for them. Because that's all I'll let it be.

Ariel and Miranda are pulling my arms out of the sockets. You're going too slow! They're complaining and complaining. In a few years they'll be gone and the house will be empty. They'll never know. A wonderful thing: why didn't you tell us? How would we ever know?

It's too late.

Sophie has grabbed Miranda's hand. Now we make a line, a company. Lumpy and Smith are on the flank. Everybody is hurrying.

He's caught us. We can't escape. We've done it. He was right. Everything is a circle.

Chapter 62

An old tarmac county road led up the coast. Otherwise Wheezle, seventy-six if a day, would never have made it. She watched the younger people hurry down the beach, noses up, so intent on something that they left the house doors and windows wide open. They didn't ask me to tag along – true. I have a right, she told herself.

The children.

It wasn't far, really, not by car. Wheezle parked by a sandy parking lot nobody ever used. Low dunes rose between the road and ocean. She slipped off her shoes and began climbing.

Halfway up the dune she saw, along the loblolly pines, she saw a big, old-fashioned tent surrounded by a phalanx of flags covered with strange symbols. She paused a little while to catch her breath.

"Hippies," she muttered and soon reached the crest.

The shoreline she saw was ancient still: a deep, endless sky, a smooth beach and dinosaur-humped dunes and, oldest and king of all, the sea itself, royal blue and emerald green.

It was a quiet time: even the ocean seemed to be drowsing.

Wheezle spotted them right away. They made a little knot of people on an empty beach: Al and Sophie, Lumpy and Mr. Smith and the two children.

Knee-deep in the surf, sunburned and worn-out looking, Dr. Pendragon. The girls splashed into the surf. Pendragon encouraged them along.

In the shallow surf the girls played with two sharks, pale bellies up and lolling in the surf.

Wheezle cried out and half-stumbled, half-surfed down the far side of the dune. She didn't notice it at first, a parrot or the like circling the scene. It flapped towards Wheezle, brilliant gold and emerald metallic feathers gleaming. It squealed and cried out angrily. Suddenly it was huge and its leathery wings beat whump-whump-whump. Sand swirled into the air. Wheezle covered her head with her hands and half-stumbled, half-ran down the smooth side of the dune, crying and calling for the happy people on the beach to come save her.

They think I don't know. I wasn't back there so long ago. Maybe I even slept a while. I recall amazing, monstrous things. The dark, ancient ones-- I remember tales about them when I was so young. They were real, weren't they? They clasp the boy to their chest. He is one of us, they intoned. We were awoken when this universe began and we are here to see it end.

What about me?

You no longer belong, they insisted.

Where do I go?

Back to yours.

I tumbled into the well. I thought it would devour me. Then all around me that's all I could find.

I returned here. Maybe I can say it's where I began. There isn't anything else. The powers are nearly gone. I can call my old friends, set up a tent. I can tell stories to anyone who wants to hear.

Look now. The tall man has stopped. Let him think…now he starts again, a child in each hand. Maybe he will let me teach them about those wonderful and monstrous things. I think he will, my Arthur. In his house I know an ancient sword, wrapped in old cloth, waits for us, gleaming.

THE END